THE FIN

CW0076156

The last part of the Retribution tr
its fastest pa

The time is now… Further threats… Misguided loyalties…
Betrayal of the worst kind...

Even knowing Ron O'Hara is somewhere in the vicinity, Jonah Powell feels it's time to finally get rid of the diamonds which have haunted his family for decades and caused so much trouble.

However, other problems start to arrive from unexpected and additional sources, some of which Jonah didn't expect. Neither did he expect Teagan Fraser to be playing on his mind so heavily.

But what does it all mean? It may be apt to call time on the curse plaguing his family and of those around him, but how can this be achieved while so many other things are at stake?

Also by Edie Baylis

THE FINAL TAKE

RETRIBUTION #3

EDIE BAYLIS

ATHAME
press

· LONDON ·

First published in Great Britain in 2021 by Athame Press.
This paperback edition published in 2022 by Athame Press.

Front cover design Copyright © Athame Press/Edie Baylis 2022
Front cover photography: kiraliffe/envato.com; shironosov/iStock
Back cover photography: Drew Hayes/Unsplash

ISBN 978-1-9161627-8-5
e-ISBN 978-1-9161627-7-8

Athame Press
Unit 13230 - PO Box 6945 – London – W1A 6US

July 2005

HEATH POINTER'S INITIAL MIX of first surprise and then elation at being granted bail, quickly morphed into confusion, then suspicion as he walked alongside his father towards the car park outside the court, seeing the total stranger sitting in the driver's seat of the Lexus – the one *he'd* been given the use of this last few months.

Ushered into the back of the car, Heath sat motionless whilst his father clambered into the passenger seat and the stranger started the engine.

Heath had been busy working out where his father had got the money from, not only to pay the solicitor who clearly knew what he was doing, including every single loophole only available to those in the know and worth their salt, but also how he'd scraped together the cash for the bail money. He had no idea how much it had all cost, but couldn't imagine the guarantor fee promising his return to court for a murder charge would be a fiver...

Walking from the court in a state of bemused trance, he'd gladly accepted the bearhug his father gave him, too elated to initially question anything. He'd fully expected to be held in custody – serving his time waiting for the trial in a prison of the judge's choosing, but instead, he'd walked.

It didn't change that he'd still got to return for the main trial, but it was a start – a very good one. If he had that same brief for his main trial too, then from what had been said, the possibility of walking away permanently was on the cards.

But now, Heath experienced the creeping feeling things were more complicated.

For a start, who was this bloke driving *his* car?

Heath silently eyed the balding head of the thick-set man driving his Lexus, his mind going at ninety to the dozen. Would no one explain what was going on? Or even think he might want to know who the stranger was?

Heath nervously picked the skin around the thumb of his left hand. He couldn't pick his nails – they'd already been chewed down to the quick during his time on remand, but picking at something was better than not. It gave his hands something to do.

Clearing his throat, Heath made the decision to break the heavy silence as they travelled in the opposite direction of his flat. It wasn't like he could return to Footlights and Dulcie Adams now she was dead.

That was another thing. All of his stuff – the stuff that mattered anyway, was still at Footlights. Like his laptop, his best clothes – everything. He didn't expect he'd get any of that back now. In fact, it had probably all been seized by the Police, never to be seen again.

He hadn't killed the old bat, but by Christ, how he wished he had. The question was, would anyone believe him?

'Erm, where are we going?' Heath eventually asked, his voice sounding horribly croaky and nervous and he resented that. But the truth was, he *was* nervous. He didn't like this one bit.

Catching the stranger's eye in the rear-view mirror, Heath shuddered. *Who was he?*

'We're going home – as in, mine and your Mum's,' Mike Pointer said. 'You'll be staying with us for the foreseeable future. At least until this court business is finished.'

'*Your* home?' Heath spluttered. 'But I...'

'It's a condition of your bail,' Mike interrupted. He had no idea exactly where Heath would go in the house once they got back, not with that lot there too. He glanced at Ron O'Hara, his strange eyes fixed determinedly on the road ahead and his mind worked overtime with how best to broach this subject with his son. At the end of the day, Heath should be damn grateful that he was no longer being detained, but he was unsure if he'd be too enamoured about his release once he found out what had been agreed in his absence.

'Are you not going to introduce us?' Heath finally blurted. The urge to scream, *"Who the fuck is this person driving my car?"* burnt at the back of his throat, but something stopped him from vocalising what he really wanted to say. That and how the hell he would stand being back into his parents' poky semi with his mother flapping around like an injured pigeon. Wasn't that the reason he'd moved out in the first place?

But the first and foremost question was who this man was...

Mike twisted his body around in the passenger seat to face Heath. 'This is Ron O'Hara. It's thanks to him that you're out of your present situation.'

Heath blinked. Was that supposed to mean something? He'd never heard of the bloke. Why would this person have stumped up all that brass for him?

He wracked his brains for the answer and failed. Was it someone his father knew from old? Should it ring any bells, because it didn't? None whatsoever.

'Erm, thank you Mr O'Hara. I'm very grateful,' Heath spluttered. 'I don't wish to sound rude, but I don't understand why you would do this. It must sound awful, but I can't think how I know you and...'

'You don't know me,' Ron O'Hara growled, his voice thick with a strong Irish accent. 'But my family knows yours. Very well.' He glanced at Mike, his expression cold, then met eyes with Heath in the rear-view mirror again. 'Yes, it cost me a pretty penny getting your sorry arse off the hook.'

'I really do appreciate it, Mr O'Hara. I hope you know that I didn't do it of course, but...'

'I don't give a flying rat's dick whether you did it or not. All I want is the information your father promised me then you'll have paid your dues.'

'I-Information?' Heath's inner alarm bells jangled. He glanced at his father, but Mike now faced forward, making no attempt to meet his son's eyes.

'Yeah, information.' Ron swerved across the lane of the carriageway, his hand slapping the horn. 'FUCKING EYJIT!' he roared, giving a Volvo driver the middle finger as he screeched past.

Heath's head clanged off the back window and he swallowed uncomfortably. *What information?* Information about Dulcie? He didn't know who had killed her. If he did, he'd have served them straight up to the cops quicker than he could shake a stick at. Whoever had done it had not only got him banged up, but had trashed his plan of getting himself onto her final will and testament, the bastards. So, yeah – there was no love lost there, but he didn't know, apart from that he must have been something to do with Jonah Powell.

'As I was saying,' Ron continued. 'All I want from you is to tell me everything you know about my niece.'

Heath frowned. 'Your *niece*?'

Taking his eyes off the road, Ron's head swivelled around to look at Heath. 'Lena O'Hara. Your father here tells me you knew her.'

Heath was momentarily taken off guard seeing O'Hara's face; his large head merged into a thick neck and his weird eyes, far too close together to be normal, made him look like a strange-looking owl. Shaking the image from his mind, Heath wished the man would concentrate on the road rather than on him. He hadn't walked from court to get mangled underneath an artic and neither did he know any bloody O'Haras. 'Lena, you say?'

'The woman from the Feathers, son,' Mike cut in, his tone sharp – *warning.* 'The one you told me about. She's gone missing and Ron understandably wants to know why. I've told him you'll tell him everything you know – everything about Lena, the Powells and the Adams. Everything you've ever been involved in.'

'What? I…' Heath felt the walls closing in around him. 'Lena's *your* niece?' She must have had a whole lot of plastic surgery because there was absolutely no resemblance between them.

'From what I understand, she went under the name Taylor,' Mike added. 'Oh, and Ron and his family are staying with us while they're over here.' *And didn't he know it.* He opened his window, suddenly desperate for air. 'But one thing is vital. Your mother doesn't know anything about any of this. We'll stop for a drink closer to home and I'll fill you in with everything and then you can tell Ron what you know.'

Heath nodded mutely not knowing what else to do or say. Actually, he had a lot he wanted to say – like to demand the car be turned around to take him back to where he'd just come from. By the looks of it, jail would be preferable to this.

ONE

July 2005

ROBERT ADAMS ALLOWED the fresh sea breeze to blow over him. Only certain things could cleanse him and they had to be the *right* things.

His backside was stiff from the time he'd sat on this bench. Hours it had been - possibly *days*. It was all the same to him.

His eyes tracked along Margate's windswept seafront and mindlessly watched the myriad of people taking leisurely morning strolls. He'd even started recognising some of the people on their daily rituals. The same route; the same coats; the same bags... Mainly old duffers who'd come here to die for want of nothing else to do.

Being as he'd begun to recognise half of these programmed fools, that in itself meant he'd been here long enough. Long enough for the seething rage and injustice to fall back down to its usual manageable level and long enough to make him functional again.

There had been one blip of blinding rage reading the report of Heath Pointer being released on bail which was not supposed to happen, but he'd got that under control now too and the plan of what he would do was now firmly engraved in his mind.

Robert scowled at a young child who had found the need to stare at him consistently for the last few minutes. He'd successfully ignored it so far, but the brat was within his personal space now. He was encroaching and there was only so long he could withstand that.

He glared at the child as harshly as he could. It was the best he could do, short of bellowing, but he couldn't do that. That would undoubtedly cause unwanted attention of an over-protective mother.

Christ, if these women were so bothered, why allow their precious darlings to push their luck?

How did they know who they were allowing their kids to irritate? He could be anyone. Even someone dangerous. And then what would those thick as shit women do?

Pleased his staring had achieved the desired effect as the kid ran off, his face screwed up in fright, Robert pulled his attention back to what was important. *Heath Pointer*. The man who had kindly taken it on the chin for the mercy killing of dear old mother - the psycho bitch.

Robert's eyebrows knitted together. Pointer wasn't supposed to get bail. The only way that loser could have swung it was if someone had stumped up a wad of cash, meaning he had an ally. The only ally Heath could possibly have would be the father - Mike Pointer. Or in other words, his *half-brother*.

Robert's rugged face crumpled into a half-smile. It still sounded strange. *His brother.*

Well brother, he thought. *I think it's time we met…*

He was the only one out of them all who knew the details of Mike Pointer's whereabouts and workplace. It was unlikely Jonah Powell and his plastic fantastic crew would have progressed that far along the trail since he'd left them to their own devices.

Yes, he'd pay his unknown brother a visit and see what reasons the man had for bailing out a murderer - son or not.

Robert almost laughed with the delicious irony. The trip

would coincide nicely with Mummy-dearest's funeral. Not that he'd be attending. Not in the way she'd have wanted anyway.

Oh, Dulcie Adams, the star of stage and her own head. Look at you now. No one gives a fuck because everyone knows what you've done..

And that was the only reason he would drive past the church at the time of the funeral - to make sure the lying cow was well and truly six feet under.

There wouldn't even be a notice in the paper. He'd made that *very* clear in his instructions. No one would get the chance to pay their last respects – not that he imagined there was one single person left wishing to mourn his mother's most unfortunate passing.

Even that damaged bitch, Teagan - the one that should have been his, had his witch of a mother not ruined everything, must by now know what her beloved Dulcie had really done.

Robert laughed out loud, not caring if anyone stared at him. How he'd have loved to have seen Teagan's face when she discovered the truth. It served her right for not being what she should have been and for spoiling his chance.

He hoped her heart shattered, like she'd shattered his. *Almost shattered his, but not quite…*

All he had to do now was to find somewhere to stay for a while. He wouldn't go back to his flat or to that haunted Footlights dump either. He'd happily leave both places to rot and moulder. It wasn't like he needed the money.

Jonah Powell and his band of not so merry men wouldn't get any easy hints on where to search for him. That's if they were looking? In reality, they probably weren't.

Robert knew he didn't figure in anyone's plans enough to warrant an effort. He never had and never would.

And that quality was invariably useful.

• • • •

JONAH LOOSENED HIS COLLAR and looked around the enforcement team. He'd put this off for as long as possible, but knew murmurings as to Saul's whereabouts were rumbling and they had to be quashed. He didn't want speculation snowballing.

Both himself and Nero had spent a good deal of time deciding the best way to play this and agreed this was the best way forward.

There was already general unease in the wings and Jonah would rather get in first. The next point of call would be the announcement about Lena, but that one could wait. He wanted nothing said about that until the very last minute before his ill-fated wedding day and there was only another two days until that.

He met Paul Bannister's eyes, the head of one of the two enforcement teams. A trustworthy man, and one Jonah was relying on to keep the rest of the team in order.

'Just to let you know we're reverting back to how things were before my brother returned. From now on, you'll resume taking orders from me, or if I'm not here, from Nero.' Jonah nodded at Nero leaning casually against the wall behind him.

Paul Bannister frowned at Jonah's words. 'What about Keith? Are they both still working on this other contract you informed us about?'

Jonah folded his arms and sighed. 'Not exactly. I'm afraid things haven't worked out in the way we'd all projected. My brother has made the decision to concentrate on pastures new and won't be returning.'

An audible gasp went up around the room and Jonah scanned the people in front of him. 'I'm not going into details of the exact reasons behind Saul's decision.' He smiled thinly. 'All I'll say is that my brother wishes to pursue other options. You all know the first and foremost importance in our firm and this job is to want to be part of it so that it works for everybody. The decision for Saul to leave was mutual and, I should stress, *amicable.*'

Jonah carefully clocked the men, reassured to see there didn't seem to be any mistrust. Surprise, yes, but suspicion, no.

'Keith Grogan has also accompanied Saul and I'm sure you'll join me in wishing them both the best.'

Seeing heads nod, Jonah breathed an internal sigh of relief. 'Team A and B are to remain as is. All jobs and contracts will stay in place. Nothing has changed, apart from that it's me or Nero you'll come to with issues. Oh, and team meetings will be held on a Tuesday, rather than a Monday.' He looked around again. 'Any questions?'

Receiving none, Jonah smiled. 'Thank you gentlemen.'

As the men filed out of the room, Jonah pulled Paul to one side. 'I'd like a word. Come to my office in an hour.'

· · · ·

'I COULDN'T BELIEVE IT when your Dad said you'd decided to move back with us for a while. What a surprise!' Tammy gushed, unable to stop herself from hugging Heath for the third time since he'd walked through the door.

She lowered her voice. 'Although it would have been much better if your Dad hadn't taken it upon himself to dump *them* on me!' She nudged her head in the direction of the sitting room where Mike sat with Ron, Kim and Kieran. 'I mean, I don't even know who they are!' she snapped. 'I can't say I like any of them much either. They're all a bit odd, if you ask me.'

Heath smiled, amazed his face still worked, but he knew better than to not play the game. He'd love to tell his mother that she was spot on with her opinions of the O'Hara's and so far he'd only met one of them. He was also itching to tell her that as much as she didn't know who they were, neither did he. Furthermore, neither did her husband, but he'd been left under no illusion how this would work and if he wanted the chance of not being sent down for a long time then he had to keep O'Hara sweet. But he couldn't say he was happy about it.

Even less so when O'Hara had outlined exactly what was expected of him.

Tammy continued waffling, but Heath had already zoned out, his mind stuck wondering exactly how his father had kept his arrest and subsequent charge hidden. It had been in all the papers and by all accounts, had even made the local TV news, but somehow – for now at least, his mother remained blissfully unaware.

It was imperative he didn't arouse suspicion otherwise regardless of what power O'Hara had over his freedom, his mother would go absolutely tits if she discovered the truth about *any* of this, but what choice did he have? The time he'd spent behind bars may only have been days, but it was long enough to make him sharply realise it was not something he wanted to do again. Certainly not for the length of time he expected would be forthcoming had this unexpected change of circumstances not occurred.

The taste of incarceration was more than enough to know that from now on he would be doing *nothing* to put himself in the firing line to being banged up. He must have had rocks in his head to even contemplate that ludicrous plan with the diamonds.

He wanted to stay *this* side of the fence and do what O'Hara needed without any comeback and the least involvement as possible and then get them all out of his life.

Heath shuddered just thinking about it. No wonder his father thought he'd lost the plot with his get-rich-quick ideas. In hindsight, he had to agree, which made it doubly worse. Now able to understand his father's reasoning, he couldn't work out why he would put him back in this situation.

Still, the sooner he could get these weirdos out of his hair, the better.

Plastering on a good-natured smile, Heath moved towards the sitting room. 'I'd better go and say hello to the rest of them.'

'You might as well,' Tammy snapped. 'We're all like bloody sardines in here. Your father had better make sure they're not here for much lon...'

'Shhh!' Heath hissed, rolling his eyes. 'They'll hear you!'

'I don't care!' Tammy snapped petulantly. 'He shouldn't have dumped this on me. It's not right.'

Heath smiled weakly. His mother would be more upset if she knew that had it not been for O'Hara, her house was about to go from under her and he'd be still in the clink, but he'd keep that to himself as well.

Heath was glad his mother opted to stay in the kitchen out of the way, but he had the overwhelming urge to join her as he walked into the thick, treacly silence of the sitting room.

His father perched uncomfortably on an arm of the sofa, whilst O'Hara sat in the armchair – the one his father usually sat in, his owl-like features not having improved. His strange close-set eyes followed Heath's every move.

Mike looked up. 'Ah, Heath. This is Kieran and Kim, Ron's niece and nephew.'

Heath would normally shake hands, but the vacant way he was being scrutinised by the additional two pairs of equally close-set eyes from these two put him right off. 'Alright?' he said as chirpily as he could muster.

'Come and sit down,' Mike continued. 'Let me tell you what we've been discussing.'

Heath grimaced as Kim shunted up the sofa just enough so he could cram himself next to her. He forced himself to sit down, his skin bristling as his thigh pressed against hers.

Why did he get the feeling he would not like what he was about to hear?

· · · ·

TEAGAN SAT ON THE window seat in the back sitting room and stared out onto the garden. She then found her eyes moving towards the gold clock on the mantlepiece and mentally calculated what sort of time Jonah might put in an appearance.

And *if* that happened, whether she would do exactly what she'd done every time she'd been in the same vicinity as him over the last few days - panic and decide to quickly retreat back to her room or to stay put and risk being in the same space as him. *The same enclosed space.*

Four walls containing him and her and hoping beyond all

hope that he'd read her thoughts, sense her all-consuming urgency for him and take her into his arms.

The persistent thought both terrified and excited her, but as much as she wanted to feel his lips on hers again, urgent and intense, she knew it was not going to happen and she would do what she'd done previously. Hastily mutter an excuse and dash off to the security of the bedroom which, at the moment, she called hers. The room which she was holding herself prisoner in.

She needed to take a deep breath and get over it. She needed to get over *everything*. Including what Saul had done.

But that was easy to say, Teagan thought sadly.

She wasn't the same person she had once been. And what had she been before?

Uncertainty bubbled. She didn't know that either.

What she was sure of was that her faith in everyone and everything was knocked for six and she no longer knew what to think about herself or anyone.

Was anyone who they said they were? Robert? Dulcie? Darren Harding? Where were they all now? What about Joe? Joe, the man she'd thought she'd loved once. That was until he'd betrayed her and almost got her killed. But now he was dead.

No sign of Robert either. Dulcie was dead too and Darren Harding - well, he'd disappeared off the face of the earth.

And Jonah... Who was he and how could she feel this pull towards him? She hardly knew him - and what she *did* know, terrified her.

Gwen was the only remotely normal, stable person out of the lot of them.

Teagan shivered, sure even Gwen was keeping things from her. And the longer she hid herself away, the harder it would be to pick herself up and start again.

She knew all of this and didn't need to keep telling herself the same thing, but she was stuck fast; unable to stop the days drifting into one another and pretending everything was ok.

Saul Powell was gone and the nightmare was over.

But was it? If that was the case, why did she feel none of this was over?

Without realising, Teagan found herself walking towards Jonah's office. The room where he'd kissed her. The room where she'd felt alive for the first time she could ever remember. *Really alive.*

Her eyes tracked to the safe where Jonah had placed the diamonds. Her face twisted into a grimace. Those bloody pink things that had caused all of this bloodshed, grief and pain.

She glanced at the fading scars on her wrists. A lasting reminder of what she'd been through because of them. And she hated them. Hated them with a passion.

Diamonds are a girl's best friend? Diamonds were her enemy and had ruined everything.

If she had the means to open that damn safe, she'd rip those cursed jewels from their hiding place and throw them down the nearest sewer to drift away from her as far as possible.

She shuddered. Just the thought of what they had brought to her and to so many other people, leaving their trail of death, destruction and misery, made her skin crawl.

Feeling suddenly very sick, Teagan had to get out of the room and away from those *things*. They were half the problem. They were in there. Within that safe. Within this *house*. Seeping their cursed miasma through the welded joints of that metal box to dissipate into the air - the air she breathed.

Hearing footsteps along the corridor outside, Teagan stumbled out of the study. She shouldn't be in there. *What if it was Jonah?*

'Teagan?' Gwen cried when Teagan barrelled through the study door straight into her. Holding her by the shoulders, she stared into her eyes. 'Are you alright? Are you looking for Jonah?'

'No!' Teagan said, fervently shaking her head. 'I-I don't know why I went in there. I...'

Gwen frowned. The girl *had* been looking for Jonah, she

was sure of it. And she shouldn't be doing that. Nothing good could come of it.

It hadn't even been a week since she'd walked in, catching Teagan and Jonah kissing passionately in this very room. Yes. Gwen may have been mortified, but at least her presence had stopped it from going any further. And she was fairly sure it would have done if not for her interruption.

Gwen sighed despondently. She'd already told Jonah she didn't want Teagan getting hurt and as much as she thought the world of Jonah, she knew he couldn't offer the girl anything other than sex. After what Lena had done, his heart would be closed and Teagan would need more than that - much more.

Although she believed Jonah had taken her words on board, Teagan would have to be warned off too. But how? How could she do that without making things worse?

Two

RON COULD NOT STOP his jaw from clenching as he walked with Kieran across the pristine gardens towards the Registry Office. Set in a rare, large expanse of trimmed lawn, well-stocked flower beds and ponds, the area housing the registry office was open to the public. Due to its pleasant surroundings, it was a popular destination during the summer months, but it wasn't remotely pleasant for him – none of this was.

The Powells were onto him. He'd known that as soon as Lena started making excuses to call him to finalise the arrangements. And those texts – they weren't quite right – something about them. But he'd got his answer when he'd called from a different number and a stranger answered.

Leading the way to a bench, he knew the chances of anyone showing up today was minimal, if not zero. If it were at all feasible that Lena would appear today for her own wedding, then she'd have already contacted him.

Ron ran his eyes over the bench, double checking he wasn't about to plant himself on any cunningly concealed bits of old chewing gum or sit on a patch of green moss to create a lovely stain on his trousers. Satisfied, he gestured to Kieran to sit down too.

There was a good view of the registry office entrance from here. It was several hundred yards away, but in plain sight of any arrivals and departures. Besides, he'd recognise his beautiful niece anywhere.

Lena had been excited for him to be here and was impatient to do the grand reveal. By God, she'd moved heaven and earth to put this into place, but now it had been cruelly snatched away at the last hurdle.

Something bad must have befallen her for this silence. Lena had always kept him up to speed and Ron had been looking forward to this day, possibly even more than she was. Ever since his brother had been murdered by those double-crossing toerag Powells, he'd been determined to even the score and thanks to Lena it had been within his sights.

He'd been so looking forward to seeing the smug smile slip from Powell's face when he realised who he'd married and that he was tied to the O'Hara's for eternity. Not to mention the financial benefit and acceleration of kudos it would bring the family. It would have enabled the O'Hara's to claim their long-awaited foothold in this city – the one they'd been all set to take had Sean not been offed.

Ron scowled. The Powells might have thought they'd won by killing his brother, Sean, then getting him incarcerated in the loony bin, but all it had achieved was putting off the inevitable.

He glanced at Kieran chain smoking. As Lena's brother, Kieran had felt she'd jumped ship to move to England. But Kieran was nowhere near as canny as himself – and certainly not on a par with Lena. He wasn't the only one - the rest of the family had all but disowned her, but *he* knew Lena better. He knew *why* she'd done it – even if the rest of the O'Hara's didn't and he wanted her to receive her well-earned reward.

The Powells had done this to her. They'd discovered her plans – but God knows how? Lena was the master of deception, but somehow she'd been tucked up.

Since then, Ron's plans had changed dramatically. He hadn't bargained on shelling out that money for the Pointer prat, but now Lena was off radar, he needed information and a base.

His mouth formed a flat line. Now he'd got both. The only question remaining was where Lena was and whether she was ok. And he intended to find that out.

Once he'd done that he'd fuck the Powells up for the last time. They were not taking any more of his family, that much was certain.

. . . .

SEEING NERO making his way down the corridor towards the office, Jonah beckoned him inside. 'Any sign?'

Nero shook his head. 'Nothing substantial.'

Jonah frowned. 'What do you mean, nothing substantial? He was either there or he wasn't.' He'd have preferred to watch the registry office himself, but it was lunacy being as he'd be immediately recognised.

By now he should have been married. Wasn't he supposed to feel something?

His eyes narrowed. Married to a liar and a cheat. Married to a woman who had faked a pregnancy and set him up so to be tied to the O'Hara's for eternity.

All Jonah felt was relief.

'There were a few people milling around in the gardens, but no one behaving suspiciously.'

Jonah sighed heavily. This wasn't what he wanted to hear. Ok, so it was a long shot that O'Hara would show up and stand waiting for the wedding party to arrive. The man clearly knew something had happened, he wasn't that stupid, but Jonah had still clung to the slight hope that he *might* have been that stupid. He slapped his hands on the desk. 'Ok well, it had to be done however faint the possibility. Now it's been ruled out, we'll move on.'

Nero chewed at a hangnail, inspecting the jagged edges. 'Any news on Adams?'

'He's gone to ground,' Jonah admitted. 'I'm not sure in what way. He's either walked away completely or he's planning something.'

Nero frowned. 'The thing I don't get is *why*? I know he's weird, but why revenge? And on who?'

Jonah faltered. 'Me.' He saw the confusion on Nero's face. He wasn't going to mention this, but in hindsight, he needed to. 'He killed his mother.'

'But that wasn't anything to do with you,' Nero countered. 'You didn't lie to him about his bloody father.'

Jonah's fingers knitted together. 'I may be wrong, but I believe he blamed his mother for involving Teagan.'

Nero's eyebrows shot up. 'What's it got to do with her?'

'You didn't hear the stuff he was saying. He couldn't bear to be around Teagan after what happened with Saul. The problem is, I think he *wanted* to be...' Jonah paused, waiting to see if Nero got the drift without having to go into gory details. Details of which he'd rather omit.

Still seeing abject frustration on Nero's face, Jonah sighed. 'I think Robert was in love with her. Or rather *wanted* to be in love with her. He blamed Saul for "tainting" her and his mother for involving her.'

Nero whistled through his teeth. 'The guy's fucked up. I still don't get how you're on his list of people to blame?'

'Because I'm the only one left – aside from Teagan.' Jonah glanced out of the study window at one of the men patrolling his large garden.

Nero followed Jonah's eyes. 'Wait, are you saying this extra security has been laid on not only for O'Hara but for *Robert*? You think Robert will try something?'

'I don't know and that's the point. I want to cover all angles.' Jonah shuffled the paper on the desk, stacking it into a neat pile. 'I need to make sure everyone under my roof is safe when I'm not here.'

'You mean Teagan?' Nero asked, studying Jonah curiously. 'Since when is she your responsibility? We've got enough regarding the O'Hara's without taking on more baggage.'

Jonah stiffened. 'She's my responsibility because of what

Saul put her though and I will not be asking or expecting her to move on until she's ready.'

Nero knew when to leave it, but he'd be blind if he hadn't noticed Jonah had been distracted the last few days. And not by the expected issues. He'd sensed the distinct change of atmosphere on the rare occasions the girl left her bedroom and entered an area with Jonah present.

'It's not just Teagan,' Jonah snapped defensively. 'Gwen is here too. If Robert is as unhinged as I believe, then I wouldn't put anything past him. I should have shot him the night he burst into the office.'

'Erm, are you…? You and Teagan…?'

Jonah laughed loudly. 'God no!' He raised an eyebrow. 'I've had enough of women to last me a lifetime, thank you. And the bloody humiliation yesterday hasn't helped! Announcing at the club about that bullshit that Lena left me said it all! Besides, I doubt whether a Powell would be top of Teagan's list of potential suitors.'

Nero laughed, secretly thinking Jonah protested a bit too much…

If he *did* have his eye on the girl, he'd do best forgetting it. Getting his leg over was one thing, but Teagan didn't strike him as the girl Jonah normally went for. As well as personally not wanting to be dragged into refereeing another complicated relationship, Jonah was like a brother to him and Nero had seen first-hand how Lena's betrayal had all but broken him. It was something he'd never thought he'd witness, but it had been close. And that he wouldn't allow to happen again.

If Teagan had designs on Jonah and him on her, then what sort of friend would he be if he didn't look after his mate's best interests?

'Oh and by the way,' Jonah said. 'I'm making moves on shifting those diamonds.'

The cigarette almost dropped out of Nero's mouth. 'What? When? Who?'

'I made a call earlier,' Jonah continued. 'Firstly, I wanted to check the old bastard was still alive and not demented.'

'Benowitz, you mean?' Nero asked. 'The guy must be at least 148 by now!'

'He's definitely alive and has no problems with his memory either. He knew exactly who I was, based on the codename,' Jonah grinned. 'I said I'd be in touch.'

Nero nodded. If anyone could offload those diamonds without it coming back on them, it would be Abe Benowitz - the smartest and most trusted fence in Hatton Garden.

'There'll never be a good, or more to the point, *safe* time to offload the bloody things,' Jonah added, spotting the worry behind Nero's eyes. 'But I want them gone. They've done nothing but ruin this family and I want rid.'

Nero shrugged. 'It's your call.'

'It is and it will happen. I just need to think how I'm going to do it first.' *And then once those things were out of his hair, perhaps he could get on with his life.*

THREE

'YOU CAN'T HIDE AWAY FOR EVER!' Gwen eyed Teagan sternly.

Teagan put down the book she'd been reading. 'I know, but I'm still struggling to come to terms with things.'

Gwen pursed her lips. 'Look, I realise you're upset about Dulcie, but she wouldn't want you to spend your life pining.' Actually, knowing what she knew now, Dulcie would probably prefer that, but she could hardly say that to Teagan, not when she wasn't aware of Jonah's suspicions about the whole thing. But it was getting harder to justify why Teagan was being kept in the dark and holding a candle for the old woman wasn't doing her any favours. Neither was her concern over Robert's disappearance helpful either, given the situation.

Teagan's eyebrows knitted together. 'I hate Heath Pointer, whoever he is!' She raised her eyes, a surprising amount of steely determination evident. 'Regardless of everyone saying there's no link with Michael Pointer, I don't believe it. It's too much of a coincidence, don't you think?'

Gwen fidgeted uncomfortably. 'Well, I... erm...'

By the looks of it, the fact Teagan had also been shielded about Heath Pointer being the one and the same as Darren

Harding would come out sooner rather than later and then she would feel even more betrayed. Not just by *him*, but by all of them for keeping it from her. She'd have to speak to Jonah about this. The girl needed to know the truth.

'I've been doing nothing but think about it. That and whether I can go to Dulcie's funeral.' Teagan's big blue eyes filled with tears. 'I mean, will Robert be there? Does he even know Dulcie's dead? I know he was dreadful to me at the end, but Christ, Gwen, Dulcie was his mother and now the bastard who killed her has been released on bail, how do you think that will make Robert feel? I'm worried he'll do something stupid when he finds out the murderer is back on the streets.'

'Released on bail?' Gwen spluttered, her heart cranking up a notch. 'When?'

Teagan shrugged. 'I saw something on the web when I was flicking through the news the other day. On the 16th I think?'

Gwen forced herself to shrug nonchalantly. 'Four days ago? I didn't see it.' *Shit*. Jonah couldn't be aware of this because he'd have mentioned it. How on earth had Heath Pointer got bail? Had he given information in exchange for freedom before the trial? Had he implicated Jonah or the Feathers?

'I keep looking for a photo of this creature,' Teagan continued, oblivious to Gwen's internal angst. 'I want to look into the man's eyes and see what possessed him to murder an old lady. But there isn't a photo – not *one*. Not that I could find anyway. Probably some solicitor protecting that bastard's personal identity.'

Gwen breathed a silent sigh of relief. At least Teagan hadn't seen a photo. 'I've got to go into work now love, but you need to get your mind off all this. Have a wander in the garden or something.' *Heath Pointer was out? How had this been missed?*

Someone would have to find out exactly what that little shit had said to the police, otherwise as well as comeback from O'Hara and possibly Robert, they could have the police on their backs to contend with as well.

Gwen was halfway out of the door when she froze. *Wait a*

minute... She turned back to Teagan. 'Did you say *funeral*? Where did you see this? This notice about the funeral?'

Teagan flushed red. 'I, erm, I didn't exactly...'

Gwen frowned. 'Then how...?'

'I... erm... phoned around every undertakers in Maidenhead until I found the one who had been given instructions and they told me... Eventually...'

Gwen gasped. 'You phoned around? Why would you want to do that? Does Jonah know?' As soon as she said it, she regretted it. *Teagan didn't know the truth, remember?*

'Why wouldn't I?' Teagan cried. 'Despite what you may think of Dulcie, I loved her. She was good to me and so therefore I want to go.'

Gwen sighed. The funeral must have been organised by Robert Adams, which meant he was around. *Somewhere...* Teagan must be told the truth about everything. Jonah must tell her about *all* of it.

• • • •

HEATH LOCKED THE BATHROOM DOOR, shut the toilet lid and sat down. He could still hear everyone's voices downstairs, but now it was muffled and not quite so chafing, offering a much needed respite to the constant clamouring noise.

He scowled at three empty toilet roll tubes tossed on the floor around the bin and then glared at his toothbrush and razor, which he'd found a space for on one of the shelves above the sink, had been shoved right to the back behind an open packet of Tampax.

Didn't these people have an ounce of manners?

How long would this go on for? Seemingly forever, by the looks of it.

His father had been purposefully vague when asked – no surprises there, but Heath had the very real and depressing sense of dread that the O'Hara's would be within this house for a very long time.

After discovering that not only had Ron O'Hara paid for his brief and bail, he'd also paid off his father's debts. For this, O'Hara was expecting a substantial payback for his generosity. And *he* was the one tasked to deliver it...

Heath hadn't been happy telling O'Hara everything he knew about the Powells, the Adams' and the most important one of all in O'Hara's mind – Lena...

He didn't want to be involved, full stop. After his brush with incarceration, he strongly wanted to avoid that in the future and didn't feel selling out the little he knew about the Powells was a good step in the direction he wanted to go.

Personally, he didn't feel he'd got much to tell – not where the Powells and Lena was concerned – his own plan had centred mainly on the Adams', but still, he'd told O'Hara all he knew and bizarrely the man had appeared impressed.

Heath stabbed in the PIN for his phone and scrolled through the news. At least he wasn't in it today, so that was something. Whether he'd remain as low-profile once the main court case started was a different story, but right now he was more concerned about everything else.

After he'd spilled his guts to O'Hara, he'd been deluded enough to think that was it. That he'd paid his dues.

Apparently not.

Finding out that not only were the O'Haras their house guests for the foreseeable future, they had also gained positions in City Car Sales – of which *he* was also expected to resume his prior role.

Heath scowled. Now he had the accolade of training Kim and Kieran? What the fuck for? He doubted that in the past couple of weeks the business had become overrun with customers. It struggling having enough for one salesman to do – let along three! Or should he say, two salesman and one sales*woman*?

Christ. Kim was a nightmare waiting to happen. Heath didn't quite know how any of it had come about, but the woman had devised a strange cling-on obsession with him. Everywhere he went, *she* was there... Every time he sat down, *she* sat next to him, yabbering away – like he cared what had gone on in her life. Stuff like how her husband had run off with another woman. How much she missed her sister. Did he think Lena was dead? What would she do if Lena was dead? Who had killed her? Had it been him who really killed that old woman? Had he seen the diamonds? She'd had a dog, but it died... Did he believe in fate? Did he think she was ugly?

Yes. She was ugly. That one was easy.

On and on and fucking ON.

Heath scowled, hackles rising. Kim gave him the creeps. The full and complete creeps.

It was difficult to believe the woman was actually Lena's sister. Alright, so Lena wore more layers of makeup than a Revlon testing lab, but at least both her eyes had pointed in the same direction!

Kim was not only battered by the ugly stick, but she bored him shitless. He also hated how she felt the constant need to keep grasping his arm when they spoke – or should he say, when *she* spoke. No one else could get a bloody word in edgeways.

Heath rolled his eyes, swallowing the urge to scream. Now not only did she live in his house, but he was expected to work with her too?

And the final insult... Ron O'Hara still had his Lexus.

A sudden banging on the door made Heath jump.

Kim's scratchy voice called through the door. 'Is that you in there, Heath?'

Gritting his teeth, Heath felt his body tremble with irritation. *She was following him to the bog now?* 'Yeah, it's me.'

'Can you please hurry? I think I'm going to be sick,' Kim whined. 'I think I've got an eating disorder. It's only just started. I read in a magazine that eating disorders are caused through emotional distress, which makes sense with what's happened to my sister.'

Heath zoned out. *Go away Kim. I don't care...*

'Heath?' The banging on the door resumed. 'Are you going to be long?'

'I'm on the toilet!' Heath lied, pressing restart on the latest level of Candy Crush. *Fuck off Kim, just fuck off.* 'Can't you use the downstairs toilet?'

'There's a spider in there. If it drops on me, I'll die!' she wailed.

A smirk crossed Heath's face. *If only...* 'If you're unwell, you'd best not accompany me to the showroom.'

He smiled at the weighted silence. That shut her up. 'Did you hear me? Go and lie down. I'll explain to my Dad why you're not joining us today.'

'No, no, it's fine. I'm ok now,' Kim blustered. 'It comes and goes.'

Yeah, course it does, Heath thought, wishing she'd attach herself to someone or something else – like the bottom of a river...

'I'll see you downstairs in a moment then?' Kim called, clumping back down the stairs.

Jesus Christ. Why couldn't he just go back to his own flat? If it carried on like this then he'd be doing just that *regardless* of his bloody bail conditions.

· · · ·

JONAH STOOD IN THE SITTING ROOM watching Teagan in the garden. Her long dark hair flowed over her shoulders in waves, blowing gently in the summer breeze and the sunlight silhouetted the shape of her legs through the long floaty summer skirt she wore far too tantalisingly.

As much as he'd love to continue what had started before Gwen had interrupted a week ago, he knew it would be a bad idea.

A no-strings fling was just what the doctor ordered after all the recent stress, as well as something to get his mind off the mounting issues, but aside from suspecting Teagan wasn't the sort to welcome a dirty quickie, he had the nagging issue it wasn't something he wanted either – not with her anyway. *He wanted more.*

And he knew better that to dilute his concentration with something that could not go anywhere. Although he'd washed his hands of ever going down that road with a woman again, he couldn't shake the feeling that it would be different with Teagan, but that was something he was not willing to risk. He'd taken on board what Gwen had said and as much as he'd hated it, she was right. He might hurt Teagan and she'd already been hurt enough.

Pulling his phone from his pocket, Jonah checked his call log. *No missed calls. Good.*

As to why he'd insisted on coming back here rather than being at the Feathers, he wasn't sure. He'd justified it to himself that he'd needed to be away from the host of sideways glances that he was sure he was receiving from the staff, but he knew that to be an excuse. He couldn't give a rat's arse what any of them thought of his ended relationship with Lena – he'd wanted an excuse to be *here*. To see *her.*

Movement in the garden caught Jonah's eye and he stiffened seeing Teagan conversing with one of the security guards. Although he'd instructed Nero to let the men know nothing should be mentioned to Teagan, he couldn't take any chances.

Making his way into the garden through the large French windows, Jonah moved onto the patio and jerked his head, giving the security guard the silent hint to disappear.

As the man walked away, Teagan turned and frowned, before hesitatingly walking towards Jonah.

'I didn't realise you were out here. How are you feeling now?' Jonah asked.

'Still upset,' Teagan answered quietly. 'I know everyone thinks I shouldn't be, but I can't help it. I thought a lot of Dulcie.'

Jonah smiled, painfully aware of her presence.

'Can I ask why there are security guards everywhere? I hadn't noticed them before as I haven't been around much the last few days.' Teagan paused pointedly. 'Is there a problem?'

Jonah scowled at the back of the retreating man. 'I always have security,' he lied. Seeing Teagan was far from convinced, he smiled. 'Ok, I'll admit I arranged extra. And before you say anything, it's for *all* of our benefit after... well, after what happened. It's not a case of treating you with kid gloves before you accuse me of that.'

Teagan couldn't help but smile at the roguish grin on Jonah's face. That was exactly what she was going to accuse him of.

Jonah fought against the urge to brush away the tendril of hair across Teagan's cheek. 'You don't have to hide in your room.'

Teagan nodded. 'I know, but I've been tying myself up in knots about Dulcie and Robert.'

Jonah stiffened at the names. 'Don't overthink anything.'

'That's easy for you to say,' Teagan said. 'There's so many things that don't add up. I... I feel things are being concealed...'

Jonah pursed his lips. 'Has it ever crossed your mind that none of us have the answers?'

Irritation flaring, Teagan swallowed it. 'I also feel awkward about... after we... I thought it easier to stay out of the way...'

Jonah truly hoped the blood rushing to his face hadn't belied itself by colouring his skin. He pushed an easy smile onto his mouth. 'Yeah, I'm sorry about that. It was a fraught time and heightened emotions got the better of us. It was silly and shouldn't have happened. The last thing I want is for you to feel awkward.'

Teagan nodded, ignoring the crushing disappointment at Jonah's words. 'Well, I do feel a little awkward, but you don't need to apologise.'

Jonah made to continue down the hallway. 'Don't over-analyse it. We're both adults and don't need to allow something so trivial to cause problems. After all, we've got more important things to worry about. Anyway, I must get on. Have a good day. I'll probably see you at some point later.'

Striding down the hall, Jonah let his confident smile fade. If only she knew how much what he'd said wasn't true. As much as it was insanity, he'd love to repeat what had happened. Plus, a hell of a lot more besides...

The woman was exquisite, but starting that old lark, especially with someone who had demons to deal with wasn't something he could entertain, despite every single one of his nerve endings telling him otherwise.

Straightening his suit jacket, Jonah moved back towards the study, overriding the impulse to glance back along the hallway to see if Teagan was still there. He had to concentrate on the next plan of action. Nero and Paul should touch base shortly and hopefully they would have good news.

FOUR

'IT'S ONE OF THESE.' Paul scanned the low-rise flats along Panama Street. 'Number 14.'

Nero nodded, looking for somewhere to park. Cars were parked nose to tail both sides of the road in resident-only permits. He grimaced. He could do without a trek from five roads back.

He glanced at Paul Bannister. The man's closely cropped sandy hair and dark green bomber jacket emphasising his massive shoulders reminded him of an action man he'd had as a boy. He agreed with Jonah's suggestion to bring Paul onto the job. The guy had been on the firm since they had and although they had moved in vastly different directions, he was a trustworthy member of the team.

Paul's long-term position as an enforcer was by no means down to lack of ability, it was his decision to remain at that level and everyone knew he was capable of a lot more should he want to pursue it. But Nero was glad Paul had accepted this assignment. Now Keith was no longer around, another man to work alongside was needed. It had to be one whose record of trust was exemplary as there were many facets which Jonah insisted remained unknown to the vast majority in the firm but themselves. The truth about Saul and Keith for one, as well as anything regarding Robert Adams and the Pointer man.

Spotting a newly-vacated space, Nero's eyes lit up. He backed the car into the non-generous gap and quietly hoped whoever was parked in front and behind had excellent manoeuvring ability should they wish to move their motors.

Turning the engine off, he leaned across to look at the piece of paper in Paul's hand. 'Number 14? Let's go.'

'I reckon we look pretty decent for a pair of bailiffs,' Nero grinned as they climbed the steps to the first floor. 'That's if anyone has the stupidity to question what we're doing here?'

'I suppose they're used to bailiffs paying calls around here!' Paul stopped at Number 14. 'This is the one.'

Banging on the door, Nero shouted, 'Bailiffs! Open up!'

Seeing a woman peer from behind her curtains from the neighbouring flat, Paul made a show of looking at his clipboard. 'No one's in. Either that, or they're laying low. How long shall we give it? We've got an audience,' he hissed out of the corner of his mouth.

'Another knock and warning then we'll go in,' Nero said. 'Mr Pointer? This is the bailiffs. We have a warrant to enter your property. It would be easier if you opened the door.' He banged loudly once more.

Letting a few more seconds elapse, Paul gestured for Nero to stand to one side. 'Right, let's see if the prick's hiding behind the sofa.' Raising his foot, he gave the door a hefty boot, the wood around the lock splintering.

Using his shoulder, Nero finished the job, the door giving way with a sad groan.

Rushing into the small hallway, both men stood in silent surprise at the shoes neatly lined up along the skirting. Continuing, the lounge displayed similar characteristics. Used to entering flea-ridden cess pits, this place was clean and nicely furnished. A bachelor pad, but tidy all the same.

'I'll check the bedroom,' Paul muttered as Nero sifted through paperwork on the coffee table in the centre of the room.

Moving to a small desk, Nero yanked open the drawers containing little and no sign of a computer.

'Most of the clothes have gone,' Paul said, returning to the lounge.

Nero nodded. 'I think we can safely say the man has been released from nick, but hasn't come back here. Or if he *did*, it was purely to grab his stuff.'

'So, the question remaining is where he's gone?' Paul sifted through the remaining paperwork on the desk. Stopping at a handful of invoices and compliment slips, he frowned. 'Do we know what trade this guy is in?'

'Jonah said the prick reckoned he was a music producer but that's bollocks.'

'Definitely a shit music producer if he lives round here!' Paul laughed. 'But these might be something?' He held up some invoices. 'Can't see the bloke purchasing three top of the range cars last month, can you?'

Looking at the paperwork, Nero frowned. *City Car Sales*? 'Where the fuck is this? Oh, White City. Yeah, stands to reason.' He glanced around the room. 'Take those with us. There isn't a lot else to see here. The guy's definitely not about, but that place is worth checking.'

Nodding, Paul shoved the invoices in his pocket and picked up an unopened packet of biscuits from the side. 'Might as well have these. Pointer won't be eating them!'

Laughing, they left the flat and pulled the broken door to rest back on its smashed hinges.

· · · ·

TEAGAN RAN HER FINGERS over the deep blue taffeta and beamed. She hadn't thought anything would brighten her mood, but as usual, Gwen had managed it.

Suddenly her face fell. Was it right to feel excited over something so frivolous as a dress after what had happened to Dulcie? Her excitement fading, she glanced at the scars on her wrists and then the markings where the needles had been shoved into her veins against her will. The scars on her wrists had faded further but were still visible and although there was little outward sign of the injection sites, *she* knew they were there.

Her skin became clammy with the prospect of everyone somehow being able to read her mind and see the signals underlining what she'd been through. Would they be able to tell she'd been subjected to those drugs? Would they treat her like an addict - the lowest of the low in most peoples' minds?

Who else knew about the situation? Had it been discussed at the Feathers and was now common knowledge? How could she go there if everyone knew what had happened?

Panic fluttered. She couldn't bear it. She just couldn't. It was ridiculous contemplating the idea to be feasible.

'Are you thinking the red one instead?' Gwen asked, holding up the velvet of one of the other dresses on the rail.

Teagan smiled weakly. 'I don't think any of them are for me.'

Gwen pursed her lips. This was what Teagan needed. It was imperative she pull herself from the rut she was in and fix her mind on something else. She smiled at the personal shopper she'd summoned from one of Oxford Street's finest department stores.

'The colour of that one would suit you perfectly, Miss,' the lady said, noticing Teagan touching the sparkling neckline of a purple cocktail dress.

'We'll take the blue one,' Gwen said quickly. That was the one Teagan preferred. She'd seen it in her eyes for a split second before she'd allowed the demons to dictate.

Teagan looked up in panic. 'Gwen, no... I...'

'Put it on Mr Powell's account please.' Gwen motioned for the personal shopper to vacate the room.

'Of course Madam,' the woman gushed, taking the blue taffeta gown from the rail and gently laying it on the bed. 'This is a beautiful one indeed.' Nodding politely, she wheeled the rail out of the room.

Teagan twisted her hands in her lap. 'Gwen, I said I...'

'I heard what you said, but it's rubbish!' Gwen scoffed. 'You love this one. You're naturally stunning and you'll look amazing!'

Teagan bit down on her bottom lip. It was true. She loved the dress, but as for looking amazing, she doubted it. No amount of beautiful dresses could hide what she now was. 'And you put it on Jonah's account? What will he think? I'm not ready to face the outside world yet. I...'

'After the amount of money Jonah spent on clothes for that tramp Lena, he won't even notice, so don't worry about that.' Gwen grasped Teagan's hand. 'Anyway, it's not for him - it's for *you*. You've got to get back into the real world and where better to start than the place you told me you'd always wanted to go?'

Teagan faltered. 'I know, but I...'

'But nothing! What better way to honour Dulcie's memory than by going to the very place where she was the star of the show?' Gwen smiled.

This was nothing to do with Dulcie, but if saying that convinced Teagan, then so be it. The girl was slipping into depression and Gwen would not allow that to happen. There was another reason too. It didn't make her feel too great, but if it protected Teagan and Jonah, then she'd live with her plan.

The women would flock around Jonah now they knew he was available again. This would highlight to Teagan what she'd be dealing with if she tried to get involved with the man.

Patting Teagan's arm, Gwen smiled. 'I'll only say this once more, Teagan... Don't allow what Saul did own you.'

Teagan remained silent for a moment. She glanced at the dress and then at Gwen. 'But going somewhere like that. I... What if everyone knows? What if...'

Gwen folded her arms. 'No one knows, aside from the people here that night and I can assure you *no one* has breathed a word about it. Neither will they.' She smiled kindly. 'You never know, you might even enjoy yourself! It's a big bash and there will be celebrities there too. It will do you good.'

Teagan chewed her lip thoughtfully. Closing her eyes, she inhaled deeply. Gwen was right. Why should Saul Powell govern the rest of her life? She owed it to herself and to Dulcie to not let this define her.

She swallowed the lump forming in her throat. She would not continue being a victim.

Looking at Gwen, Teagan smiled. 'Ok. I'll come.'

FIVE

MIKE TRIED HIS BEST to chat to the customer, but it was difficult with Ron O'Hara watching him through the glass of the fishbowl office at the back of the showroom. He didn't need to turn around to know his every move, word and mannerism was being scrutinised because he could tell. The hairs on the back of his neck stood alert.

It was like being alive throughout an autopsy.

Suddenly noticing the displeasure on the customer's face, Mike ransacked his brain for what he'd said or missed. It could have been anything because the sad fact was, he wasn't concentrating. He could have been speaking gibberish for all he knew. The amount of control he had on his brain was minimal. 'Sorry Mr... erm, Mr...?'

'Ashford. I'm Mr Ashford,' the man spat, eyeing Mike with disdain. 'Just forget it. The deal's off!'

Mike frowned. *Deal? What deal?*

The customer shook his head in contempt. 'People like you shouldn't be in business. You haven't got the first clue!' Seeing the expression of utter blankness on Mike's face, the customer shook his head once again. Throwing the colour brochure for the BMW at Mike's feet, he stamped across the showroom towards the door.

Chewing his cheek in bewilderment, Mike drifted back to the office. He needed to sit down or have a drink or something. What was the matter with him? He'd never get anywhere like this. He needed Heath back to deal with things. He couldn't do this anymore.

'You'll never pay back your debt at this rate,' Ron said, his tone that of utter boredom as Mike moved back into the office.

Mike jumped, somehow having forgotten the all-seeing eye was still there. 'What? I...'

'That bloke just offered you the asking price for that beamer and you just muttered something about fish!' Ron spat. 'What the fuck have fish got to do with anything?'

'Fish?' Mike parroted. 'I... I don't know.' And he didn't. In fact, he hadn't the first clue.

'Jesus wept!' The beginnings of a smile formed on Ron's face 'Good job Heathcliff and my two will be working here tomorrow.'

'His name's Heath, not Heathcliff,' Mike muttered. How could he forget that Wednesday Adams and her equally strange brother were encroaching on his business tomorrow? The answer was, he couldn't and neither could Heath, which would explain, amongst other reasons, why his own son could barely bring himself to speak to him.

He wiped his hand over his sweaty brow. Heath would prefer languishing in the nick rather than this, he knew he would.

'Bollocks to this!' Ron pushed himself out of Mike's leather chair. 'I'll leave you to it. I've got someone I need to meet up with.'

Mike nodded, hiding the glee he felt at O'Hara's departure. He watched the back of the man's misshapen bulbous head leave the showroom, then shortly saw the Lexus pull out of the forecourt. *Something else Heath wasn't happy about.*

He put his head in his hands. What could he do? O'Hara had him over a barrel and he was stuck.

Mike toyed with locking up the showroom and scooting off to the pub. He was in no rush to go home to sit with *them* and put up with Tammy's wrath on top. None of this was good.

Inwardly sighing as the buzzer signified a customer had entered the showroom, Mike realised his plan to lock up was thwarted, but on second thoughts, without O'Hara here there was a small percentage he could make up the lost sale.

'Good afternoon. Have you...' Mike stopped abruptly, staring at the mirror image of himself - just on a slightly bigger scale, standing in front of him.

'Mike Pointer, I presume?' Robert Adams said, his face unsmiling. 'I'm guessing you know who I am and now that retarded ape who's been here half the day has gone, I suggest you begin by telling me who he is and why your son has been released on bail?'

Mike suddenly thought perhaps Ron O'Hara remaining here might have been preferable to this.

• • • •

'I DON'T BELIEVE THIS!' Jonah fumed. Standing up from his desk, he shoved the paper into Nero's hands. 'Look! Have you seen it?'

Nero dragged his eyes from Jonah's furious face to look at the article in the paper's entertainment section:

Blow for Club Owner

Well-wishers were disappointed to be informed the big celebration planned following the wedding of one of London's most prestigious club owners, Jonah Powell, would not go ahead.

The ceremony itself and the following party was unexpectedly cancelled at the very last minute following Miss Taylors disappearance.

Lena Taylor, 27, was due to wed Mr Powell, 40, at 1pm on 20th July, but staff and guests were only told of the cancellation the evening before.

One guest, who did not want to be named, said, "It's so disappointing. We're all utterly shocked."

The future isn't looking bright for Jonah Powell now his wife-to-be has jilted him at the altar and disappeared with his unborn baby. A source also informed us over speculation whether there could be a link with Mr Powell's brother, Saul, who also recently left the family firm unexpectedly.

'Was it not bad enough having to pretend she left me? Now they've made me out to be a right sad cunt! Who the fuck told the papers this?' Jonah raged, pacing up and down.

Nero shrugged. 'It could be one of hundreds. Basically, anyone who was invited.' He waved his hand. 'Don't let it get to you. It's just idle gossip - you know how it is.'

'Yeah, I know how it is,' Jonah seethed. 'But I don't appreciate being made out to be a loser.' His eyes narrowed. 'Only the staff are aware that Saul has "left", so it must be one of them.'

He continued pacing, his face getting redder. 'When I find out who spilt their guts like a stuck fucking pig, they'll be finding themselves another job.'

'People love to talk,' Nero reasoned.

'Not about this they shouldn't!' Jonah spat. 'Putting it around that Saul's left the firm could ring alarm bells?'

Nero silently agreed. The last thing they wanted was anyone thinking something was suspicious.

'They've all but printed Saul's run off with my fiancée and kid!' Jonah raged. 'This is your fault. Yours and Gwen's. You came up with this idea and it's made me look like an idiot. Everyone must be laughing behind my back!' Grabbing the whisky decanter, Jonah poured himself a large one and gulped it down.

Nero grinned. 'Look on the bright side. There'll be loads of women queuing up now they know you're single. A good excuse to while away the time at that event this weekend?'

Jonah ran his fingers through his hair and inwardly snarled. This may be something and nothing to everyone else, but being made out to be a bloody fool bothered him. He didn't like it and neither did he want to spend the evening grinning and being pleasant to hordes of people simpering or clamouring for his attention either. But like it or not, he had to put in an appearance. It would only look worse if he didn't.

He'd prefer spending the time paying a visit to this car sales place that Nero and Paul had uncovered, but Nero was right. They had to bide their time and do things properly so as not to bring any attention down on them - from anyone. If O'Hara was there, or connected to there, they didn't want him getting advance warning.

They had already lost track of O'Hara once and couldn't do so again, but they couldn't sit on their hands in the interim either. That would give O'Hara, and possibly Robert, the chance to strike first.

'We need to make a move on this City Car Sales place,' Jonah said, perusing the calendar. 'Give it a couple of days, say Friday, then get yourself down there and see what, if anything, is going on.'

• • • •

RON SWIGGED FROM HIS PINT and drummed his fingers on the table in the Nag's Head. Pulling out his phone, he stared at the screen, still hoping for a text from Lena - that is, the *real* Lena. He'd be able to tell her way with words and her mannerisms anywhere.

Heath had said something interesting too. When he'd gone to the Feathers to see Lena, he'd been told she wasn't there. According to Ron's calculation, that was either the day or the day before he'd last spoken to her - as in, *her* - not the tramp pretending to be her.

The thing was, even if Lena wanted to get in contact with him now she couldn't because he'd had to ditch his old number.

No, he was kidding himself. She'd been offed.

Feeling the anger bubbling, Ron grabbed his pint and took another mouthful. Everything was taking too long. *Far* too long.

'What I don't understand is if Heath has a membership to the Feathers, why doesn't he just go back and do more digging?' Kieran asked, slurping at his pint of Fosters.

Ron stared at Kieran incredulously. Sometimes it was impossible to work out how this boy was a product of his brother's. He had no common sense. Actually, not just common sense - *no* sense. Thick as shit summed it up better.

He fumed silently. He could have done without being lumbered with Kieran and Kim. Between the pair of them, they weren't a patch on Lena. Where his brother's kids were concerned, Lena had definitely not only got the lion's share of the looks, but also the brains.

And if his bloody wife, Noeleen, hadn't got on her high horse about not wanting to be on "bastard English soil" then Kieran and Kim wouldn't have pushed to take her place.

Ron scowled, not knowing which was worse: stuck here with his moaning wife or this pair of retarded dummies.

Sighing deeply, Ron stared at Kieran. Asking stupid questions about Heath only underlined why the boy wasn't doing anyone any favours. 'Heath can't go back to the Feathers because there's a good chance they've worked out who he is.' Finding out Heath had given his real name to the club meant the prick wasn't much more intelligent than Kieran, so it was pointless him pushing his luck going back there, especially with the cops around his neck about this court case.

'But *I* could go,' Kieran offered, grinning excitedly. 'I wouldn't mind spending some time watching those hot chicks dance.'

Ron's mouth flattened in distaste. *Yeah, wouldn't that be*

helpful... Not.

'Alright, you Irish bastard?'

Looking up sharply, Ron's face split into a wide grin. Standing up, he shook Stan Leyton's hand animatedly. Giving him a slap on the back, he grinned. 'Stan! Long time no see! Pull yourself up a chair. I got your message. So have you got something for me?'

Stan placed his pint on the table and stared at Kieran until he shifted his chair so another could fit in between. 'That I have Ron, that I have.'

'I always had faith in you, Stan,' Ron grinned.

Stan grinned back at Ron, his yellowing teeth more grisly than usual in the light of the low-hanging stained glass shade of the overhead light. 'I can confirm someone of interest has been in touch with Benowitz.'

Ron's eyes lit up. *Just as he'd suspected.* It stood to reason once Powell realised he'd lost the trail on him since chucking his phone overboard on the ferry crossing, he'd move quickly to fence those jewels. Now, after all this time waiting to get his hands on those diamonds, as well as the bastard whose family had screwed his up, plus probably killed his beautiful niece, it was time for the final take.

The list of the Powell's wrongdoings was endless and now it was time for payback. 'Are you sure it was Powell that got in touch?' Ron hissed, leaning across the table.

Stan stubbed his roll-up out in the ashtray. 'As sure as I can be,' he shrugged. 'I didn't actually see or speak to the bloke myself, as when he phoned he spoke directly to Benowitz.' He raised an eyebrow. 'But Benowitz *did* tell me a massive earner had landed, plus I overheard the code name...'

Ron's ears pricked up. *This sounded promising.* He'd know that codename anywhere. If Powell wanted to make it known to the age-old jeweller in London renowned for dealing with the hottest gems on the planet, then he'd have used the very codename used during the heist itself. The one Ron had heard his brother use in relation to the job which had killed him, along with that snake in the grass, Michael Pointer. 'And what was it, may I ask?'

Stan took his time supping his pint of bitter, eking out the suspense for as long as possible. 'I heard Benowitz use the word *Unicorn.*'

A flush of relief washed over Ron. *At last. At fucking long last.* 'And what's the upshot?'

Stan shrugged his broad shoulders. 'That's all I know. Benowitz just said it would be coming up soon and that it was nothing I needed to deal with...' His face cracked into a grin. 'But what I *do* know is that although Benowitz is keeping this one to himself, he'll still need my skills for setting up and arranging the subsequent details. The old duffer can't work a mobile, let alone cope with sending a fucking text, so yep... you've guessed it... That will be down to *me...*'

Ron swigged down the last of his pint. 'Then my friend, keep your ears to the ground. I need to know everything - no matter how small.'

'What sort of code name is Unicorn?' Kieran blurted.

Ron's head swung around seeing the gormless, yet inquisitive expression on Kieran's face. This kid was a liability. He'd have to get him sent back home before he ballsed something up.

Six

WHILST HEATH WAS BUSY showing Kim and Kieran the ropes, Mike took the opportunity to steer O'Hara onto the City Car Sales forecourt well out of earshot.

Ron glared at Mike. 'You didn't think to tell me this last night?'

'I could hardly discuss it in front of Tammy and everyone else, could I?' Mike cried. The fact that Tammy had even crammed around the table with them for dinner was a turn up for the books and a step in the right direction. It showed that she wasn't about to divorce him. She'd be even *less* likely to divorce him if this worked out and the O'Hara's got out of his life and his house. If he could do that he'd be in Tammy's good books again.

As it turned out, meeting his half-brother hadn't been too bad. After the initial surprise and then worry, he'd found himself quite liking the man, despite his brusque and odd manner. And he couldn't be more grateful for what had been offered.

Mike just hoped and prayed O'Hara would accept it. If he worded it correctly and in the way Robert instructed, then he just might.

'Why do I smell a rat?' Ron stared at Mike suspiciously. 'Why the fuck would a random bloke want to do this?'

Mike had asked himself the very same question, but as long as it got him away from this nutter, he didn't much care. 'He's not a random bloke though, is he? He's my brother.'

'Yeah, so you said, but why haven't you mentioned you were friendly with this brother?' Ron asked, getting perilously close to Mike's face.

Mike stepped back, forcing a relaxed look on his face. 'To be honest, I've been so tied up worrying about Heath and everything else, it didn't cross my mind. It was only when I realised he could help with your plans did I think it a good idea.'

Ron thoughtfully rubbed the stubble on his chin. 'So this Robert Adams wants to buy your debt from me and help me with the Powells? Why?'

'Because the end result is what he wants,' Mike explained, hoping he was getting this the right way around. It made little sense to him either, but who was he to look a gift horse in the mouth?

He put his hand on O'Hara's shoulder in a friendly gesture, even though it made him feel like he may be immediately turned to stone. 'On the big scale of things, I'm not much use to you, but Robert is. He knows a lot more than me'.

'But that will mean he'll expect something in return.' Ron spat. *He wasn't sharing the diamonds with no fucker. Especially not one born from a two-faced cunt and a slag from the Feathers.*

Mike shrugged. 'Surely it's worth talking to him?' *Come on O'Hara...* If O'Hara didn't agree, then he was knackered because Robert had made it very clear if he failed to get O'Hara on side, his next planned visit would be to Tammy. And then Mike *really* would be finished.

Mike could see the greasy cogs in O'Hara's mind crunching and hope flickered. 'I wouldn't mention anything to Heath about this though. As you know, he's had a few run-ins with Robert Adams. I guess I'm just lucky the man doesn't hold a grudge because of my son's part in trying to rip off and then kill his mother.'

O'Hara jerked his oversized head and Mike initially thought the man was about to have a seizure, until he realised it was his way of showing grudging agreement. He grinned, the glimmer of freedom sparkling. 'I'll arrange a meet then, shall I?'

'If it's a setup, I'll hold *you* responsible,' Ron growled. 'And believe me, you don't want that.'

Mike kept his grin in place, but internally he was disintegrating, hoping more than anything that wasn't the case.

· · · ·

ROBERT SAT IN FRONT of the small chest of drawers he'd turned into a makeshift desk and glared at the laptop power cable snaking over the bed.

What sort of crummy dump only had one plug in a room? He squinted at the screen, the reflection of the bare bulb hanging from the ceiling obscuring half of the LED display.

Christ, this was irritating. Still, at least he'd found somewhere to stay that was cheap and out of the way, yet close enough to everywhere he needed. It was also somewhere that didn't ask questions and accepted cash rather than card. This was good, because there couldn't be any trace as to his whereabouts. *None whatsoever.*

Whether his car would still have all four wheels intact by the morning was a different story, but it was a risk he had to take because he'd be using this place as a base for however long it was needed.

Robert clicked his mouse and opened the tracking program. He scanned down the alerts. Last time he'd looked, the trace was still showing loud and clear and he could only hope the tiny device he'd slipped deep into Jonah Powell's wallet before he'd left the man's house was still transmitting. That or the man hadn't felt the need to replace his wallet lately.

He clicked on the number he'd assigned to Jonah Powell's

tracker and held his breath waiting for it to handshake. *Bingo. It was still transmitting perfectly well.*

Robert's lips curled into a smile. He'd keep an eye on that very closely now he'd got Mike Pointer on side.

Unscrewing the quart bottle of brandy he'd bought from the off licence, he took a swig. Cheap shit, but drinkable. *Just about.*

Mike Pointer - what a useless spineless prat that man was. It would have been embarrassing were he in a position where he was forced to involve him in family gatherings, but that was not something likely to happen.

One thing was apparent and to see someone with a likeness so close to himself was bizarre, but it had been easier than expected informing Mike Pointer that he would be assisting. The guy had as much balls as a eunuch.

Robert hadn't even tightened the thumbscrews before the prick spilled everything he knew like verbal diarrhoea.

Ron O'Hara indeed? And staying at Pointer's house?

It seemed everyone was thinking along the same lines. Everybody wanted to get at Jonah Powell.

Robert's eyes narrowed as he watched the screen scrolling through lists of numbers. No one wanted to get at Jonah Powell more than he did - it was just his reasons were completely different from everyone else's. But that was ok. He'd let anyone who wished think they were all singing from the same page carry on. As long as it got *him* what he wanted, then how that was achieved was fair game.

And he *would* be getting what he wanted because Teagan would be paying too. She'd disappointed him in the worst way and he'd had enough of being disappointed.

Being as that two-faced little cocktease decided she'd rather move on to the second Powell since the first one was no longer available, it was only reasonable he should retaliate. There was no need why he couldn't. It wasn't like the police were looking for him in connection with his so-called mother.

Robert smiled. Oh, he'd been clever. *Very clever indeed.*

Patiently waiting for them to get in contact with him over her demise had been the best idea. Of course, he'd made sure everything had been perfectly laid out so they'd suspected no one other than who they'd arrested for it. And if Heath Pointer had even attempted to turn it back on him, if he'd been clever enough to work things out, which he clearly wasn't, it wouldn't have made a blind bit of difference. As far as the police were concerned, Pointer had been caught red handed.

Robert grinned. *He'd made sure of that too.*

It went without saying when the detective finally got hold of him, Robert had acted suitably devastated. Admittedly, that bit was hard, but he hadn't spent years studying aspects of the human psyche and how people behaved for nothing.

Even arranging the funeral was easy. He'd done it all remotely, citing working away as the reason. He hadn't even had to step foot in the undertakers. Knowing his lying hag of a mother was somewhere in a chilled drawer within the building would have irritated him profusely. *No thank you.*

Money was a wonderful thing. It brought anonymity and if there was a big enough paycheck at the end, people would do exactly as required.

But now Heath Pointer was out, thanks to that bloody O'Hara idiot, which could cause problems if he wasn't careful.

Robert focused on the screen, quickly scribbling coordinates in his notebook, then setting the search to alert him with updates.

O'Hara would play into his hands, Robert was as sure as he could be about that. He'd paid close attention to everything Jonah Powell and his monkeys had carelessly spouted during the time they'd trusted him, so he'd garnered a nice bit of information about the Irish twat.

But it would be interesting to know if the Powell's still trusted him or whether they had worked him out?

Robert shrugged his large shoulders and swigged another mouthful of brandy. It hardly mattered. Powell would always be ten steps behind. And when O'Hara got in contact, which he would, the neanderthal would be eating out of his hand.

Once Robert let slip what had become of O'Hara's most treasured niece, the man would do anything and everything to make Powell pay.

And he would pay. *With bells on.*

Robert's lips tightened. Then he'd take back what was his. *Teagan Fraser.*

Not because he wanted her for himself - not like he'd believed for a very short confusing time that he had. She'd just done what treacherous witches did - played with people's heads and made them confused, but not anymore.

Teagan would become his because he was going to keep her. He'd keep her as an experiment and teach her not to play with people. A fundamental lesson in manners.

SEVEN

HEATH'S SKIN TINGLED. 'What do you mean?' he spluttered. Had no one listened to a word he'd said?

He stared at his father incredulously. The man had had a change of heart about just about everything since Ron O'Hara arrived on the scene, yet he was reluctant to explain why. 'You're sending *them* there?' He nodded towards the lounge where Kieran was drinking bottle after bottle of Budweiser and Kim gawped vacantly at the television whilst shoving peanuts into her mouth. 'I told you before VIP membership is like rocking horse shit. There's a massive waiting list.'

'If you knew so much about anything then you'd know on certain nights of the year anyone can buy tickets,' Ron interjected. 'And as it happens, I've bought two for "Mr and Mrs Sutherland" for Saturday night. None of us can go to see what's going on, but *they* can because no one knows them.'

Heath's eyes darted back to his father, but found him grinning inanely at O'Hara's reasoning. What was the matter with everybody? Was it only him that could see Kieran and Kim combined had less brain cells than an amoeba? They would do something which would lead the Powells straight here. Heath didn't want the Powells being led here - or more importantly, anywhere near *him*. He didn't want to be involved at all, yet thanks to his father's promises to O'Hara, he'd been dragged right back into it.

Heath fidgeted on the spot, knowing it was the information *he'd* told O'Hara that was now the fuel enabling the man's vendetta on the Powell firm and *if*, or rather, with those two being involved, *when* Jonah Powell discovered who was the fount of information, his life would be more over than it already was.

'I can see by the look on your mug that you're not liking my plan,' Ron spat. He didn't like it much either. Kieran and Kim were pointless individuals, but he was getting desperate. 'If you hadn't fucked things up in the first place, then it would be *you* going to the Feathers, Heath, so pull your head in and reflect on what you've done before you question my logic.'

Heath felt like screaming. What *he'd* done?

Whatever he'd done, which wasn't a fat lot, would be chickenfeed compared to what those idiots, Kieran and Kim could unleash.

· · · ·

GWEN SMILED AT THE GROUP of girls scheduled to dance at Saturday's big event. 'Is everyone clear about who's doing what? We'll have lots of celebs on the night and there'll be press interest in the fabled charity auction, so it's important everything runs to plan.'

Seeing everyone nod enthusiastically, Gwen smiled. 'Good stuff. Right, crack on and let's hope we have a successful night on Saturday.'

As the girls filed out of the room, Gwen pulled one of them to one side. *She knew it was an underhand thing to do, but she needed to do something.* 'Could I have a word?'

Gwen waited until all of the other girls had left and turned to Terri, looking at her expectantly. *Yes, she'd do nicely.*

Although not the brightest button, Terri was one of the sweetest natured girls out of the troupe. A fantastic dancer with the most amazing body, she was a pretty thing. Best of all, the girl had a fascination with Jonah. Most of them did, but the difference was, this one wasn't demanding. Terri was down to earth and not high maintenance – the *opposite* of Lena.

A willing, no strings attached fling was just what Jonah needed to be deflected from his worries. *And Teagan.*

If there was any part of him left from the old days, which Gwen was sure there was, then this would make the perfect opportunity. She smiled brightly. 'I was wondering if you'd like to be the one to help Mr Powell call the auction?'

'M-Me?' Terri exclaimed. 'You've picked *me* to stand on the stage with Mr Powell?'

Gwen nodded. 'Yes, why not? Mr Powell was only asking about you the other day,' she lied. 'I think you two would make a very striking couple for the press photos.' *Sneaky, sneaky.* But if this girl grabbed Jonah's attention, and there was no reason why she shouldn't, then it would work out well.

'Wow!' Terri exclaimed. 'I'm honoured. I'd love to.' She clapped her hands excitedly. 'Mr Powell really asked about me?'

'He certainly did. It's his way of dropping me a hint that you should be the one I ask to accompany him,' Gwen lied.

Terri could barely contain her excitement. 'I can't believe it! Thank you! I can't wait!'

'Make sure you look your absolute best,' Gwen winked. 'You never know, you might get a drink out of him afterwards.' *And with any luck - a bit more besides.* 'Get yourself off home and I'll see you in the morning.'

She watched Terri almost skip from her office in delight. Switching the light off and locking the door behind her, Gwen made her way down the corridor.

Pausing outside Jonah's office, she tapped on the door and stuck her head around it. 'I'm heading home now, love.'

Jonah nodded absentmindedly, not moving his eyes from the diary. His schedule was bloody chockablock. He'd love to head home himself, but couldn't see that happening for a good while yet.

Gwen walked into Jonah's office. He looked tired and stressed. 'I know what was said in the paper about the wedding got to you, but you're still hosting the auction on Saturday, aren't you?'

Jonah, still firmly fixed on his schedule, reached for his whisky. 'I haven't got a lot of choice!' he snapped. 'People will only speculate further if I don't.'

'Good. Business as usual, as it should be,' Gwen said. 'Oh, by the way, I've arranged for Terri Mason to accompany you for the auction.'

Jonah glanced up. 'Who?'

'Terri. One of the dancers. You'll like her and she'll look great in the press photos,' Gwen chirped.

Jonah waved his hand dismissively. 'Ok, whatever you think.'

'Don't stay here all night. You need a break.' Gwen left Jonah's office, quietly shutting the door behind her.

She wouldn't mention she'd also talked Teagan into coming as her guest. The Feathers would be jam-packed on Saturday and Jonah would be on the stage most of the night dealing with the auction.

As one of the biggest events on the Feathers annual calendar, he wouldn't have time to mingle - apart from with Terri Mason. With any luck he wouldn't even notice Teagan's presence, but Teagan would see *him* and Terri's close proximity. Knowing how flirty Jonah was when he played up to the crowd should be enough to dissuade Teagan from having any more silly thoughts.

It wasn't perfect and not something Gwen would usually consider doing, but sometimes it was necessary to be cruel to be kind. She loved Jonah and had come to care about Teagan deeply too, so it was the least she could do to ensure no more hurt befell either of them.

· · · ·

HEATH MURMURED LAZILY as he relished the feel of the soft mouth teasing his raging arousal. In his half-awake state, he groaned, his hips moving to the expert sucking and licking.

Now, this was some way to start off the day.

Not quite able to rationalise where he'd been last night to grant him this bonus, he found himself unable to question or worry further. His hand moved lower and feeling the hair of the woman working him to heights unknown, he pushed her head down further.

Groaning louder as his wave of climax started to roll, Heath's eyes fluttered open. His orgasm was too far underway to stop when his eyes focused on Kim positioned between his legs and could do nothing as Kim milked every last drop from him.

Sweat poured down Heath's face from the horror discovering who had just given him the best orgasm he'd had in a long time. *How the hell had this happened?*

He rolled his body away from Kim. 'W-What are you doing?' he panted, his limbs disturbingly jelly-like.

'Morning,' Kim said brightly. 'I tried to wake you up, but you were sparko so I thought this might work!'

'You can't just come here and...'

'You were the only one who came,' she winked, wiping the back of her hand across her mouth. 'Aren't you going to reciprocate?'

'I don't think that's a good idea.' Scrambling off the bed, Heath pulled his clothes on.

This was the sort of thing he'd had nightmares of when he been in nick: waking up in the morning with some random bloke. He'd heard all the stories about that kind of thing happening, but thankfully it hadn't. Now it had happened - just with *her* instead. And he didn't know which was worse.

'You'd better get out of here before someone spots you,' Heath cried. The last thing he wanted was Ron O'Hara accusing him of ruining his niece. *Jesus.*

Kim flapped her hand. 'Chill out. It's fine. They know I'm

in here. Being as Kieran wasn't up for it this morning I thought I'd give you a surprise instead.'

Heath blinked. Even though he'd tried his best to avert his eyes from Kim, now he couldn't help it. 'You what?'

Was he living in a parallel universe? Did she just say what he thought she'd said? With her brother? No, no, NO!

Feeling bile fast track up his throat, Heath launched himself from the bedroom and burst into the bathroom, hastily locking the door behind him. He leant back against the wall and regulated his erratic breathing. That made what had just happened even more unpalatable.

He gingerly peered into his boxer shorts to make sure everything was still intact and turned the shower on, wasting no time diving under it. *What the fuck was going on?*

Heath allowed the water to cascade over his face, feeling grubbier than he could remember. He couldn't stay here with this lot. This was too weird and he wanted nothing to do with it. But one thing was for sure, it wouldn't be happening again. He was out of here as soon as possible and in the interim, he'd invest in a heavy duty fucking bolt for the bedroom door.

EIGHT

GWEN GLANCED AROUND CASUALLY, or at least she hoped it looked that way, rather than an on-edge rabbit caught in the headlights. That was more of a truthful description of how she felt.

She pulled the collar of her light summer jacket higher, wishing she'd worn a more substantial one. For mid-July it was decidedly chilly and the fine drizzle was seeping into her. Still, it seemed apt to be overcast and rainy for a funeral, rather than blue sky and sunshine.

Not that there was anything to mourn over this particular passing.

Gwen looked at Teagan's head bowed as the coffin finished its descent into the ground. Short of the vicar, herself and Teagan, there was no one else present.

Her eyes scanned the churchyard once again. *Nobody.*

Jonah had major concerns about Teagan's safety where Robert Adams was concerned, but Gwen doubted him to be an issue. Her opinion was Robert would remain as far away as possible. O'Hara was the main issue, but either way, she didn't want to hang around here any longer than necessary. Now the vicar had wrapped things up, they could get going.

She could have asked one of the security Jonah had employed to watch their back from a discreet distance, but then they would report back and he'd know she'd gone against his wishes.

Jonah wouldn't be happy to discover she'd accompanied Teagan to Dulcie's funeral, or hadn't talked her out of going in the first place, but considering he didn't want Teagan to know the truth about Dulcie, Robert or Heath, there was no justifiable reason Gwen could think to give the girl why she should not attend, especially when it was so important to her.

Gwen placed her hand lightly on Teagan's arm. 'Shall we make a move?'

Teagan smiled weakly. 'Yes. I think everything's done here.' She glanced once again in the direction of where Dulcie's coffin had been lowered and silently said her goodbyes. As upsetting as burying Dulcie was, the fact that Robert hadn't shown was even more upsetting.

He must have organised the funeral. At least, she was as sure of that as she could be from what the undertaker had hinted. The only plausible reason to explain Robert's absence was that he wasn't coping with his mother's death. It was the only explanation. Either that or he had lost it trying to deal with what he'd done to Saul Powell.

Teagan frowned. Jonah hadn't come out and said Robert was the one responsible for taking Saul's life, but he hadn't denied it and that spoke volumes.

Her hands dug deeper into the pockets of her black jacket. How she wished she could do something to help Robert. The thought of him being alone with his suffering was dreadful. Despite his harshness towards her before he'd disappeared, Robert was a good man – he just thought too deeply. Dulcie had always said Robert retreated in on himself during difficult times.

Seeing the eagerness to leave on Gwen's face, Teagan dejectedly followed her back to the car.

'I wouldn't mention anything about coming here today to

anyone,' Gwen muttered, scanning the car park.

Teagan nodded. She already got the gist she wasn't supposed to be here, but no one had explained why.

Had Teagan's mind not been so preoccupied and Gwen not been so concerned about their attendance being discovered, they may have glimpsed Robert Adams standing in the trees to the left, they might also have noticed he'd been watching the entire time they'd been at the graveside.

They might have also heard his mobile ringing, but unfortunately they missed that too.

• • • •

'I HATE TO SAY THIS, but I'm really liking the look of this one,' Paul grinned, admiring the bodywork of the black Jaguar S-Type taking centre stage in the showroom.

'We're not here to buy a fucking car though, are we?' Nero jibed good-naturedly, admitting the motor Paul was drooling over was a particularly nice set of wheels.

'Maybe not, but I can still look. It's not as if anything else of interest is going on.' Paul tried the door handle of the Jaguar, pleased when it opened.

Clambering in, he lounged back into the cream leather of the driver's seat. 'Not sure I wouldn't get confused looking for the non-existent gear stick and missing clutch,' he said, eyeing the shining Walnut fascia.

'I'd have thought sitting back and doing sod all would be just up your street!' Nero laughed.

Paul was one of the hardest working men he had worked with at the firm, making all the years he'd worked alongside Keith pale into insignificance with the difference between the two men's work ethic.

Nero frowned. But Paul was spot on with there being nothing of interest here, apart from the cars. He had no idea how this firm shifted any motors at all. Almost half an hour they'd been here and were yet to see a single salesman. Not *one* person had jumped on them and that was most unusual for a car showroom. Normally they had to be beaten off with sticks.

The only person they had seen was the back of a youngish-looking bloke through the panoramic glass of the rather posh office at the back of the showroom, so busy on his mobile phone they hadn't even been noticed.

'Ah, good afternoon gentlemen,' Mike Pointer said, striding towards them through the showroom. 'Have you seen anything that interests you?'

'Not really,' Nero muttered cryptically. 'Although now I'm thinking I'm changing my mind...' This was a Pointer without a shred of doubt. The man was the spit of Robert-bloody-Adams. So similar he'd almost laid the tosser out the minute he'd clapped eyes on him. He glanced at Paul, giving him an almost imperceptible nod.

'I've just taken delivery of a couple of new motors, but I hope you've been taken care of well in my absence?' Mike continued unwittingly.

'I'm quite interested in this Jag, but unfortunately no one's been available to ask.' Paul nodded in the direction of the office. 'Apart from him, but I think he's dead because he hasn't looked up from his phone in half an hour.'

Flustered, Mike looked at the back of Kieran's head. *The useless bloody twat.* He'd told him to keep new customers talking until he or Heath were free to deal. And where was Heath? *God, this was embarrassing.*

'I can only apologise, Sir. We've recently taken that young man on and he hasn't quite got to grips with things yet,' Mike blustered. 'My son would normally be here and will be back shortly, I expect.'

Nero made a big point of looking around the surprisingly lavish showroom. This place must have set the Pointers back a fair few quid. 'Family business?' So Heath Pointer was definitely out of nick and back working with daddy?

He had to be careful and couldn't be entirely sure Heath Pointer hadn't previously seen him when he'd sneaked his way into the Feathers. *He couldn't be recognised.* 'Nice place you've got here.'

'Thank you.' Mike puffed his chest out with pride. Thanks to his change in luck, things were definitely on the up. Once O'Hara was on his merry way he could put this whole unfortunate business to one side and forget it ever happened. 'As I've discovered during my many years in car sales, one has to speculate to accumulate,' he gushed pompously.

Paul glanced at Nero, fighting the urge to laugh. *What a jumped-up deluded dick this bloke was.* 'Have you got the keys for this motor?'

Mike's face split into a wide grin. 'Of course. I'll go and fetch them straight away. We can take it for a test drive.'

Watching Mike rush towards the office, Nero hated to spoil Paul's fun, but he couldn't risk Heath returning. 'Actually, that will have to wait. We're running late for a meeting.'

Paul stared at Nero. 'What? Wh…'

'We'll arrange it for another day?'

Mike retraced his steps and fumbled in his pocket for a business card. 'Just call when you have a time in mind.' He handed a card to both men. 'Bear in mind this beauty won't hang around for long.'

Nero smiled coldly. Jerking his head to Paul, they walked from the showroom, Paul's face resembling a slapped haddock.

NINE

HEATH THOUGHT it was a good time as any to check on his flat. O'Hara had buggered off on an "errand" and his father would be gone most of the afternoon picking up a cheap pair of Audis from some dodgy Polish blokes.

Personally, Heath thought the motors must either be nicked or cut and shuts, but didn't see the point in questioning his father's decision. Let him get on with it - nothing to do with him.

Besides, there had been no customers all morning and no sign of any this afternoon either, so it was unlikely a coachload of people with bags of cash would descend if he took an hour out. He wasn't being stuck in there with Kieran and *especially* not Kim.

Kim had stared at him all morning, the castors on her office chair squeaking as she subtly inched closer bit by bit, her hand brushing against his thigh on more than one occasion. And as much as he didn't want to, the image of Kim in the sack with her own brother, or worse, in *his* bed again kept seeping into his mind. Something he could not allow to be repeated and the main reason for coming back to check on his own flat.

Rounding the corner into Panama Street, Heath already felt

relief wash over him to be back on his own territory.

He'd only been back once since leaving jail and that had been but a fleeting visit to quickly grab some clothes, even though most of his stuff was still at Footlights. It wasn't like he'd be getting that back.

He glanced up at the block of flats with appreciation, not thinking he'd have ever looked forward to being back at this crummy dump as much as he had done lately. But the time he'd been in nick and since being forced to move into his parents, along with the Munsters, he'd thought of little else.

Leaving his car at the side of the road, Heath clambered up the stairwell to the first floor and walked along the litter-strewn walkway. He just wanted to make sure everything was still connected. Most importantly, the Internet, and then he was moving back. *Tomorrow if possible.*

He no longer cared it would break his bail conditions or that someone may want to pay him a visit. He'd rather live in fear of being murdered in his bed by Jonah Powell or Robert Adams then waking up being pawed by Kim O'Hara again.

Whistling to himself, Heath took a furtive glance over his shoulder as he approached his flat. It never hurt to be alert.

His cheerful whistling and visions of escape rapidly diminished seeing the splintered doorjamb.

What the...?

Christ. The Powells? Had they been here looking for him? It must have been them. When? Were they still here?

His heart upping a notch, Heath hovered by the smashed door. *Should he go in?*

Gingerly pushing the door, he had to shove harder to get past the mound of unopened mail stacked behind the door. Heath's panic intensified as he half wondered whether his father had kept the services up to date whilst he'd been inside, like he'd promised. If he hadn't, then the internet might have already been cut off and would take a bloody age to sort out again. Jesus, what a pain in the arse...

Urgh! What the hell was that?

Any thoughts of lack of internet were bypassed by the sudden assault of the stench hitting Heath's nostrils. His hand flew to cover his mouth and nose and he involuntarily gagged as he made his way down the hallway.

His shoes were still lined against the wall, but that smell... Something was very wrong. It smelt like a combination of shit and rotting fish.

Pushing his way into his lounge, he froze as he took in the scene. His once neat and tidy living room looked like Beirut! Where his 43-inch flat screen TV had once sat, there was now a gaping, tell-tale space. His framed prints on the wall had disappeared and even his fucking sofa had gone west.

What the fuck? And that smell...

Gingerly moving into the room, Heath gagged once more spotting a pile of faeces where there had once been a very nice and expensive grey-striped rug, which had also miraculously disappeared. As well as the pile of shit, there were plastic bags and rubbish all over the floor.

Just about everything worth anything had gone. Even his little desk in the corner was missing, the contents scattered across the floor to mix in with the myriad plastic bags, fag ends and half-eaten pot noodles.

The place had been burgled, but by who? And who the fuck had taken a dump in the middle of his lounge floor, the dirty bastard?

Careful where he put his feet, Heath dropped to his haunches and peered at one of the many plastic bags. *It had something in it... Something gloopy.*

Bending closer, dubiously about to touch it, he backed away quickly.

Glue. It was fucking glue!

Jesus Christ. That's what the stench was. Glue mixed with piss and shit. *For Christ's sake.*

Anger rattled through Heath's body. There was no way he could live here with it in this state and he was fucked if he was tidying it up. Besides, everything had been half inched, apart from his shoes and those he wouldn't touch with a bargepole in case he contracted hepatitis.

Catching sight of a pile of discarded hypodermic needles in the corner, nausea rose. Not even bothering to look in the bathroom or the bedroom for fear or what he may find and fairly sure it would be more of the same, Heath stumbled from the flat he'd once called home.

'Oh, it's you!'

Heath swung in the direction of the voice, only to see the woman from two flats down. Wearing a dressing gown, despite it being mid-afternoon, the woman hadn't even bothered covering her sagging breasts with the loosely fitted garment.

Trying not to stare, he struggled to form words, the stench from within the flat clinging stubbornly to the inside of his mouth and nose. 'What the hell has happened?' he finally spluttered.

The woman shrugged dismissively. 'First of all some bailiffs turned up looking for you and kicked your door in.' She rolled her eyes in distaste. 'That same night a bunch of junkies took up residence. About six or seven of them. In and out all hours they were, making a right racket. They finally disappeared yesterday, thank fuck!'

She tutted loudly. 'We don't want wankers like that around here. When are you moving back to clean it up? Hilda next door reckons you can smell the stench through the wall.'

'I won't be back,' Heath spat. 'The place is wrecked and all my stuff has gone.'

'I didn't see the bailiffs take anything, but they weren't here long. Must have been the junkies, but then that lot would sell their own fucking grandmas.'

'You'd know,' Heath muttered under his breath, his worry reigniting. 'These bailiffs? What did they look like?'

'Like bailiffs. You know - the usual, mean-faced, hard cunts? Don't they all look like that?'

Again, not something Heath would know, but were they bailiffs or something to do with the Powells? What had they taken, if anything? And how did they know where he lived?

Fuck, fuck, fuck! That stupid Feathers membership card was how. He'd put his bloody address on there... They were on to him, knew he was out of nick and had come looking...

'Ere, you alright?' the woman squawked. 'You've gone a funny colour.'

'Yeah, yeah, I'm ok. Gotta go,' Heath mumbled, staggering back along the walkway to the stairwell.

So, by the looks of it, the Powells were after him and his flat was trashed. He had no choice but to remain at his parents with the freak collection now.

Fuck and bollocks. This was a disaster.

Still, there was safety in numbers, even if it meant being stuck with them.

• • • •

RON SAT IN THE LEXUS in a road behind an industrial estate in Shepherds Bush. This was where he'd arranged to meet Adams, so where the fuck was he?

If that loser, Pointer, had sent him on a wild goose chase in a bid to steer him away from things then the man would sorely regret it. He didn't like the fucking idiot at the best of times. Mike Pointer was a Grade A slopy-shouldered bastard, but then that was hardly surprising, being the offspring of that wanker, Michael Pointer Senior. But then, Adams was another one of that waster's offspring, so he was suspect to start with. Not to mention Adams' unexplainable offer to pay Mike and Heath Pointer's debts. What could there possibly be in it for the man?

Becoming more and more convinced this was a set-up, Ron fingered the Glock concealed within his inside pocket.

If he'd got the gist correctly, Adams had worked with Powell until recently, which meant he still could be...

Furthermore, when he'd phoned the number Pointer supplied, Adams hadn't sounded in any way cordial. He'd spoken as if he were a nuisance and would have thought, being as Adams was desperate to broker a deal, he'd at least have been afforded some courtesy, but Robert Adams' manner was short and downright rude.

Ron scowled. Had his urge to find what had become of Lena blindsided him?

For fuck's sake. Mike Pointer had turned him over and sold him out to the Powells, he just knew it. Was he losing his touch? Why hadn't he worked this out before?

That was it. He wasn't hanging around waiting to get jumped. *No way Jose.*

Shoving the key back into the ignition, Ron made to start the engine, his jaw clenching at the blinding headlights of another car appearing from out of nowhere, blocking off the only way out from this dead end road.

Fumbling for his pistol, Ron readied himself, squinting into the darkness as the headlights of the car in front died and a figure stepped from the car.

What the fuck was Mike Pointer doing here? He hadn't told him where he'd arranged to meet Adams.

Wait! That wasn't Pointer...

He stared at the big man advancing towards the Lexus. This was Adams? Holy shit! This guy and Pointer were almost identical...

Ron peered into the darkness further, his fingers still poised on the trigger of his Glock.

There was one astute difference immediately clear between the two men: this one had something behind his eyes that Mike Pointer did not. And that alone made Ron hesitate firing his gun through the windscreen into the man's chest.

The look in the man's eyes told him that perhaps it may be worth having this meet after all.

• • • •

AS HE ANSWERED THE QUESTION, Robert saw O'Hara's sadness turn to rage.

'She's definitely dead?' Ron questioned, mentally chalking up exactly what he would do to the Powells for this.

'Definitely,' Robert confirmed, his voice void of expression. 'A right mess she was - they made sure of that.' His eyes remained fixed out of the windscreen of O'Hara's car into the blackness beyond.

He would love to tell this Irish wanker that his beloved niece was a piece of work who had deserved everything she'd ended up with, but he didn't. It made no difference to him, but he didn't like this man's attitude. He thought he was a somebody, when in reality he wasn't. None of these people were worth jack.

'You're rather flippant, Adams,' Ron barked. 'You're the one wishing to make contact with *me*, not vice versa, yet when I called, you spoke as if you were doing *me* a favour. Bloody rude, truth be known and you're fucking late! That's no way to do business now, is it?'

Robert's eyes narrowed. 'You phoned me in the middle of my mother's funeral, Mr O'Hara, so it wasn't the best time to talk.' Not that he was actually part of it, but he'd been there long enough to see Teagan, along with that old trout from the Feathers. No sign of Powell, but Teagan, yes. It meant she'd purposely sought out the time and location of the funeral, which also meant she didn't know. *Didn't know the truth...*

It was better than he'd thought and would make things so much easier.

'What are you smiling at?' Ron barked. *The man had just buried his mother and he was grinning?* 'I take it you had as much liking for Dulcie Adams as the rest of us?'

'Something like that,' Robert muttered.

'Getting back to my niece... Who did it?' Ron spat, swivelling towards Robert and grabbing his arm. 'Tell me which one of them killed my Lena. I need to know.'

Robert yanked his arm from O'Hara's grip. 'Do not put your hand on me,' he hissed, driving home the point.

He waited until O'Hara's arm retreated, then sat patiently a moment longer, enjoying making this saddo wait for the scraps. 'Saul Powell killed your niece, Mr O'Hara. As you are well aware, the Powells discovered what she was planning and for that, she had to die.'

Robert had thought about telling O'Hara it was Jonah who had killed Lena for added amusement, but the truth gave him more leverage.

Ron swallowed hard, the combination of anger and pain upping its stranglehold. Lena had died trying to get just desserts for the family? He itched to ask how she'd been killed, but refrained. If he knew how much she'd suffered there was a risk it might break him. It was one of the few things in this world that could and that he couldn't risk. Not when he had Saul Powell to deal with.

'I saw the paper,' Ron barked. 'It made out Lena ran off with Saul. I know the baby was fake, as she told me about that, but I just knew she wouldn't have run off. She'd have contacted me first.' His eyes narrowed. 'Where the fuck has Saul Powell gone? You're going to fucking well tell me, Adams, because I'm having him.'

Robert cracked his knuckles and savoured the moment. *God, he loved this.* Making people believe they had a chance for retribution, only to pull it out from under them, like a badly fitting rug. Like what Teagan had done to him. She'd made him believe he had a chance to be normal - to be normal with *her* and then she'd spoilt it. She'd fucking spoilt it. They'd *all* fucking spoilt it.

'Tell me where that cunt is,' Ron screamed. 'You know where he is! I'll hunt him down and take you down with him if you don't tell me what you know.'

Robert smiled coldly. 'Your threats don't bother me, Mr O'Hara. There's nowhere you can take me that I haven't already been, so save your Boy Scout shit.'

Ron stared at Robert incredulously. *Boy Scout?* He was no fucking Boy Scout! What was wrong with this bloke? As much as he didn't want to admit it, the man was beginning to unnerve him.

'Saul Powell's dead, Mr O'Hara,' Robert said quietly, his

eyes like a dying fish. Vacant. *Hollow.* 'I killed Saul Powell. I stabbed him through the heart.' His face broke into a smile. 'He looked surprised as he died. It was beautiful.'

And it had been. Fear and surprise - the qualities of which would make a stunning photograph. If only that swift glimpse of emotion could have been captured for eternity.

Robert shook his head. It was important he didn't go off on a tangent. He raised his hooded eyes, watching O'Hara process the information and battling whether to offer thanks for taking retribution for his niece, or being irritated he had missed out on doing it himself.

These people were so predictable. Saul Powell wasn't killed because of Lena, Robert knew that much. Saul Powell was killed because it was *necessary.* Saul Powell had soiled his possession. He'd made Teagan unusable and ruined his plan.

He absentmindedly scratched his chin. There were other things to discuss. *More pressing things.* 'So, Mr O'Hara, shall we discuss what we're here to discuss? About our mutual benefit?'

Ron inhaled deeply, still trying to get his head around any of this. Adams was certainly a strange one. And his Lena was dead. He'd known deep down she must be, but it still hurt. *Really* hurt and that had to be paid for. *Everything* had to be paid for.

Another member of his family the fucking Powells had taken. Another life wasted. He fixed his scowl on Adams' reptilian eyes. 'I want my dues from them. I want to make them pay.'

Robert nodded. 'And you want the diamonds and y...'

'I suppose you want half of those too?' Ron interjected. 'I'm not prepared to deal on those.'

Robert shrugged. 'They're all yours, Mr O'Hara. I want nothing to do with them. The diamonds mean nothing to me. I've already given them back to Jonah Powell once.'

Ron blinked. *He hadn't expected that.* 'Then what do you want?'

Robert smirked. 'One thing will suffice and that is Teagan. That will automatically spawn the remaining thing I desire, which is to hurt Powell. *Here...*' He tapped his temple.

'Who the fuck is Teagan?'

Robert glared at O'Hara. 'Teagan is mine. Powell thinks he has the right to her, but he doesn't. She is *mine* and no one else's.'

Ron's brain whirred at an alarming rate. This bloke really was a loon. Could he work with someone like this? And why would he have given the diamonds back to Powell?

'This, I think is yours,' Robert placed a bag on O'Hara's lap.

Almost reluctant to peer inside the carrier bag, but unable not to, Ron stared at the rolls of money.

'This is what you paid for Mike Pointer's debts and what you stumped up to get the son out of prison. It's all there,' Robert smirked. 'I'll take over any ensuing amount on that subject from now on.'

Ron blinked. *This nutter had just handed him over 100K in cash and all he wanted was a girl?*

'Do we have a deal, Mr O'Hara?' Robert asked. 'That money is yours and I'll help you get the diamonds. I know exactly where they are. You help me get Teagan and in turn hurt Jonah.'

Ron couldn't help but smile. The guy was insane, but hell, yeah, he'd got himself a deal. 'The only problem is, Powell is about to get the diamonds fenced and that could happen any time. I have no way of knowing.'

Robert grinned and tapped his nose. 'But I do. It's called technology.'

Ron frowned before realisation dawned. 'It was *you*? You were the one who put a tracker on me?' His eyes narrowed, suspicion bubbling again. 'How do I know this isn't a set-up? How do I know you're not reporting this back to Jonah Powell? He knows I'm on to him. You could be part of that and Mike Pointer could be too.'

Robert laughed. The first time he'd laughed in a long while. 'Of course I had you tracked. That's what I do. But, your question is why would I not set you up now? That's easy. Powell has got what I want and you haven't. There is no logic in setting up the only person who wants something that will help achieve what I want. And Mike Pointer? That man is so fucking stupid to do anything, short of obey.'

Ron shook his head in bewilderment. *Mad, but efficient.* 'Then, Mr Adams, I'd say we have a deal.' Extending his hand, he shook Robert's firmly.

TEN

TEAGAN'S HEART BEAT like a drum as she walked with Gwen up the steps to the Feathers' entrance.

'Don't look so nervous,' Gwen said. 'You look fabulous!'

The blue taffeta dress fitted Teagan like a glove and she'd almost liked her reflection.

Almost.

But she was nervous and worried, despite what Gwen said. Worried that everyone here knew who she was and what had happened. Although she looked good on the outside – a thousand miles away from how she'd looked a few weeks ago, she felt anything but good on the inside. Still, the excitement of seeing the place that was so important to Dulcie and her dancing days tempered down the nagging dread. She'd promised herself to get back out into reality and she was damned if she would let anything stop her.

As a doorman opened the large double doors with one fluid motion, Teagan's excitement gained pace. She could barely believe she was finally entering the renowned Feathers club of Soho.

'Evening, Mrs Vella,' the doorman said, his bulky frame encased in a smart uniform and top hat. He nodded to Teagan.

'Evening Miss.'

Teagan smiled nervously and followed Gwen into the lobby, looking around in amazement.

Although it had changed slightly, she recognised the foyer from one of the first photographs she remembered seeing at Footlights the day she'd started work for Dulcie.

Teagan stared at the massive gold-embossed feather emblem behind the reception desk. Dulcie had stood just there with several other dancers in that photograph. *This was amazing.*

Leading the way, Gwen slipped off her jacket. 'I'd normally sling this in my office, but being as you're with me, I'll make proper use of the facilities,' she winked, indicating for Teagan to leave her blue bolero with the attendant. 'Let's go to our table.'

Depositing her jacket, Teagan nodded her thanks to the attendant, then nervously walked with Gwen up the brightly illuminated staircase. 'We're going to the VIP suite?' she exclaimed excitedly, her anxiousness diminishing. Her eyes darted around hastily taking everything in.

'Where else?' Gwen smiled as the door to the VIP suite was opened by two further doormen and tall thin flutes of champagne were placed in both hers and Teagan's hands.

Sitting down at their reserved table high up on a raised dais, Teagan gasped, her eyes drinking in the stage with its sumptuous curtains. The whole place was just as she'd imagined based on what Dulcie had said and the photographs she'd seen. Actually, it was even *better*.

A waiter wheeled over a silver ice bucket holding a bottle of Dom Perignon and placed it on the centre of the table. A small sliver of sadness washed across Teagan as she thought how she'd have loved to have seen Dulcie here in her heyday. Perhaps with her lover Michael Pointer - the romance of the century. Her face fell. The romance of the century before it was ruined by those diamonds...

'You look stunning,' Gwen whispered, squeezing Teagan's

hand. 'Now relax, sit back and enjoy the show.'

Gwen subtly glanced about, unable to see Jonah. The place was packed to the rafters and the show was about to start. Hopefully, by the end of the evening things would play out in the right way for everybody, if her plan worked out.

· · · ·

'WE'RE ONLY HERE to look at what's going on,' Kieran said, watching his sister. 'Try not to gawp as if you've never seen anything but the inside of a pub before, will you? And don't forget you're Kim *Sutherland* tonight, ok? Whatever you do, don't even think about breathing the name O'Hara.'

Kim ensured she kept up the act that had taken so long to perfect. 'Why's that?' she asked innocently.

'Too complicated to explain and you wouldn't understand,' Kieran snapped. 'Trust me on this and don't say that name. You'll get us killed - not just by this lot in here, but Uncle Ron will want to kill us too.'

Kim nodded and turned her attention to her new clutch bag. She was well aware everyone thought she was thicker than two short planks, but she'd show them. She'd show *all* of them.

Everybody, including Uncle Ron made no attempt to conceal their lack of faith in her and struggled to give her more responsibility than making a cup of tea, but their attitude had its advantages. Because everyone branded her as pointless, they invariably forgot she was even there. And that meant she became privy to things. Things that no one counted relevant if she overheard. After all, she was too *stupid*...

Well, she heard everything, but said little. And she would soon make them all realise they'd underestimated her. Lena might have been the shining star of the family; the prettiest; the most intelligent and the one who had the nous to turn water into wine, but whatever had happened, her sister had failed. And from what Kim had overheard, no one was getting any closer to finding out what had actually happened to Lena. Neither was Uncle Ron any further in getting his hands on the diamonds that her father should have had dibs on. The diamonds her father had *died* for.

She would show them all she wasn't the retarded muppet they believed her to be. She would become invaluable in getting to the bottom of everything and when that happened, she would be as revered as her sister.

Kim smiled. She had no idea how she would do it yet, but if she continued acting dim but happy-looking, people would keep talking over her like she was a deaf mute like they always did. And it would be *that* which would get the answers Uncle Ron needed. Then and only then would everyone change their tune.

Kim watched Kieran's attention fully centred on the beautiful dancers doing one of their famed burlesque routines on the stage, their lithe bodies moving in unison like mercury.

How she wished she could be up there doing something like that - having all the men stare at her with unconcealed lust and the women looking with combined adulation and envy.

Was that how Lena felt when she'd once danced at this club? Put on a pedestal and admired by all? And then the cherry on the top - snaring the rich and powerful club owner, Jonah Powell; the one Uncle Ron and everyone hated.

Well, she wouldn't mind a bit with Jonah Powell. He was ever so handsome.

Kim smiled secretively to herself. She'd overheard enough of Uncle Ron's phone conversations with Lena about the national glossy magazines she was featured in. Unbeknownst to Kieran, Uncle Ron or the rest of the family, Kim had made a point of following her sister's life from afar for years. She'd bought all the magazines about Lena and Jonah: the happy couple.

Kim almost felt she knew Jonah Powell, she'd seen his face in the papers, magazines and on the Internet so much. Yes, she'd have loved to have been in Lena's shoes. That beautiful lifestyle, massive house, fancy holidays... Except, she wouldn't have got herself killed.

Even if Uncle Ron and Kieran refused to believe it, Kim knew her sister was dead. That's why it was so important to make it *her* mission to get the answers.

A twinge of irritation glimmered as Kieran all but salivated over the dancers and she scornfully eyed the tightening crotch of his tuxedo trousers. She'd spent *hours* getting ready tonight and not one person had complemented her on her appearance.

Snaking her hand under the table, Kim palmed her hand over Kieran's crotch.

'What the fuck are you doing?' Kieran hissed, pushing Kim's hand away. 'You can't do that.'

'We're supposed to be married according to our identities tonight, aren't we?' Kim spat, her patience wearing thin. 'Have you forgotten?'

'I know, but you don't have to *really* do that! What's the matter with you?' Kieran glanced at Kim, then quickly turned his attention back to the dancers.

Kim's eyes narrowed. She turned away, continuing to watch the show with interest, pretending she was thoroughly enthralled, when really she was silently fuming.

Lena had taught her to do whatever was necessary with anyone to bide time, gain a foothold and control. Well, she'd been doing it for years now and was past being treated like an idiot. It stopped *here*.

She would get her well-earned pay-out this time.

ELEVEN

POSING FOR THE UMPTEENTH photograph from the clamouring press in front of the stage, despite not relishing tonight's big event Jonah found himself relaxing as the auction got underway, no doubt aided by the large whiskies consistently being placed in his hand.

Putting his arm around the small waist of the girl Gwen had picked to accompany him, Jonah found it relatively easy to get into the swing and adopt the persona expected of him on nights such as these.

Despite how he felt inside and all the things tumbling around inside his head that in his opinion, deserved priority over *this*, he knew how things worked. He hadn't forgotten he had a club to run and a reputation to uphold. That in itself must be fastidiously maintained whatever the cost. But to his surprise, it was nowhere near as hard going as he'd expected and found, dare he say, he was actually half-enjoying it.

As the spotlight swivelled onto him once more, Jonah gave the waiting crowds his trademark smile - the one that according to Gwen, had all the ladies' hearts melting and the men wanting to emulate him.

'Right, Ladies and Gents - the next lot in our fabulous

auction tonight is a pair of beautiful Cartier earrings modelled by my stunning assistant, Terri.'

With a flourish, Jonah's arm swept towards Terri. Taking her hand he kissed it and led her forward to hold up the box of diamond studs. An enlarged image of the jewellery projected onto the large screens suspended from brackets around the room.

Silently glowing that Jonah still had hold of her hand, Terri smiled widely, feeling quietly confident he mirrored her interest. Why else would he specially ask Gwen to arrange for her to be part of this otherwise?

He'd been attentive and nothing but charming tonight. Best of all, there would be plenty of photographs of the pair of them in every paper by the morning.

Terri's eyes sparkled with delight. Word had also reached her that photographers from the glossy magazines were in attendance. Now, that would be something. *Just think, her pictured with Jonah Powell in OK magazine...*

She'd made sure she looked the part too. She'd splurged a fortune on this stunning red strapless dress and would have to been blind not to notice the scores of appreciative looks she'd received. She just hoped she was impressing Jonah as much.

What she wouldn't do to be his - even for one night. Anything more than that would be what dreams were made of. *Lena Taylor had managed it, so why not her?*

Satisfied everyone had got a good look at the earrings on offer, Jonah turned to Terri. Running his finger under her chin, he tilted her face up to his and winked before turning back to the crowd. 'Let start the bids for these gorgeous earrings at £500... Nowhere near as gorgeous as Terri here, but she's not up for auction I'm afraid, folks!'

Jonah's comment got a good-natured response from the crowd and he grinned, now well and truly in the swing of things. 'Don't forget Ladies and Gents, this auction is for Great Ormond Street Hospital, so don't be shy with your money. A stunning present for the lady in your life.'

Terri heated with desire at both Jonah's touch and his words. Leaning into him, she relished his arm slipping back around her waist.

Jonah pointed into the crowd. 'One bid there for £500? Thank you Sir... Do we have an increase on that? £550...? Yes? Over there in the corner...? Wonderful! Another £600 there...? Thank you Sir...'

From the table, Gwen watched the proceedings as the bidding continued. This was going well. And by the looks of it, Jonah was on form. Even if it was all an act, he played the part well and it was having the desired effect. She glanced at Teagan. 'Enjoying it?'

'Yes, it's fascinating.' Teagan hid her disappointment as she reached for her champagne. The auction was good, but what was going on with the beautiful girl on the stage wasn't. Who was she?

Disappointment rumbled. She desperately wanted to ask Gwen what was between Jonah and the girl, but she couldn't.

A man approached the table. 'Sorry to intrude Ladies. I'm Max Roland – entertainment reporter from OK magazine. Mrs Vella, isn't it? I understand you organise the auction every year, so may I have a photo?'

'Of course,' Gwen said, standing up.

'And your companion?' The photographer eyed Teagan appreciatively. 'I'm presuming this beauty is one of your luscious dancers?'

'No,' Gwen laughed, watching colour flood to Teagan's cheeks. 'This is a friend of mine. A family friend...'

'Would you stand with Mrs Vella for the photo, Miss?'

'Oh no! I couldn't possibly,' Teagan blustered.

'Yes you can. Come on!' Grabbing Teagan's arm, Gwen pulled her to her feet. 'This is Teagan Fraser.'

'Beautiful.' The photographer snapped away. 'Thank you Ladies. Much obliged.'

'I can't believe you made me do that,' Teagan said, sitting back down.

'Oh, let your hair down,' Gwen laughed.

Teagan forced a smile. She'd wanted to but didn't much feel like celebrating any longer.

. . . .

TEAGAN KNEW SHE SHOULDN'T continue drinking the glasses of champagne which kept appearing in a never-ending supply. Instead, she should have enjoyed the opportunity of being dressed in the most beautiful gown and being in this famous and sumptuous setting surrounded by celebrities as a welcome reintroduction back to the world she'd been hiding from for the past however long.

But try as she might - and she *had* tried, she was drowning in the crushing disappointment since the moment Jonah entered the stage with that girl.

They were obviously having a fling and judging by the chemistry simmering between them, had been for some time. By her reckoning, this meant Jonah must have been seeing this woman, and probably plenty more besides, behind Lena's back. Despite the sort of person Lena turned out, for Jonah not to believe in treating a relationship as anything other than for his own gain, stung.

Teagan had heard about his reputation - even Gwen had said so before now in not so many words, but for some reason, the few occasions she'd spent with him - the way he'd spoken to her had seemed genuine with a surprising depth of feeling. She'd never believed he was like that, but she'd been wrong. *Very* wrong. And it was stupid of her.

Teagan necked the remains of her champagne, her eyes still fixed on Jonah, who looked absolutely jaw-droppingly gorgeous, unable to stop torturing herself with the way he stared at the blonde on his arm.

Now the auction had ended he was doing an interview with the press and the blonde was stuck to his side like glue. Teagan couldn't fail to notice Jonah's arm firmly around the woman's waist, his fingers lingering just that little bit lower to brush the girl's buttocks. It wasn't an act for the crowds - it was *real*.

Feeling hot and suddenly very claustrophobic, Teagan's panic surfaced. *What had she been thinking?* Why on earth would Jonah Powell be interested in someone like her - lacking in confidence, live-in carer for old people; abused by his brother? Not forgetting the track marks from drugs as an added feature of her physical appearance.

Jonah had seen her in states she'd be mortified for even a dog to witness, yet she'd been so deluded, so *deranged*, she'd thought the one kiss they'd shared could have meant something?

He'd already made it clear. He'd even *said* it had been a silly mistake. A kind way of saying she was a misjudgement, a pity thing.

Teagan sighed. This whole evening was a bad idea, but at least it had shown her the truth of her situation and what she needed to do.

Grabbing her small clutch bag picked by the personal shopper to match the colour of the dress, Teagan stood up unsteadily, the urge to remove herself from this uncomfortable situation snowballing.

'Are you alright?' Worry creased Gwen's face as Teagan steadied herself against the side of the table.

Her guilt had increased as the evening progressed. She'd hoped Teagan would be put off by Jonah's public affection towards Terri for the benefit of the press. She'd admit she'd hoped Jonah would take it further, but in no way had she expected Teagan to take things so badly. And judging by what she was seeing, Teagan had taken it very badly indeed.

'I need to get out of here for a moment.' Teagan heard the slur in her own voice, making the embarrassment grow further. She was drunk and felt sick. *This was dreadful.*

'Sit back down,' Gwen urged, reaching for Teagan's arm. 'You look pale.'

'I don't.' Teagan snatched her arm away, almost losing balance. 'I'm going to the Ladies'.

'I'll come with you,' Gwen said, concern barrelling.

'No, please. I want to be on my own.' Teagan stumbled off in the direction of the Ladies cloakroom over the other side of the club and Gwen could only watch from a distance.

As soon as Teagan came back she'd arrange for a taxi to take them home.

• • • •

KIM MOVED TOWARDS the Ladies cloakroom once more. This champagne was going through her like no one's business, but as it was all being paid for courtesy of Uncle Ron, she wanted to make sure his generosity was not wasted.

She hadn't managed to get anything much of interest like she'd hoped, but the night was still young. She'd been hoping to wangle bumping into Jonah Powell and get him ensconced in a conversation. It was a bit of a longshot, being as from the minute he'd stepped onto the stage to hold the auction, he'd been in demand from everybody and she hadn't stood a cat's chance in hell of getting him alone.

That's if she'd have even got the time of day from him, what with the assortment of stunning women surrounding him.

Jonah was even more gorgeous in the flesh than his photos and he was hot enough in those and bloody hell, did Kim envy that pert little blonde he'd been with on stage with! The way they'd carried on, *her* luck was in tonight, that was for sure.

Kim grinned. They hadn't seen her, but she'd seen *them*. On her way down the corridor to the Ladies she'd seen Jonah and that blonde bird dart into the disabled toilet. And she knew *exactly* what they'd gone in there for.

A glimmer of an idea formed. Maybe the blonde would be potentially useful to Uncle Ron? It was feasible, so maybe the night had been more use than she'd thought?

Pulling open the door to the toilets, Kim bundled herself into the nearest free cubicle, sighing with pleasure and relief at emptying her bladder.

She yanked a heap of toilet paper from the gold feather

emblemed holder and bunched it up. *Nice, posh quilted paper.*

Kim frowned, hearing whoever was in the next cubicle vomiting. The smell and the sound made her feel quite queasy. Hastily finishing, she pulled her tights up and flushed the toilet.

Trying to ignore the stomach churning sound still coming from the cubicle, Kim washed her hands and busied herself with retouching her makeup. In the mirror's reflection she saw a woman emerge from the cubicle. The woman was absolutely stunning, despite having offloaded the contents of her stomach.

'Are you alright?' Kim asked tentatively.

Teagan smiled sheepishly. 'Better than I was. I don't usually drink much and I've drank far too much, as you can probably tell!'

Kim smiled. 'Happens to us all. I love your dress, by the way.'

'Thank you,' Teagan said, her face falling slightly. 'Not sure why I bothered really…'

Kim raised her eyebrows. 'Man trouble? Whoever he is, he's a dick. You're stunning!'

Teagan leaned unsteadily against the vanity unit. 'He's far more interested in everyone else. I don't know what I was thinking.'

She busied herself washing her hands, then looked at her reflection. Her eye makeup was a bit smudged, but apart from that, she looked better than she'd thought. She still felt far too drunk and shouldn't be moaning about her personal problems to a complete stranger, but saying it out loud made her feel a hundred times better than she had ten minutes ago.

The time in here had also given Teagan space to come to a decision. Despite everything, tonight had given her one thing - it was time to move on.

She'd shied away from doing so before now, partly because she hadn't felt able - her confidence had taken a hell of a kicking lately, but she could easily now see she'd been hoping for something to develop between her and Jonah. That had been the other part of her reticence to move on. It was a ridiculous notion and tonight had underlined *exactly* how ridiculous it was.

'I'm Kim by the way.' Kim watched the woman closely. She looked like she'd got the weight of the world on her shoulders. 'Are you a member here?'

'God, no!' Teagan said, quite liking the girl she was chatting to. 'I'm Teagan. I'm here with a friend, but this place isn't somewhere I'll be frequenting.'

'Oh?' Kim said, her ears pricking up. That was the name mentioned when she'd overheard Uncle Ron and Mike talking yesterday evening. It couldn't be the woman they'd referred to could it? Something to do with that bloke Uncle Ron had met up with?

She chewed the inside of her lip carefully. Maybe it was the same woman? And if it was...? Surely it was worth a punt? Nothing to lose either way.

'You don't like the Feathers then?' Kim continued. She'd do *anything* to make coming here a regular occurrence.

'It's not that, but I'm moving soon,' Teagan explained, doing up the button of her small bag. *And that was a definite.* She'd be moving out as soon as possible. Probably over the next few days if she could arrange a small flat quickly enough.

'Is this because of that man trouble?' Kim pressed, raising an eyebrow. 'He's not beating you up or that sort of thing is he?'

'Nothing like that. It's just...' Teagan looked down at her hands, her despondency returning. 'I just need to get away.'

'You moving away from London?'

Teagan shrugged. 'I don't know. I need to find somewhere and it depends what's about.'

Kim's brain ticked over quietly. She opened her clutch bag and tore a piece of cardboard from the top of her cigarette packet. Fishing out her black eyeliner, she scrawled her mobile number down and handed it to Teagan. 'If you ever need a chat...'

Looking surprised, Teagan took the number. 'Thank you, that's really nice of you.'

'No worries,' Kim grinned. 'Us girls have to stick together where men are concerned! Let me know if you get stuck for somewhere to stay because I might have a room coming up in my flat this week...'

Well, she didn't - not even slightly, but if this woman turned out to be the one referred to in that conversation, then Uncle Ron would fall over himself to get a flat sorted for her tout suite. In fact, this might work out quite nicely for everyone.

'I really appreciate that. I'll keep it in mind,' Teagan smiled, a twinge of optimism returning. So there *was* somewhere she could go. And it wouldn't mean being completely on her own either. Something to consider anyway.

'I'd best get back.' Teagan pulled open the outside door to the Ladies, then turned and smiled. 'Nice to meet you Kim.'

'You too.' Kim following Teagan out, watching with interest as the woman stopped dead as Jonah Powell and the blonde emerged from the disabled toilet looking ruffled and still kissing.

TWELVE

AFTER THE HORRIBLE INCIDENT of the other morning, Heath was doing as much as possible to give Kim a wide berth. Now he no longer had the option of going back to his own place and was stuck at his parents, he'd had no choice but to go for Plan B. He'd subtly attached a heavy-duty lock to his bedroom door, blagging his mother the banging she'd heard was him fixing the hinges.

Hopefully she'd never notice or if she did, by then he'd have thought of a suitable excuse why he'd felt the need to turn his bedroom into Fort Knox.

He checked his phone once again, disappointed to see no new alerts from Rightmove for a suitable flat to rent. Not one that he could afford anyway. *God, it was no use. He was stuck.* And now as well as being adamant the Powells had been to his flat and were on the lookout for him, there was still the horrible creeping feeling Robert Adams was lurking ready to kill him for murdering his bloody mother.

Not that he had murdered the old boot, but everyone else thought he had and that was all that counted when push came to shove.

Heath's face crumpled. Someone had set him up for

Dulcie's murder and it stood to reason it was the Powells. Who else would want Dulcie Adams out of the way like that, apart from them? The Powells knew he was aware of too much about how they operated and what they'd been hiding. Even Ron O'Hara, the psychotic bastard, believed the Powells had killed Lena. They probably had, which meant they'd be gunning for *him* in case he opened his gob to the cops about all of their wrongdoings.

Christ, this was such a bloody mess.

Heath ignored the trickle of sweat running between his shoulder blades. He'd purposefully not said a word to the police about the Powells. He wasn't stupid. They had their fingers in so many pies it wouldn't have been difficult for them to get to him whilst he was a sitting duck in nick and that was something he'd wanted to avoid. But in hindsight, maybe he should have told the cops everything? Remaining in prison was preferable to any of *this*. And working in the showroom on a bloody *Sunday* was the final insult.

He glanced at Kim through the window of the office as she tapped away at the keyboard. What exactly she was doing, he wasn't sure. He wasn't sure what *any* of them were doing, apart from Kieran, who had been tasked with making sure the cars on the forecourt were clear of dust. *All he was good for, the thick bastard.*

Even Kieran had started giving him filthy looks. Heath didn't have a clue why, but wished he'd take his weird-looking eyes and fuck off. He wished *all* of them would fuck off. It was becoming more and more difficult to bear being around any of them.

Why O'Hara had forked out all that money sending his two strange relations to the Feathers last night was a mystery too. It was just an excuse for a jolly because from what he'd gathered, absolutely nothing had been deduced from the extortionately-priced outing. It wasn't a surprise because Heath wasn't sure what they had expected to see.

It was hardly likely Jonah Powell would walk around with

a case of diamonds and Lena's corpse under his arm just to make things straightforward, would it?

Heath stared at Mike. The worst part of all was his father seemed utterly oblivious - like this was normal. His father had got uptight with his initial plans and schemes, yet when it was *O'Hara's* plans, that was different and absolutely fine.

Well, it wasn't fine. Not from where Heath was standing.

His hackles rose just by looking at the odd outline of Ron O'Hara sitting in his father's office with his back to the glass and the vision of staving in the man's head grew stronger.

Heath had *so* had enough of them being here, as well as at his parents' home. He wanted them to go away.

· · · ·

DRINKING A PINT OF WATER, taking paracetamol and forcing herself to eat several pieces of toast had done nothing to assuage Teagan's hangover. Neither had lying awake half the night with her mind going round in circles, imagining all manner of scenarios, as well as half-listening for Jonah to return from the Feathers.

Not that it would have made any difference, because despite all of her wild imaginings as to what his absence may mean, what she'd seen with her own eyes was enough to know *exactly* what had happened.

She may have been drunk last night, but not anywhere near incoherent enough to have missed Jonah and that woman all but falling out of the disabled toilets, so fiercely entrenched with each other to be blind to her presence.

Another wave of nausea washed over Teagan. She'd seen Jonah's mouth on that woman's, the hunger in the way his hands moved on the blonde's body, the way their clothes were ruffled. It didn't take rocket science to work out what they'd been doing - and what they were both desperate to continue elsewhere.

And she'd wished it had been *her*.

Sickening jealousy and disappointment coursed through

Teagan once again like it had been doing since last night and ever since Jonah had rebuffed her after that one kiss they'd shared.

Now she had the answers like a billboard sign on Piccadilly Circus, but even so, it didn't make things any easier. Just *worse.*

Grabbing one of the Sunday papers from the breakfast table, Teagan scuttled back to the safety of her bedroom as quickly as possible, terrified she would run into Jonah if she remained downstairs. She didn't want to see him. She couldn't bear looking at him knowing how she felt, whilst knowing what he'd done.

But the chances of running into him were zero because he wasn't here. It was obvious he wouldn't have come back last night. Why would he?

Not that it was any of her business, but it hurt. Hurt more than it should.

Shutting the bedroom door, Teagan flopped onto the bed, her head pounding and flicked to the entertainment section of the paper. Her heart lurched. She'd expected to see it, that's why she'd looked - to torture herself further, but *this...*

Teagan stared at the photograph of Jonah and that woman. The picture was in black and white, but her brain filled in the deep red of the woman's sexier-than-hell dress and the dazzling blue of Jonah's eyes. She didn't need colour to imagine that.

She ran her finger down Jonah's chiselled face on the image, his body language shouting his longing for the woman in his arms.

Look at the way he was touching her. They looked like a couple meant to be together. It was captured on film and could be argued by nobody.

Biting back unwanted tears, Teagan read the accompanying article stating the success of the charity auction. But the auction took a back seat compared to the article's fascination with "Jonah Powell's new love interest, Terri Mason".

Terri Mason? That was her name?

Suddenly feeling very ashamed, Teagan closed the paper

and chucked it aside. Didn't Jonah deserve some happiness after what Lena had done? The way she'd treated and betrayed him?

Of course he did.

Teagan frowned. That was if what he'd said was accurate? Judging by his carrying on with several women at the same time, maybe he wasn't as bothered about Lena's lies as he'd made out. After all, he *had* said he'd never much cared for Lena. By the looks of it, he didn't much care for *any* woman, short of what was between their legs.

Standing up, Teagan glared at the blue taffeta dress that she'd so loved dumped on the chair. All it resembled now was how money was thrown around to gain favour.

Well, she didn't want anything from Jonah Powell and must have been stupid for thinking otherwise.

Bundling up the dress, she stuffed it into the bottom of the wardrobe and slammed the door loudly. That's what she thought of Jonah Powell's account at Oxford Street department stores to dress his harem of women.

Feeling marginally better at her decisive action, Teagan moved across the bedroom and stared at the contents of the clutch bag she'd drunkenly emptied onto the bedside table last night.

She picked up the torn piece of cardboard with a phone number on it. The scrawled eyeliner had smudged, but not enough to make the numbers illegible.

What was that girls name again? The nice one that she'd chatted to in the toilets?

Kim. That was it. Her name was Kim.

Carefully placing the phone number back on the table, Teagan sat back on the bed. A house share would be the perfect solution. It would be cheaper than renting by herself and this way she wouldn't be on her own either. Remaining in London would also give her more options for work, which was something she needed to return to sooner rather than later. She'd spent enough time quivering in the shadows with her tail between her legs like a frightened puppy.

This way she could get back into real life - one which didn't include people who had turned her life into a waking nightmare, plus she'd no longer be faced with seeing Jonah, knowing he felt obliged to give her free bed and board out of pity.

Grabbing a hairbrush, Teagan dragged it through her tangled tresses. Remaining here was impossible.

Time to stop hiding, she told herself. *Pick yourself up and move on.*

Picking up her mobile, she dialled Kim's number.

• • • •

IT HAD ONLY been by chance Robert noticed it because he didn't usually make a habit of buying the Sunday papers.

He had no interest in weekly listings of nonsensical TV programmes due to be on. Neither did he have any interest in twee stories about blind kittens, overpaid football stars or crap recipes concocted by alleged celebrity chefs, but something had drawn him to the newspaper stand that morning and there was good reason for that.

Listening to his inner instinct, Robert had flicked through the paper and had almost got to the back when he'd seen it: An article about the Feathers charity auction.

There he was in all his black and white glory: Jonah-fucking-Powell, the thieving lying bastard.

Picking up a different paper, there were more pictures of the man, but this time with a woman. He was all over her. Powell's fling with Teagan hadn't lasted then?

Back in his room at the B&B, Robert gazed at the cutting in his hand. 'Oh dear, Teagan. It didn't take your lover long to realise just how soiled you are, did it?' he spat.

Swallowing down the building urge to laugh, Robert grabbed the next paper. Powell really thought he was royalty. *Look at all the celebrities in the Feathers. Aren't they special.*

Robert stopped. *There she was. Teagan.*

Look at the miserable bitch. Look at how her full lips turned down slightly at the corners, probably stuck like that after the amount of times they'd been round both Saul and Jonah Powell's cocks. *The share and share alike brothers.*

'You whore,' Robert muttered, feeling an unfamiliar throbbing in his trousers. His anger turned to rage.

It had happened again. How could she have this effect on him after what she had done? After giving her body in exchange for drugs? She was that wanton, that *desperate* for someone between her legs, Teagan had allowed that filthy bastard to inject her, then fuck her. Then, no longer able to have Saul, she'd resorted to Jonah, who interestingly, had also now binned her off.

Robert stared once again at the pile of newspapers stacked up in the middle of his sagging bed and a wide smile replaced his scowl. He'd grabbed every single copy of every paper he could find in newsagents and garages in a five mile radius and bought every single one.

He stared at the pile of cuttings he'd made and placed neatly on the table so far, then his eyes moved to the ones he'd started sticking to the wall.

Half a wall of identical photographs of Teagan. Her traitorous whore-body in that tight tarty dress.

Yanking the next paper from the pile, Robert cut around another image of Jonah Powell.

Snip. Snip. Snip.

Grabbing one of Teagan, he turned over the two pictures to face each other and began rubbing them together. 'That's right, Teagan. Ride Jonah – go on!'

The thin newspaper crumpled under Robert's thick fingers as he rubbed the two images together faster. 'Fuck him again, that's right. Harder.'

As Robert's arousal became stronger to the point of pain, his anger increased. 'But you can't fuck him anymore,' Robert panted, the paper ripping under his fingers. 'He's left you for another slut. You've been replaced like I knew you would be. No one wants you.'

Grabbing the scissors, Robert stabbed at the newspaper. 'You treacherous bitch!' he roared, the rage that this woman had done this to him again, intolerable. His hand frantically pushed down the erection straining against his trousers, willing it to go away. He didn't have sexual feelings. *Never* had sexual feelings. Not unless he specifically *allowed* them. And he didn't.

The only time that it happened without his consent was because of her and he resented that. It wasn't right this whore caused his body to react without him allowing it.

Robert's jaw clenched. She'd tricked him. Tricked him into thinking he could be like everyone else, when he couldn't.

His stabbing against Teagan and Jonah's images became more frenzied until he felt that strange sensation of release flood from his groin up through his body.

Confusion and the seeping knowledge of shame that once again this whore had somehow commanded control over his body, Robert snatched up his new bottle of brandy. Raising it to his lips, he greedily drank and waited until his heart picked up its normal rhythm.

Picking up another newspaper, he resumed cutting out more copies of the same image. He had to cover the wall. It was vital he covered *all* of it.

• • • •

'I THOUGHT I HEARD you come downstairs earlier?' Gwen said, glad she'd finally clapped eyes on Teagan.

Swinging around, Teagan concealed the handful of plastic sandwich bags she'd taken from the kitchen drawer in her pocket. 'Yes, I did, but just for a drink and I then went back to bed,' she lied, inching towards the door. She indicated to the sink. 'I need another one.'

'How are you feeling?' Gwen asked, eyeing Teagan knowingly. 'A little bit rough, I don't doubt?'

'I'm sorry about leaving early.' Teagan blushed. 'You didn't have to come back with me.'

'I did,' Gwen said. 'You know that no one is to go anywhere unaccompanied.'

Teagan nodded contritely. Yes she knew, but Jonah's version of Fort Knox all seemed mainly for *her* benefit. Not that she could see any plausible reason for it. He'd already said there were no major problems for her to worry about, so it was pointless. Just another reason underlining why being involved with these people and staying here was as far away from normal as it could be. And she needed *normal*.

It also begged the question how she would get away to Kim's flat without the security patrolling the house and grounds spotting, stopping and questioning her. She'd have to think of a way because she was not being a prisoner of Jonah Powell's any longer.

Teagan turned her attention back to Gwen. 'Accompanied or not, I spoilt your night and I'm sorry. Now you see why I rarely drink,' she laughed, but it came out sounding like a strange gurgle rather than anything else.

Gwen laughed good-naturedly. 'You spoiled nothing. Did you enjoy yourself though? Was the Feathers how you'd imagined it to be? I know Dulcie told you all about it.'

How it stuck in Gwen's throat to talk with false fondness about that two-faced conniving woman. She'd love to tell Teagan the truth about what the old woman had *really* been like, as well as the rest of it and then maybe Teagan would understand why it was imperative to remain vigilant.

'It was fascinating,' Teagan said. That was partly true. Seeing the place she'd heard so much about had been wonderful until her eyes fully opened to exactly how deluded she was. 'I saw lots of *interesting* things...'

Gwen headed to the pile of newspapers on the kitchen table. 'You made quite an impression on everybody.'

Teagan's heart sank. Did she really have to look at those photos of Jonah and that... that woman again. Her teeth clenched as Gwen flicked through one of the papers.

'Remember that journalist who asked for our picture? He

was from OK magazine which isn't out until tomorrow, but we've been snapped by other papers too,' Gwen cried excitedly, pointing to a photograph.

Teagan edged closer. *She was in the newspaper?* She hadn't seen that. It must be a different paper from the one she'd seen. Peering over Gwen's shoulder, she gasped at the photograph. She barely recognised herself. She looked like a *celebrity*.

'You make me look like the local bag lady!' Gwen remarked.

Teagan was unable to believe how refined she looked in the picture and glanced down at her baggy T-shirt and pyjama bottoms. 'Good job they can't see me now, isn't it?'

Gwen turned back the previous page. 'I can't believe these two either. How photogenic are they? Cameras speak volumes, don't you think?'

Teagan's feeling of well-being nosedived seeing yet another photograph of Jonah and Terri Mason.

Ignoring Teagan's change in demeanour, Gwen clasped her hands together. 'They look so good together.' She sneaked a glance at Teagan out of the corner of her eye. 'Terri's ever such a nice girl too. Just what Jonah needs.'

She knew she had to time this right for it to have maximum impact and hopefully seal the deal once and for all. 'Yes,' she continued. 'Thanks to Lena, Jonah hasn't been in the right place for a relationship for some time, but Terri's always understood that. She's in the same game, understands the pressures of the lifestyle and doesn't expect things that can't be offered. She's been really good for him. Uncomplicated.'

'Good luck to them,' Teagan said, moving to the door before the tears of frustration and disappointment flowed.

So that was it. Proof Jonah had been having a thing with Terri for a while, like she suspected. 'I'm off back upstairs now. I'll see you later or tomorrow.'

Except I'll be out of here soon, Teagan thought as she reached the stairs. She'd pack what few bits she had tonight and the moment she received confirmation from Kim the other woman had moved out and there was an opening to slip past security, she'd be taking it and out of here forever.

Thirteen

NO ONE GLANCED UP when Heath wandered into the office, apart from Kim. Heath didn't want Kim to notice him. She was the *last* person he wanted looking at him and that was saying something.

'Adams will let you know when Powell moves?' Mike asked.

'That's what he said, but he's a weird fucker. Plus he looks just like you!' Ron laughed heartily. His face screwed up in mirth, but his strange eyes remained static in his potato-shaped head. 'Apart from he has ability. Unlike you...'

Mike wondered how it was possible to contort a face so much without it impacting someone's eyes. O'Hara's were glass-like and it was most off-putting.

Neither did he care if this nutjob felt the need to insult him. O'Hara and Robert Adams were welcome to each other. If their collaboration meant they both got the hell out of his life and his office, they could insult him all day long. 'I'm glad you got things sorted between you,' he said, ensuring his voice came out pleasant, rather than being forced through his tightly clenched teeth.

'Hold on a minute!' Heath cried, stuck from fully moving

into the office because his legs had ceased to work hearing the conversation. 'You're dealing with Robert Adams?' His eyes darted from O'Hara to his father. 'When did this happen?'

A sickeningly smug smile crept over Ron's face as Heath's presence was finally noticed. 'Oh, didn't your father tell you? Yes, Adams paid your good old Dad a visit and he very kindly put him in touch with me.'

Motionless, Heath watched as O'Hara rub his shovel-sized hands together with morbid fascination. He then turned his accusing glare to his father. 'Why didn't you tell me? You know he...'

'I didn't want to worry you,' Mike cut in, cursing both himself and O'Hara for not being more attentive. He'd already made it clear Heath was not to know about this. 'They're dealing with things together now, so it's nothing to do with us.'

'Of course it's to do with us!' Heath yelped. 'Robert Adams thinks I killed his mother!'

'That's because you *did*!' Ron cackled triumphantly, ecstatic at Heath's discomfort.

'It wasn't me!' Heath protested. 'How many more times? It was the Powells. It had to be!'

Ron dismissed Heath's worry with a flap of his hand. 'Adams ain't interested in you anyhow.'

Mike nodded. 'It's true. From what Ron said, Adams holds no grudge. Jonah Powell will be intercepted when he visits a fence with the diamonds.'

Heath glowered. 'But why should Adams cash in? It was *me* who did the groundwork where those jewels are concerned.'

Ron stood up, his massive frame making Heath feel like a twelve-year-old. 'Listen, you pointless shit,' he growled. 'You've already had your cut - you're out of nick, aren't you? You're out, you have no bill to pay for that top brief, so pull your fucking head in. As for Adams getting a cut, like I was about to say before you took it upon yourself to steam into our *private* conversation, Adams will be getting sod all. I'm having the diamonds and then I'm having Jonah Powell. All Adam wants and all he'll get is some bird that he's got a weird obsession with.'

Heath blinked rapidly. *He didn't buy that for one minute.* His worry increased. 'What bird?'

Ron shrugged. 'How the fuck do I know? Some chick with a stupid name - Trebor or something like that.'

'Teagan?' Heath spluttered. *Surely it couldn't be?*

'Aye, that's the one,' Ron grinned. 'The bloke must be mad.' He shrugged his huge shoulders. 'I fully expected him to demand a share of the diamonds, but no! He's paid 100K for you and your father's debts, he's helping me fuck the Powells over – what's left of them, and his price for all of this is the girl.'

Heath's mouth flapped up and down, unable to form coherent words. *Hold on...* 'What's left of them? What do you mean?'

Ron ran a thick finger across his own neck. 'Saul Powell, the mad bastard, he's brown bread. Adams finished him off.' He rolled his owl-like head. 'I'm a tad pissed off about that, truth be known. I wanted to be the one to finish the cunt that killed Lena, but I'll settle for the other Powell. They're all the bastard same, anyhow.'

Health blinked. *Robert Adams had been the one to kill Saul Powell? Jesus H Christ...*

'If this Adams bloke wants the same Teagan I met on Saturday night in the Feathers, then I don't blame him. If I batted that side of the fence, I wouldn't say no to her either!'

Kim's voice came from nowhere. Without moving her eyes away from the screen she pretended to concentrate on the mailshot she was setting up, smug in the knowledge everyone had suddenly turned to stare at her and were interested in what she said.

For once in her life they'd noticed she was here. And better than that – she had information that could be *vital.*

She couldn't have planned it better herself. But she would hang on to the small bit she did know, and that was from last night's call, the girl had taken up her offer. She'd hold onto that just a few hours more so her ability would be, at long last, appreciated. She wanted them to be grateful for the information. And they would be, that was a definite. Then Uncle Ron would do what was needed and she could phone the girl back to confirm all was good.

. . . .

'GWEN NOT ABOUT?' Jonah muttered, seeing only Nero as he stuck his head around the office door.

'She's catching up with the girls. One of them has called in sick so she needs to jig the rota around.' Nero chucked a magazine back on Gwen's desk. 'I'm waiting as I want a word with her myself.'

Jonah moved into Gwen's office, not bothering asking who had rung in sick. With any luck it would be Terri Mason. Not that he'd wish ill on the girl - she was lovely, but he regretted more than he thought possible his dalliance with her on Saturday.

He knew everyone was itching to see if there was any truth behind the articles scattered across just about every London paper about the supposed "chemistry" between the two of them and the resulting speculation over Terri being a contender for the new love interest in his life. Jonah just wished they'd all bugger off and concentrate on reporting things of importance.

He also had a creeping suspicion that Terri was also hoping there would be further instances of what had occurred, but there wouldn't be.

Jonah ignored Nero's inquisitive gaze and helped himself to a liberal measure of the whisky from Gwen's decanter, grateful she had the sense to keep it topped up.

That had been half his problem on Saturday. He should have remained more on guard. His ill-conceived notion of being slap-dash with the amount of spirits he'd put away to dull down the irritation of performing to the masses had been a badly thought-out plan.

Sure, it had loosened him up to get into the swing of the event and neither would he deny that Terri was a gorgeous woman, but he'd been stupid to think sleeping with her was enough to sort out what was really in his head.

And the only thing *really* in his head was Teagan Fraser.

'There'll be none of that left soon!' Nero nodded at the glass in Jonah's hand.

'And your point is?' Jonah picked up the magazine from Gwen's desk. 'Is this the latest issue?'

'I was about to look at that when you came in,' Nero grinned. 'I presume Gwen bought it because the auction is covered in there. 80K raised for the hospital from what I've heard.'

Jonah nodded, skimming through the pages. 'That's really great news.'

Nero jerked his head at the magazine. 'I wonder if they've billed you and Terri the hot new romance of the century too?'

Jonah gave Nero a clear warning look. 'Do you not think I've had enough of that bullshit?'

Nero held both his hands up and moved away, turning his back so Jonah didn't see the slight grin on his face. *Gwen was right. Getting his end away was just what Jonah needed.*

Finding a double page full of colour photographs of the event, Jonah leant over the magazine, internally cringing at the main photograph.

What a surprise - him and Terri. He cringed further reading the caption:

> *Jonah Powell and stunningly attractive Terri Mason - a dancer from the club, made a striking couple compering the GOSH bidding. A hint of something more to come between this gorgeous pair perhaps...?*

The chosen photograph had been cleverly picked from many available: Jonah's hand blatantly resting on Terri's buttocks showcased to perfection in her skin-tight red dress; him leaning toward her, looking as if he was about to shove his tongue down her throat... He couldn't deny the photo hadn't captured Terri gazing at him with the same unharnessed longing he'd displayed towards her.

The camera never lies, Jonah thought. It may not have lied in entirety, but in this instance the truth certainly wasn't anywhere near the vein they billed it as.

Clever, very clever. But it was a one off and he should have known better. After what had happened with Lena, he should have well and truly learned his lesson.

Taking Terri Mason against the wall in unbridled passion may have been what his body had longed for and what had urged him to bypass logic, but all it had achieved was to make him feel like shit. And he'd feel even more shit if Terri thought there was more to it. It may have given him much needed physical release, but as for anything else...

Dragging his eyes from the condemned photograph, Jonah flicked through the article text and glanced at the other photos showing crowded tables around the Feathers; celebrities posing with the items they had bid on and won and the dancing girls on stage.

A good article, apart from that picture of him. More fodder for the gossips, he didn't doubt.

Was that it? Any more?

Turning the page, Jonah froze. Although there were four other photographs, his eyes were transfixed on only one. *A photograph of Teagan and Gwen.*

Teagan was there on Saturday? Why hadn't he seen her? Why hadn't anyone told him she was present?

Heat rushed up Jonah's spine and pooled to burn relentlessly in his chest. She was stunning. *Ravishing.*

He slowly dissected the image on the glossy paper. Teagan's strapless dress clung to all the right places; the colour a hundred different shades of deep blue at the same time. His gaze moved to one of her legs tantalisingly showing through the side-split of the dress…

His throat constricted at the unflawed skin of Teagan's shoulders and up to her beautiful, no *stunning*, face. Perfectly made up, her eyes resembled deep ocean pools and her dark glossy hair cascaded over her bare shoulders.

Christ.

Jonah knew she was gorgeous, but she looked something else here. He feverishly read the caption accompanying the photograph:

> *Gwen Vella, organiser of the renowned annual charity auction at the Feathers, is pictured with a stunning family friend - Teagan Fraser, a lady who we hope to see more of when we cover future events at this salubrious Soho club.*

He gulped at his whisky, his throat dry. 'I didn't know Gwen had invited Teagan,' he said, the audible crack betraying his wish to act nonchalant. 'Why didn't anyone say?'

Nero studied Jonah carefully. 'You were busy. You didn't have time to mingle.' Jonah's reaction proved everything and it was a lot, *lot* worse than he or Gwen could have imagined. *Jonah was in love with Teagan.*

'She's… She's beautiful…,' Jonah muttered, only half-aware he'd uttered the words out loud.

Nero tentatively moved towards Jonah and took a deep breath. He'd told himself he would do this if the need arose and from what he'd seen, it had. 'Listen mate,' he began. 'And I'm talking to you as a *mate*, rather than as my boss. You need to forget whatever you're thinking.'

Jonah's eyes snapped up, containing a note of warning, but Nero continued regardless.

'She's not in the right place and neither are you, after well… after Lena.' Nero placed his hand on Jonah's shoulder. 'I know it's none of my business, but if you care about Teagan, which I think you do, then you'll leave her well alone. For *both* of your sakes an...'

'You're right. It's none of your fucking business!' Jonah shrugged Nero's hand from his shoulder and threw the magazine back onto Gwen's desk. Necking the rest of his whisky, he walked to the door with a look that spelt out there was no room for further conversation. 'I'm leaving for the night. Make sure Gwen sorts the rota out.'

Halfway through the door, he turned back. 'I want you and Paul in here at 9AM tomorrow. We're visiting Benowitz.'

Leaving Nero to stand alone in Gwen's office, Jonah strode up the corridor, his head spinning. As much as he was tempted to knock Nero out for his impertinence in infringing on his personal business, he knew his friend of old was right. He must put aside any ideas he had about Teagan. The one thing he would not do was hurt her any more than she'd already been hurt.

FOURTEEN

IT HAD TAKEN a fair bit of wrangling and a shed load of money to twist the estate agent's arm into making the apartment in Holborn available immediately without jumping through the usual hoops of bullshit rental paperwork, credit bollocks and identity checks. Money was a great incentive and something that if the price was right, would always out in the end.

The rental price per calendar month was toe-curling, but then again, central London flats, especially ones bigger than a postage stamp, were daylight robbery. But Ron would take it on the chin because he had to show willing. Adams had stumped up a massive amount already, plus he'd supplied the gen Powell was on the move in the direction of Hatton Garden. No guesses where he was going.

This was also backed up by the text he'd received from Stan Leyton last night letting him know Powell was due to visit Benowitz today. There was no rush to move on that just yet.

Powell wasn't stupid. He wouldn't take the whole haul of diamonds there on spec. If Ron knew anything, the smallest diamond would be taken, along with detailed information about the others. Benowitz would then be left to do his job of finding a buyer and the best price. And that might take some time.

These things had to be done carefully - especially with something so smoking hot.

Now Stan had proved he was good for his word and placed to get all of the info from the horse's mouth, Ron would wait patiently until it was time for the main intercept. Then the diamonds would be his - with a kosher buyer conveniently lined up too.

But being as today proved Adams' tracking worked and worked well, it was quid pro quo. Ron had to move things forward with Adams' side of the bargain - *the girl*.

And for Kim to have come up with such a gem of information was another shocker.

Ron gazed at his grubby fingernails, thinking perhaps he'd underestimated the girl. Maybe she was more like Lena than he'd given her credit for, but time would out.

One thing he hadn't underestimated though, was Kieran. He was definitely a rock short of a lobster.

He stared at his nephew playing a death-defying game of Snakes on his mobile. Scowling, Ron snatched the phone from Kieran's hand and launched it over the other side of the room.

Kieran watched his phone bounce off Mike Pointer's living room wall and onto the floor. He scrabbled up from the sofa to grab the mobile and stared at it. 'What did you do that for? You've cracked the bloody screen!'

Ron grabbed Kieran by the scruff of his shirt and pulled him towards him. 'I asked you to help your sister cart her stuff over to the new place, so why the fuck are you sitting here playing stupid games?' He pushed Kieran away with force.

Kieran stumbled against the armchair, his face screwing into a scowl. 'Why should *she* get a posh flat while the rest of us are cooped up here?'

Ron scraped his fingers across his balding head. He would punch this shit-for-brains in a minute. 'Did you not hear what was discussed last night? Why are you even here if you're doing nothing but taking up space and oxygen? Tell me that?'

'I just want to know why can't I go as well?' Kieran

whined. 'There's room.'

'No there's not!' Ron spat. 'The Teagan girl will hardly want to move in somewhere with *you* kipping on the bloody sofa, will she? We have to do our part so Adams gets what he wants. At least your sister has done something to contribute. You might want to think about that.' He jerked his lumpy head in the direction of the door. 'Now fuck off and sort it!'

Kieran stormed from the room, his expression that of a sulky child. Pushing past Heath in the hallway, he stomped upstairs.

Heath quickly backtracked to the kitchen. He'd been loitering outside the lounge to hear what was being said, but he didn't want O'Hara to spot him. He'd only get roped into it and he didn't want to be dragged into carting Kim *or* her stuff about.

Turning the tap on, he filled one of the few remaining glasses with water and gulped it down.

The initial relief he'd felt hearing Kim was moving into her own apartment had morphed into concern. Aside from being astounded how she'd cleverly and surprisingly supplied a bona fide lead into securing Teagan, it also amplified that although he was more than glad for one of the O'Haras to be out of the house - especially *Kim*, it didn't change his growing unease.

Heath had previously suspected Robert Adams had a thing for Teagan, but not a thing in the *normal* sense of the word. It was strange and he couldn't quite put his finger on it.

Whilst in prison, the one thing that had haunted Heath was out of all the things he'd orchestrated, or helped orchestrate, was his part in involving Teagan. The girl had never had anything to do with any of this, yet she'd been brought into it on every level. This alone wouldn't have been quite as bad if she was a nasty piece of work, but Teagan was actually a nice person. And that fact was starting to chafe.

Could he really sit here and justify allowing this lot to sacrifice her to Robert Adams? The man had a screw loose.

If Robert was capable of killing Saul Powell, then what *else* was he capable of?

. . . .

PAUL WALKED WITH NERO behind Jonah as he strode briskly towards Benowitz Fine Jewels on Greville Street. It had been ages since he'd been to Hatton Garden and wouldn't have minded a ganders at the nice pair of cufflinks which had caught his eye in the shop they'd just passed, but there was no time for such luxuries.

He frowned. The unusual atmosphere in the car on the way down had been unsettling. The silence wasn't the type between people who were comfortable. It was heavy and laced with resentment. Something had occurred between Jonah and Nero, but Paul didn't know what and he was hardly in the position to ask.

Bad feeling and outstanding issues meant minds weren't on the game. Arranging a fence for burning hot stolen jewels worth millions wasn't something that could be done safely with half-baked concentration and getting tucked up and involved with this decades old heist was not top of Paul's bucket list.

Coming to a halt outside Benowitz's shop, Paul looked up at the non too special chipped black façade. The small frontage was dwarfed in comparison by several of the other jewellers on this strip. A less ostentatious front for the best jewellery fence in London?

A bell tinkled when Jonah pushed the door and walked inside the shop, Nero and Paul behind him.

A stocky, balding man behind the counter looked up. 'Good morning, gentlemen. How can I help you?'

Jonah stared at the man. This was definitely not Benowitz - he was about eighty years too young for a start. 'I have a valuation appointment with Abe Benowitz,' he said, feigning interest in the trays of gold sovereign rings under the glass counter.

'Is he aware of what it's concerning?'

Without looking up, Jonah muttered, 'Yes, we spoke on the phone. It's a *Unicorn* piece.'

'One moment please.' The man got up from the counter and moved through the door behind.

Nero glanced at Paul as they waited in silence. This place wasn't what he'd expected at all. He'd heard of Benowitz - who hadn't, but this place looked more akin to a pawn shop than a renowned jeweller in the centre of Hatton Garden.

The door opened and the man stepped out. 'Please go through, Sir.' He then turned to Nero and Paul. 'If you gentlemen wouldn't mind waiting here?'

Jonah followed the short, stocky man into the back room, seeing a tiny, withered and ancient man sitting at a cluttered desk surrounded by piles of boxes and jewellery trays.

'Thank you, Stan,' the old man said, bidding his assistant his leave.

With great effort, the old man pushed himself to his feet and extended his arm. 'Jonah Powell, I take it? I am Abe Benowitz.'

'Pleased to meet you, Mr Benowitz.' Jonah made sure he didn't shake the man's bony hand as firmly as he would normally do, worried it might break.

'Take a seat.' Benowitz indicated to a green leather-covered chair and smiled widely, exposing a surprising amount of remaining teeth for one so old. 'You look a lot like your father, boy,' he said. 'A good man he was. A good man.'

Jonah pulled a silver cigarette case from the inside pocket of his suit jacket. 'You dealt with my father on many occasions and he spoke very highly of you, Mr Benowitz, hence me coming to you now. Let me show you what I've bought, if I may?'

Benowitz's rheumy, but alert eyes watched Jonah carefully. 'I didn't think I'd live to see the day the *Unicorn* jewels were rediscovered, yet alone be requested to be moved. Why now?'

Opening the case, Jonah extricated a small piece of material and placed it on the desk. 'It's been a long time coming, I agree, but now is the right time. I need them gone.'

Benowitz studied Jonah for a few seconds in silence, before nodding. His gnarled fingers unwrapped the scrap of black fabric.

'That's one of the smallest for your inspection,' Jonah said, watching Benowitz examine the diamond. He tried not to let his eyes wander and instead watched the old man go about his work.

Pulling the long-armed light towards him, Benowitz first studied the small pink diamond on the black material, his loupe eyeglass wedged snugly in his right eye.

Picking up a pair of long tweezers with surprisingly nimble fingers, he clasped the tiny jewel and held it up to the light, turning it slowly. After what seemed an age he placed the diamond back on the black material. 'How many have you salvaged in total?'

Jonah reached into his pocket and pulled out a selection of close-up photographs. 'These are all the small ones we have.' He pointed. 'That particular one is the same one you've got in front of you to put the sizes into perspective.'

Benowitz put on a pair of wire rimmed glasses and peered closely at the photo. 'Yes, all around 0.3 to 0.4 carats.'

Jonah stared at Benowitz in fascination, wondering how he needed specs to see a photo clearly, yet nothing but the loupe to analyse intricate elements of a tiny jewel. He placed the other two photographs in front of the old man. 'These are the larger ones. I photographed the stone you have there next to them again for comparison.'

Benowitz studied the pictures, a whistling noise sounding from between his teeth. 'That one…' His arthritic fingers pointed to a medium-sized diamond on the left of the photo. 'That's a light pink, but the others…' His head swivelled to the other photo. 'They look like vivids.' He tapped the tiny gemstone in front of him with the tweezers. This one's *definitely* a vivid.' His old eyes raised to Jonah's. 'I presume you know the difference?'

'The vivid pink are the most valuable?'

Benowitz nodded. 'Correct. It looks like all but one are vivid.' His face cracked into a wide smile. 'These,' he pointed to the photo of the medium-sized jewels, 'I'd say come out just under two carats a piece, but these...' He pointed to the largest diamonds. 'Those two are at least fourteen carats each. You've got yourself a fine haul here, son.'

Jonah smiled. 'Can you shift them?'

Benowitz sighed deeply. 'I can, but as you'll appreciate, shifting something of such significance isn't easy and will involve a fair amount of risk...'

Jonah grinned. Benowitz may be older than the Doomsday Book, but the old boy would drive a hard bargain. 'Name your price. You will be substantially rewarded for your troubles.'

'Just like your father,' Benowitz smiled, tapping the side of his head. 'Sensible.' He looked up, his old eyes twinkling. 'As it happens after your phone call the other day, knowing what it was concerning, I made a couple of preliminary calls. Just to test the water, you understand...'

Benowitz's old fingers wrapped the tiny diamond back in its black cloth. 'I have a couple of potential buyers. One, a Russian and the other, South African.'

Jonah frowned, not much liking dealing with the Russians.

Seeing Jonah's expression, Benowitz continued. 'There are few places where items with such an intricate history, shall we say, can be moved undetected and made into saleable pieces. The nature of how these were acquired limits our options.'

Jonah nodded. Nothing he hadn't expected. He also knew he'd have to take a cut of the actual price for that very reason. The buyer would be taking a big gamble whether they could be safely offloaded the other end. Of course, Benowitz would want a percentage. All of that was fair enough, but the most important thing wasn't the money, it was getting them gone.

'When?' he asked. 'When do you think you could arrange the deal?'

Benowitz frowned. 'I'd like to say two weeks? Maybe more. Maybe less...'

'And the price?' Jonah's eyes met with Benowitz's. He may want them gone, but he was no mug.

'Obviously I'd have to see them in real life before I can give a final figure, but that's too risky to happen until the day of the deal.' He waggled one of his extraordinarily long fingers. 'Look around the £17 million mark. I'll need to hang on to this small one to show the buyers the quality.'

Jonah nodded once more. 'And your cut?'

'40%.'

Jonah couldn't offload these things without Benowitz's knowledge and contacts, but 40%? On the same vein, Benowitz was the best and no one else could do a better or safer job. '30%,' he countered.

The corner of Benowitz's mouth twitched. '35%'

Jonah grinned and stood up. '35% it is, Mr Benowitz. Get in touch when we can move on it. The sooner the better.'

FIFTEEN

'HI BABE,' Kim trilled down the phone. 'Just to let you know my flatmate has confirmed she's moving out today, so the room is all yours if you still want it?'

Teagan grinned. She hardly knew this woman, yet it already felt like they were good friends. A warm feeling replaced the sad hollow clattering inside her heart. It would be nice to have somebody she could have a laugh with and believed she might be able to do that with Kim.

If nothing else, this recent business had taught her one thing: Men couldn't be trusted. First Joe, then Darren, Saul, Robert and now Jonah. Her lips tightened. She'd never trust another man again.

These last few years had revolved around work which hadn't left much room for anything else, aside from the one proper relationship she'd had, and even that one with Joe had turned out to be fake.

No, she was done with it.

She hadn't even had any girlfriends to let hair down with or talk to for years. Her one best friend from school, Nadine, she'd lost contact with several years ago. The last she'd heard, Nadine had moved to America. Although they'd sworn to remain in contact, it had never happened and she'd never had the chance to strike up a friendship with anyone else, so sharing a place with Kim would be good.

'I've just thought,' Kim continued. 'You haven't seen my flat or the room yet. Did you want to have a look around before you make a final decision?' She had everything crossed Teagan wouldn't want to. It wouldn't be until later today that any furniture or any basic living stuff, like plates and cooking things were being delivered.

Uncle Ron would have a fit when he saw the bashing his credit card had taken, but he wanted the job done didn't he? Furnishing a two-bedroom flat from scratch didn't come cheap, so it was a good job he had a cracking credit limit.

Kim smiled. The knowledge that now she was important - that she was finally being taken seriously and that everyone was for the first time, treating her like a *somebody*, was the best feeling ever.

In fact, now she was intrinsic to everything they had to involve her in everything. It was brilliant. The only problem was Kieran. He'd been a right sulky bastard since she'd got the flat.

'What do you reckon?' Kim repeated, aware Teagan hadn't answered her question. A small glimmer of worry flickering, hoping she hadn't changed her mind. 'You checking it out first or not?'

Teagan smiled to herself. There was little point. Even if the flat was a dump and her bedroom the size of an airing cupboard, it was preferable to being here. 'No, I haven't changed my mind and I don't need to check it out. It sounds fab!' Suddenly hearing a crash in the background, she frowned. 'What was that?'

Kim swung around, glaring at Kieran who had just dropped one of her boxes. It had better not be the one with her makeup in it. 'Just my clumsy boyfriend!' She forced herself to laugh. 'He's helping Cilla, that's my flatmate, load up her car.'

'I didn't realise you had a boyfriend,' Teagan said. 'I hope

I won't be a gooseberry?' The last thing she wanted was to live in a love nest, watching a loved-up couple drooling over each other. *Maybe this was a bad idea?*

Sensing she'd said the wrong thing, Kim hastened to backtrack. 'Don't worry about him, he doesn't live with me.' She laughed shrilly. 'He's always working and I don't see him all that often. There are no gooseberries here, so when are you moving in then, Teagan?'

Teagan felt the grin slide back onto her face. 'How about tomorrow? Would that be ok?'

'Tomorrow would be perfect! I can't wait!' Kim squealed, mentally calculating how long it would take them to put all the furniture together, whilst making the gaff look lived-in. 'Grab a pen and I'll give you my address.'

Sitting on the window seat with the phone wedged in her neck, Teagan grabbed a piece of paper and a pen, stiffening seeing Jonah's car pull up the driveway. She fought the urge to remain staring as he, along with Nero and Paul got out of the car.

Leaving here was the right thing to do, but how to broach it with Gwen and Jonah was more difficult.

She knew they'd insist on her staying, but how could she explain the real reason why she wanted to leave? Aside from not wanting to remain in this house with all the dreadful things that had happened, she would not stoop to embarrass herself further by saying out loud that she had to get away from Jonah because he was all that she could think about.

His ego was big enough as it was.

• • • •

JONAH HELD UP THE BOTTLE to Nero and then to Paul. Seeing them both shake their heads, he shrugged and poured himself a large one before plonking himself down in his favourite chair.

He'd felt a lot better about this living room since replacing the three-piece suite and all of the things Lena had insisted he buy. He'd never liked them and he certainly didn't want anything remaining in his house that she had touched, let alone chosen.

He looked between Paul and Nero in turn. 'Hatton Garden went ok.'

'Who was the short, balding bloke?' Nero asked. 'I didn't much like the look of him.'

'One of Benowitz's,' Jonah said. 'He wasn't party to anything we discussed, I made sure of that.' He swilled the whisky around in his glass. 'Hopefully, the diamonds can be shifted over the next week or so.' He shrugged his big shoulders. 'Although I don't want to deal with the Russkies, if they're the only ones willing to take the risk, then I'll take it too.'

Nero nodded, his eyes tracking out of the large patio windows, seeing one of the security guards Jonah had insisted upon. 'You've still got them stationed here?'

A muscle under Jonah's left eye twitched. Aside from giving him advice on his love life, would Nero question every decision he made? 'Why wouldn't I?' he snapped. 'We still need to be conscientious about O'Hara and the rest.'

Hearing a floorboard above creak, Jonah glanced at the ceiling. *Teagan was upstairs again.* He hadn't seen her since the weekend and he was desperate to set eyes on her, even if just to know she was ok. The security would be doubly in force for as long as she remained here. He would and *could* not risk her coming to any harm.

'There's been no sign of Adams, though. Not a peep. I don't think we'll hear from him again,' Paul added. 'The guy sounds like a fruit loop and has gone to ground. Come to think of it, I haven't seen Teagan lately either. How is she these days?'

Silently flinching, Jonah shrugged. 'Ok, as far as I know.' He'd seek out Teagan tomorrow and see if he could make her feel less uncomfortable. She didn't have to tiptoe around. He just hoped he could control the urge to take her into his arms. She deserved more than he could offer her, he knew that.

Nero watched Jonah's attention focused on the ceiling where he could hear footsteps. There was no guessing who they belonged to and why Jonah's attention was elsewhere.

Jonah knew Nero was watching him and resented the intrusion. 'You haven't got any further with locating O'Hara, I notice? It's *imperative* we locate him.'

Nero inwardly scowled. It was true he'd got less further along with the O'Hara situation than he'd hoped and didn't much like that fact. 'As you know, there wasn't a lot to report on the City Car Sales. We know Heath Pointer's there and some other young muppet, but no sign of O'Hara. I'm a bit stuck on where to go next.'

'We've still got to arrange that test drive though,' Paul added, not having forgiven Nero from dragging him away before he'd had chance to give that nice Jag a burn up.

Jonah nodded, his attention back on the matter in hand. 'Arrange the test drive,' he said. 'Nero was right. We can't be sure if Heath Pointer clapped eyes on him at the Feathers, so make it just you, Paul. See what else you can dig from the father. Put pressure on if necessary.'

'I'll arrange it then.' Paul grinned, reaching for his mobile.

• • • •

RON STARED AT THE BACK of Kim's head, irritated she'd ordered so much clobber and even more irritated she expected everyone to ponce about building her flat-pack furniture tonight. With the amount of cash she'd got through, he'd have at least expected it to be already bloody assembled. Still, that Teagan girl was supposed to be moving in tomorrow. Kim had worked fast and Ron had to grudgingly admit he was impressed.

His eyes swivelled to Mike yabbering excitedly on the phone to a potential customer and waited until the call had ended. 'You don't do yourself any favours acting over-excited. It reeks of desperation.'

'Ah, but this is the guy who came in the other day. The one interested in the S-Type.' Mike glared at Heath. 'And if *he* hadn't buggered off whilst I was taking delivery of the Audis, I'd probably have already sold it to him. On top of that, Phone-Boy over there sat through the whole thing, not once giving them any assistance.'

'Ron scowled at Kieran. 'Is that true? You ignored the customer?' Getting up from his chair in Mike's office, he gave his nephew a clip around the head.

'OW!' Kieran yelped.

'What's the matter with you, you prick? Did you not notice them?'

Kieran rubbed the back of his head. 'I noticed them. I just didn't like the look of them. They looked like a pair from the Sopranos!'

Ron rolled his eyes. 'For fuck's sake! Is there anything you are capable of?'

Ignoring O'Hara and Kieran's squabbling, Heath tapped his password into the computer. *He didn't like the sound of this.* 'What day did you say these people came in? Two of them you say?'

'Christ on a bike!' Ron cried. 'Are you lot fucking paranoid or just plain stupid? It's just two blokes looking at a car. Not everything revolves around you Heath!'

'It was Friday last week,' Mike said. 'The day I took delivery of the Audis.'

'The footage shouldn't have been overwritten yet,' Heath said. 'Call it a hunch...'

'Do you think it was the actors from The Sopranos?' Kieran asked, suddenly interested.

Ron rolled his eyes and plonked back down in the chair watching Heath move the cursor to the relevant CCTV footage. *Was he the only sane person here?*

Locating Friday's recording, Heath moved the timeline along until two men entered the showroom. He peered closer, pausing the video and zoomed in on the faces, cold sliding up the back of his neck. Prickly bits moved from his fingertips and along his arms, up through his chest and up into his nose. He'd seen that man before.

Heath's forehead creased as he homed in tighter on the man who rang every single alarm bell in his head, acutely aware the office had gone eerily quiet.

Suddenly the memory of where he'd seen this man hit him like a shovel to the side of his head.

That man. It was him...

Heath's eyes moved across the man's face, his large head sitting on the thick neck and the hands like shovels...

That man was driving the car the night he'd witnessed Jonah Powell running from Footlights - the night Helen Shepherd had been killed. This man had been driving the car Jonah Powell clambered into...

Heath's attention moved to the second man on the CCTV footage. Now that one wasn't the other man there that night, but *this* one was.

Suddenly aware he was making strange strangulated sounds, Heath's head jerked away from the screen to see both O'Hara, his father and Kieran staring at him.

'What is it?' Mike asked, his face showing the first twinge of apprehension at his son's expression.

'T-This bloke,' Heath stammered, pointing to the image on the left of the screen. 'This is one of Jonah Powell's crew.'

'What?' Ron spat, moving closer to the screen. 'Are you sure?'

Heath nodded. 'Categoric. I don't recognise the other one, but this one is for definite. It was the night Jonah Powell legged it from Dulcie Adams' house. The night Helen Shepherd was shot.'

Ron's head swung around to Mike. 'Who the fuck is Helen Shepherd?'

'Long story.' Mike frowned. 'But if he's one of Powell's men, then so is *he*.' He pointed to both the men on the screen.

Ron sighed dramatically. 'When are they coming to test drive the Jag?'

'Only one is coming and that's tomorrow at 2 o'clock,'

Mike spluttered, his face white. 'He's not coming to test drive the Jag though, is he?' Fear pulsed through his body. 'He's coming to kill me. To kill all of us...'

'That's what *he* thinks,' Ron muttered.

Sixteen

'GIVE ME THE ADDRESS,' Robert barked, leaning across his makeshift desk for a pen. He sighed impatiently, hearing the rustling of paper down the other end of the phone line. That showed how unorganised this idiot was. Phoning someone up to give them an address without even having it to hand? *Pure stupidity.* Another reason why the fool's business had run itself into the ground. 'I would have thought O'Hara would have called to tell me this himself, rather than you,' he snapped.

'Ron had something he needed to do.' Mike pulled yet another receipt out of his pocket, along with a Twix wrapper. *Where the hell had he put the bloody address?* He'd had it just a moment ago and now it was gone. Becoming more flustered, his hands frantically felt around all of his pockets.

He'd have preferred if O'Hara phoned Robert Adams up too. The man might be his own brother, but he couldn't deny he didn't much like him. Something about him.

O'Hara always had something to do. A bit like last night when Mike agreed to help O'Hara and Kieran build that furniture for the flat and what had happened?

Within half an hour of getting started with the disturbingly huge amount of large boxes containing Kim's flat-packed furniture and its accompanying Chinese instructions, O'Hara had buggered off, stating he got to see a man about a dog. More likely he'd fucked off to the pub.

Mike could hardly blame O'Hara for that, but it had meant leaving *him* to deal with it.

Heath had been there, but he wasn't on form. Usually good with stuff, he'd been distracted, clearly uncomfortable. If Mike didn't know better, he'd say his son was worried. Worried about the plan to move the girl from Footlights into that flat with Kim O'Hara. But Heath had been more than happy to play the girl himself in his schemes to get those diamonds, so surely he'd hardly bother developing a conscience now?

Besides, it wasn't like anything would happen. Heath had already said Adams had a thing for the Teagan woman, and although he was a bit of an oddball, he wasn't about to murder a woman he wanted to be with, was he?

As for Kieran, well he'd been as much use as a chocolate teapot.

O'Hara hadn't shown his face again until goddamn midnight and it was almost 2AM before they'd wrapped up.

2 bloody AM.

Mike's teeth clenched. He was absolutely ball-bagged. He'd put together enough furniture to stock IKEA and if he ever saw another instruction sheet again it would be too soon. All he wanted to do was go to bed, but instead he'd got that test drive this afternoon hanging over his head.

'I haven't got all day!' Robert barked.

Mike almost dropped his mobile from fright. *Christ, he'd forgotten he was even on the phone!* That was what happened when he was overtired. *Damn O'Hara for all of this.*

Fishing around in his trouser pocket, Mike suddenly spotted the address on the table in front of him. It had been there all along. 'I've got it,' he blurted. 'Have you got a pen?'

'It's probably dried up the amount of time I've waited,' Robert snapped, fingering the remaining images of Teagan waiting to be stuck to the wall.

He glanced up at the montage covering the entire back wall. It was so frustrating. From the pile of cuttings he'd got left over, he'd only needed another fifty papers to cover the whole second wall, but despite having gone back out the other day to purchase more, he'd only managed to get his hands on a couple and that wasn't enough. There couldn't be any gaps without pictures.

His jaw clenched. Now this pilfering idiot was jerking him about?

Robert's mind sharpened as he scribbled down the address his brainless half-breed brother finally blathered off.

'Are you still there?' Mike asked.

'Yes, I'm still here,' Robert snapped. 'Teagan's definitely moving there?'

'She'd better be after the amount of bloody furniture I've built,' Mike muttered. 'Kim said she's coming today.'

Robert's heart lurched. 'Today? What time?'

'Time?'

'Yes. Time. What time?' Robert would gladly wrap his hands around this man's neck by now if he was within reaching distance. Alas, he wasn't.

'I don't know what time. Kim just said today,' Mike said, put out. He didn't know *everything*.

Cutting the call off abruptly, Robert stared at his mobile. He had to be there. He had to see Teagan with his own eyes to remind himself what she'd done. His eyes tracked back to the wall. 'I'll see you today,' he said loudly as if the black and white newsprint could hear.

Shoving his phone back into his pocket, he picked up his car keys, then stared at the address.

He'd go now. He'd go and wait. He'd wait all day. It was fine. Teagan would arrive at some point and he would be watching and waiting. In the meantime, he would work out what he would do when that time came.

• • • •

LEAVING THE NOTE on the sideboard in the main sitting

room, Teagan felt this would be the best place. The place where it would most likely be noticed quickly.

Not ideal, but there was no way Gwen or Jonah would let her go *regardless* of her reasons if she'd broached it with either them. This was the only way and the only window of time to make her move too, so there was no other option but to take it.

Pacing up and down the square reception hall, Teagan's ears remained tuned for the approach of the taxi. It was a gamble giving a time, but she couldn't walk from here. She might be seen and that would be worse.

Gwen and Jonah were both at the Feathers, along with Nero and the other men of Jonah's who came to the house on a frequent basis, but they could come back any time. There was never a set time when one or another of them might drop in to check on her.

She had, however, thought she'd stalled things, downplaying the need for suspicion. This morning first thing, Teagan had acted purposefully upbeat, pretending to be eager to see the article in OK magazine Gwen had told her about and which she'd promised to bring back to show her when she returned from work this evening.

Because of this she was confident Gwen had no reason to believe she wouldn't be here, therefore hopefully removing the chance of one of them coming back during the day. At this precise moment, all of the security guards were around the grounds, rather than some of them being out front of the property, so if this bloody taxi got a move on she'd be away without anyone being any the wiser.

Hearing the crunch of tyres on gravel, Teagan's stomach flew to her mouth. Peering through the window and seeing the outline of the taxi, relief flooded her.

Taking one last look around the place where several people had been brutally murdered only weeks ago, Teagan grabbed her oversized handbag - the largest thing she could safely use to stash the bare minimum of essentials in without bringing attention and rushed out of the door.

SEVENTEEN

MIKE TRIED HIS BEST TO KEEP HIS COOL. O'Hara said if he followed the instructions, all would be well. But it wasn't well. His hands were clammy and he felt sicker than he thought humanely possible.

Putting his foot to the accelerator, Paul took the roundabout a little bit too quickly, the normal flood of adrenaline pumping as it always did when speed came into the equation. How he longed to put some decent tunes on and blast the music. He'd love that. It had been ages since he'd had a decent burn up and this car was the dogs.

He grinned hearing the roar of the V8 under his control. *Yeah, quality car, this.*

Paul glanced at Mike in the passenger seat, his dark navy pinstripe suit overtight and swallowed a smirk as the man's foot twitched over an imaginary brake pedal. 'She handles well, mate,' he grinned. 'How much did you say you wanted for this?'

Momentarily diverted from his fear that if he didn't die at the hands of this scary-looking member of the Powell firm - the very firm baying for their blood, then it looked like he'd end up as a fatality in a hideous head-on collision the way this nutter was thraping the car, Mike's eyes darted to the driver, resisting the urge to undo the top button of his shirt so that he could breathe.

He'd just been asked how much for the car?

Could it be possible this was Heath's over-active imagination and these men had nothing to do with the Powells at all and merely wanted to buy a car? Like a normal person?

In his panic, Mike couldn't remember how much he'd put the Jag up for. *Quick. Think, think.* '38K, if I remember rightly.'

O'Hara had warned him not to get side-tracked. He'd said this man may attempt to lull him into a false sense of security and to answer no questions, making sure he stuck to the main roads. And he had.

In fact, the driver had taken the very route Mike had suggested, with no attempt to suddenly veer off down unknown lanes where there could be a trap. There was nothing suspicious, but that didn't stop the strong sense of foreboding.

Remain alert, Mike, he chanted silently, glad to see there was only a mile to go before they would reach the safety of the forecourt.

Paul scowled when the traffic along the A40 to White City drew to a crawl. How he hated the London roads. Barely any space to slam the accelerator down. He'd been lucky to even get one decent blast. But the downside was that he'd got side-tracked. The whole point of this sojourn was to do digging.

His eyes flashed to the landmarks. *Bollocks.* They were almost back. He really was a sucker for a decent motor. *Still, no time like the present...*

'Did your son turn up in the end?' Paul asked.

Mike stared at Paul, confused. 'My son...?'

'Yeah, the other day you said your son works with you?' Paul blasted the Jag's horn at the car in front for not pulling off the second the lights turned to green.

Mike flinched. *Jesus. Calm, calm... He was only chatting... Nothing to worry about...* 'Oh yes. He'd been to pick up some invoices,' he blustered, unsure why he was explaining anything.

'And you said it's a family firm? Any other relations working there?' Paul pressed. Now his mind was focused he could smell this man's nervousness. His *fear*. Mike Pointer was hiding something. 'Who's the muppet? Phone Boy? He's the only one there again today. Is that wise, considering his attitude to customers?'

'He wasn't *my* choice,' Mike snapped, before remembering himself. 'I mean, you can't choose your family, can you? I had to offer him a headstart in the business.'

'Oh, so he's family too?'

'No, he's just... Well, I mean, he's a family friend.' Mike corrected himself. *Now it was getting obvious*. This man was subtly grilling him because he knew exactly who he was. This was no coincidence. His shirt clung to his back under his suit jacket and he almost cheered with relief when the City Car Sales sign came into view. 'Ah, we're back.'

Paul scowled. *He'd ballsed this up. He should have used his time better. Jonah would not be pleased.* 'Can I take it round again?'

Finally giving in to the strong urge, Mike stuck his fingers into his collar for much needed air. He felt like he was choking. 'Can't, I'm afraid.' He forced a smile. 'I've got another test drive booked in ten minutes. You could always book in for a second another time?'

He pointed to the carport to the left of the showroom, where for some reason, O'Hara wanted the car parked. 'Pop it in there if you wouldn't mind. See what you think of the reversing sensors and camera.'

'It's got a camera?' Paul grinned, impressed. 'Fancy stuff!' At least he'd deduced Pointer was hiding something. He may not have properly grilled this dick, but he'd redeem himself by hanging around and tailing that muppet boy - the one Pointer was being cagey about.

Yeah, he'd do that. That might bring some leads. He had the strong suspicion the young lad was the key to something else.

Swinging into the forecourt, Paul pulled in front of the carport. 'I'll stick it next to that white motor,' he said, slamming the Jag into reverse. 'How does this camera thing work?'

'It's this here.' Mike pressed a button and pointed to the inset screen on the dashboard which changed from listing the speed and journey time to the view of the carport. 'The camera is inlaid in the back,' he said, proud of his knowledge.

'That's fucking ace, that is,' Paul grinned, genuinely impressed. 'It would take a bit of getting used to not having to look behind or in the mirrors.' He backed into the carport, his eyes glued to the screen.

Mike breathed a sigh of relief. Now he could get away from this bloke.

Paul froze seeing a figure on the screen pointing the barrel of the gun at him from behind. 'What the...?'

Mike didn't even get chance to look before the window of the Jag blew out and the man slumped forward onto the steering wheel, the horn sounding relentlessly as the body slumped against it.

He only began screaming from the bottom of his lungs when a lump of Paul Bannister's brain tissue slithered from where it had landed on Mike's cheek down onto his shirt.

• • • •

ROBERT WAS STIFF AS A BOARD. Four hours he'd been here and still no sign. He pulled out a folded newspaper clipping from his wallet and ran his finger down the outline of Teagan's body.

He'd also checked the tracker. Powell's transmitter was signalling static and had been all morning. The man was at the Feathers as expected. Or at least his *wallet* was.

Robert's nose wrinkled like it always did when he happened to think of an alternative to put the kybosh on a well-laid plan. There was always the possibility that Powell was not at the Feathers. He could have left his wallet and be somewhere else. He could even be accompanying Teagan to the new O'Hara flat?

Robert shook his head with irritation. That was a stupid theory. His brain-damaged moron of a brother had already said Kim had told him "man-problems" were Teagan's reasons for leaving the Powell residence and it didn't take a neurosurgeon to work out *exactly* who the man-problem was in Teagan's life at the moment.

Public humiliation was a better way of describing what Powell had done to her. Being binned off in favour of a slut who made a living getting her tits out on stage was insulting to anyone, but in Teagan's case, it was just desserts.

A smirk slid across Robert's face. Teagan would have no men problems now Powell was out of her life and *he* was taking back his rightful place. The place that he should have never walked away from in the first place.

Robert's decision to leave Powell's place had been uncharacteristically rash. If only he'd bypassed the disgusting knowledge and ridden it instead then he could have started Teagan's well-deserved punishment long before now. But he'd been fortunate in arranging a way to amend his mistake. Had O'Hara not been open to doing what was asked, then his task would have been more laborious.

Still, it was important to have faith. The world was now his oyster. Robert always had faith. It never failed to come good and sometimes he had no concept of why he would ever doubt himself.

But where the bloody hell was Teagan? It was plain to see she wouldn't have told Jonah of her new location, so why wasn't she here?

Robert meticulously folded up the clipping, checking the folds mirrored the original ones. It had to be identical to when he'd first folded it, otherwise the link would break.

Leaning back in the driver's seat, he flexed his stiff shoulders and rolled his neck. His plan would be difficult and it would be hard pretending, but it had to be done. If it worked, which he was hopeful it would, then it could cut a chunk of time off and he could get straight into what was needed.

The vision of having the real-life, flesh and blood Teagan in his room at the B&B with the backdrop of the wall covered in her image would be a sight to behold. One that would be better than *anything*.

Robert's concentration spiked sensing Teagan had arrived. *Yes, there she was.* His pulse accelerated. He was never wrong. His instinct was something he'd meticulously groomed to the point of precision. It had always served him well and yet again, hadn't disappointed.

Clambering from his car, Robert popped the boot and pretended to look in it, counting down the seconds before Teagan would pass so he could put his memorised plan into action.

EIGHTEEN

HEARING HER NAME, fear flashed over Teagan's face. They'd found her. One of Jonah's men had somehow found her. Had they tailed her in the taxi?

She'd asked the driver to drop her half a mile away from the address to avoid any chance the taxi firm may be located and encouraged to spill the details of the fare collected from the Powell residence, but they'd found her anyway? *How?*

Almost too terrified to focus, Teagan's thoughts diverted from one to the next. Should she run for it? What should she do? She couldn't be forced to return to Jonah's house. *Wouldn't.*

'Teagan,' Robert repeated, stepping out from behind the boot of his car. 'It's me.'

Suddenly recognising the voice, Teagan swung around with relief. *Robert?* Apprehension then overtook her. 'What are you doing here?'

Robert smiled amiably; his act honed to perfection. He pointed to the CPU in the boot. 'Dropping this server off for a client who lives just across there.' He pointed to a row of town houses opposite. 'What are *you* doing here?'

Teagan faltered. 'I... I... erm...'

Robert shut the boot and walked around the side of his car, leaning casually against the back door. 'I'm really glad I've bumped into you,' he said. 'I've been trying to think how I could get into contact with you without involving the rest of *them.*'

He stuck his hands in his pockets so she wouldn't see the relentless twitching of his fingers. 'I owe you an apology for upping and leaving the way I did.'

Teagan studied Robert. He looked well, but sad and tired. The apprehension she'd felt diminished. 'Are you alright? I hoped you be at Dulcie's funeral... Oh, Robert, I'm so sorry... You must be devastated.' Without thinking, she reached out and placed her hand on his arm.

Robert counted to five slowly in his head. He'd been practising this. It stopped the immediate urge to flinch; to punch this soiled whore in the face and rip her leprous, infected fingers from his jacket sleeve. *The plan, Robert. Breathe.*

'I-I couldn't face it...' he murmured. 'I wanted to go, but then everything just hit me suddenly. Listen, I need to explain...'

'You don't need to,' Teagan said, her heart breaking for the man who had once shown her so much kindness. 'I understand. I...'

'I said some dreadful things to you and I'm so sorry.' Robert forced himself to look into Teagan's traitorous, lying eyes. His concentration moved to her mouth, knowing *exactly* where it had been. *Whore. Tart. SLUT. I'm not sorry. Not sorry for what I'm going to do to you. Not even forever.*

'I understand,' Teagan interjected, placing her other hand on Robert's chest. 'I really do.'

Robert's eyes flashed with fury as he battled to override the overbearing need to rip Teagan off him and push her into the gutter where she belonged. Where *all* of them belonged. *How could she understand. How could any of them understand?*

Instead he quickly replaced his mask. 'No, I really do need to explain.' He moved away under the pretence of reaching into the car for his cigarettes. 'Too many things happened... Things you don't know about... After a while it all went boom in my mind. I couldn't handle it.'

'I know...' Teagan whispered. 'I know what you did to Saul, but it's ok.' As soon as she said the words, she questioned whether she should have. She'd seen something in Robert's eyes and the last thing she wanted was make him feel worse. This poor man had to live with killing Saul and then his mother dying with their problems unresolved... 'I know you did it for me. Saul was evil, Robert. You did the right thing.'

Robert turned away to light his cigarette. He had to pull his head together. He was losing it. Losing the thread. *Concentrate. Concentrate.*

It wasn't for you, Teagan, you bitch, he thought, acid bubbling within his mind and threatening to spill into his words. *There is nothing I will do for you, apart from take everything so you know exactly how you have made me feel.*

Sucking in air through his nose, Robert turned around and took a drag from his cigarette. Now was the time. She believed he was damaged, like her. He was nothing like her and never would be.

'I want to make it up to you. I want to put things right.' He took another long drag from his cigarette. 'There's other stuff you don't know. Those people you've been staying with... I need to tell you about them. You need to get away because they're poison.'

Teagan stiffened, apprehension mounting once again. *What was he saying?*

'I shouldn't have left you there. I should have taken you with me, but I wasn't thinking straight. I *couldn't* think straight,' Robert continued, his lies gaining pace. 'Please leave that place.'

'I...' Teagan was about to say she had already left and had no intention of ever returning, but something stopped her. She stared at Robert, trying to read him.

'I've moved to London now,' Robert said. 'I couldn't go

back to my flat in Maidenhead.'

'Oh, but what about all your lovely furniture?' Teagan gasped. 'And Footlights?'

Robert looked at Teagan, slightly bemused. *Footlights? The scourge of his bloody life. And furniture? Like that mattered? Like any of it mattered? Only one thing mattered and this was it. Teagan was as open and stupid as she'd always been. She'd learnt nothing. Nothing at all. It was almost comical.* 'Why don't you come and stay with me?'

Teagan smiled. *Everything was alright - Robert was fine.* 'That's really kind, but I'm moving in with a friend. That's where I'm heading now.'

'A friend?' Robert cried, feigning surprise. 'Where?' *As if he didn't know...*

'Just there.' Teagan pointed to the block of flats behind her. 'I'm sharing a flat with a girl called Kim. It will be a fresh start.'

Robert stared up at the flat. *Yes, he knew exactly where she'd be living.* With a girl who would now be tantamount to his plan. As much as he was disappointed Teagan hadn't made things easy to bypass all the extra work now needed, her reaction proved no one had told her anything. That's if those retarded thugs had even worked any of it out themselves? Teagan was still amenable and in a way that would make the end result even more satisfying.

'I'm so glad you're ok,' Teagan said. 'Please keep in touch.'

'It's been nice to see you Teagan. Here's my new number.' Robert held out a scrap of paper with the number of the Pay-As-You-Go phone he'd picked up last week. 'Call me when you get the chance to talk and we can meet up.'

'I'd like that,' Teagan took the number. 'I'd best get myself in there. Kim will be waiting.'

Everyone's waiting, Robert thought, winching a smile back onto his face. He waved as Teagan walked up the path to the block of flats. He wouldn't be waiting for his phone to ring. *Not for long, anyway.*

• • • •

MIKE WAS STILL IN SHOCK. The several brandies that O'Hara insisted he drink had taken the edge off for a while, but no matter which way he looked at it, he couldn't delete the image of half that bloke's head splattered all over his suit. And the Jag was wrecked too...

It was all very well O'Hara saying the back screen could be replaced and the inside valeted, but how would it be explained? *"Hi, yes, a full valet please. You know, the works... We need to make sure all tracks of gore and brain tissue have been removed otherwise it will be a bastard to sell..."*

'Are you going to sit there all night like that, Mike?' Tammy asked, her concern replaced with irritation. 'If you won't tell me what's wrong, then either stop sitting there like that or go somewhere else to do it.'

Mike willed his fingers not to tremble as he reached for his glass.

'Sitting there drinking all night hasn't helped,' Tammy moaned. Studying her husband, her face paled. 'Has the business gone tits up?' Her hand flew to her mouth. 'Oh my God, it has hasn't it? You behaved like this a couple of months back and wouldn't say why and now you're at it again.'

Moving to stand in front of her husband, she folded her arms across her chest. 'If things are going down the pan, I have the right to know. It affects me too.'

Mike didn't want to look at Tammy. How could he? Little did she know how close they'd already been to losing the business and their house. To losing *everything*. And they would have done too if it wasn't for Ron O'Hara. But look what that had brought. *A living, waking nightmare.*

Now, as well as Heath's freedom teetering on the brink, it looked like *he* would lose his freedom as well. It wasn't likely the police would let someone with a body riddled with bullets in a car at the car salesroom he owned carry on as normal, would it?

Sweat poured down the back of Mike's neck. Surely it was only a matter of time before the police came looking and then he'd be banged up for eternity.

'MIKE!' Tammy screeched, slapping her hand on the kitchen table. 'What's going on?'

Mike's eyes flew to his wife as if noticing her for the first time. 'I'm sorry, love. I'm out of sorts.' *Understatement of the bloody year.* 'Everything is fine with the business, really it is. I just don't feel well. I think that sausage roll I ate at lunch was a bit iffy.'

And it would be even more iffy if O'Hara didn't return and tell him what the upshot was. The nutter had acted like shooting a man in the back of the head - and a man from the *Powell* firm at that, was something and nothing. O'Hara had merely instructed Mike to go home and that he'd sort it, but that was *hours* ago.

Raising his head, Mike saw Tammy was still staring at him suspiciously. *Go away, please go away.* 'Honestly, I'm fine. Everything's fine. I'm just not feeling well.'

Tammy's face screwed into a scowl. 'You're well enough to bloody drink though?' she spat. 'You'll moan about being hungover tomorrow.'

Hearing the front door slam, Mike's head jerked up.

'Oh great!' Tammy spat. 'Now *they're* back. I'm going to bed. It's late.' Stomping across the kitchen, she barged past O'Hara and Kieran as they entered, not bothering acknowledging them.

Mike looked over his shoulder as Tammy's footsteps stamped up the stairs and into the bedroom.

'What's the matter with her, the miserable bitch?' Ron muttered, pulling his cigarette packet from his pocket, then plonking himself down at the kitchen table.

'What's the matter with *her*? What's the matter with *you*, more like?' Mike had had enough of this lunacy. 'Are you going to tell me what you've done with... with that *thing* or don't you deem me important enough? We'll go to prison for this,' he hissed, staring at O'Hara accusingly. 'Are you insane? You've been ages! Where have you been for Christ's sake?'

Ron casually lit a cigarette. 'Cor, you don't half flap!' An irritating grin formed on his face. 'As I said earlier, it's all in hand. It's sorted.'

'What do you mean, *sorted*?' Mike cried. 'How can it be sorted? What have you done? Glued his fucking head back together?'

Hearing Kieran chuckle as he helped himself to a bottle of Budweiser from the fridge, Ron glared. 'Don't be a prat, Mike. All you need to know is that it's sorted. Other news is the Teagan girl has safely moved in with Kim, so everything's going nicely.'

'You call *that* going nicely? You murder a Powell bloke in one of my cars whilst I'm sitting next to the fucker and that's *nice*? Meanwhile, all you're bothered about is this girl moving into Kim's flat?'

Mike pulled his hair, sure it would detach from the roots and flutter from his head to lie on his shoulders. *A bit like that man's head...* Nausea rose once more as the vivid image of the scene in the carport returned with a vengeance.

Tapping his ash in the ashtray, Ron sighed loudly. 'As I said, I told you I'd sort it and I have.' He spoke slowly - methodically, like he was comforting a child. 'The body has been delivered as planned.' He glanced at his watch. 'And someone should stumble across it any time now. Powell will get our message loud and clear. Tonight he will realise he needs to watch his step and that I'm gunning for him.'

Mike blinked once, then twice and then reached for a top of brandy. 'Oh, that's great that is! Advertise your grudge with Powell. Wonderful...'

Getting up from his seat at the kitchen table, Mike paced up and down and glared at Kieran playing the snakes game on his mobile again. *What was the matter with the boy?*

He raked his fingers through his hair, genuinely amazed it was still attached to his head. 'There will be retaliation for this,' he yelled. 'The Powells will know it was you - or *us* and there's no knowing what they'll do.' Mike increased the speed of his pacing. 'Christ, Ron, they've already killed Dulcie and set Heath up for it, so how do you think they'll react having one of their own men butchered and dumped on their doorstep? This is unhinged! Jesus!'

Ron laughed at Mike's meltdown. 'The Powells are bullshit. They weren't the ones who killed Dulcie Adams. Neither did they set Heath up. They're not that fucking clever!'

Mike stopped pacing and stared at O'Hara in disbelief. 'What? What do you m...?'

'It was Adams!' Ron laughed, loving Mike's flabbergasted expression. 'I know, it's brilliant, isn't it? Robert Adams killed his own mother and framed your boy. And before you ask, I know this because Adams told me himself.' He stubbed his fag end out in the ashtray. 'I'm playing Powell and this is only part one. Eye for an eye, remember and I owe them at least two.'

Ron's face cracked into a sinister smile. 'Robert will be happy now that bird of his is ready and waiting at the flat and I can carry on with my payback - which in case you hadn't noticed, started today.'

· · · ·

PRESSED AGAINST THE KITCHEN DOOR, Heath did not dare breathe in case his presence was noted. He could feel a vibration moving up his legs and prayed his knees didn't start knocking together and making a racket. *It was Robert? Robert had killed his own mother and set him up to take the blame?*

His initial rage turned to dread. Without a doubt the man was psychotic and now he'd got his sights set on Teagan? O'Hara said Teagan was ready and waiting... She'd walked into a trap...

Heath's heart pounded, sweat trickling down his back underneath his shirt as he forced air into his lungs. This changed things. Could he really stand by and let whatever was planned for Teagan go ahead? He didn't know what Robert Adams was planning, but now knowing how he worked, it wasn't going to be good.

He knew he'd been set up over Dulcie Adams' murder, but he'd thought, he'd presumed, he'd been *convinced*, it was down to Jonah Powell. It made sense for it to be Powell, but all along it was Robert?

Heath leant forward, his clammy hands clawing at the thick layers of gloss paint on the lounge door jamb and knew at that moment that with all certainty, he would have to warn Teagan. This couldn't go on. He needed to get to that flat and warn her that she was being set up. Robert Adams was more unhinged than he thought. *A hell of a lot more.*

He focused on the noises from the lounge. They were still arguing in there, but would any of them come out? He couldn't risk them knowing he'd overheard.

Backtracking, Heath crept up the stairs and into his bedroom. Shutting the door, he shot the bolt home. Even though Kim was no longer here he still wanted the protection it offered.

Flopping onto his bed, Heath put his head in his hands. He couldn't go to that flat and warn Teagan because Robert would be watching the place. *Waiting.*

Bile rose into his throat. His only other option was to go to Powell. But could he risk betraying his father and the nutjob Ron O'Hara to tip Jonah Powell off? Or could he live with being the one person who, at this moment in time, could stop anything happening to Teagan at the hands of that seriously unhinged bastard, Robert Adams? *Impossible decisions.*

NINETEEN

STILL DRESSED IN HER STAGE CLOTHES: the jewel-encrusted leotard, plumed headdress and overdone makeup, Terri had literally jumped straight from the stage the second the curtains closed in her haste to reach Jonah's office before anyone else had the chance to collar him. Rushing down the corridor towards the main office, she prayed her sky-high heels wouldn't snap and slow her up.

Since the weekend, she'd been the talk of the dressing rooms. All the girls were pea-green with both fascination and envy. Gutted she'd been the first to score the jackpot when such a prize was open to all.

Who would win the attention of Jonah Powell had been the main topic of conversation since word spread Lena was off the scene.

Terri still had to blink to believe her own good fortune. In her wildest dreams she'd never have believed Jonah Powell would pick *her* from all the gorgeous girls at his disposal, but he had. He'd picked *her* and now she had a real chance to make something of herself.

The taste of what life would be like by the side of this man was intoxicating, to say the least. The press clamouring for photos, being treated with the utmost reverence and celebrity status, not to mention the mind-blowing quickie in the toilets on Saturday had been but the start of it.

Back at her flat - yes, Jonah Powell had accompanied her to her very own apartment - the night of passion they'd shared had been something else. The man was a tiger between the sheets and she'd barely been able to catch her breath. All night they'd hungrily explored each other's bodies.

The reality was better than the dreams she'd had and what she'd longed to happen for ages. Of course, she'd have preferred it if Jonah had hung around the next morning, rather than take off not much past first light. Apart from wanting luscious morning sex with the man, she'd have loved nothing more than to show him off to her flatmates. But she wasn't too disappointed. Being as Sue and Jenna had heard the previous night's passion through the thin walls it hadn't taken long for the gory details of the night they'd spent together to pass along the Feathers' grapevine.

The only question on everyone's lips now - including hers, was would they become an official couple?

Terri's heart glowed with a mixture of happiness and anticipation. The newspapers thought so. As did the magazines.

Fancy being in a magazine... She could still hardly believe it herself.

But although she'd been in work every day since, she'd yet to speak to Jonah alone. She'd hoped he'd have sought her out by now, but she wasn't too disconcerted. After all, he was extraordinarily busy.

Starting to get out of breath from her exertions, Terri rushed along the final part of the corridor, her heart leaping seeing Jonah leave his office, locking the door behind him.

'Mr Powell!' she cried, scuttling towards him. She'd wondered whether to call him Jonah. She'd moaned that very name over and over on Saturday night, but figured that until they went official, it was professional to refer to him as Mr Powell in public. But that would change very soon, she was sure of it.

Almost running slap bang into Jonah as he stopped abruptly, Terri smiled up at him. Going giddy at his ice blue eyes, she fluttered her heavy false lashes, all too quickly imagining the feel of his full lips over every inch of her skin once more.

'Hi,' she breathed. 'Are you busy? Thought we might grab a drink?'

Jonah smiled as genuinely as he could while extricating himself from Terri's cornering ability, glad he'd already locked his office door.

He could hear the phone ringing from inside the office and if the door was still open, he'd be tempted to go back and answer it. One; that's what he always did because work took precedence, and two; it would offer an excuse to get away from this woman.

But he'd do neither of these things and the phone could keep on ringing because tonight he was going home and that was priority. 'I'm leaving for the night, Terri,' he said.

'Surely you've got time for a drink first?' Terri purred, running her hand down the lapel of Jonah's suit, refusing to allow her disappointment to show. 'The show's only just finished.'

Jonah removed Terri's hand from his chest. 'I'm really sorry,' he said. 'I've got things I need to take care of at home.'

Feeling confident, Terri leant closer. 'Anything *I* can help with?'

'Unfortunately not. Maybe another time? Goodnight.' Turning on his heels, Jonah walked away before Terri could say anything else and hoped she didn't follow.

He berated himself for his response. What he'd said made it sound it was a possibility another time. A heavy pang of guilt flooded him. He knew what Terri was angling at - she believed there was a likelihood of her becoming a frequent or permanent fixture in his life and Jonah knew he would have to disappoint her. But how he wished he didn't. It would be so much easier to have a no-strings fling, but he couldn't. If he couldn't have Teagan, then he wanted no one. *It was as simple as that.*

However, it was true he had things to sort out at home. Time may be getting on, but he needed to have that talk with Teagan. He wanted her to feel comfortable and as much as his heart leapt with the prospect of speaking to her, it was bittersweet. Nevertheless, he still had a duty to uphold.

Deciding to leave the Feathers via the stage door rather than the main entrance to cut down the risk of getting stopped by anyone, or worse, bumping into Terri again, Jonah yanked open the heavy steel door. He'd walk round to his car from here.

Striding down the stone steps, he cursed under his breath almost tripping over a pile of bin bags at the bottom.

Which fucker thought it acceptable to dump half the contents of a trade bin at his stage door? One of the girls could have tripped and broken her ankle because of this.

His face screwing into a scowl, Jonah thought about going back inside to grab Nero or Paul to sort out someone to clear this mess, but aside from not having seen either of them tonight, he didn't have time to mess around otherwise by the time he got home it would be too late to expect Teagan to want a conversation.

No, he'd just do it himself.

Rolling up his jacket sleeves, Jonah grabbed the top of one of the bags. *Jesus Christ, that was heavy! What was in it? Bricks?*

Using both hands, he pulled the bag, the thick industrial plastic slightly tearing.

Sweating from exertion, Jonah got a better grip of the black plastic and was about to pull again when he caught the sight of something poking through the ripped area.

It looked like hair...

Squatting down, his heart thudding painfully, he ripped at the bag.

'Fuck!' Jonah cried, stumbling onto the steps in horror as Paul Bannister's face was revealed behind the plastic, the back of his head missing.

• • • •

GRAVEL FLEW IN ALL DIRECTIONS as Jonah screeched into the driveway of his house. Jumping from his car, he didn't bother locking it and raced up the steps, his fingers fumbling in his pocket for his front door keys.

Whether Teagan liked it or not and regardless that it was now 2AM, he'd be having a conversation with her. A very important conversation and one which could not be put off for another time - even a minute.

Glancing over his shoulder, he was heartened to see two security guards in the shadows. He shoved his key in the door and barged in.

'Gwen?' he roared. 'Teagan? Down here now!' Ripping off his suit jacket, Jonah threw it haphazardly against the coat stand, not caring that it ended up in a crumpled heap on the floor. That could wait. *This couldn't.*

'GWEN! TEAGAN! Come down here now. It's important!' Jonah moved towards the sitting room only for Gwen to rush straight into him.

'Oh thank God!' Gwen cried, white-faced. 'I didn't think you'd ever get ba...'

'Go and fetch Teagan,' Jonah barked, pushing past Gwen into the sitting room. 'I need to speak to you both urgently. I don't care how late it is, it's important.'

Gwen remained frozen to the spot. 'I tried calling you at the Feathers, but I couldn't get hold of anyone. I...'

'Please get Teagan,' Jonah yelled, getting irritated. 'I haven't got time to fuck about.' He was damned if he would get berated for not picking up the phone. Not while he'd had bodies to move and deal with.

'She's gone,' Gwen said, watching Jonah slop whisky he was pouring down the front of his trousers at her words.

Jonah swung around. 'What?'

'Teagan's gone. I-I tried to call you... I...'

'What do you mean, *gone*?' Jonah stared at the whisky soaking his front in confusion, not knowing how that came to pass. 'Gone where?'

'Left.' Gwen moved into the room, her eyes wide. 'I had no inkling until I got back and found this note...' She passed Jonah the piece of paper she'd found propped against the gold clock on the overmantle.

Snatching the paper from Gwen's hands, Jonah scanned the words:

Dear Gwen,

Thank you for everything. I hope everything goes well for you and the Feathers too. You've been a good friend and I would have preferred to tell you in person, but you'd try to talk me out of leaving and I couldn't allow that. This is the right thing to do.

I can't remain here anymore. It's not good for anyone and I need a fresh start.

Please pass my thanks to Jonah too.
All my love
Teagan
X

'Fuck!' Jonah muttered, dropping into the chair. *Teagan had gone? Where and when? How? She couldn't. Not when someone was targeting them. It was too dangerous. Shit!*

'I don't know how she left unnoticed. Security saw a taxi, but thought it was me...' Gwen said. 'Maybe this is for the best? Teagan clearly felt she needed to leave, so...'

'You don't understand! It's started. It's fucking started and she's not safe!' Jonah jumped from the chair and paced around the room. 'Jesus Christ, Gwen, Teagan's in danger and I'm not sure which angle it's coming from.'

Gwen guessed Jonah would take this badly, but this was more than that... Fear wormed its way into her insides and twisted. 'What do you mean, it's started?'

'Exactly what I said. That's why I needed to talk to you both,' Jonah barked, his eyes wild with rage and worry. *Teagan was out there somewhere. Unguarded. A target.* 'Paul Bannister's body was dumped at the stage door tonight. I found him. He'd been left there as a message. A message to *me*.' He watched the shock register on Gwen's face. 'The back of his head blown off. Gone!'

'W-What? How...? Wh...?'

'It was O'Hara. It *had* to be. Nero couldn't find a link, but there must be one. The Pointers' car sales place – I don't know?' Jonah's pacing became frantic.

'Wait! Slow down. I'm not following. A car sales place?' 'Why would...?'

'The Pointers own a car lot in White City. Paul took a car for a test drive. I told Nero not to go in case he'd previously been eyeballed by the Pointer lad and it looks like he was. Christ, Gwen! I sent Paul into a bloody set up. A fucking trap!'

Gwen tried to make sense of the avalanche of information. 'And O'Hara's involved?'

'Why else kill one of my men?' Jonah spat. 'O'Hara's involved with the Pointers somehow and he's sent that message. He's going after everything associated with me. It's got to be him. This is the sort of thing he'd do.'

He poured himself another large whisky. 'We've got to find Teagan. If Pointer is involved, which he must be, then O'Hara will also be aware of Teagan's association with me via Heath, don't you see? She's in danger, big time.'

'But I thought comeback on Teagan was more likely to be from Robert Adams?' Gwen reasoned. 'Isn't that what you said before? What reason would O'Hara have to go for Teagan?'

Jonah fumbled for his cigarettes. 'That I don't know. I don't know where that cunt Adams is either, but Teagan cannot be out there on her own. Do you not understand? That goes for you too, Gwen. Until I can take O'Hara out we're all targets.'

Gwen nodded. 'I see. And where is... where is Paul? His body?'

Jonah gulped at the whisky. 'Nero's at the Feathers dealing with that until I decide what to do. I may no longer be able to help Paul, but I can ensure no one else gets offed as part of O'Hara's payback. That includes everyone else at the club too. The girls, *everyone*. But we have got to locate Teagan and bring her back to where she is safe.'

Gwen sat quietly, thinking wherever Teagan had gone was probably safer than being around here or the Feathers. She hoped so anyway because she couldn't help but feel part of the reason behind Teagan's unexpected departure was down to what she'd made out was going on between Jonah and Terri Mason.

TWENTY

'I'M SICK OF THIS,' Nero fumed, slamming his fist down on the workbench. 'This ain't right!' He glared at Paul's body laid out on the table. 'Look at the fucking state of him!'

Jonah nodded. He understood Nero's wrath and felt the same, but what could they do?

'We've lost a good bloke because of those wankers and this is the best we can do? Hole his body up in a fucking lock up?' Nero spat. 'We should never have gone to the car sales place to start with. I had a hunch that Heath Pointer prick might recognise me.'

Jonah had already racked his brains for what to do with Paul's body. He was loathe to send the man to a car crusher for his final resting place, but there was no other plausible solution which wouldn't involve the police or bring attention to everything else. And that they could not do.

Aside from stitching themselves up over countless matters, it would also mean he would be unavailable to get his hands on O'Hara. And furthermore, find Teagan. He had to put an end to this and do it fast.

'You said the Pointer lad wasn't at the showroom when you visited, so it must have been via CCTV,' Jonah mused.

'Then they must have had their suspicions of us from the off to watch it in the first place. Why else would they, apart from to get an ID from the Pointer lad?' Nero's fury built further. 'I'm going to kill the cunt!'

Jonah shook his head sadly and pulled the tarpaulin back across Paul's body. 'There's no way around this. I'll call Talbot to pick him up.'

'He's going to the crushers?' Nero pulled his hand down his face in exasperation. 'For fuck's sake!'

'Sorry, mate,' Jonah said. 'Not a lot else we can do under the circumstances. He had no wife or anything, did he?'

Nero shook his head. 'Divorced, but not amicably. His parents are long dead and no siblings, as far as I know.' His mind swirled. Up all night dealing with this, he was shattered, but not as shattered as from losing his mate.

He'd liked Paul. Liked and respected him. Now he was gone and Nero couldn't help but feel responsible. 'The Pointers must be harbouring O'Hara because I don't believe they've got the balls to pull a stunt like this.' His head swung up, an idea forming. 'I'm going to the house.'

'House?' Jonah frowned, alarm bells ringing. 'What? Pointer's house?'

Nero nodded, grabbing his bomber jacket. 'Yep. I'm going to locate the address the car sales place is registered to. That's most likely the home address and I'll turn the fucking place over until I find O'Hara.'

Jonah sighed. 'You can't. At least not yet.' He hadn't spoken to Nero of the major fear which had kept him wide awake for what remained of the night. The few hours before dawn had been spent sitting in his study, unable to get the vision of Teagan being held hostage again out of his mind. But this time being held hostage by O'Hara and the thought of that made every single nerve ending grate.

'You want me to sit here and do nothing? *You* want to sit here and do nothing? We know it's O'Hara.'

'What if he's got Teagan?' Jonah blurted, his throat dry.

Nero threw up his hands in frustration. 'Why would he have her? She's gone, that's all. She fucked off because it was the sensible thing to do. We *all* think it was the sensible thing to do, so leave her be.'

A further glimmer of unease radiated from Jonah's mind. *Had Nero and Gwen expected Teagan to leave? Had they known she was planning it? Encouraged it even?*

Regardless of what anyone said, he wouldn't rest over Teagan's welfare until all the possible threats were out of the picture. 'Whatever happens, you can't steam into Pointer's gaff.' Jonah eyed Nero carefully. We'll get the place watched and if he's there, we'll move on it.'

Pulling his mobile from his pocket, Jonah stabbed the digits for Talbot's car crusher into it and nodded towards the tarpaulin covered body. 'I'll get this sorted now. Go home and get some sleep.'

'I don't need sleep. I want this dealt with,' Nero muttered.

'Then get yourself back to the Feathers. Remind the men they're on stand-by. O'Hara is out to score points and I need to ensure everyone there is covered. We don't know what he'll aim for next and it might be the Feathers.'

. . . .

TEAGAN BUSIED HERSELF fiddling with the small amount of bits and pieces she'd brought with her. It hadn't taken long to arrange everything, but that wasn't the point.

She looked at her hairbrush and comb on the white, mirrored dressing table and smiled, feeling a tremendous sense of relief. Last night was the first night for months, and especially the last few weeks, that she'd slept soundly and today she felt both refreshed and positive.

Moving was definitely the right thing to do. By not being in that house she no longer had the constant reminder of what Saul Powell had done and what had happened because of his actions. Furthermore, there were no security guards and, more importantly, no *need* for them. It was liberating and only served to show how people involved with the wrong side of the law were forced to live. Forever looking over their shoulders to check they weren't staring down the barrel of a gun? That wasn't the kind of life she wanted or could live like for anybody.

Not that there was the option…

Teagan pursed her lips, purposely pushing away the encroaching thoughts. She would not think of Jonah Powell. *That* part of her life was over. And good riddance. He'd shown his true colours and she once again questioned how she could have been so naïve to think someone such as him; someone who was capable of, and had done so many dreadful things, could ever behave in any other way.

But she *had* thought it possible for a short while. And she'd wanted it. Even *dreamt* of it.

It was irrelevant. Jonah hadn't been interested in her, short of something to pass the time that once, but had they not been interrupted, Teagan shamefully admitted she'd have let him do whatever he'd wanted.

Good luck to Terri Mason. If the poor woman was happy to take the scraps of Jonah's life thrown to her like a dog when the fancy took him, then more fool her. If the woman was content with or would accept him putting it about with countless other women, then perhaps they deserved each other?

Teagan studied her reflection and mentally shrugged, grateful Gwen had restored her faith in herself after Saul. And that had been Jonah's plan. He'd known her to be especially vulnerable at that point, so he'd taken that very time to exert his charms.

A slight smile crept over Teagan's face. And by God, he had plenty of charm, but she wouldn't cry over her stupid, girlish thoughts any longer. *This was her fresh start and so far so good.*

The apartment was beautiful - so much better than she'd hoped. And there was her worrying it might be a dump. She couldn't have been more wrong. Teagan glanced around the light and airy space of her bedroom.

Kim had made her feel welcome too. Last night they'd ordered an Indian takeaway and shared a bottle of decent white wine whilst getting to know each other. Teagan liked Kim a lot. The woman had even lent her some clothes, which was really good of her, but she needed to go shopping and kit herself out with her own stuff.

She could, she suppose, arrange for her clothes to be collected from Jonah's house, but it wasn't worth the risk. It wasn't worth it at all.

Walking to the window, Teagan stared down onto the street below. Frowning, she squinted through the bright sunlight. She must be going mad. She was sure that was Robert's car - the one she'd seen him in yesterday, but it couldn't be. He wouldn't be back to deal with that client opposite already?

She shook her head in bemusement. No, she was imagining things. Besides, it had gone now. All that sleep, coupled with last night's wine and good company had scrambled her head.

Teagan smiled. Seeing Robert yesterday had made her feel a lot better. His disappearance had bothered her deeply. She knew his abrupt leaving had riled people, but she'd always believed there was a genuine reason behind it. And there was.

Seeing him and hearing the explanation from his own mouth yesterday meant a lot. Including his apology. All of it combined laid a lot of things to rest in her mind.

She briefly toyed whether to let Jonah know she'd seen Robert and would be lying if she said she wasn't considering it, but then promptly dismissed the idea. Considering she didn't want them to know of her whereabouts, neither did she wish to throw poor Robert to the mercy of Jonah's vile temper.

It was no secret he was furious about Robert's disappearance, although he'd never gone into details why. The man was so egotistical he'd no doubt taken it as a personal affront and sought to repay Robert's "betrayal", as he most likely saw it, with the mindless violence she'd heard all about, or whatever else he hid behind his posh suit and shiny club façade. A bit like everything about Jonah…

She wouldn't put Robert in that position and would not be responsible for anyone else becoming privy to one of Jonah's attacks. She knew his sort now. He didn't fool her any longer.

Teagan nodded to herself, confirming her decision. She might have been dragged into Jonah's way of life, but not anymore. She would not be party to any more of his lies to fuel his deluded sense of grandeur.

Her thoughts then turned to Gwen. The note she'd left should have been discovered by now, if it hadn't been last night and she did feel a little bad about that. Gwen had been good to her and Teagan couldn't help but feel she'd betrayed that kindness by disappearing like a thief in the night.

And Jonah? Did he know she'd gone? Maybe, maybe not?

Against her will, Teagan found herself wondering how he'd reacted. Had he been angry? Dismissive? Nonplussed? Shrugged his shoulders and rolled his eyes in irritation? His ice-blue eyes? *Those* eyes.

Stop it!

Moving across the bedroom, Teagan grabbed her handbag. She'd go clothes shopping right now. Kim was at work this afternoon, but they'd planned to go for drinks tonight and she couldn't wait. It had been so long since she'd had a laugh and was enjoying this new lifestyle already.

She found herself grinning. The money she'd saved would keep her going for a few more weeks and she intended to enjoy it.

With a spring in her step and a new sense of purpose, Teagan left the apartment.

TWENTY ONE

ROBERT WATCHED THE TRACKER with interest. It had moved somewhere different - a location he hadn't seen before. Jotting down the coordinates, he opened Google Earth and flicked up another tab in Chrome, opening an instance of Street View.

His forehead crumpled in concentration. *An industrial unit?* Jonah Powell was at an industrial unit, or very close to one.

Robert scratched his chin thoughtfully. A lock up for ill-gotten goods? Drugs? Could be either or probably both... It was unusual for Powell not to be at the Feathers or the house though.

At least watching Powell's whereabouts was deflecting Robert's mind from the frustration of waiting for Teagan. Knowing she was almost within *touching* distance, yet he had to wait. *Must* wait.

But it was difficult. All the extra minutes, hours and days sitting on his hands, waiting for the right time was torture. Complete and utter torture. But he must do things properly and in the correct order. That was imperative.

Robert scowled. He had to keep alert. His impatience was starting to make his brain malfunction. He didn't ever malfunction, so that was worrying.

He shouldn't have taken himself off to watch her flat again last night, but the urge had been too strong. The call was too loud, too insistent to ignore. But he still shouldn't have done it. It was hard. *So* hard.

Robert jumped at the unfamiliar ringtone of his PAYG mobile; the shrill noise disturbing his inner plan. He didn't like different ringtones; they sounded wrong.

It might be Teagan? Maybe she wanted to meet up today?

It might scupper O'Hara's plan of getting more info from her via that strange niece of his, but that wasn't Robert's problem.

Snatching the mobile from his pocket, he glanced at the screen:

Unknown number

Robert stabbed the answer call button. 'Yes?'

'I've had a call from my contact.'

O'Hara's nasally voice grated in Robert's head. *Not Teagan... Disappointing.* 'And?'

'The deal is happening next week.'

Robert remained silent. He liked silence better than noise. His mind churned with what O'Hara's words meant. *Another week of waiting. Watching.*

'Did you get that?' Ron asked. 'I want JP's movements recorded in case he tries his luck and brings the deal forward. If he speaks to Benowitz without my contact being aware, we won't know, so any movement on him in that direction needs acting on.'

'I'm already watching him,' Robert muttered. *As if he wouldn't be.* He wanted to know every footstep Jonah Powell made too. And not because of the fucking diamonds. He wouldn't have him moving towards Teagan. He may try to pull her back to complete his harem and that would not happen.

Teagan was *his*.

'Any interesting movements so far?' Ron asked, glad

Robert seemed on the ball. The man was more than useful and for a bargain price too.

'Not unless you count an industrial estate,' Robert said, his irritation mounting. *A week? He'd got to wait another week? Unbelievable.*

'By the looks of it, Powell took receipt of my present.' Ron chortled, then frowned at the silence the other end of the line. 'Don't you want to know what the present was?' Most people would ask what he'd meant, and Ron thrived on being the centre of attention.

Robert sighed. *He didn't care a jot.* 'Not really...'

Unperturbed, Ron continued regardless. 'One of Powell's henchmen met with an accident last night.' He laughed again, the noise sounding like a build-up of phlegm.

'Fascinating...' Robert muttered.

Ron absentmindedly flicked through a magazine whilst he waited for Adams to comment. *He had to want to know more details, surely?*

Finally getting the hint that Robert really wasn't going to push for anymore tit-bits of his cleverness, Ron sighed loudly. 'You know you can't move on your girl until all aspects of the plan are in place?'

Robert snarled inwardly. *Teagan was not his girl and never would be. She was a necessity.* She was what was needed to restore equilibrium. The equilibrium that she had damaged. And this prick, this Irish munter, was telling him he had to wait?

He didn't have to do anything he didn't want. And O'Hara would serve better if he remembered that one very simple fact. 'How long do you expect me to wait?' he snarled.

'As I said, a week. Kim will work on your girl for info on Powell whilst we wait for the deal to happen. It will all come together at the same time. It *has* to come together at the same time. Then she's all yours.'

'I'll let you know of any movements,' Robert said curtly, then ended the call, unable to listen to that nauseating piece of pointless shit any longer.

Hearing the call disconnect, Ron shook his head in amusement. *Weird fucker.* He continued skimming through the pages of the magazine.

What absolute drivel women read these days. There was sod all in this rag, apart from photos of celebrities and bullshit about where they'd been. Who in their right mind cared? He didn't know who half of these people were, let alone give a toss what they did in their sad, jumped-up lives. *Ridiculous.* Even Kim must have thought this rubbish pointless, otherwise she wouldn't have left it behind.

He was just about to launch the OK magazine in the bin when he stopped, his hand freezing on an article.

What was this? Jonah Powell's new love interest?

Ron's eyes flashed with delight. *Terri Mason...?* His eyes ran over the woman's slender body, his tongue trailing across his fat lips. *Very nice...*

Ron read the rest of the article with interest. It hadn't taken Powell long to replace Lena. And, by all accounts, the man was loved-up with this new tart?

Aw, how heart-warming. Not...

Ron stared at the lust in Jonah Powell's eyes centred on the stunning blonde in the photograph. Yeah, Powell liked his blondes, didn't he? Blonde and big-busted. Tits like bazookas. *Like Lena.*

Except this bird was merely a scutter whore from Powell's oh-so-popular stage.

Lucky you, Powell, Ron thought, his mind ticking over. So he'd found someone he wanted to be with? Someone to figure prominently in his life? The burgeoning romance of the century?

Ideal...

His mouth twisted into a sneer. *Eye for an eye, Jonah, remember?*

Ripping out the page from the magazine, Ron stuffed into his pocket, pleased numero dos had just been identified.

It had come to him too, rather than him searching for it. The best way and the way that showed him some things were just meant to be.

. . . .

GWEN FIXATED ON the worries taking centre stage in her mind. Paul Bannister was dead, Teagan had gone AWOL, Nero was baying for blood and Jonah, well – he'd reached the point where his increasing obsession with protecting everything and everyone was becoming uncontrollable.

How could people be expected to go nowhere unaccompanied and to be alert at all times if they weren't told *why*?

Her eyebrows knitted with concern. What Jonah was expecting her to police was impossible, given the criteria. He wasn't thinking about this clearly.

Now, Gwen admitted she didn't know all the ins and outs, but the one thing she *did* know was the person in the least danger was Teagan. If Jonah knew the true reason why the girl had left, then he wouldn't be anywhere near as concerned as he was.

But she could hardly admit she'd all but warned Teagan off and purposely set him up with Terri Mason. After the other things she'd hidden from him over the years, she doubted Jonah would be as forgiving this time around.

The trouble was, all of this only went to show the plan to help Jonah had not worked half as well as she'd hoped. With regret Gwen realised, if anything, her meddling had made things worse.

Only half-listening to the dressing room chatter around her, Gwen was suddenly aware the focus was centred on her. Flustered, she looked up.

'Are you off with the fairies?' Sally, one of the dancers, asked.

Gwen laughed. 'Did someone ask something?'

'Molly's moaning that we shouldn't have the hen do for Josie until we can all go.' Sally rolled her eyes.

'It's true!' Molly pouted. 'Don't you think so Gwen? It's not fair otherwise.'

Sally thew a rolled-up flannel at Molly's head. 'Oh, piss off, girl! When have you ever heard of a time when all of us were off for the night. Get a grip! There would be no show if that were the case!'

A loud burst of laughter ensued, which Gwen joined in with. *She loved these girls.*

'I'll just have two hen nights then! One for each shift,' Josie grinned, beaming widely.

'You're lucky to get one, let alone two before that one becomes the star of the show,' Sally grinned, placing her hand on Jodie's stomach, the tell-tale roundness of early pregnancy accentuated by the gold lamé of her skin-tight leotard.

'I've got a couple more months before I'll need strategically-placed feathers attached to my costume!' Josie laughed, tenderly placing a hand on her belly.

'We've also been trying to talk Terri into joining us at the weekend, but she's still sulking about being binned off by you-know-who... That's how she sees it anyhow, but we're not so sure.' Sally nodded at Terri staring forlornly into the illuminated mirror the other side of the dressing room.

'Hey, you'd know, Gwen. Put us *and* her out of our misery, will you? Has Mr Powell binned Terri off or what?' Molly sidled up to Gwen, her overdone stage makeup looking sinister at close range, like a giant over-painted doll.

Gwen smiled uncomfortably. Her plan hadn't affected just Jonah and Teagan. It had affected Terri too. How she wished she'd never had the idea. If she'd have known it would hurt people, she'd never have done it. She'd genuinely thought she was doing it for the good of Jonah and Teagan and hadn't in a million years believed Terri would take everything so seriously. Plus, she'd thought Jonah would keep up the no-strings liaison as a deflection for his worries. *Looks like she'd got it wrong...*

'Come on, Gwen, you *must* know...' Sally pushed.

Gwen frowned. 'I may be close with Mr Powell, but we

don't discuss his personal life. Besides, even if I *did* know, I wouldn't tell you. It's none of anyone's business what Mr Powell and Terri do in their own time.' She wagged her finger in a mock-stern fashion. Although she made light of the questioning, the point had to be made clear the girls were overstepping the line.

'Are you coming on Saturday?' Josie asked. 'Please say you are?'

Gwen shook her head and winked. '*Some* of us have to work.'

Even if she wasn't, she wouldn't go. It would only cramp their style. A lot older than them, she'd feel like their mother tagging on, plus they wouldn't speak as openly with her there. She was still their boss and she wanted the girls to have a good time. As Terri Mason was finding out to her detriment, mixing business and pleasure did not work.

'Where are you off to?' Gwen asked, hoping to God Jonah didn't get wind of this planned outing otherwise it would be *her* neck on the chopping block. She would, however, try to meet his demands half-way and send security along – subtly, of course.

'The tapas bar and then on to a club,' Josie chirped. 'Not sure which club, just not *this* one!'

Everyone laughed once again. Everyone apart from Terri, and Gwen decided she would see what she could do about talking the woman out of her doldrums and joining her friends on Saturday. It sounded like she needed it and, to be honest, it was the *least* she could do for Terri, considering she'd been the one to cause the problem for the poor woman.

TWENTY TWO

'LOVING THE DRESS, BABE!' Kim swigged at her glass of wine and looked Teagan up and down. 'You look hot!'

Blushing, Teagan beamed widely. 'Thanks. As you can tell, I had a spot of retail therapy this afternoon. I overdid it a bit and spent way more than I intended.'

Kim flapped her hand dismissively. 'Ah, you can never have enough clothes, honey. A girl's got to look her best!' She tottered over to refill Teagan's glass.

'Are we going out? I'll be sloshed before we even get anywhere at this rate,' Teagan laughed, again more than enjoying Kim's company, but well aware she didn't fare too well with too much wine. The last thing she wanted was to throw up over her new clothes and embarrass herself for the second time in front of her new friend.

'Soon,' Kim said. 'Just a couple more and then we'll shoot off.' She smiled widely, pleased how easy it was to mould this woman.

Despite not thinking she would, she'd found herself beginning to like Teagan Fraser, but not to the point of forgetting the overall aim of this meticulously concocted plan. 'That's if we don't get accosted by the press...' she added cryptically.

Teagan paused, her glass halfway to her mouth. 'The press?'

Kim smiled knowingly. 'Don't tell me you haven't seen that photograph in OK magazine? Don't get me wrong, I knew you were at the Feathers the night of the auction, otherwise I'd have never met you, but wow... you're a dark horse!' she winked. 'It said family friend... You know the lady who runs the cabaret, right?'

Teagan's good mood evaporated slightly. 'Erm, well, I know her, yes, but I wouldn't go so far as saying I'm a family friend. I'm not sure where they got that from.' She needed to play this down. She wanted no reminders of the Feathers or the people associated with it.

'Hey, in that case you must know the owner, Jonah Powell?' Kim plonked herself on the sofa next to Teagan and grabbed her hand. 'Come on, spill the beans! Tell me what he's like. Oh my God! He's as gorgeous in real life as the photos isn't he? We saw him coming out the bogs with that bird, remember?' She fanned herself with her hand. 'Phew, I wouldn't mind a bit with him!'

Teagan suddenly wished she was anywhere else but here. 'I've only seen him once or twice,' she lied.

If she let on that she'd lived in the same house, let alone *kissed* the man, she'd never hear the end of it. Neither did she want to acknowledge that Jonah Powell was excruciatingly handsome and even more so in the flesh, even though it was true. Furthermore, she didn't want to discuss the night they'd seen him with Terri Mason either. She didn't even want to *think* about him. That was the whole point of moving away, was it not?

Sensing Teagan had clammed up, Kim changed tack. She'd wait until the woman got a few more wines down her neck then she'd splurge her guts in more ways than one. Her eyes narrowed. Especially if she believed they were sharing confidences...

'Oh, ignore me,' Kim laughed. 'I'm a sucker for a handsome man in more ways than one, if you get my drift...' She winked conspiringly. 'Saying that, I screwed up with my husband. Pig ugly he was! I think I must have been pissed when I married him!'

'I didn't realise you were married!' Teagan gasped. *She'd thought Kim had mentioned a boyfriend?* There was so much she didn't know, but that was hardly surprising being as she hardly knew the woman.

'*Was* married is the operative word,' Kim lied. Actually, she'd never been married at all. Sometimes she forgot exactly what she said to people and she must concentrate this time. Too much was riding on it. 'He's dead now.'

Teagan's hand flew to her mouth. 'Oh my God, Kim, I'm so sorry, I...'

'Nah, don't be. He was a wanker. A raging alcoholic who beat me up and ran off.' Lying about her life was so easy. Kim had learned a huge amount by watching how Lena got what she wanted. *Talking of sisters...* 'Yeah, the bastard ran off with my sister. Until they both got killed in a car accident.'

'That's dreadful,' Teagan cried. *Poor Kim.* Yet, despite all of that heartache she was still so friendly, so chilled out and full of fun. A genuinely nice person.

'It was difficult, I'll admit,' Kim sniffed, switching on one of the many expressions she'd learned to pull from on cue. 'But, life goes on.' She stood up from the sofa. 'Talking of which, shall we hit the bar?'

'Yes,' Teagan smiled, all traces of uncomfortableness now forgotten.

Linking arms with Kim, Teagan happily walked from the flat and down to the road below, too preoccupied to notice Robert's car parked in the twilight.

• • • •

ROBERT FELT THE FAMILIAR BURN of rage spread around his mind and rode the gratifying feeling of satisfaction it brought.

This position was perfect to get a decent view and worth every single second of the time he'd waited. It would also be worth the stiffness he would undoubtedly suffer tomorrow from holding himself at such a strange angle for so long.

Holding his phone steady, he captured another selection of photos, his mind festering with contempt.

That had to be the fourth glass Teagan had tipped into her mouth in an hour, the cheap drunk. Only certain types of women drank like that. And *she* was one of them...

Robert's lips curled into a sneer, his expression turning to one of incessant rage watching a group of three men at the bar. Every single on of them had their eyes on Teagan as she sat without a care in the world, acting like a fishwife with the other grotesque parody of a female at the table they shared.

Only tarts went to wine bars - a classic haunt for women with no morals to prostitute themselves to well-paid males present in establishments such as these.

How he resented stepping foot inside a place such as this. And worse, actually having to buy a drink.

Robert watched Teagan from afar, her mouth covered in lipstick which left a disgusting imprint around her wine glass. The red gash of her mouth gaped in mirth at something the other woman said. Most likely preening over their admirers.

He clicked his camera several more times. Once he found somewhere to get the copies printed from his phone he'd have more coverings for his wall.

This woman with Teagan - this was Kim? The woman, who if O'Hara was to be believed, was his ticket to infiltrating the needed information?

Robert's eyes narrowed. *Well, Kim, you'd better get a move on because I'm getting impatient.*

The urge to slash his Swiss army knife through Kim's neck for slowing up his mission intensified. Every time he saw Teagan it made him angrier. Angry with *himself* as well as her.

How he'd allowed himself to be fooled. To be changed.

Almost. He despised that this little harlot possessed the power to trick him into thinking things he couldn't think. But he'd come to his senses and stopped himself falling foul of her guiles just in the nick of time.

Why had she come into his life? Why had his bitch of a mother picked her? Why could all of them not have left him alone? He'd been fine before. *Absolutely fine.*

Frantically taking more pictures, Robert realised to his horror that his fingers were shaking. He couldn't wait much longer. All of the other people in this shit hole; this collection of tarts and fake pimps with their bottles of cheap wine blurred out. The only face in focus was Teagan's; her face flushed from too much alcohol. She was laughing at him. Fucking *laughing* - he could see it. She was looking straight at him and laughing.

Soon she would pay for her obscene thoughts, her vulgar way of living and her behaviour.

Robert's heart ramped up to an alarming speed, the thumping pounding painfully in his chest and echoing loudly in his ears.

His jaw ached from clenching as he watched a man approach Teagan's table and involuntarily jerked forward before reining himself back in. *He had to leave. He was losing control.*

Robert hastily pushed his way through the throng of people in the busy bar, ignoring the irritated looks he collected along the way.

Reaching the pavement outside, he slipped into the shadows before allowing himself to breathe a deep lungful of air. He must cleanse the filth he'd allowed to enter his body from the segment of repulsiveness he'd just been trapped in an enclosed space with.

TWENTY THREE

HEATH SAT IN THE OFFICE in Kensington, thinking the place looked more like Buckingham Palace than a lawyer's firm. The small, but exquisitely furnished waiting room with its leather chesterfields, marble fire surrounds and coffee tables piled with neatly positioned magazines was all very nice, but Christ, this lot didn't half have some money.

His eyes focused on the fish in the pristine tank inlaid in the wall. It felt he should be wearing a tuxedo to even sit here, let alone have a meeting with the man getting paid a fortune to keep him out of prison.

Heath had already done his weekly stint of reporting to the cop shop to satisfy the bail conditions and wished more than anything that this was over, but it could be months and months before his case came to court.

Now he knew Robert Adams had framed him in the first place, that the man was now paying for this lawyer was even more disconcerting than when O'Hara was footing the bill.

Heath pushed his hair off his forehead away from his eyes.

How could he get away with warning Teagan what Robert Adams was planning? If he managed it, would she even believe him? Would she believe *anything* he said when she discovered he'd lied about his identity and wasn't Darren Harding after all?

Maybe she already knew? If that was the case, then thanks to the papers, she'd also be aware he'd been charged with the murder of Dulcie Adams. The Dulcie Adams she'd thought so much of.

If he got in touch with her she may even call the police in her terror and accuse him of harassing her? But if he went to Powell instead and somehow avoided getting immediately shot, then that would scupper things too. If Robert Adams discovered Heath had betrayed him, or if Powell took retaliation against Robert, then who would pay this bill?

He glanced back around the waiting room. If he didn't have a decent brief, he'd go back to prison. Just because he had a shit-hot defence lawyer didn't mean his release was assured, but at least he stood more of a chance than without one.

Christ, there was no easy solution to this. What the fuck was he going to do?

'Mr Pointer?'

Heath looked up to see the lawyer's starch-faced secretary had glided undetected into the waiting room.

Forcing a smile, he stood up and prepared himself to listen to what his brief had to say. With any luck he'd be informed the case had miraculously been dropped due to insufficient evidence.

Of course, this was unlikely, but it was better than thinking about Robert Adams because it was getting him precisely nowhere, apart from one step closer to being locked up or murdered.

Maybe he should just mind his own business and keep the hell out of everything?

• • • •

TEAGAN NERVOUSLY wandered into the sitting room. Again, she'd overdone it last night and the last part of the evening was a worrying blur. Much to her unease, she couldn't remember getting home. But she must have done because she was here. As was Kim.

Worry strummed along Teagan's veins. She may well be enjoying her newfound freedom, but what use was that if she was so stupid as to get so drunk she couldn't remember what she'd done or where she'd been? With what had happened in the not so distant past she should know better and it was an extremely foolish attitude to take.

Teagan pushed open the lounge door a crack, not wishing to burst in for fear of what she may find.

'Ah, there you are!' Kim cried. 'I thought you would sleep all morning!'

Moving fully into the room, Teagan's eyes darted around. 'Yes... I...'

'Morning!' Kieran brushed past Teagan and walked into the lounge.

Kim laughed loudly seeing Teagan staring at the stranger. 'You should see your face, Teagan. It's a picture!' She cut Kieran a knowing look. 'This is my boyfriend.'

'Erm, hi,' Teagan said awkwardly.

'We met last night.' Kieran looked Teagan up and down, his eyes lingering a lot longer than they should.

Pulling her dressing gown tighter around her, Teagan's eyes darted to Kim. *They'd already met?*

'She won't remember,' Kim grinned at Kieran, then turned to Teagan. 'You were mashed, babe. I had to call my fella to help get you home.'

Teagan's cheeks burned scarlet. *How embarrassing.* 'I'm so sorry. I...'

'And then I couldn't get rid of him,' Kim chuckled. 'Not that I minded having company in my bed.' She snaked her hand onto Kieran's crotch.

'Kim!' Kieran snapped, batting Kim's hand away.

Teagan looked away in embarrassment, but Kim continued nonplussed. 'Don't mind him. He'll be off soon, won't you?'

Kieran nodded, staring at Teagan inquisitively. 'I hear you're a bit of a celebrity? In with all the gangsters and murderers from the Feathers?'

'W-What?' Teagan stuttered.

Kim's high pitched laughter trilled loudly to disguise the hefty warning nudge to Kieran's ribs. 'You were having a bit of a rant last night, Teag, but don't worry. We won't repeat it.' She narrowed her eyes conspiringly. 'Although you'd make a fucking fortune if you sold your story to the News of the Screws. The papers would *love* to hear what you told us!'

A wave of dread flooded Teagan. *Oh God, what had she said? She'd been talking about the Feathers? About Jonah? What exactly?*

Her eyes darted to Kieran who was still studying her intently. *She hadn't said anything about Saul had she?* Teagan felt like passing out.

'She hasn't got a clue, look,' Kim laughed.

'That's a dangerous place to be... Not knowing...' Kieran tutted disapprovingly.

Watching Teagan's reaction was all Kim needed. The silly cow really had no clue what she'd said. In all truth, Teagan had said very little, but it was enough to keep Uncle Ron happy for now. It was also enough to hold a tight leash on the woman by letting her believe she'd said more than she had. *Perfect.* But Kieran needed to pull his head in. She didn't want him asking Teagan too many questions and causing suspicion. Slowly and gradually was the way to do it.

Kim slapped her brother's bare leg. 'Take no notice of him. You don't need to worry. We won't say anything to anyone, I promise.'

Teagan felt the heavy weight in the pit of her stomach sink further. She had no way of knowing what she'd said and was too worried to ask, but she'd obviously said something and something which prompted Kim to need to promise not to speak of it. That wasn't a good sign.

Struggling to think of what to say, Teagan hurried out of the room. 'I'm going back to bed,' she muttered.

'Why do I have to pretend to be your boyfriend?' Kieran

hissed once Teagan's bedroom door slammed. 'And you don't have to keep pawing me!'

Kim rolled her eyes. 'Oh, get over it! It's not like I haven't seen it before – you're my brother, for Christ's sake! Besides, we've got to make things look realistic. Who else would you be otherwise?'

Kieran sighed. *Maybe, but that didn't mean he had to like it.*

TWENTY FOUR

RON LOOKED EXTREMELY PLEASED with himself as he pulled the magazine page from his pocket. Unfolding it, he flattened it on the kitchen table and prodded the image of Jonah Powell. He grinned proudly. 'As suspected.'

It felt so much of an effort for Mike to drag his eyeballs away from the spot on the floor to stare at whatever O'Hara was indicating, it was as if a crane cranked his vision in the relevant direction. He didn't want to look at what was being shown to him. He didn't want to look at *anything*.

When Kim moved out he'd truly thought things were looking up. He'd actually been stupid enough to think it signified the beginning of the end with light at the end of the tunnel, but that was the most misguided assumption. Sitting next to someone while they had their head blown off by an uninvited houseguest had put paid to that, along with the general consensus that *he* was the one with the problem for daring to find this unusual and disconcerting behaviour.

Apparently, he was causing problems by acting out of sorts and subsequently risking bringing suspicion down on them. *"Even Tammy's starting to suspect something,"* O'Hara had said, berating him and instructing him to get a grip.

Mike blinked at the image in front of him, not even really seeing it. How the fuck was he supposed to get a grip? Even Heath was acting odd and if he'd known O'Hara would be lying in wait like a spider when he got home he'd have stayed at the car lot.

'Yeah, look at her. She won't be difficult to spot. What a little cracker, eh? Can't say I blame the man myself,' Ron said, jolting Mike from his distraction.

As Mike stared at the crumpled paper the colours and image of the photograph came into focus. The girl in the tight red dress was certainly a looker, but who was she? 'What's she got to do with anything?'

It was only after the words had left his mouth did he notice the man in the photograph with his hand on the woman's pert backside. *Oh fuck, Jonah Powell. That's what the woman had to do with it.*

Seeing the realisation sinking into Mike's addled mind, Ron grinned. 'Get us a top up, me old mucker?' He waved his empty beer bottle in Mike's direction and then tapped on the magazine page. 'Yep, interesting confirmation from my lovely Kim this afternoon. She got our Little Miss pissed as a fart last night and she moaned about Jonah having chosen this hottie over her. Most put out she was.'

His gnarly teeth became more grotesque as his smile widened. 'So, it seems it's true that the wonderful Mr Powell has got it bad for this slapper. And...' He leant over the table conspiringly. 'Apparently he's been carrying on with the slut for some time. You know what that means, don't you?'

Mike didn't know what it meant and didn't want to either, but regardless of what he wanted, he suspected he'd be forced to listen anyway.

'It means this piece of shit was betraying my Lena the whole time,' Ron spat. 'Another reason to make him pay.'

Mike nodded enthusiastically. Or at least he hoped it looked that way. 'Erm, what happened with... you know... with that man?' To him, that was the only thing that mattered. Not some chick in a red dress.

On the other hand, there was a part that didn't want to know what had become of that man's body in case it was bad. Visions of the riot police outside his house at this very second waiting for the right moment to riddle him with bullets, stuck in Mike's mind.

Throwing caution to the wind, deciding it would be the quickest and easiest way to stop this nightmare in the long run, Mike jumped to his feet and moved to the fridge to obediently fetch O'Hara another beer. If he was going to be taken down he'd rather it be now rather than later.

He blinked when nothing happened. He hadn't been shot or tackled to the floor, so he was wrong. *Again.*

Ron nodded appreciatively as the new beer was placed in front of him. 'If you're talking about that body, Powell's got receipt of the stiff and what he does with it is *his* concern.'

'But what if they go to the police,' Mike blathered.

Ron laughed loudly. Ripping the bottle top off with his teeth, he spat the lid on the floor. 'They won't go to Old Bill. They're working out what to do.' He grinned manically. 'And they don't have a clue.'

Mike's phone beeped and he pulled it from his pocket, glad of the distraction, until he saw it was a text from Robert Adams:

    Call me

'Who is it?' Ron peered across the table.

'Robert wants me to call him,' Mike muttered. *Adams was supposed to be dealing with O'Hara, not him.* 'I thought it might be Heath. He had an appointment with that lawyer of yours earlier, but I haven't seen him since.'

Ron nodded at the phone. 'That's probably what Adams wants - the latest bill. After all, he's paying for it.'

Mike turned his phone around in his hand. 'I think it's dawning on Heath that going to prison could well be a reality.'

'That lawyer can get anyone off. Murder's a doddle for that

bloke, so Heath doesn't need to fret!' Ron laughed.

'Would someone like to tell me what I just heard? My son could be going to prison for murder, did you say?' Tammy screeched, bursting into the kitchen.

Mike swung around in horror. 'Tammy love,' he blustered. *Shit. Fuck. Just when he thought things couldn't get any worse.* 'You must have misheard.'

'I misheard nothing!' Tammy cried. 'You said Heath could go to prison!' She pointed to Mike. 'I heard you! You must think me stupid! Stuff has been going on since *they* turned up and so you'd better tell me exactly what's happened, otherwise I'll go to the police and let *them* get to the bottom of it.'

Mike stood up, his eyes pleading. 'Don't do anything rash, sweetheart. You've got the wrong end of the stick. You've...'

'Wrong end of the stick?' Tammy screeched. Pulling her hand back, she delivered a stinging slap to Mike's face. 'Get away from me, you bastard! You bring this freak of nature into my house - Uncle Fester and his Munster family and since then everything's been cloak and dagger.'

Mike raised a hand to his stinging, reddening cheek and glanced at O'Hara watching the proceedings with a strange sense of combined detachment and amusement.

'What do you know about this? Is it true?' Tammy yelled, pointing to O'Hara. 'You! You know something, that's for sure. In fact, this is all down to you isn't it? What have you done to get my boy into trouble?' She swung back to Mike. 'And you, you pointless bastard. You allowed this thing to come in here, into my house and...'

'Tammy love, calm down,' Mike begged. 'The neighbours will hear and...'

'I don't care!' Tammy glared at O'Hara once again. 'There's been nothing but misery since you took it upon yourself to descend on us. I don't know you, I don't want you here and neither does Mike, so get out of my house!'

Seeing O'Hara's lack of movement and sensing Mike approaching, Tammy batted her husband away. 'Did you not hear me, Ron?' she screamed once again. 'Get out of my house!'

'Hmm... Point one...' Ron smiled slowly. 'This wouldn't be your home at all anymore had it not been for me "descending", as you put it...'

'What's that supposed to mean?' Tammy spun to face Mike. 'What does he mean by that? Mike, what have you done?'

Tammy's voice was at screaming pitch and Mike closed his eyes in despair. If the neighbours weren't getting all of this, the rest of Shepherds Bush certainly was. 'Tammy... I...'

'That's it! I've had enough!' Tammy stomped past O'Hara. 'If both of you want to play it like this, then I'm calling the police. Let's see what *they* have to say!'

With sweat now running freely down Mike's back, he glanced at O'Hara, who wasn't reacting to Tammy's outburst whatsoever. If she called the police, she would drop everybody in it. *This was a nightmare. A complete and utter nightmare.*

The police would find traces of that man's body in the Jag, he knew they would. *Jesus.* And he still had the suit upstairs. O'Hara had told him to burn it, but it was one of his best and he couldn't bring himself to do it. He just couldn't. O'Hara had assured him everything would all be ok, but it wasn't. *It wasn't alright at all.*

Lurching forward, Mike grabbed Tammy's arm. 'Please darling, don't call the police. You're...'

'Get the fuck off me!' Tammy spat. Grabbing a frying pan, she whacked Mike in the elbow.

Howling with pain, Mike stumbled into the table, watching his wife reaching for the cordless phone.

'You've wrecked both mine and our son's life! What have you done Michael, you waste of space?' Tammy screeched, her eyes wild.

'Tammy...' Mike struggled to push himself up from the table, sure that bloody cast iron pan had bust his arm. 'Please...'

Rising from the chair, Ron grappled the phone from

Tammy and clamped one of his meaty hands over her mouth.

As Tammy's screaming became muffled, Mike was momentarily relieved for the respite from the ear-splitting noise, but his relief turned to abject horror when, in slow motion, he watched O'Hara calmly snap his wife's neck in one manoeuvre right in front of his very eyes.

. . . .

ONE THING WORSE than sitting outside the Feathers contemplating whether to go in, was sitting outside the Feathers contemplating whether to go in whilst being in a Nissan Micra.

Heath scowled, the resentment for Ron O'Hara building by the second. Why should he be stuck with this poxy car whilst O'Hara got use of the Lexus? That had been *his* motor to use, not O'Hara's, yet now he was having to make do with *this*.

He glared at the dome of the plastic dashboard and felt like smashing the silly little clock through to the other side of it. It wouldn't take much effort.

Heath stared at the Feathers' frontage; its gleaming gold façade shining out into the night like a beacon and enviously watched well-dressed couples walk up the steps to the foyer. Those people had nothing on their minds other than the show they were about to watch and the lashings of expensive champagne they would drink.

He felt like screaming. Why couldn't his life be simple? Why couldn't he just enjoy normal things, like normal people? He hadn't been doing too badly before getting the outstanding brainwave that it was a really good idea to attempt the retrieval of diamonds that should have been his grandfather's from a firm full of violent psychos.

Just think, had he not had the amazing foresight to get involved with this in the first place, he'd have missed out on meeting all of these *lovely* people - like his supposed Uncle Robert, who'd killed his own mother and framed him for murder, or Ron O'Hara, who was planning on screwing over everybody.

If it were possible to rip his own head off and spit down his neck in utter contempt for his blatant stupidity, then Heath would have already done it.

Pulling his mobile from his pocket instead, he stared at it. No texts, but then he couldn't say he was surprised. He hadn't expected Teagan to reply to the message he'd sent earlier, especially when, out of desperation, he'd tried calling too, only for an automated voice to drone, *"this number has not been recognised"*.

Teagan had changed her number as he thought she might have. There had been no activity on Teagan's Facebook profile for over a month either. The last time she'd commented or posted anything was way back in June, so that was a dead end too.

Heath knew he could get the address of Kim's flat from his father, but not with Robert Adams watching the place, which only left *here*.

He looked back at the Feathers club, uncomfortably aware the doorman was starting to take an interest in the mint-coloured Nissan Micra parked for no apparent reason for over half an hour the opposite side of the road.

Heath fumbled with the collar of his shirt, feeling worryingly short of breath.

From his meeting earlier, the lawyer was still adamant he would walk free and was doing his upmost to speed the process up. This was good - sort of, but could he really risk jeopardising his freedom for Teagan?

He'd even toyed with the idea of mentioning that he had new information to prove his innocence to the brief, but it seemed absurd to expect the lawyer to start prosecuting the very person paying his invoices, so he'd said nothing. Paying Jonah Powell a visit was the only option.

Unless he went to the police? He could tell them what he knew of Robert Adams, what he'd done and his plans for Teagan?

Heath's face contorted into a scowl. But if he did that, the whole story would come out, including his own part in it. He'd be done for fraud and perverting the course of justice. Then, not only would he have everyone and their dog on his back, he'd also have to spend the rest of his life under witness protection, probably squirrelled away in a bungalow in Clacton under the name of Kevin.

Everything was a bloody hideous risk and he didn't know which way to turn.

Heath pulled out his Feathers membership card. They'd have to let him in with this? As long as he could get past the henchmen baying for his blood, knowing he was the one who had ID'd and therefore caused the death of one of them, that was…

Perspiration beaded on Heath's brow. *Fuck. He needed to rethink this.*

The sudden ringing of his mobile made him jump out of his skin. His nerves were shot to buggery.

Dad calling…

Oh, not now. Not in the middle of this…

Heath buttoned the call and shoved his mobile into his pocket. He couldn't deal with his father flapping. The man was becoming more of a nervous wreck by the day and it was making Heath feel even more jittery.

It was no use. He couldn't concentrate.

Shoving the key into the ignition, Heath started the car and pulled away from the Feathers, consoling himself with after he'd thought through his plans a bit more he'd know what to do. It was a poxy excuse for further procrastination and he knew it.

TWENTY FIVE

ON ONE HAND Heath found the house being so quiet, pleasant. On the other hand, it was strange. More worryingly still was that his father was still there.

It was a Saturday. Never since he could remember had his father not opened the car lot on a Saturday.

Had he not been truthful the business was saved?

As Heath crammed what remained of his toast into his mouth he stared at his father who hadn't spoken the whole time he'd made his breakfast. The man hadn't even moved and possibly hadn't blinked. 'Are you not going into work today?'

The toast continued going round Heath's mouth as he willed himself to swallow it. His mouth was dry and he wasn't hungry, but after yet another night of little sleep, he had to make the effort to eat something, else he'd hit the deck.

By the time he'd got back last night everyone had gone to bed and now, in the interim, they had all disappeared again. His life was turning into more of a parallel universe every day. The sleepless night may have given him plenty of time to think, but it hadn't bought him any closer to making a decision about Teagan.

Dislodging the lump of half-eaten bread from the roof of

his mouth with a swig of tepid tea, Heath looked back at his father. He looked like a cardboard cut-out. 'Dad? Did you hear me?'

'Hmm?' Mike muttered disinterestedly.

Heath frowned. 'I said, are you not going into work? Are you alright?'

Mike was unable to look at his son. *How could he look at him?*

'Where is everyone?' Heath peered over his father's shoulder through to the lounge. 'Where's O'Hara and the idiot, Kieran? And Mum?' He watched the colour drain from his father's already pale face. 'Dad?'

Under the table, Mike dug his nails into the palms of his hands. *Could he actually say what O'Hara had instructed him to say?*

He felt empty, like he'd been gutted by a taxidermist and couldn't function enough to blink without physically reminding himself to do so. How would he ever act normal again?

Mike's eyes moved to the kitchen window out into the garden before rapidly looking away. *He couldn't look out there. Maybe if he didn't look it would all go away?*

'Dad?' Heath repeated, his worry growing. 'Are you going to tell me what's going on? Has the business fallen through after all?'

His heart-rate increased. What would he live on now? He had no means of getting money from the diamonds and nothing else was on the agenda. God, he may as well go back to nick. He'd end up in the equivalent of that either way the way things were going.

'It's your mother...' Mike's voice sounded like it didn't belong to him.

Heath tensed. 'What's the matter with her? Is she ill? Where is she?'

Mike shook his head forlornly. 'She's not ill...' *She's dead, but I can't tell you that.*

'Where is she then and what's the matter?' Heath cried,

becoming impatient. 'You look mental and you haven't opened the car lot. What's going on?'

Mike stiffened, sick of everyone shouting at him. Everyone always shouted at him. The last thing Tammy did was shout at him. He'd let her down in the worst way imaginable. All of this was his fault. *His*. And now *this*... 'She's left me...'

He wasn't sure how he'd said it. How he'd actually forced the lie from between his lips. Why wasn't he telling Heath the truth? Why was he hell bent on protecting the person who had killed his wife?

But was he protecting O'Hara or *himself*? Protecting himself from Heath knowing exactly how pathetic he was? Protecting himself from admitting to his own son that he'd stood by whilst Ron O'Hara had murdered Tammy?

Mike's nails dug further into his hand to see how deep he could dig them in. He deserved the pain. He deserved the *utmost* pain.

He could hear Heath saying something, but the words were muted, muffled - like Tammy's screams when O'Hara put his hand over her mouth. *Before he'd snapped her neck...*

It was an accident, O'Hara had said...

Aware Heath was shaking him by the shoulders, Mike pulled himself back to reality, Remember this was the best thing to do for everybody. The best way to deal with the mishap...

Mishap? His wife was dead. Tammy was fucking dead...

'Your mother's left me, son,' Mike repeated, the lie no longer feeling like his. It was a means to an end. And the end of this was all he could hope for. It was a bad dream. A *very* bad lucid dream that he no longer wanted a part of.

'Left you? What do you mean left you? When?'

Heath's voice filtered into Mike's mind and he stared through his son as if he were not there. 'She walked out last night. She wants a divorce.'

'Divorce?' Heath spluttered, trying to read his father's face and finding it shut off - closed. 'That's crazy. She can't just divorce you! Is this because of *them*?' His head jerked towards the empty sitting room where the O'Haras normally sprawled themselves across the furniture. 'I'll speak to her. Where has she gone? I'll phone her mobile. I'll...'

'You can't son...' Mike said, drowning in the lies of his own making.

'I can! I'll...' Heath abruptly stopped seeing the pink case of his mother's iPhone on the kitchen worktops. 'She hasn't taken her phone? Why wouldn't she take it?'

Mike shook his head in disbelief with both himself and with everything. 'I don't know... I...'

Heath's eyes moved to the hooks on the back of the kitchen door. The ones where his mother hung her handbag. And there it was. *The handbag.*

If his mother left the house not taking a phone, she certainly wouldn't have left without her handbag.

Mike stared back into the garden, a single fat tear rolling down his unshaven cheek and a steady trail of cold dread crept around Heath insides, twisting and gripping as it snaked between his intestines and stomach.

He didn't want to think what he was beginning to think, but the gnawing reality that he should think about it gained pace.

'Where is she, Dad?' Heath asked quietly. 'What have you done with my fucking mother?'

• • • •

'I'M WELL AWARE it's none of my business Jonah, but the least you can do is make the girl feel less used,' Gwen said, her tone stern.

Jonah bristled. Placing his crystal tumbler on the desk, he raised his eyes. 'Are you seriously berating me for this business with Terri Mason? No disrespect, but what has it got to do with you?'

Softening her stance, Gwen sat down and looked at Jonah pointedly. 'Like I said, I know it's none of my business but the poor girl is gutted. She's not had a second of attention from you since the auction.'

Jonah pulled his hand over his face in frustration. 'What are you? My bloody mother? Christ, Gwen, I'm forty years old for God's sake, not fourteen!'

Gwen tried to mask the hurt. No she wasn't Jonah's mother, but she'd known him since he was a boy and had always looked out for him. In reality, this time she hadn't behaved in a way she was proud of and with stinging guilt, acknowledged she expected Jonah to do something in order to assuage her guilt over the grief she'd caused.

Feeling even worse, Gwen wondered whether she was turning into one of those manipulative people, the sort of people she hated - the sort who only ever did things for their own gains. She picked at her fingernails. 'You're right,' she said. 'It really is none of my business. It's my own fault for asking Terri to help you at the auction. I could see she was overjoyed.' She looked at Jonah sadly. 'And I encouraged her by allowing her to think you'd specifically requested her.'

Jonah raised his eyebrows. 'Why would you do that?'

Gwen sighed, deciding to come clean. 'I thought it would take your mind off things. I didn't mean any harm, but she's taken your lack of interest hard. The other girls aren't helping as they're ribbing her about it.'

Jonah's temper spiked. 'To deflect me from Teagan, you mean? I know you didn't approve of what you *think* you saw, but you had no right.'

'I know and I'm sorry,' Gwen blinked away the forming tears. 'I know I'm not your mother, as you quite rightly pointed out and I never can be. I also know I've let you down in the past by not telling you about me and your father but...'

Jonah knocked back his whisky. 'You've been good to me Gwen, but my business is *my* business.'

Gwen nodded, contrite. 'I'm sorry.'

'There was nothing between me and Teagan anyway, but that doesn't mean I don't need to make sure she's ok.'

Although what Jonah said was true, it didn't change that he *wanted* there to be something between him and Teagan. The unfamiliar feeling was both disconcerting and irritating. He stared at Gwen. 'Did you know she'd planned to leave?'

Gwen shook her head resolutely. 'No, I did not. Genuinely. But I won't pretend I don't think it's for the best.'

'Perhaps I might agree with you if O'Hara or Adams weren't playing dangerous games and we knew where she was.'

'It was definitely O'Hara behind what happened to Paul?'

Jonah shrugged. 'I'm pretty certain.' He stood up from the desk. 'I will however, catch Terri over the next couple of days and have a word.'

Gwen nodded. 'Thank you. It would help. I don't like seeing any of my girls down.'

Jonah waited until Gwen left his office before sighing. Did he not have enough to deal without *this* in addition? Although he did feel a twinge of guilt for brushing the girl aside, it hardly ranked alongside everything else.

And Gwen purposely fitting him up? He may still have the air of the man who had a string of women in tow, but that was *before*. And now he only wanted the one. *The one he couldn't have*.

Twenty Six

IT HADN'T BEEN TERRI'S PLAN to agree to the hen night, she wasn't in the mood, but then she'd spent enough time wallowing in her own self-pity, not to mention the constant digs from the others over her failure to keep Jonah interested and she was sick of it. The girls were jealous. She'd got further than the rest of them and yes, it was a pisser Jonah hadn't wanted more and her dreams of being treated like a Queen had gone down the pan, but realistically, worse things could happen so it was about time she sorted herself out.

Staring into the mirror, Terri applied another coat of gloss and smacked her lips together. Turning her face from left to right, she grinned at her reflection. A night out with the girls to celebrate Josie's wedding was just what the doctor ordered.

Hearing a beep of the horn, she glanced at the clock. *That must be the taxi.*

Finishing her glass of wine, Terri took one more look at her reflection. Satisfied everything was in order, she grabbed her bag and rushed out of the door to meet the others at the tapas bar.

· · · ·

FROM THE LEXUS, Ron watched the girl teeter in her stilettoes along the pavement from the apartment block and smiled to himself as he started the engine.

She was nowhere near as glamorous as she'd looked in the magazine, but then it was amazing how an evening dress added class. Put the girl back in a low-cut, skimpy top and a short skirt and she looked every inch exactly what she was - a stripper and a slut.

The hours he'd spent down the road from the Feathers watching until the girls finished the afternoon show was a gamble. Terri Mason might have been rostered for the evening show too, but the gamble had paid off. She'd left and after getting a good eyeball by zooming in on his phone camera, he was satisfied it was her. Enough to follow the woman back to her flat anyway.

It could also have been a waste of time keeping watch there. She might have been in for the night and all he'd have got for his trouble was a stiff arse, but he'd thought the chances of that on a Saturday night were remote and he'd been right in his assumption.

Terri Mason was off out.

As the taxi pulled away, the girl's blonde hair visible through the window of the cab, Ron allowed two other cars to pass before he picked up the tail.

As much as he hated the painfully slow and drawn-out pursuit of hanging around watching targets, it would be worth it in the end.

'Will this take all night?'

Ron glanced to his left. 'Probably, yes. Problem?'

Kieran pursed his lips. 'No, there's no problem.' Actually, there was. He'd been hoping to have a night to himself. It was Saturday for fuck's sake and Kim and that other dozy bird were off out again and he was starting to feel side-lined. That he didn't like.

Ron grinned to himself. Kieran was that forgettable, he'd almost forgotten the boy was even here. Still, if this worked, he'd need two pairs of hands. All things considered, Kieran had done alright last night and it wasn't like he was snowed under with henchmen to do the grunt, but he would be soon. He'd have *everything* soon.

He centred his eyes back to the taxi as it moved slowly through the traffic towards Leicester Square and lighting a cigarette - probably the hundredth he'd smoked since this morning, he wound down the window a crack. Where Terri Mason was going he didn't know and it could still all be a waste of time yet, but it was worth a punt.

Besides, anything was better than remaining in the house with Mike Pointer. The bloke was getting on his tits. Face like a fucking slapped haddock, sitting unresponsive like he'd had a bloody lobotomy, the fucking idiot.

What exactly had the man expected when that stupid bitch of a wife had gone nuts on them? He'd been trying to shut the silly cow up for fuck's sake. Screeching and wailing about calling the Old Bill and shouting their bloody business so fucking loudly that everyone in a ten-mile bastard radius would hear? He wasn't to know she had a weak fucking neck, was he?

Ron stared at his hands on the steering wheel and grinned. Either that or he was just too damn efficient. Probably the latter. He'd had enough practice - especially in the old days. But it didn't change that it was yet another issue he'd have to sort.

It was bad enough he'd had to rely on temporary measures for the time being. It was hardly like he could fanny about sorting that out while all of this was going on. Why did extra things always crop up at the most inopportune moment?

Had Kieran not turned up last night he'd have been in a right quandary. For once the dolt had come up with a good idea. Well, not a good idea, but an idea that would suffice, at least until there was more time to deal with it. At the moment, time was of the essence and he couldn't spend time buggering around sorting collateral damage.

Approaching Leicester Square, Ron saw the taxi indicate to pull over. Laying off the accelerator, he allowed the Lexus to drop back, not caring just how many cars he offended behind him.

Finally pulling over, he waved the traffic past, watching Jonah Powell's tart get out of the taxi and walk confidently along the pavement.

His lips curled in contempt as the girl tottered along in those ridiculous stripper shoes.

If the cap fits.

Terri Mason stopped outside The Tapas HQ and Ron's mouth twitched into a smile. So, she was eating and then no doubt moving onto somewhere else. *But where and with who?*

It was a shame she wasn't meeting her star-crossed lover, because that would be downright funny. But Adams would have contacted him if Powell had moved.

Ron glanced at his mobile. *Nope. Nothing from Adams.*

Kieran watched the door to the tapas bar close behind Terri Mason with interest. 'What do we do now?'

'We wait, that's what we do. We wait for as long as it takes.' Ron grinned. And when the time was right, he would move on the opportunity.

· · · ·

'GET THAT DOWN YOUR NECK.' Kim lined another round of tequila shots on the bar and nudging Teagan, winked mischievously. 'Come on, you slacker!'

Teagan watched Kim jigging from foot to foot in her stilettos and smiled, not really wanting another shot of the burning liquid. She'd already had several on top of the wine and didn't want a repeat of what had happened on Thursday night. Still unable to recall what she'd said bothered her and although she was reticent to put a dampener on her new life, she couldn't ignore the niggling sense of disquiet.

Her initial excitement of sharing an apartment with Kim had diminished. She'd tried to reconcile her unease being down to things being different to what she'd been used to. After all, the nightly outings to bars and chatting about personal stuff wasn't something she'd had any experience of.

Kim had been open about her own life and Teagan was honoured her new friend should feel comfortable enough with her to tell her all manner of personal details.

From what she'd said, a lot had happened to poor Kim, but there was something wrong and she couldn't quite work out what. Whatever it was, it stopped Teagan from being as open and transparent in return.

Maybe it was just because she wasn't used to having anyone to confide in or maybe it was because the things she could say were too risky to talk of? Maybe it was because she was being asked to many questions?

Teagan frowned. It wasn't just the stream of questions Kim asked either.

She glanced at her new friend actively scanning the busy club, trying to catch the eye of a group of well-dressed, decent-looking men not too far away from where they perched on their high bar stools.

Why would Kim want to encourage attention when she'd got Kieran?

And he was another one…

Teagan fiddled with her slice of lime, taking as long as possible to squeeze it into her shot glass.

Although Kim's boyfriend was pleasant enough, there was something odd about him. There wasn't any specific thing, apart from his over-interest in her background that worried her, but *something* definitely didn't sit right.

Kim had sensed Kieran's questions had made Teagan uncomfortable and said he was like that with *everyone*, but why was he so interested in her?

None of it felt right and the more time she spent with the pair of them, the odder everything felt.

Sneaking another quick glance at Kim, Teagan took the opportunity to lower her shot glass and tip the contents onto the floor. The less she drank, the less chance there was of saying something she shouldn't.

Kim turned back to Teagan. 'Are you ready to down it then? Oh, you've already finished? That was quick! I'll get you another.'

Teagan was about to protest but her attention was instead grabbed by the group of loud women entering the club, making their way over to the other side of the long crescent-shaped bar.

She recognised that woman. That woman in the short pink dress. That was the woman in the magazine - the photos with Jonah. *That was Terri Mason, Jonah's girlfriend.*

Teagan's heart sank. It had only just gone nine and there was no way Kim would be willing to make tracks and head home for several hours yet.

TWENTY SEVEN

JONAH ENDED THE CALL and shoved his mobile back in his pocket. 'Thursday.'

Nero raised his eyebrows. 'What's Thursday?'

Jonah swilled the whisky around his glass. 'The deal with Benowitz.'

'How exactly will it work?' Nero asked, already knowing it was a tricky operation to pull off without leaving any traces in the event of things going tits-up.

'The details will be arranged throughout the week. The instructions will come through gradually so as not to create a trail.'

Although Jonah wasn't overly pleased with the confirmation the buyers were Russian, the prospect of getting those cursed diamonds as far away as possible was something he looked forward to. Although he would feel better about it if he knew where Teagan was. Her lack of whereabouts bothered him.

Gwen was a disappointment too. She may have been doing what she thought best, but it wasn't her call to invade his personal life.

Reading between the lines, Jonah wondered if Teagan's

sudden departure could be anything to do with his association with Terri Mason. His brow furrowed. That stuff wasn't true - not to the extent it had all been blown out of proportion.

Dare he hope to think Teagan had left because of that? If she had, then wouldn't that mean she was bothered? That she cared? That she felt the same way as he did?

He shook his head to himself. That was another thing. He'd promised to let Terri down gently, rather than avoiding her, which to his shame, he was doing.

It was a mess. All Gwen had achieved with her so-called "trying to help" tactics was to cause people needless upset.

Jonah watched Nero closely. The man wasn't as stoic as usual. Paul's death had grated especially hard on him. Yes, it was shit and something that would be avenged, but as much as Jonah didn't like admitting it, they were getting nowhere with O'Hara. Being thin on the ground with high-up competent men was taking its toll.

Jonah folded his fingers together. All of his men were competent, but he'd only ever had a select few within the inner circle. Now that inner circle was too small to deal with even *half* the things on their plate and this worried him. It left the firm and all the people he'd vowed to protect, vulnerable and that was not pleasant. It certainly wasn't what he would class as a working solution. 'Any word on Pointer?'

Nero shook his head. 'I've had scouts trawling everywhere to try and pinpoint O'Hara and his link with Pointer. I've even gone back to Heath Pointer's flat, but the place has been turned over.' He stood up. 'I know you said to hold off, but it's pissing me off. We need more hands on deck. I need to go back to the car sales place and tail Pointer senior, but I can't do everything.'

Jonah frowned. This was where Adams would have been useful. He'd have located the required address within minutes with his technical know-how.

Jonah may be a dab hand at running a firm and dealing with rackets, but how he wished he wasn't so much of a dunce when it came to computers. Nero was right. He couldn't do everything. Neither of them could be in four places at once. They had to maintain a business-as-usual approach for the firm and the club's reputation, but it was bloody difficult when they were so low on manpower. It wasn't as easy as just recruiting someone. Not for a job like this. That level of trust took time - the one thing they didn't have, but one thing was certain and Jonah couldn't risk Nero.

'You mustn't go digging around City Car Sales,' Jonah said. 'We know O'Hara is connected, but after the stunt he pulled with Paul, that's exactly what he'll be expecting – us looking for retaliation.'

'I *do* want retaliation,' Nero spat, his eyes flashing.

'You and me both, but we're not walking into a trap. That's what O'Hara's counting on. He's trying to flush us out and knows we're down on numbers.' Jonah finished his whisky. 'I'm counting on you not to lose patience. I know it's frustrating, but we mustn't play into O'Hara's hands.' He placed his empty glass on his desk and stood up. 'Right, there's someone I need to talk to. I'll be back shortly.'

Moving into the corridor, Jonah made his way down to the stage side of the club. The show was almost over. Now was a good time as any to get this business with Terri Mason ironed out.

• • • •

THE TWO DANCERS tripping along the corridor chatting amicably immediately quietened seeing Jonah Powell striding towards them.

'Good evening ladies.' Jonah made sure he acted in his normal way around the staff. The last thing he wanted was anyone getting wind of his growing unease. There could be no chinks in the armour.

The girls glanced at each other, beaming wildly. 'Good evening, Mr Powell,' they chorused in unison.

Jonah smiled. 'Is Terri about?'

The two women exchanged glances yet again and Jonah felt

like slapping Gwen. By the looks of it he was the talk of the dressing rooms and the whole club. Christ knows what Terri had spouted about the one night they'd spent together.

For a split second, he felt like walking away out of principle, but he didn't. After all, he'd been the one to behave somewhat unchivalrously.

'Did you not hear me?' he snapped, his hackles rising. 'Terri Mason? Where is she?'

Seeing the women's faces startle with his uncharacteristic harshness, Jonah stared at them coldly, his resolve to remain pleasant, gone. *People needed reminding who the fucking boss was around here.*

'Terri's not on rota tonight, Sir. She's gone out with the others,' the tall blonde said.

Jonah frowned. *Bollocks*. He thought most of the girls did both the afternoon and evening shows? Gwen must have changed the line-up. *Hang on...* 'Did you say, gone out with the others? What do you mean?'

The brunette folded her arms and glanced at her blonde colleague, a miffed expression on her face. 'We should have all been able to go, but there isn't a night when half of us aren't working, so we've had to miss out. Josie said she'd do it twice, but I doubt whether that will happen what wi...'

'Hold on!' Jonah put his hands up to silence the women. 'I haven't got the time nor the inclination to get involved in your squabbles. Where have the other girls gone?'

The two women looked at each other as if Jonah was a sandwich short of a picnic for not being up to date with the goings on. 'It's Josie Fletcher's wedding next week, Mr Powell. She's holding the reception here. You've been invited, of course.'

Jonah waved his hand, wishing they get to the bloody point. 'Right? And?'

'They've gone on her hen-night,' the blonde pouted. 'It'll be a good night too. I'm re...'

'Who organised this?' Jonah snapped.

'Josie did, Mr Powell, but she checked with Gwen to make sure it wouldn't affect the rota. All the girls who have gone tonight aren't back on shift until Monday and...'

'Where have they gone?' Jonah barked, not caring if the rota was to pot or not. Gwen had sanctioned the girls to go out even though he'd told her quite plainly that no one was to go *anywhere* unaccompanied? *No social stuff. Nada. Not until further notice.* He hadn't cared how she implemented that, but she knew it was vital. He'd *told* her, yet she'd okayed half his girls to go off on a bloody hen night?

'I asked you where they've gone?' he roared again.

'T-They've gone to The Tapas HQ and then on to Percy's nightclub,' the blonde woman stammered.

Turning on his heels, Jonah stormed down the corridor, glancing into Gwen's office on the way. It was a good job she wasn't in there otherwise he'd most likely rip her head clean off, the stupid, *stupid* woman.

Bursting back through the door of his office, he jerked his head in Nero's direction. 'We've got to go.'

Nero didn't have time to question anything before Jonah grabbed his jacket and was back off down the corridor.

• • • •

HEATH HOPED his absurd thoughts stemmed from wild figments of his imagination. He'd failed to get a word of sense out of his father. All the man had done was sit and cry. And by cry, *really* cry. Huge, heart-wrenching sobs, choked with suffocating pain. He'd never seen his father cry before and it wasn't a pleasant experience.

Apart from that, his father had done nothing, except drink whisky and mutter illegible cryptic stuff which made no sense. He'd repeated the same thing over and over and Heath had become more worried than angry for a while. His father hadn't been himself for ages and was getting worse. Was he finally having a breakdown?

He wasn't sure what to do. Hours had passed and there was

still no sign of O'Hara or Kieran. For once in his life he could have done with them being around to see if they had any clue as to what the fuck was going on. And he had the gnawing suspicion they *did* know. Or at least knew more than what his father had divulged, which was basically sod all.

He looked back at his father, now slumped in an armchair in the lounge, a small trail of dribble hanging from the corner of his mouth.

Shaking his head, Heath walked along the hallway to the crammed utility room that doubled up as the home office. Entering the tiny space, he reached over the washing machine to one of the overhead cupboards, careful not to knock the laptop from its precarious position balanced on the pointless desk wedged between the washing basket and the tumble dryer.

Opening the cupboard, praying there wouldn't be an avalanche, Heath was relieved to spot the torch kept for emergencies.

Whether this was an emergency or not remained to be seen and in reality, it seemed a ridiculous thing to do, but the need to rule the absurd notion out burnt as strongly as it did when he'd first noticed his father's unexplained obsession of looking in the direction of the shed at the end of the garden.

Taking the torch, Heath tiptoed past the sitting room. Waking Mike from his alcohol-induced slumber was unlikely, but he couldn't take undue risks. He also hoped after an entire day of absence, the O'Haras wouldn't decide now was the right time to return.

He only needed five minutes. *Five minutes to quiet the nagging in his head.*

Stepping out the back door into the garden, Heath flicked the torch on and moved swiftly along the overgrown path to the shed. He glanced over his shoulder, the bright yellow light from the kitchen illuminating the patio. No movement from within the house which was good.

Stepping into the darkness further up the path, Heath reached the shed, his apprehension growing. *What was the matter with him? It wasn't like he was scared of the bloody dark.*

Shoving the torch into his mouth, he held it in between his teeth as his hands moved to the rusty padlock. His fingers fumbled with the combination of numbers, hoping he recalled correctly, although it had been some time since he'd offered to cut the grass, let alone get anything out of this shed.

His mother always wondered why Mike insisted on buying such a big shed when all it contained was a lawn mower, small tins of paint and a selection of unused garden tools.

Heath grinned wryly. It had always been his father's plan to tinker with bits and pieces - maybe even an old bike as a project, but as usual, had failed to get around to putting that plan into practice. A bit like everything else the man had planned or promised.

Come on, he thought impatiently, changing the last digit on the padlock from a 3 to a 2. He'd been *sure* he could remember the number, but if he couldn't...

A-ha!

Feeling the lock give, Heath wiggled the padlock off and after a final glance towards the house, opened the shed door.

Once inside, he nervously swung the torch around, half expecting a plague of mice to scurry over his feet, but there was nothing. No resident family of rodents or unfortunate wasp nests he'd disturbed. Just the usual things.

He moved the arc of light from the torch around further, still confused as to what he'd expected to find. *It was all very silly.*

Lawnmower, hoe, rakes, paint... Old boxes and a selection of tools which had an intended purpose when purchased, but sat unused. Along with the compost bin - again, another incentive his father had wanted to try. Making his own compost and becoming the next Alan Titchmarsh.

The furthest Heath's father had got to being green-fingered was buying trays of bedding plants on offer at B&Q and even then, most of them had wilted or died before he'd got around to planting them. That's if he'd even managed that half the time.

And compost bins weren't supposed to be kept in sheds. They should be out in the garden with cuttings and grass in them, shouldn't they?

Shaking his head with irritation, Heath took another look around. *Nope. Nothing here.* In fact, he'd bet there wasn't even one thing in that bloody compost bin. *What a waste of money.*

Stomping across, he yanked the plastic top from the large, black plastic container and pointed the torch inside.

Yelping with shock and fright, Heath dropped the torch. *Fuck. FUCK.*

Scrambling on the floor, raging panic threatening to render him useless, his fingernails clawed across the wooden floor to find the torch. *He had to get out of here.*

With his breath coming in ragged pants, Heath's fingers closed around the torch and then purposely looking away, placed the lid back onto the compost bin.

Stumbling out of the shed, he wanted to run back to the house, but had to replace the padlock first. He *must.*

With trembling fingers, Heath swallowed down the rising bile and sang tunes in his head to aid his concentration.

Get the padlock on. Twizzle the numbers around. Come on!

Getting it in place, Heath legged it back down the path, amazed he didn't trip in his blind haste. Slamming the back door behind him, he leant up against it, willing his heart not to give out.

He hadn't needed to look twice to know what he'd seen. Those shoes, along with the legs that were attached to the feet wearing the shoes, belonged to that of his mother.

Twenty Eight

ROBERT SAT PATIENTLY in his room at the B&B and eyed his montage with pride. The many copies of the photos he'd printed from his phone camera had done well in covering the second wall. Still another two walls to go, but nothing would be as gratifying as *her* being here in person. It shouldn't be too long to wait now.

According to O'Hara, that dim Kim bitch was doing the business with getting Teagan to spout information and the man reckoned he'd soon have enough gen to go ahead.

Soon Robert could take what he'd become involved in this whole thing again for, but that day had better hurry up because he was fast running out of patience.

He lined up his pens on his makeshift desk in the way he preferred them: silver, gold, then black. Making sure the top of each pen lined against a score on the table, Robert sat back and smiled.

Although it wasn't ideal, he'd made the decision not to follow Teagan again. He'd taken a stupid risk the other night by going to that bar and could easily have been spotted. He couldn't have anything spoil his progress.

He was close to the final take and he would have it.

Robert's jaw clenched as he glanced at his mobile again, the vision of Teagan spilling into his mind.

No more messages since O'Hara had texted earlier. The last text received read:

```
T on the lash with K again tonite.
Not long now.
```

It might not be long in O'Hara's world, but it was bloody eons where Robert was concerned. Every time he imagined Teagan in a bar with all the other slappers, behaving like *them*, it made his blood boil further.

It had been tempting to ask O'Hara where Kim and Teagan were going but he hadn't. He'd only get the urge to follow and he mustn't. Besides, the stupid Irish cunt wouldn't know because he was too wrapped up in his own agenda.

Robert glared at the tracking system. Powell's tracker was still handshaking. He was still at the Feathers. *No surprise there.*

He was about to minimise the tracker and concentrate back on the document he was working on, when he stopped. Peering at the screen, he watched Jonah Powell's tracker begin to move.

Robert's eyes darted to the clock in the corner of the laptop screen. It was too early for Powell to leave the Feathers. He'd watched the man's movements for so long he could set the usual leaving times by clockwork. Very silly for someone such as Powell to have a set routine…

He watched the tracker coordinates moving out of Soho. Was Powell going home?

Wait...

When the tracker headed in the opposite direction, Robert leant forward. Frowning, he pulled his mobile back out of his pocket and stabbed in a text to O'Hara:

```
Where r u?
```

Pressing send, Robert tapped his fingers impatiently on the desk, adrenaline pounding as the response came in:

```
Am outside Percy's. Leics square.
Target and group inside for 1hr. Am waiting.
```

Robert clenched his teeth. O'Hara's idea to tail the tart Powell was involved with was all very well and good for whatever he was planning, but it didn't help *him*.

His eyes moved back to the tracker, his frown deepening as he compared the new coordinates to the map. Adrenaline surged. It looked like Powell was heading to Leicester Square too.

```
P on move. Heading towards L sq
```

Pressing send, Robert's focus centred on an instinct burrowing into his brain:

```
Wheres T and K gone?
```

His pulse increased in line with the rising adrenaline. Was Powell heading to the same place? If so, why? Had he discovered O'Hara was lying in wait for his girlfriend?

He glanced back at the tracker. It was definitely heading in the direction of Leicester Square. Of course, Powell could be going somewhere else, but if he wasn't...

As the phone beeped, Robert snatched it up again:

```
Don't no where K and T are. Wheres P now?
```

Swallowing his annoyance, Robert stabbed out a terse reply:

```
P approaching. Stay clear.
```

Shoving his phone into his pocket, Robert turned back to his screen and continued watching the coordinates.

• • • •

HEATH SHOOK LIKE A LEAF. He hadn't dreamt it. He'd seen what he'd seen and couldn't unsee it. His mother - his very own mother was in the compost bin in the shed.

He stared at his father, still comatose in the armchair and felt like battering him to death. He'd known about this, that's why he was in this state. He *knew*, yet had said nothing. Had he witnessed it?

Thoughts crashed and rolled around Heath's brain. Who had done this? Had the Powells been here, threatened his father and his mother had stepped in, ultimately paying for the intrusion with her life?

A mixture of rage and terror coursed along Heath's veins, every single hair on his body standing on end.

He froze, hearing a sound. *What was that? Where they back?* Had the Powells returned to finish off the rest of them? Or was this to do with Robert Adams? Had buying O'Hara's debts been a ploy – a front to get to the family?

Heath didn't care what O'Hara said. Robert Adams believed he'd killed Dulcie and what sane person would shrug that off and pay that man's debts? Adams was weird, granted, but not *that* weird.

He choked back the suffocating tears. This was *his* fault. His mother had been killed because of what was believed he, himself, was responsible for. Except it hadn't been him. None of it had. He'd killed no one.

Christ, this was a nightmare.

It filtered into Heath's mind to call the police before dismissing it a nanosecond later. That would help no one. Being as they already believed him capable of murder, they would surely suspect him of murdering his own mother?

He dragged his shaking fingers through his hair and fumbled for his mobile. He'd have to call O'Hara. The man should be here helping him get to the bottom of who was behind this.

Suddenly going cold with a frightening unwanted realisation, Heath found his eyes moving back to his father, hate steadily building towards the dejected figure of the drunken man in the chair with a patch of dribble soaking the front of his shirt.

What if his father had done it? What if he'd killed his wife because he was scared she'd find out about what he'd allowed to go on from within their own home?

It was no secret Heath's mother had been, to put it mildly, unhappy with the O'Hara's presence from the start. What if she'd discovered the state of the business, that her home was at risk and that the O'Haras had their family over a barrel? His father had kept the debts secret for months and the shit would definitely have hit the fan if she'd found out.

Maybe she'd found out and his father had lost it? The man had become gradually more deranged, unstable and unable to cope for months. *And if he'd finally snapped...*

Heath scrolled through his contacts, stabbing the call button for O'Hara, his eyes not moving from his father as the phone rang out. *Come on, pick up, pick up.*

Hearing it go to voicemail, he abruptly ended the call and slammed the phone on the table. Where the fuck was O'Hara? Heath needed some help before he lost it completely and allowed the extent of what had happened to fully seep into his consciousness. Because when that happened, and it would, he'd be able to deal with nothing.

His mouth quivered, the unwanted vision of his mother, his dear mother coming into his mind.

Powell or Adams had murdered her, Heath was sure of it. His father surely couldn't have done it?

His eyes tracked back to the slumped figure.

Or could he?

Jumping up, Heath shook his father by the shoulders. He wasn't having this. His father would tell him what the hell had gone on and he'd be telling him now.

. . . .

'JUST DO AS I SAY,' Ron spat, pushing Kieran down the corridor towards the toilets, glancing around for CCTV. The music in the club was doing his head in and he couldn't think straight with that bloody crap racket going on.

His face twisted into a scowl. *Stay clear, my arse*, he thought viciously. There was no way in hell if Powell was heading here like Adams thought, that this opportunity could be allowed to go to waste.

This wasn't the way he wanted to do things. It would cause unnecessary risks, like *major* ones, but this might be the only chance to pull this off and he would not lose that.

The sudden vibration of Ron's phone made him pull it swiftly from his pocket. It could be Adams texting important info.

He glanced at the screen:

```
HP calling
```

Buttoning the call, Ron shoved it back into his pocket. What the fuck was that prat, Heath Pointer, ringing for? That lot were bloody liabilities. He wasn't in the position to be having a chat with that dickhead.

Even if he'd been happily in the pub having a well-earned pint, he wouldn't want to talk to that idiot. And he certainly wasn't doing it *now*. The quicker all of this was brought to a close so he could fuck off back to Ireland, the bloody better.

'Do you think Powell knows we're here?' Kieran muttered, not liking that he was lurking in a corridor rather than being in the middle of the action of the club. There were some banging tunes and instead he was hanging around outside the bogs? Plus, he'd seen Kim. Why should she enjoy herself when he couldn't?

'If Powell's coming here, then he must know something.'

Ron shrugged. 'Either that or he doesn't want his new missus out partying. Whatever happens, I'm getting in first.'

Kieran scowled. 'After that, can I crack on with my Saturday night?'

'No, you bloody can't.' Ron's hands formed fists. He should be astounded the boy would say something so bloody ridiculous, but sadly, nothing this muppet did surprised him. He wouldn't even bother spelling out it wasn't wise for him to hang around afterwards. 'If I thought too deeply about how much of a liability you are I'd never sleep again.'

'Alright! Keep your hair on. It's just Kim's in there and I...'

'Kim's here?' Ron peered past Kieran to see if he could spot Kim through the small glass pane leading from the dark corridor back into the main body of the club. 'Where?'

Kieran shrugged. 'Over the other side. I spotted her as we came through.'

Ron tensed and reached for his phone. 'Is the other girl with her? That Teagan girl?'

'Yeah, when isn't she? They're joined at the fucking hip and d...'

'Shut up!' Ron hissed, stabbing out a text, hoping there was enough signal in this rabbit warren of corridors to send it. 'You put the car where I said?'

Kieran nodded. 'Out the back in the alley near the fire door, like you s...'

'Good. We've got no time to waste. Get into position like I told you. Do you think you can cope with that?' Scowling, Ron scurried into the club, leaving Kieran to wait in the corridor.

Finding a place at the bar, Ron focused on the raucous group of drunk women the opposite end of the bar; the ones who had accompanied Terri Mason. Further scanning of the area uncovered the woman herself standing on the outer circle of the group, her face like a slapped arse. She didn't look like she was enjoying herself all that much, which was good because he needed her to make a move towards the toilets in the next few minutes. If she didn't, and Adams was correct about Powell being on his way, then time would run out.

There was no way he could do what was needed in the middle of the club.

Subtly moving his gaze, Ron could just about make out his niece and that Teagan woman over the other side. Kim looked like she was enjoying herself and they seemed to be getting a fair bit of attention from a group of men, but he didn't give two hoots.

Teagan was of no interest to him personally, short of what information she knew, but that part was Kim's job, not his. Adams would be interested though...

Ron pulled his mobile from his pocket. Should he taunt Adams with this knowledge to wind him up or just keep schtum?

TWENTY NINE

KIM SUBTLY NODDED towards the man at the bar buying yet another round of drinks. 'Mine's the dark one, but what do you think of the blonde one?'

Teagan fidgeted. She didn't want to chat to these men and wasn't interested in the blonde one, or *any* of them come to mention it. She hadn't come out to go on the pull. Neither did she want another drink. She could already feel unsteadiness in her legs and the prospect of being out of control caused panic to flood.

'I'm feeling a bit dodgy,' Teagan shouted in Kim's ear over the loud music. 'Do you mind if we go?'

'Go?' Kim cried, her scarlet mouth agape. 'We haven't been here long and it's not even 10.30. What are you playing at?'

Teagan fiddled with the clasp of her handbag. 'I'd just rather go home.'

Kim shrugged. 'Don't be a twat!' She jumped off her stool. 'Come on, let's go to the bogs and have a snort of this coke I've got. It will buck you up a treat.'

Teagan shook her head. The forced introduction she'd had to drugs, courtesy of Saul Powell was enough for her to know she wouldn't touch anything like that with a bargepole. 'I don't do coke or that sort of stuff.'

Kim raised her eyebrows. 'You're joking? You had a thing with Jonah Powell and you're telling me you don't do gear? Pull the other one!'

Kim's laugh exposed her teeth and made Teagan think of a braying horse. 'I didn't have a "thing" with Jonah Powell and as far as I'm aware he didn't do drugs either.'

Kim rolled her eyes melodramatically, the vast amount of tequila she'd knocked back making her more brazen with her comments than she should be. 'Oh righto! You're telling me the guy who controls most of this side of the river's supply of gear and you didn't get any freebies? Not what I'd call a worthwhile shag!'

How Teagan wished she'd never opened her big mouth and let it slip anything had ever occurred between her and Jonah. Not that it had really. Certainly not what Kim assumed. 'Look, can we just go bef...'

'Did you see them?' Kim whispered. 'Spill the beans! I bet you did. The diamonds? Did you see them? What are they like?'

Fear rolled along Teagan's spine. *Jonah had said no one knew about the diamonds.* Her stomach churned as her clammy hands gripped her bag. *Best to play it stupid.* 'The what? I...'

'Shh! They're coming back with our drinks,' Kim hissed, silently rebuking herself for asking about the diamonds. Uncle Ron would kill her if he knew she'd mentioned them, but Teagan had downed just as much tequila as her and wouldn't remember the conversation by tomorrow. Whatever happened, there was no way Kim was being dragged out of this club by Teagan. Not whilst there were free drinks on offer.

'Here you go, ladies.' The blonde man squashed into the small remaining space next to Teagan, making sure his thigh pressed against hers. 'Fancy a dance?'

• • • •

ROBERT REMAINED GLUED to the tracker and his brows

furrowed further. Pressing refresh, he waited for the coordinates to log the next movement, but there were none.

Powell had stopped two roads from Leicester Square. *He must be going to that club. Shit.*

Watching the tracker move off again, but this time very slowly, Robert frowned. Powell was now on foot.

His instinct was correct. There were only two reasons Powell was in Leicester Square; he was either meeting that whore, Terri Mason, or he knew O'Hara was on the scene. Either way it wasn't good.

Slamming the lid of his laptop, Robert snatched his phone from the side:

```
P in Leics Square. Get out now.
```

He stared at the phone, hoping O'Hara would feel the vibration from the incoming text message, then jumping up from the rickety chair, he paced around the room. *Come on, respond O'Hara. Fucking Respond.*

O'Hara had to leave Percy's club or whatever dump he was in quick smart. Robert had never heard of the place, but then it wasn't like he was a frequent user of London night clubs.

It was impossible to know how much headway, if any, Powell had made with O'Hara's whereabouts. Neither was he sure if Powell even knew what the man looked like, but could only assume he did. If O'Hara was recognised and Powell got his hands on him, that would cause no end of problems.

Robert's face screwed into a scowl. He trusted O'Hara as much as he could throw him and would bet his last quid it wouldn't take long for O'Hara to bleat about his plans for Teagan if it offered him a bargaining chip with Powell.

He paced around the room frantically. He knew he shouldn't have bothered holding off with his plans to get Teagan to suit O'Hara. Why had he been so stupid to allow himself to wait until O'Hara got what he needed first? Why had he not moved on it the second he knew of her whereabouts?

If O'Hara didn't get out of there now, the whole plan would be ruined. *Bloody ruined.*

Hearing a text message arrive, Robert's thick fingers fumbled in his pocket. This had better be O'Hara telling him he'd left.

```
Don't stress. It's all in hand. BTW T and K in
here too but hnvt seen me.
```

Robert blinked and breathed deeply before he spontaneously combusted.

Grabbing his car keys and jacket, he flew out of his room, slamming the door loudly, not caring if it fell off its woodwormed hinges and loped down the stairs with massive strides.

He wasn't about to let this unfold the way it was heading. Teagan was in the club and Powell was there too. Or would be soon. He had to reach her first on the off chance Powell had a change of heart and wanted Teagan for himself over that other tart after all.

Robert had waited patiently for this moment and it was not going to be ruined. Powell would not take Teagan from him this time.

• • • •

CLUTCHING HER HANDBAG, Terri forced a smile. 'I'm just popping to the loos,' she shouted in Sally's direction.

Getting no response, Terri moved from the group, her eyes despondently searching for the toilets. It didn't make any odds whether the girls had heard what she'd said or not. They wouldn't even notice she'd gone.

Despite her plans to have a good night, it wasn't working. Apart from the expected digs about being binned off by Jonah whilst they had their drinks and eaten at The Tapas HQ, she couldn't get her head in the right place.

Easing her way through the crowds, Terri moved towards

the door leading to the toilets.

The rest of the girls had been chucking the drinks down their necks and having a generally good time, but she couldn't bring herself to enjoy it. She was struggling to keep up and had only managed to down a fraction of what she'd normally put away. That was most unlike her. On their rare nights out she was usually one of the first to down the shots like there was no tomorrow and jump on tables, but tonight, the alcohol had done nothing to loosen her up or put her in a better frame of mind - the opposite, if anything.

Pushing open the door to the toilet corridor, Terri frowned. Tonight was Josie's night and it wasn't fair to put a negative slant on the celebrations. Perhaps she should go home, rather than drag everyone into a downer?

Glancing up, she saw a young man walking up the corridor from the Gents toilets and forced her mouth into a pleasant smile.

She'd freshen herself up, make her excuses to the others and then head off. She'd get over Jonah's stinging rebuff in time - just not as quickly as she'd hoped. It had been a long time since a man had engendered such an effect on her and that irritated more than anything else.

His loss, Terri told herself with fake bravado as she continued down the corridor.

'Thanks,' she muttered as the man stood to one side to let her pass, her smile quickly turning into a frown when he stepped in front of her, causing her to bump into him. 'Wh...?'

Stepping out of the darkness from behind, Ron clamped his hand over Terri's mouth and dragged her along the corridor, glancing over his shoulder to check no one else was about.

With wide eyes, Terri fought against being manhandled, but whoever was frogmarching her towards the metal door at the end of the corridor was too strong. 'MMMPHH' she squawked, the thick nicotine smelling fingers pressing against her nose as well as the hand over her mouth taking its toll.

'Shut it!' Ron hissed, glancing around. Even though he'd

already checked for CCTV and found none, in times such as these he had a habit of double checking. 'Door!' he barked to Kieran, hoping beyond all measure the stupid fool could cope with opening the bloody thing.

Terri's mind raced with panic as the metal fire escape door was booted in by the young man that she'd thought at first glance to be so polite. *How wrong she'd been.*

'HHMPHHH!' she cried, the muffled sound pointless. No one would hear her from down here. Would the others notice she hadn't returned? Her hands flailed wildly, hoping to gouge whoever's stinking hand was over her mouth.

Grabbing Terri's arm with his free hand, Ron twisted it and yanked it down behind her back, hearing the satisfying sound of it dislocating at the shoulder. As her frantic muffled wailing increased, he tried not to laugh. She should be grateful he hadn't broken it, but maybe he'd surprise her with that later. *If there was time...*

Shoving her through the door to the wide alleyway outside, Ron jerked his head at Kieran, watching him push the fire door closed. The stupid fuckers at this shitty club hadn't even bothered alarming their doors. *More fool them.*

'NNNGH!' Terri grunted, pushing back again the man with all her might despite her useless arm.

'Shut up, bitch,' Ron spat, glancing around once more. He knew it was a risk, a *big* risk, but there was no one about. Even if someone happened to stumble up this alley, it would only be a drunk or a prostitute - no one to worry over. And he couldn't wait. It was her own fault. The stupid slut shouldn't press against him like the whore she was, should she?

Slamming Terri face down against the boot of the Lexus, Ron fumbled with his zip, his other hand still firmly over her mouth. He ignored the insistent vibration of his phone clamouring for attention within his pocket. It would be that Pointer dickhead again. *Well, he could wait.*

Terri squirmed and twisted in impotent hopelessness. This man, whoever he was, was using his knee and thighs to pin her legs against the bumper, the weight of him crushing her already half-smothered face down into the cold metal of the car boot.

She tried to bite his hand, but couldn't open her mouth over the vice like grip. *Wasn't anyone going to help her?*

Terri stared at the young man standing motionless to the left of the car, her eyes pleading. Panic increasing, she attempted a further futile struggle. 'NNNNH!' she wailed, rapidly running out of steam.

Ron freed himself from his trousers, barely able to control his lust. This one was a fine looker even if she was a cheap tart. And what made all of this even more satisfying was, if Adams was correct, Powell would shortly be in the premises looking for this lady of his. *This one's for you, Lena*, he thought.

'What are you doing?' Kieran finally noticed why the woman Ron was so insistent on grabbing wasn't yet in the boot like they'd planned. 'You can't do that here! What if someone sees you?'

'Shut the fuck up!' Ron gasped, hitching up Terri's already barely-there skirt. 'Who's to notice?'

'NNNH!' Terri squawked, wincing with pain as the man pushed himself roughly into her. Panic swirled and spiralled in her mind and agony throbbed in her arm twisted at a strange angle where she was bent double over the car boot.

The car was silver, she thought, concentrating on something that may help later on. It looked silver, but it was difficult to tell in the dark. It was definitely light-coloured. What type of car was it?

Absurdly, Christmas carols played on repeat in her mind as she fought to keep her brain from crashing into a place where it could never return.

'What was that?' Ron grunted, thrusting harder. 'You calling for your boyfriend? Think he'll come and save you?'

'NGGNHH!' Terri wailed, her face pressing harder into the metal as the man thrust harder.

'What a shame… Powell's not here? Well, he won't want you now, you slut!' Ron spat. 'Now he'll realise the hard way not to fuck with my family!'

Tears escaped from Terri's eyes. *This was to do with Jonah? Some kind of payback?* Even if she'd been able to speak, there was no point explaining Jonah didn't want her. Her whole body began trembling.

'Get her in the boot. We've got to leave!' Kieran urged, looking around him for the tenth time.

'I said, shut up!' Ron grunted. He was almost done. *As was she...*

Terri barely noticed the hand over her mouth move to around her neck. She had no energy, but nothing hurt anymore. It didn't matter any longer either.

THIRTY

MIKE GRADUALLY BECAME AWARE of a constant shaking like the world was moving around him. *Was this the end? An earthquake?*

Being buried by rubble to die a long and lingering death from starvation, undiscovered for weeks trapped under the complete and utter collapse of his home would be a fitting end to match the crumbling shreds of his pointless existence. A worthwhile and welcome release from this torture. 'I'm sorry Tammy,' Mike slurred, his eyes still closed. 'I'm so sorry...'

'Dad!' Heath shouted, increasing the severity of the shaking. 'Dad. It's me!'

Four times he'd attempted to rouse his father over the last half an hour. *Four bloody times...*

Short of lobbing a pint glass of water over him, he'd tried everything, and he'd been just about to do that out of pure frustration when there was a response from the drunken idiot.

Heath was at his wits end. He'd called O'Hara twice with no response either. In fact, it was worse than that. O'Hara had cut off the call, so it was clear he wasn't going to help.

Continuing to shake his father's shoulders, watching his lolling head ricochet off the armchair's headrest, Heath was determined to bring the man round from his self-imposed stupor. He needed answers. He *had* to have answers. 'Talk to me!'

'Hmm?' Mike burbled. 'Leave me alone. It won't help. Nothing will help... Not now... It's all ruined... In pieces... I...'

'DAD!' Heath spat. 'Open your fucking eyes. Do you hear me? Open your goddamn eyes!' Raising his hand, he slapped his father hard around the face. 'Wake up, damn you!'

Mike's bloodshot eyes finally opened and he looked around him, first with fear, then with confusion. He squinted, adjusting his focus to the sudden light of the sitting room. 'Wha...?'

Squatting down on his haunches, keeping a grip on his father's shoulder, Heath looked into Mike's bleary eyes. 'Tell me what's happened. What happened to Mum? I need to know and I need to know *now*.'

Mike eyes filled with tears, his gaze looking through Heath as though he was transparent. 'Your mother... Oh God... Your mother... she...'

'Don't even think about telling me this rubbish about her leaving you. I know she didn't,' Heath screamed, his fingers digging into Mike's skin. 'Tell me the truth, Dad. Who did it?'

Mike blinked. 'Did it? Who...? Tammy?' As his mind gradually caught up, he felt himself slipping back towards the black hole. He wanted to stay in that hole. He didn't want the memory of what happened to Tammy surfacing. If he pretended she'd left then he wouldn't have to think about what had really happened. *That's if it had? Maybe he'd dreamt it? It could all be a horrid dream. Tammy had gone out and she was fine. Oh, thank God.*

'She's not here at the moment,' Mike muttered.

Heath gritted his teeth. He would punch the truth out of his father if he kept denying it. 'Stop this shit!' he roared. 'I know she's dead so you might as well tell me how!' He got to his feet. 'I know she's dead because *I* found her.'

Mike stared at his son in horror. *Dead? Oh no, no, NO! He hadn't been dreaming.* His eyes flicked in the direction of the garden.

'Can you imagine what that was like, Dad?' Heath spat. 'Have you any idea? You told me she'd left you. You *lied*. You know she's in the shed. What the fuck? In the shed in a fucking compost bin?'

Mike blinked, his bloodshot eyes unfocused. *O'Hara put his wife in a compost bin?* 'S-She can't be... She can't...'

'Was it you?' Heath lurched towards Mike. Grasping him around the throat, he almost lifted his father from the armchair, such was his rage. 'Was it you who killed her or was it the Powells?'

'The P-Powells?' Mike spluttered. *Heath thought he'd killed his own wife?*

'Has Jonah Powell been round here threatening you? Did he kill my mother?' Heath's frantic need to know the truth was spiralling out of control. 'Was it him? I need to know!'

Mike was unable to make sense of any of this. 'No, the Powells haven't been anywh...'

'Robert Adams then? Was it him or was it you? Did my mother find out about your debts, you piece of shit?'

Mike put his head in his hands, the more he sobered up, the worse the crushing sense of hopelessness became. 'It... I...'

'You're pathetic! You killed her own wife? You killed my mother?' Heath roared.

'NO! No I didn't!' Mike wailed. 'I couldn't stop him. He just did it in front of me and...'

'So it *was* Adams?' Heath screamed. 'I'll kill him! I knew he'd want his own back because he thinks I killed Dulcie.' He yanked his mobile from his pocket. 'I'm calling the police. I don't care if I go back to jail. I'm having Adams for th...'

'YOU CAN'T!' Mike stumbled to his feet, his flailing arms grasping for Heath's mobile.

Heath pushed his father back, the action taking little effort to make him to lose his balance and fall to the ground. 'I'm not having my mother put in a fucking compost bin. This is...'

'It was O'Hara!' Mike blurted. 'O'Hara killed my wife.

He's going to kill all of us.'

Heath stood motionless in front of the gibbering mess of his father, watching as his body shook and dissolved in floods of tears. *O'Hara? O'Hara killed his mother?*

• • • •

'FUCKING HELL, LOOK WHO'S COMING!' Sally's drink sloshed down her dress as she danced drunkenly. 'Where's Terri? Loverboy's here!'

All the other girls laughed, eagerly watching Jonah Powell striding through the crowds, the throngs of people parting like the Red Sea.

Josie didn't laugh. Being pregnant, she was the only sober one amongst them and could tell by the look on her bosses face that he would not find his and Terri's sex session an amusing topic of conversation to be discussed by members of his club's dancing troupe. The girls were a great laugh and she loved them dearly, but they were loose cannons when the drink was inside them. And she, for one, wanted a job at the end of the day.

Sally tottered over to Jonah, drunkenly winding her arm around his neck. 'Come now, Mr Powell. We know you can't bear to be away from us, but this is a hen night.'

Jonah's eyes narrowed as he pulled Sally's arm from around his neck.

'Don't be like that, Mr Powell. I'm not trying it on. I wouldn't tread on Terri's toes. Us girls don't do that to each other, do we ladies? Sally looked at the others for encouragement only to find their laughter had diminished, but her drunken brain couldn't process that fast enough before her mouth was back in gear.

'If you're looking for Terri, she's gone to the loo, but she's been ages.' Sally's mouth cracked into a smile, her hand now resting on the lapel of Jonah's suit. 'Hey, you know what she's like with toilets... so if you're quick, you might get chance for another sh...'

'Enough!' Jonah roared. Grabbing Sally's hand, he ripped

it from his chest and none too gently pushed her away, the combination of her sky-high heels and drunkenness making her stagger and fall backwards. 'You all need to get out of here *now*!'

As several of the girls rushed to help Sally off the floor, shock on their faces, a man loomed forward. 'Here, you just pushed that bird over!' Swinging his fist, he landed a hefty right hook on Jonah's jaw.

Stumbling backwards from the impact, Jonah's eyes flashed with fury as he launched himself at the equally large perpetrator, his fist connecting with the man's nose. In slow motion, the man left the floor and landed on his back, knocking into several of the other clubbers. The sound of glasses smashing and women screaming almost overtook the thumping bass pounding from the speakers.

'Get out of here NOW!' Jonah roared once again to the women.

'I'm going to have you, you cunt!' Rage twisting his face, the man hurried to scramble off the floor, blood pouring from his nostrils.

Jonah swung around. *This could be a diversion tactic to get to his women from the Feathers.* 'Go now,' he repeated to the girls, waving his arm in the general direction of the door. As they scrabbled for their bags in the chaos even Sally looked as frightened as the rest of the women.

Seeing three bouncers approaching, Jonah contemplated whether to take on the man getting up from the floor and kick him back to where he came from with a boot to his already broken nose or deal with the bouncers who looked far from amused. Deciding the man getting up from the floor was the most immediate threat, Jonah wasted no time in planting his boot firmly into the man's face, sending him sprawling back to the drink-soaked dance floor.

'How many more times have I got to tell you to leave?' Jonah yelled at the women frozen in shock at the unfolding spectacle.

'What the fuck's going on?'

Feeling his arms grabbed from behind, Jonah twisted out of the grip and swung around, his face contorted in fury. He faced a bouncer even broader and taller than he. 'You want to ask that prick!' he spat, nodding at the man on the floor.

The bouncer's face broke into a wide grin. 'Mr Powell!' He nodded to his colleagues to stand down. 'Is this bloke giving you trouble?' He turned to the other bouncers eyeing him suspiciously. 'It's Jonah Powell,' he repeated, giving them a knowing look. He for one wanted no problems with the Powell firm whether they'd caused a fight in the club or not. Neither would his gaffer, he knew that much.

Jonah brushed down his suit, his eyes focused on Nero quickly making his way over. 'A bit of a misunderstanding.'

'Misunderstanding?' The man with the newly broken nose was dragged to his feet by two of the bouncers. 'This cunt pushed that woman over and then lamped me!' His eyes narrowed as he glared at Jonah. 'I'll have you, mark my words.'

Nero squared up to the man, his frame towering over both the man and the bouncers. 'I'd be very fucking careful with what you promise, mate!' *Jesus Christ. He'd only been seconds behind Jonah, yet it had still kicked off.*

The head bouncer jerked his head in the direction of the exit. 'Get this joker out of here.' He glared at the man with the broken nose. 'You're fucking barred, mate.'

Jonah watched the man being none too gently escorted to the exit whilst shouting threats and curses. *Was that anything to do with O'Hara? Unlikely, but still not worth taking a chance over.*

Nodding to the head bouncer and ignoring the wary glances of the other customers, Jonah turned back to the huddled group of women. 'Why the fuck are you still here?'

Josie burst into tears, her evening ruined and Jonah felt like ripping his hair out. He could kill Gwen for this. Her lapse of judgement in allowing this night out had caused even *more* problems.

'Can we offer you a drink on the house, Mr Powell?' The head bouncer asked. His boss would go tits if he knew Jonah Powell had left his gaff unhappy - their rep as a club would go down the fucking plug hole.

'Thank you, but no.' Jonah glanced towards the bar. 'We're leaving.' He turned to the group of women. 'Is everyone here? Where's Terri?'

Sally wiped her hand across her nose, her pride wounded from ending up on the deck. 'She went earlier. Think she went home.'

Nero frowned. 'Did she say she was going home?'

'No, but she went in that direction. She's been nothing but a miserable bitch all night,' Sally spat. 'No guesses why...'

Jonah swallowed his increasing anger. He'd be having words with everyone about this tomorrow. This outing could have put everyone at risk and would not be happening again.

'Get them out of here Nero. Call as many cabs as you need.' Jonah shoved a wad of notes into Nero's hand, then scanned the room once more to double check no one else was about. These girls were so rat-arsed he was surprised they could even remember who was here in the first place.

As his eyes passed across the room and scanned the bar, he froze. *Was that...?* The woman sitting at the bar whose eyes had locked with his... *It was. It was Teagan.*

'Get them out. I'll follow shortly. There's someone I need to speak to,' he muttered.

THIRTY ONE

THE COMMOTION over the other side of the bar was the last nail in the coffin for Teagan. She wasn't staying any longer. She'd had her fill of violence and grief and didn't want to witness more of it, or worse, get dragged into it.

She pulled at Kim's arm to get her concentration from the dark-haired man she was draped over. 'I'm going now.'

Kim turned around and drunkenly wrapped her arms around Teagan's neck. 'You can't, babe. I'm enjoying myself.' She glanced at the blonde man hovering impatiently next to Teagan. 'Don't leave. You're definitely in there and he's hot!'

Teagan untangled Kim's arms from around her and dropped from the high stool, her legs wobbly. 'I really don't feel good so I'm going, but you stay. I'll call a taxi and see you at home later.'

'But babe, you...' Kim was about to protest further, but feeling the sudden and very tempting hand of the gorgeous dark-haired man that she more than fancied, snake under her mini-skirt, she changed her mind. *Teagan was a right dull cow. If she wanted to leave, then let her.*

Uncle Ron might not be happy that she'd allowed the girl to wander off, but he'd never find out. Besides, she'd already got *tons* of info from Teagan. She'd grilled her for days. Uncle Ron wouldn't have had *half* that information if it wasn't for her.

Plus it was because of *her* they'd even found Teagan's whereabouts. Kim grinned to herself. She'd done more than enough already, so was buggered if she was losing out on a good night with this hot bloke she'd bagged.

She ran her tongue across her lips suggestively and gazed at the dark-haired stranger. Yep, she was onto a winner with this one and had every intention of taking him back to her flat.

Christ, even Uncle Ron had to appreciate she needed a break from time to time. *And that time was now.*

Satisfied Kim was too enthralled with the dark-haired man to press the issue of remaining at the club, Teagan took a deep breath and hoped she wouldn't make a fool of herself by falling over as she headed to the exit. There would be plenty of taxis outside.

Turning, she made to walk off when the blonde man grabbed her arm. 'Where are you going? You're not leaving are you?'

The feel of the man's hand tightly around Teagan's upper arm brought back memories she did not want reminding of. *He's not Saul*, she told herself, but fear spiralled regardless. She forced herself to smile. 'Yes, but thanks for the drinks.'

The blonde man stepped in front of Teagan, his stance forcing her against the bar. 'What, so you're fucking off after accepting drinks off me all night?' he said, a twitch at the corner of one eye belying his anger.

Teagan's heart accelerated. 'It wasn't like that. I don't feel too good. I...'

'You a cock-tease?' The blonde man spat, moving closer. 'Some blokes get offended by that. We don't like being used by tarts out for free drinks.' He tightened his grip on Teagan's arm. 'I'll come with you and make sure you get home.'

'Thank you, but I'll be fine.' Teagan fought to control her escalating panic. The man was penning her in and there was no way she was leaving with him. Her eyes darted to Kim, but found her lips locked to the mouth of the dark-haired man.

Putting his hands on Teagan's waist, the blonde man pulled her against him. 'Dance with me.'

'She said no.' Jonah pulled the man away from Teagan by his shirt collar. 'So get the fuck off her!'

'Who the bloody hell do you think you are?' The man snarled, squaring up to Jonah.

'If you don't know, then you will shortly,' Jonah spat, his eyes flicking to Teagan.

Seeing who was standing in front of the blonde man, Teagan all but passed out with a combination of first relief, and then pure unbridled panic. *Jonah?*

Her heart beat like a drum. *What was he doing here? Wait, he was here with Terri Mason, not here for her.* But he was still here and she couldn't have him around. She'd got away from all this and wasn't being put back to square one. The man took over too many of her dreams as it was.

Confusion rolled in Teagan's brain. 'Jonah, it's fine, honestly. I...'

'Yeah, it looks like it. Come with me.' Jonah grabbed Teagan's arm.

'She's my bird,' the blonde man barked. 'You can't just come in here and...'

'Leave it,' the dark-haired man hissed in his mate's ear. 'That's one of the Powells.'

The blonde man took a step back. *The Powells? He wasn't getting involved with them.* Raising his hands in submission, he smiled. 'Sorry, mate. No offence.'

'Teagan?' Kim squawked. 'Aren't you going to introduce us?' Staggering from her seat, she lurched towards Jonah. *Jonah Powell was here?* Here right in front of her? Uncle Ron would be gutted he didn't frequent the clubs.

Jonah glared at the blonde man who had backed off completely and blanked Kim. 'We need to go, Teagan.'

Teagan stiffened. 'I'm not going anywhere wi...'

'It's important.' Jonah placed his arm firmly around

Teagan's waist. Pulling her into him, he pushed through the crowds. To anyone else they look like a normal couple as he effortlessly steered her towards the exit.

Teagan felt giddy with the feel of Jonah's body pressed tightly to her side and found herself moving like an automaton out of the door. She watched Jonah nod to the bouncers and willed herself not to do anything stupid in front of this man. She'd already embarrassed herself enough.

. . . .

ROBERT WOULD HAVE gnawed his teeth down to stumps had his jaw not been already locked solid from clenching it. He was cutting it fine, but taking a wrong turn approaching Leicester Square, he'd ended up shunted the whole way around a one-way system crawling with London's Saturday night traffic. Every single second meant time he could not afford to lose.

His eyes moved to the app on his phone. Powell's tracker was still handshaking at the same location somewhere around here and had remained immobile for ten minutes.

Ten whole minutes Powell had been inside the very same place as Teagan.

Sweat ran between Robert's shoulder blades and he slammed his fist on the horn at the taxi in front stopped to let out passengers. 'Fucking move!' he roared, his knuckles white on the steering wheel.

He craned his neck around the black cab at the large neon lettering visible from his position down the road. *There it is. Percy's nightclub.*

Perspiration beaded on Robert's brow, not knowing how to play this. Should he abandon the car and run up to the club or what?

Was he going in to make sure Powell was nowhere near Teagan? She may no longer even be in there, but if she was, what would he do if Powell was already with her?

Robert fingered the outline of the Swiss Army knife in his

pocket - the one which had dispatched Powell's brother. Or should he use his mother's gun, safe and loaded in his boot?

Think rationally, Robert, he thought, his brain whirring. Didn't they check for weapons on entry to clubs? *Damn and blast it.* He had no idea about the rules and regulations concerning nightlife, so how the fuck would he know?

Think. Think!

The taxi in front moved off and Robert continued up the road, swerving to the side directly opposite Percy's, scowling at the skimpily-dressed women queuing to get in. It was almost 11 o'clock and they were still arriving in their droves, the tarts.

Right. Now what?

Robert glanced at the sign on the road. *No waiting. Drop off only.*

He was staying here whatever it said, but should he go in? He looked back at the tracker. The fucker was still in there.

He'd go in. He go in and look for himself.

Robert was about to get out of the car when a group of people leaving the club caught his eye. Immediately recognising the man with the group of drunk, staggering women, he froze. *Nero.*

Shuffling down in the driver's seat, Robert watched Nero flag down a taxi, then a further three, systematically piling a group of girls into each car. It was unlikely he'd be spotted. The giant of a man was too busy walking from cab to cab handing money to the drivers to notice him parked the other side of the road. Those girls must be from the Feathers. Either that or Nero had bought the services of twelve hookers. Neither would surprise him, the filth.

But where was Powell?

Robert frowned. He hadn't spotted Terri Mason either and he'd seen her face enough times after collecting those photos of Teagan for his montage, so he'd have recognised her immediately. Terri Morgan wasn't with the rest of the scutters, so she must still be in the club with Powell.

Robert's face twitched with the ghost of a smile. This meant

Powell must be sticking with her rather than setting his sights back on Teagan.

Seeing Nero clamber into the last cab, Robert relaxed a little as the taxis pulled away and straightened himself up in his seat. Now was the time to go inside.

Unclipping his phone from its dashboard holder, Robert shoved it into his pocket and was reaching for the door handle when he froze once again, his heart lurching into his throat.

Powell. And Teagan was with him. No. No. NO!

Crouching back down in the seat, Robert buzzed with rage as Jonah Powell ushered Teagan into the car he'd conveniently parked virtually outside the club.

Robert's fury intensified. He was too late. Powell had his dirty hands on *his* property.

As Jonah's car started, Robert's shaking fingers fumbled with the ignition. Was Teagan being taken back to the Feathers or to Powell's own home again? The only way to find out was to follow.

THIRTY TWO

'GET THAT WILL YOU?' Ron muttered, slinging his mobile at Kieran.

Fumbling with the phone, Kieran's fingers struggled to answer it. His nerves were shot to ribbons. There was a woman in the boot and Uncle Ron was thraping through the streets like no one's business. He didn't need this. He didn't need any of it. He glanced at the screen:

```
RA calling
```

'It's Adams,' Kieran muttered.

'Adams is calling me on *that* phone?' Ron snarled. 'Fucking answer it then!'

Finally forcing his fingers to work, Kieran put the call on loudspeaker. 'Hello?'

'Where's O'Hara?'

Kieran glanced at his uncle. 'He's next to me, driving the car.'

'Why the fuck are you calling me on this phone?' Ron screamed, his shouting deafening Kieran.

'Powell has Teagan', Robert barked. 'I got to the club and

before I could do anything I saw him leave with her. She's *mine*. You promised me Teagan and now he's got her. Are you in on this? Was this part of your plan?'

'You what?' Ron spat. 'What are you talking about?'

'You know full well what I'm talking about,' Robert raged. 'You text me at the last bloody minute telling me Teagan's in that poxy club knowing I wouldn't get there in time. This is a set up and...'

'Fucking stop right there,' Ron began, his temper igniting. Adams had the audacity to accuse him of working alongside Powell? Was the bloke mental? Furthermore, he couldn't be saying this over the mobile. 'You need to stop talking ab...'

'You knew this would happen! Why else would Powell now be at your niece's flat?' Robert ranted. 'Powell's not interested in that Terri whore - he wants Teagan, but she's *mine*! You promised I'd get her once she spilt the info you wanted to your stupid bitch of a niece and I fell for it, you cunt!'

Ron's mind span. This couldn't be right. He glanced over his shoulder, the banging in the boot resuming its incessant knocking. 'They're at Kim's apartment? *My* Kim's apartment? Powell is there now?'

'That's what I fucking said, isn't it? I'm outside now. He's gone in with her and hasn't come out. Waiting for you, is he?' Robert snarled.

Without even looking for traffic behind, Ron swung the car across the road onto the other side of the carriageway amongst a plethora of blasting horns.

'What the fuck?' Kieran screeched, his head banging off the passenger window. 'What are you doing?'

'Change of fucking plan,' Ron growled. *Powell was at Kim's flat with Teagan?* If Powell was more interested in that silly cow, why the fuck had he got this other tart trussed up in his boot. *Fuck. FUCK!*

There was little point doing what he'd planned now. *Bollocks!* He'd wasted his time. All along the bargaining chip and his leverage was living with his niece? *For Christ's sake.*

Shovelling his meaty palm over his balding head, Ron stamped harder on the accelerator. 'Adams, do *not* go into the flat under any circumstances. Stay where you are and watch where Powell goes.'

'You want me to sit here whilst that prick is with my property?'

'Yes I do and if you don't, then I'll call Powell myself and tell him what you're doing and where you are,' Ron spat. Not that he would, but he had to weigh this up. And before he could do that, he needed to get rid of the contents of the boot. 'Text me when he leaves. And Adams... never use this number again.'

• • • •

GWEN WAS FURIOUS. She handed Josie another tissue from the box on her desk, then glared at Nero. 'Where exactly is Jonah now?'

Nero shrugged. 'On his way back here, I presume.'

Gwen frowned. 'You presume?' Nero looked as stressed as she felt herself.

'He was right behind me as we left, but then said he needed a word with someone. Probably smoothing over the scene at Percy's,' Nero explained, unhappy being lumbered getting this lot back to the Feathers like a childminder. Now he was getting grief from Gwen?

Gwen pursed her lips and ran her eyes over the group of drunk, morose dancers. Jonah had steamed in and ruined the girls' night out? They had little enough time off to enjoy themselves as it was. It was a rare occurrence they went out for a laugh together, well, half of them at least, and Jonah had pulled the plug on it? And not just pulled the plug on it, but *spectacularly* pulled the plug on it, causing every single one of the girls to be upset and half-traumatised. And none so much as Josie. The girl was beside herself. Her special night had been completely ruined.

Gwen frowned. Tonight's show was about to close, she was absolutely shattered and now the other half of her staff had been dumped on her, all of them upset and pissed out of their heads.

'I still can't believe Mr Powell shoved me over!' Sally wailed, thick streaks of mascara running down her cheeks. 'I'll have bruises and everything.' She glared at Gwen. 'I should put in a complaint. He might be the boss, but he can't go around attacking us like this.'

'I don't think he pushed you over, Sally,' Josie reasoned. 'You were all over him. He moved you away and you stumbled in your heels.'

Sally's eyes narrowed. 'I wasn't all over him! He's a fucking looney. And he *did* push me over. Why else would that bloke have stepped in?' She looked around the other girls for support. 'It's true, isn't it girls? He then smacked up that bloke who tried to help me!' She stood up unsteadily. 'Look at the state of my fucking knees. How can I go on stage on Monday looking like this? He's a nutter. A fucking nutter!'

Gwen raised her hand. 'Ok, Sally. I think that's enough.'

Sally sniffed in derision. 'No it's not enough! It's always the bloody same. These people think they can get away with anything. Jonah Powell started it, yet the other bloke gets thrown out? How fair is that? No one respects blokes who hit women.'

'Where's Terri?' Gwen asked, worry prickling. The way Sally was ramping up the situation would snowball if she couldn't control it, but she was far from happy herself. Although it was unlikely Jonah had attacked Sally, *something* had occurred. She looked at Nero questioningly.

'Terri left early,' Nero said uncomfortably.

'Yeah well, she'd been miserable all night. She's been the same for days and that's because of Mr Powell too! Look how he treated her!' Sally barked.

'Just stop it all of you!' Josie sobbed, standing up. 'It's *my* hen-night that's been ruined, not yours!'

Gwen steered Josie back into her chair. 'Calm down, love. This isn't good for the baby.' She turned to Nero. 'We need to get these girls home and talk about this tomorrow.'

'I want to talk about it *now*,' Sally cried. 'Jonah Powell doesn't own us. We might dance at his club, but it was our night off and he can't tell us we aren't allowed to go out!'

Gwen frowned. Jonah had said the girls shouldn't be socialising, but it was ludicrous. *Hang on.* Where was the security she'd arranged? Had they not accompanied the girls like she'd instructed?

'Jonah Powell's blaming you, you know?' Sally continued, her eyes flashing malevolently. 'He's livid. Says you were wrong for saying we could go.'

Gwen's eyes darted to Nero and watched him shrug slightly. *So it was true?* Jonah blamed *her* for him storming into a club, beating up a random bloke, pushing one of the girls over and ruining everyone's bloody night? *He blamed her for that, did he?*

She bristled with anger. Enough was enough. She'd told Jonah he couldn't keep the staff under lock and key in their own time without a damn good explanation, yet he wasn't prepared to give them that?

This was preposterous. There was no way she was getting it in the neck for this. For God's sake, there was no danger to the girls. Jonah was paranoid and stuck in an obsession to exact revenge on people that didn't even exist anymore. He had to knock this damaging attitude on the head.

Gwen grabbed her bag. 'Nero, call taxis for every single one of these girls please.'

Nero frowned. 'You want me to call taxis?' *What was he? A fucking booking clerk? Twice tonight, this was.*

'Yes I do.' Gwen snapped. 'I'm going to sort this out and I'm going to sort it out now.'

Jonah had put a spanner in everyone's night and was blaming her for his own paranoia over this stupid O'Hara and that bloody weirdo Robert. Both of them had long gone, yet he was still acting like this, whilst keeping everyone in the dark?

It wasn't acceptable and she would tell him that *right now.* Being as he hadn't even had the decency to return to the

Feathers and instead sloped off somewhere, she'd go home and confront him because he would be bound to be there. Tomorrow she'd move back to her own place. She needed her own space and living at Jonah's house wasn't helping. Besides, there was no longer any reason to be there.

It was time Jonah let this go before he damaged the firm and the club's morale any further. She'd make him listen this time. No more pussy-footing about not wanting to upset him.

Leaving Nero in her office with the girls, Gwen slammed the door and stomped down the corridor towards the stage door exit. This was the quickest way to her car and she was having this out with Jonah before he disappeared to bed, barking at her that they'd talk about it in the morning.

No, they'd talk about this as soon as she got back. *Blaming her indeed.*

Her face set in a fierce scowl, Gwen opened the stage door and ran down the steps, freezing on the final one and an ear piercing scream left her mouth before she could stop it.

Thirty Three

JONAH LOOKED AROUND the tastefully decorated, upmarket apartment. Anything to deflect him from the burning need to pull Teagan into his arms, press his mouth against hers, rip her clothes off and make her his...

Teagan hovered next to the fridge, wanting to pull out the nicely-chilled bottle of white wine she knew to be inside, but she was unwilling to give Jonah an excuse to stay. If she offered him a drink, it would be dangerous. Every single nerve fibre was crying out for his touch and she didn't trust herself.

No matter how much she wanted to, dreamt of or needed to, she couldn't go down that road.

She shouldn't have even allowed Jonah to usher her into his car when they left Percy's. She should have had more sense. And she should *certainly* have not allowed him to bring her back to the apartment. Wasn't the whole point of being here to make a clean break? Now he knew where she lived and was right in front of her.

When she'd protested about getting in his car, Jonah had been so convincing. He'd made whatever the issue was sound like a matter of life or death, even though he was vague as to the reason. Yet here they were and she was still no clearer what it was all about.

He wasn't interested, he'd made that crystal clear, so what was this all about? More to the point, she wasn't risking her sanity by putting herself back in the position of being around him. She would not become a notch on Jonah Powell's renowned bed-post, regardless of how much her body wanted to.

Jonah watched Teagan's hand moved away from the fridge's handle. 'Whose apartment is this?'

Teagan hesitated. *What did it matter whose apartment it was?* 'A friend of mine - Kim Sutherland.' she replied tersely, folding her arms across her chest. 'Are you going to tell me what's going on or is it normal for you to drag someone from their night out without an explanation? You said it was important I leave, but you still haven't told me why.'

Jonah's eyes flashed with a brief flurry of irritation, yet Teagan's abruptness only made him want her more. *Control, Jonah.* 'Why did you leave?'

Teagan faltered. 'Leave where? The club or your house?' Her eyes moved to Jonah's mouth. He was standing too close. *Far* too close.

'You didn't seem to be having too much of a good time with that jerk in the club.'

'Something else you took it upon yourself to control.' Instinctively, Teagan moved from where Jonah might corner her, his very presence diluting her resolve. She moved her gaze to his ice-blue eyes. 'If you're talking about leaving your house, then it was the right thing to do.'

A nerve twitched in Jonah's neck. 'The right thing? What, to disappear without saying a word? Worrying everybody sick?'

Teagan frowned. 'I don't want to be around your type of lifestyle...' *There, she'd said it. Of sorts.* 'Do I have to spell out that I've had more than my fill of violence, drugs and all the sorts of things *you* sanction.'

'I might be intrinsic in supplying those things, but I'm not my brother, Teagan.' Despite the irritation, Jonah's voice was surprisingly soft.

Teagan's heart lurched, her hand itching to touch the chiselled line of Jonah's jaw. She knew he wasn't Saul. He was the very opposite.

Stop it. It changed nothing. 'You still haven't explained what was so important to warrant dragging me out of that club. Are you going to tell me what is going on or is this a weird game of yours?'

Jonah's expression hardened. 'There's no game, Teagan.' Sighing, he walked across to the window. Facing away, he looked down onto the street into the dark night. How could he phrase this without freaking her out? 'Let's just say that I would prefer it if you were somewhere I knew you were safe.'

'Safe? You said everything was over?' Teagan stared at Jonah's back, his large frame filling a good part of the window.

Jonah battled with himself whether to tell her everything or not. Which would be worse? Which would keep her the safest and not put her back in the nervous state she'd been in after what his twat of a brother had done? He turned slowly. 'I can't be sure. There might be someone. Someone who is out for me or...'

'Or those bloody diamonds, you mean?' Teagan snapped.

Jonah bit down on his bottom lip. 'Figuratively speaking, perhaps.' He studied Teagan closely. 'Has anyone been in this flat or that you've noticed hanging around outside? Anyone you know?'

'Like who? What's this about? Why would someone be here in connection to you?'

Jonah pulled his cigarettes from his pocket and nodded at them. Getting no reaction from Teagan to suggest otherwise, he lit one, smoke curling from between his lips. Should he mention Adams? That man was more of a worry than O'Hara where Teagan was concerned. The way he'd reacted; the way he'd disappeared and not been seen since...

He knew everyone believed Robert Adams had disappeared

from the face of the earth, but Jonah wasn't so sure. There was something... Something continually prodding in the back of his mind.

Sensing Jonah was weighing up what to say, Teagan's irritation bristled further. 'Do you not think you should just bloody well tell me?'

'How much do you know about this Kim person?' Jonah asked. 'I've never heard you mention her. Who does she have visiting here? Who does she know?'

Teagan snatched an ashtray from the work surface and flounced across the open-plan area in the living room, plonking the ashtray down on the coffee table in front of Jonah. 'Since when did you ever ask me about my friends? I do have friends, you know? It's hardly like we've ever had that kind of conversation. In fact, I don't think we've had *any* kind of conversation.' *Not entirely true.*

'That woman tonight? Is that Kim?'

'Not that it's any of your business, but yes,' Teagan spat, getting hot under the collar as embarrassment rose. Now *she* wasn't being honest. She didn't have any friends to speak of and was fast thinking Kim wasn't much of one either.

'She didn't seem the type I'd expect you to get on with,' Jonah muttered, raising an eyebrow.

'And why's that? Because she's not boring like me, you mean? Or too attractive?' Teagan cried, the uncomfortable rush of forming tears burning. How did this man have the power to make her feel so self-conscious? How did he have the ability to make her behave like a sulky twelve-year-old?

Biting the inside of her cheek, she turned so that Jonah wouldn't see her escalating anger.

'That's not what I meant,' Jonah said softly, unable to stop himself from placing his hands on Teagan's shoulders. 'I don't think you're boring and you certainly could never be anything but beautiful.' His voice was gravelly, low and he instantly regretted the words leaving his mouth.

It took all of Teagan's strength not to melt underneath

Jonah's hands, until she remembered Terri Mason - the woman's face in her mind clear as day. Jonah was playing her like he played all women and he was using that power right now to deflect from the strange insistence she remain behind closed doors. 'I think you should leave,' she muttered, unwilling to turn around and meet his eyes.

Jonah removed his hands from Teagan's shoulders. 'I can't until I know you're going to be safe. I'd like you to accompany me back to the house.'

Teagan's eyes widened. 'You want me to go back there? To be around nutters, drugs and cloak and dagger shit? You must be joking! I'm not doing it, Jonah. I'd rather be murdered by these so-called invisible threats than go back to that house.' Her eyes narrowed. She was about to betray herself but she couldn't help it. 'Besides, I can't imagine Terri would be pleased...'

'Terri?' Jonah spluttered. 'What's she got to do with this?'

'You tell me?' Teagan flapped her hand, her cheeks flushing scarlet. 'Oh, just forget it. It doesn't matter.' *What had she said that for? She'd made herself look ridiculous again.*

'There's nothing between me and Terri,' Jonah said. Raising his hand, his fingers brushed Teagan's cheek. 'Teagan... I...'

All possible logic leaked from Teagan, Jonah's fingers firing electric sparks across her skin. She found her eyes pulled to his. 'But, I...'

'It's you I want,' Jonah murmured, trailing his fingers under Teagan's chin and tilted her face up to his. 'You must know it's you I want... I've been trying to keep away...'

Teagan's lips parted. *Don't fall for it... do not fall for it...* 'But you and Terri... It's...'

'There is no me and Terri. The one incident the press made a big deal of, well, that was a mistake on my part. I would have done anything to get my mind off you,' Jonah whispered. 'You're in my head... You're all I can think about... All that I want...'

Teagan's blood crashed in her veins. *She mustn't do this.*

She mustn't. Her eyes focused back on Jonah's mouth, his fingers still burning her cheek. 'Jonah, I...'

Unable to stop himself, Jonah's mouth moved towards Teagan's, his body throbbing with need. He'd come to warn Teagan, protect her, but the pull was too strong and his resolve flew out of the window, along with any sense of right or wrong.

Before he could talk himself out of it, the need too fierce, his lips met hers. Feeling her mouth yield, he pulled her against him, one hand on the small of her back, the other, his fingers wrapping in her hair. His mouth explored hers, his need for this woman who had haunted his mind so vividly, crushing.

Teagan gasped at the intensity of Jonah's kiss, her arms instinctively moving around his neck, her hands pulling his suit jacket from his shoulders.

It all happened so quickly, so fast; his fingers plunging into her; the rollercoaster of crashing sensations pushing all other thoughts from her mind as the building pressure within her intensified.

Moaning with desperate need, pulling each other free of clothes, Teagan allowed herself to be pushed on to the sofa where Jonah entered her quickly and confidently. She held onto his big arms as he looked down at her, his eyes focused and intense. At first he moved slowly but forcefully – each powerful thrust making her gasp and cry out with steadily building want.

His mouth came back down onto hers, his arms hooking her legs higher as he increased his pace. Moaning into his mouth, her hands clutched at his buttocks, the intensity inside her unbearable.

As Jonah's pace upped to breakneck speed, Teagan clawed at Jonah's back, his hips pounding relentlessly, only breaking from his kiss to loudly cry out as she experienced the hardest, most intense climax she'd ever had. Her orgasm was still thundering through her as Jonah followed suit, growling as he spilt into her.

Spent, his mouth traced down over her breasts, hearing her thundering heart pounding.

Moving his lips from Teagan's skin, Jonah leant on one elbow, his free hand brushing a tendril of hair off her cheek. 'Wow,' he murmured. 'That was something else.' His mouth searched for hers once more, but she pulled away.

Frowning, Jonah raised himself so that Teagan could move from under him. 'What's the matter?'

Wrapping her arms around herself, Teagan shuffled to the edge of the sofa, self-consciously reaching for her discarded clothes, barely able to get her head around what had just happened.

Jonah was correct in as much that had been something else. It had been *fantastic*, but what had she been thinking? She'd never had random sex before. And with him of all people?

She'd worked so hard to free herself from the hold this man had over her in her mind and knew immediately without having to analyse it, that along with the stellar way her body had reacted, he would now be even further entrenched in her brain than he was before.

She knew what the problem was and it wasn't going to be one that could be easily resolved, if *ever*. She didn't want to admit it to herself, let alone anyone else, but she'd fallen for him and that was bad.

Not only would she not deal with his philandering ways where other women were concerned, she couldn't cope with his lifestyle. She couldn't be one of those women comfortable with a man being constantly under threat from either the police or lunatics.

'Teagan?' Gently touching her arm as she pulled on her knickers and straightened her skirt, Jonah frowned. 'Have I done something to upset you?'

Teagan shook her head and averted her eyes from Jonah's bare muscular chest, the thick ridges of his abdominal muscles all too enticing. 'No... It's just...'

'I want you,' Jonah blurted, unable to help himself. That may have been the most intense sex he'd ever had, and he'd had lots of good sex in the past, but this was different. He wanted to *be* with this woman.

Teagan couldn't even look at Jonah, her cheeks scarlet. 'You've just had me, haven't you?' she snapped, playing down her embarrassment and confusion.

Jonah grabbed Teagan's arm. 'I meant, I want you, as in I want to *be* with you.' He turned her face to his. 'I was advised to stay away and that I shouldn't get involved and hurt you, but I won't hurt you. That I can promise.'

Pulling away once more, Teagan stood up, her legs still shaking. 'Who advised that?'

Jonah shrugged. 'It doesn't matter. It was thought I'd do you no favours with what happened with... with...' He didn't want to bring his brother into this. He could see the doubt on Teagan's face and suddenly felt uncomfortable. He'd never felt the need to explain himself before, but right now he felt he should. 'I don't want anyone else...'

Teagan could barely believe this man wanted her as much as she wanted him. He might be lying, but she instinctively felt he wasn't. 'It's not just that... I mean, there are things with...'

'The diamonds are going,' Jonah interrupted. 'They will be out of my life on Thursday.' He sighed loudly. 'I won't stop being who I am, Teagan. For you or anyone. I can't and I won't, but I *am* getting rid of those things that have caused all of these problems. By Thursday that will be over.'

Teagan's eyes widened. 'You're getting rid of them?'

Jonah nodded. 'I am. I've arranged to sell them. I want them out of my life and I want *you* in it instead.'

Teagan bit her lip. *Could she do this?* 'But the rest of it... All the...'

'I can't change that. It's my life and my legacy.' Jonah pulled Teagan towards him. 'The rest we can work out, but I promise you the diamonds are going.'

Teagan felt the pull, the magnetism, the need. *He'd really get rid of those things? Could she live with everything else he did?* Her eyes rested on Jonah's mouth. *Could she?*

As Jonah lowered his lips to hers, Teagan knew she was

gone. *This man...*

Hearing the shrill ring of his mobile, Jonah scowled. 'Ignore it. If I can, you can.'

'I won't move back to yours, Jonah. I'm staying here,' Teagan said. *Things had to be taken one step at a time, but what was she saying by that statement? She wasn't sure.*

Jonah nodded. 'Ok, but I'm putting on security here whether you like it or not.' He held up his hand to silence Teagan's expected protest. 'Once the diamond sale is done, then I'll revisit it.' He moved to kiss Teagan, but the mobile rang again.

'You'd better get that,' Teagan said. 'It could be important.'

'Unlikely...' Jonah muttered, reluctantly picking his mobile from the floor. He looked at the screen. Nero. He'd kill him for interrupting. 'Yes?' he barked.

Teagan watched Jonah's face pale as he listened to the voice.

'I'll be right over,' Jonah barked. 'Arrange some security to be sent here immediately.'

Teagan blanched hearing Jonah read off the address of her apartment before disconnecting the call. 'What? What is it?'

'Something's happened. Look, I'm really sorry, but I'm going to have to go.'

Teagan stared wide-eyed. 'What? What's happened?'

Jonah buttoned his shirt and shrugged on his jacket. 'It's not to do with you, so don't worry, but I want you to come with me. You can wait with Gwen.'

Teagan shook her head. 'I'm staying here.'

Jonah frowned. He didn't want to leave Teagan here, but he could see she was resolute. His men were on route here and he had to get back to the club with what had just happened, so he had no option but to accept her choice. 'I've got security on its way over.'

'I've already said I don't wa...'

Jonah held Teagan's face gently with both hands. 'I need you to trust me. I'll explain everything later, but don't go out or let anyone in. *Please*, Teagan. Just until I can work out the lie of the land.' He pressed his mouth quickly onto hers. 'Promise me?'

'Ok, ok,' Teagan nodded, breathless even from that short kiss.

Jonah grabbed his car keys. 'I'll be in contact as soon as I can.'

And he was gone.

Teagan slumped onto the sofa, her head spinning and dread pooling. She stared at the sofa where she had not ten minutes past laid with Jonah. The heavy need for the man was replaced with worry. Did that phone call not underline exactly what life would be like with Jonah Powell? Had she made an extremely stupid decision?

It may be a stupid decision, but her heart gave her little choice. Despite the nagging dread, for the first time in weeks, she felt that her life was coming together.

It was only as she contemplated this did she begin to think perhaps she should have mentioned that she'd seen and spoken to Robert Adams; that she'd bumped into him outside this very apartment.

Teagan shook the thought away. Whatever had happened at the Feathers obviously wasn't good and there was no point in adding to the problems by telling Jonah something that was, in reality, of no consequence.

THIRTY FOUR

ROBERT WAS IMPOTENT with both rage and confusion. He'd barely moved a muscle since the call to O'Hara had ended. Not because he was reluctant to go against the man's instructions, but because he felt unable to do anything else.

His mind swirled with combinations of how he could do what his instinct screamed - to go into that apartment *regardless* of Powell and take Teagan.

If Powell attempted to stop him, then he'd kill him stone dead. He should have done it long before when he'd had the chance. *Stupid, stupid.*

Robert's eyes tracked back to the apartment window. Although the blinds were open, he could see no movement from within.

He'd only seen Powell once since they'd entered the building. He'd been standing at the window looking down onto the road. Had O'Hara called Powell like he'd threatened? Had Powell been searching for a sign of his whereabouts?

Robert frowned. His car was in view of the full length window, so Powell could have easily seen the motor. Ok, so the apartment was on the third floor, and the man wouldn't have been able to see anyone within the car, but there would be a good enough view of the car itself.

Robert sneered, knowing he'd made himself easy to spot by not changing motors. He still drove the very same car he'd owned whilst staying at Powell's house – another slip up, but even so, the man wasn't investigating.

Powell may have not been looking at the car at all?

The creeping disgust Powell and Teagan were now otherwise engaged pushed back into Robert's mind and his hands clenched into fists.

Either that or they had left the building. Was there another exit apart from the main entrance?

His face screwed into a scowl. He should have checked. His desperation was making him slack. How he despised people with no attention to detail and now he was becoming one of them.

He refreshed the tracker app on his phone. The coordinates had not moved, so Powell was still in the apartment.

The lines in Robert's forehead furrowed further. What if Powell *had* spotted him and called that freak, Nero, and more henchman and was waiting for them to arrive. That would give him time to rut on Teagan like the animal he was.

That was it. That's what Powell was doing.

Glancing in his wing mirrors, Robert checked the road behind him. Not a soul about.

His jaw set. He wasn't waiting to become Powell's latest victim.

Robert only had one target, aside from Teagan and he had no wish to kill her. Not yet. Not until he'd done what he'd dreamt of doing. The only target was in the flat with the woman that would shortly be his. That, and anyone else who interrupted his plan.

Scrambling from the car, Robert made a dash for the boot. Opening it, he lifted the carpet and reached for the loaded gun wrapped in a towel stashed under his spare tyre.

Rushing back to the driver's seat, Robert slammed the door and carefully unwrapped the gun, his nose wrinkling at the faint scent of the washing powder his mother had used since he could remember. He'd have to store this thing in something else. He wanted nothing clinging to anything in his possession reminding him of *that* woman.

Placing the gun on the passenger seat and detecting movement in the direction of the apartment out of the corner of his eye, Robert's head flicked up. His hand moved back to the gun, his fingers closing around the cold metal.

Jonah Powell was leaving.

Robert sat motionless, watching Powell run down the steps of the apartment entrance, his face twisted with rage.

His heart plummeted, mentally calculating the distance needed to shoot Powell whilst making sure the man was near enough to see his identity. He didn't want Powell dying without knowing who'd pulled the trigger. That would take away a good percentage of the enjoyment.

It was only then Robert noticed Jonah wasn't looking in his direction at all. He was acting like he saw nothing, short of the route to his own motor.

Amazed, Robert watched Jonah throw himself into the car and screech off down the road.

• • • •

HEADING WITH SPEED towards Kim's apartment, Kieran dared to glimpse at Ron and nausea rose once again. He wasn't happy how the night had turned out. Ron had said nothing about offing that bird. Neither had he mentioned he'd planned to rape her first either.

Squirming in the seat, Kieran realised in all actuality Ron hadn't told him *any* details of what was planned, apart from using Terri Mason to teach Jonah Powell a lesson. But then Kieran hadn't asked either…

Would it have made any difference if he had?

Kieran stared at his fingernails, his stomach roiling at the encrusted blood trapped underneath them. If his uncle had spelt out the plan, would he have refused any part in it, or would he have gone along with it like he usually did? Most probably the latter and that acknowledgement didn't sit comfortably.

He'd really believed joining his uncle on this mission would grant him access to the big league and make him a *somebody*, but all it was doing was getting him closer to a life sentence in nick. To top it all off, he was still treated like an utter dunce. Even Kim had more kudos because of the info she'd gleaned.

Kieran's teeth clenched, betting Kim was still throwing herself at that bloke in the club or by now, even shagging him back in her apartment. If Powell was also there, like Adams said, perhaps Kim was having a go with him too?

And what had he been doing on a Saturday night? Driving corpses around in a boot...

Kieran wanted no more part of this. He wanted to go back to Ireland. He glared at Ron. 'Where are we going now?'

Ron's head flipped away from the road, his owl eyes shooting daggers. 'Where the fuck do you think we're going? To make sure Adams hasn't ballsed anything up, that's where we're going. If he's gone in the flat and kicked shit off because of his stupid obsession, then we're fucked. And so is he...'

'I just want to go home,' Kieran whined. 'Someone will find that body soon and they'll know it's us.'

'Right bloody waste of time that was and all,' Ron griped. 'Powell's not interested in that silly tart and I'm right pissed off about that.'

Kieran risked another sideways look at his uncle, noticing for the first time exactly how ugly the man was. Resentment simmered. 'In that case, you didn't have to kill her.'

'Don't be fucking stupid! Of course I did!' Ron turned to glare at Kieran. 'You really are thick as shit, aren't you? That tart was supposed to be leverage, but it's the other one he wants – that Teagan, therefore we have to make sure Adams doesn't get her first.'

Kieran internally flinched from yet another reference to his stupidness, then jumped as the burner phone pinged.

'See what that is,' Ron shouted, swerving around the next

corner.

Kieran opened the text message. 'It's off Adams. He says Powell's left the flat and looks to be heading back to the Feathers.'

A wide grin wormed its way onto Ron's face. 'Looks like the body's been found then. At least Adams hasn't used my personal phone to update me this time.'

Kieran gripped the door handle as Ron's speed increased. 'If Powell's left, why are we going to the flat?'

Ron rolled his eyes. If he could afford to take his hands off the wheel, he'd clout the dolt. 'We need to make sure Adams is obeying orders.'

Kieran felt sick with the inference. 'You're planning on removing Adams?' *As well as a weirdo, the guy was a big bloke and wouldn't be easy to take down.*

'If necessary,' Ron snapped. He'd have nothing infringe the change of plans. 'Adams wants Teagan and now she's on her own he might make a move, but he can't because *we* need her.' His mouth twisted into a snarl. 'She's the one whose absence will pay Powell back for Lena. As I said, we wasted our time with that other one.'

'But you can't remove Adams,' Kieran exclaimed. *Uncle Ron was losing sight of the aim and he called him stupid?*

'I can do what the fuck I like!' Ron barked.

'The whole point of this was to get the diamonds and avenge my father, wasn't it? We need Adams to track the diamonds deal and if you're only concentrating on getting one over on Powell where women are concerned, then won't that ruin the rest? The deal's only a few days away.'

'Lena is more than just *women*,' Ron snarled. 'She's your sister and I want her avenged too. I know what I'm doing and don't need your analysis, thank you.' His fingers gripped the steering wheel harder. *Bollocks and shit.* The idiot nephew was right. They *did* need Adams a while longer, not that he would admit he'd missed that oversight.

He'd have to keep Adams sweet until the diamonds deal

went through. Then as the final parting gift to Powell and his wank firm, he'd take the woman from under his nose. And this time he'd get the *right* one. 'Text Adams back and tell him to get the fuck away from the apartment. We're almost there and if he's still lurking, he'll wish he wasn't! After that, we'll go and clear up Pointer's missus.'

Kieran's fingers fumbled to enter the text to Adams. Now he was expected to deal with yet another one of Ron's bodies. This night really was the worst. How the hell would he get rid of some old trout shoved in a compost bin? There were too many bodies piling up. They needed to get those diamonds and get the fuck back onto the ferry to Ireland before they got nicked for the whole bloody lot. Uncle Ron was being careless offloading people left right and centre like a loon and he wouldn't pay for his uncle's madness. *No fucking way.*

THIRTY FIVE

ROBERT PUNCHED the centre of his steering wheel, not caring if it made him drive erratically. It didn't matter. *Nothing* mattered apart from getting to Teagan.

A low growl erupted deep from the back of his throat. He could hardly believe how his chance, his one big opportunity to get what he wanted, had slipped from his grasp like fine sand.

Despite what O'Hara threatened, once Robert had witnessed Powell rushing from the apartment it was obvious the man's departure had sod all to do with him, so, as far as he was concerned, things were good to go.

He'd been about to step from the car and find a way in when everything got trashed.

Robert *knew* he would have succeeded. Teagan hadn't reacted negatively when she'd seen him the other day, so she was unaware of anything he'd suspected she might have been told. He was *sure* he could have talked her into accompanying him by convincing her it was the best and *only* thing to do.

And if she hadn't... If she'd resisted, then he'd have taken her anyway. One way or another, Teagan would have been beside him right now.

And he'd wanted her to see the montage. That alone was

important.

Robert's mouth twisted into a scowl. When he'd seen O'Hara pull around the corner, he knew it was over. He could have screamed. He should have pre-empted the Irish bastard would check to make sure the instructions to leave were obeyed.

Getting Teagan when O'Hara was on the scene was bloody impossible. Robert knew the ugly old cunt wouldn't stand by and allow it, so he'd had little choice but to move off.

A vein in Robert's temple throbbed worryingly as he swerved into the road of his B&B. Pulling up suddenly, the tyre scuffing against the high kerb, he killed the engine and stared out at the deserted road ahead.

Just look at it. Not a soul about. It would have been ideal - the perfect time and that balding Irish retard had blown his plan out of the water. *Again.*

Hands clenching into fists, Robert leant back against the car's headrest and closed his eyes to regulate his laboured breathing.

No matter how much he refused to allow the knowledge of Jonah Powell being inside that apartment, most likely with his hands all over Teagan; his tongue in her mouth; his body possessing hers while she begged for it in her slut-like way, it was all he could visualise.

Robert snarled. He didn't want to visualise it because it ruined his countenance and control. It spoiled his concentration and that was bad.

Snatching his mobile phone from the passenger seat, he opened the tracker, his blood pressure spiking seeing Powell's coordinates at the Feathers. That fucker wouldn't have even been aware Teagan was missing. Robert would have been away on his toes with her by his side long before Powell had the first clue. That's if he ever noticed. The wanker had gone round there with the sole intention of sticking his dick in Teagan, infecting her like his bastard of a brother had, purely to spoil the equilibrium. *Nothing else.*

People like Jonah Powell worked like that. And wanton

tarts like Teagan Fraser gagged for it.

Ripping open his car door, Robert stormed from the motor towards the B&B.

That was it.

Tomorrow he'd go to his so-called brother Mike's house. He didn't give a jot it was somewhere *else* O'Hara had instructed him to stay away from in case it was being watched. He didn't care about any associated risks along that vein. He'd go round first thing and get that dickhead to do some of *his* bidding for once.

· · · ·

STANDING IN THE small private cellar of the Feathers, Jonah stared at Terri Mason's corpse spread on the tarpaulin, grateful Nero had moved it from the bottom of the steps and into this private area without anyone seeing.

'It's a good job the girls were busy in the dressing rooms and the other half Nero shepherded back from Percy's were getting into taxis,' Gwen said, her eyes red from crying. 'Seeing Terri like this would finish them. I don't know how we'll break it to them.'

Jonah's rage intensified, unable to pull his eyes away from the knife wound in Terri's neck – the one which had undoubtedly killed her. The angry red marks accompanying the stab wound looked like she'd been half-strangled at some point too. And the additional act prompting her underwear to be missing and leaving bruises on her hips and thighs, he could only hope was inflicted after her death. Sadly, it was more likely to have happened while she was still alive.

His jaw ached. *Terri had been raped and murdered.* If Gwen hadn't pushed her on him in the first place, this wouldn't have happened. She wouldn't have been a target.

Jonah stared at Gwen coldly. 'You still think it was ok to allow the girls to go out unaccompanied?'

Gwen didn't think she could feel any worse if she tried. She'd been wrong. Jonah wasn't barking up the wrong tree at all. These people were still very much around. 'I-I asked security to accompany them. I-I thought it would be ok. I...'

'You didn't think there was any risk, more like! You thought me paranoid!' Jonah raged. He'd just about had enough of Gwen sticking her nose in and overriding his decisions. 'You thought you knew better? Well, you don't! You know fuck all!'

'The security didn't go with the girls like I asked,' Gwen blustered, clutching at straws. 'I don't understand why.' *She'd screwed up and knew it.*

Jonah swung back, his eyes bright. 'Because you don't call the shots around here. *I* do. You might want to remember that!' He turned to Nero. 'Talking of security – are they at that address I gave you?'

Nero nodded. 'Yes. They went immediately and I've had confirmation they're in position. Who's at that address?'

'Teagan. I saw her at Percy's, so now I can make sure she's protected too. O'Hara's going for anybody connected to me – that much is obvious.' Jonah frowned. Although he wouldn't feel comfortable until Teagan was exactly where he could see her, perhaps her not being around him and in the direct line of fire at the moment was the best thing.

But if O'Hara knew or found out Teagan was the woman he longed for - the woman who hopefully would now figure deeply in his life, then he didn't want to think what that could mean. 'We need to locate O'Hara and put an end to him as soon as feasibly possible.'

It was imperative the Irish bastard was located and destroyed and everybody would be put on that task from this moment forward.

'That's who you stopped to speak to at the club? Teagan?' Gwen asked, glancing at Nero.

'Yes, that's who I stopped to speak to,' Jonah snapped.

'You chased after *her*, rather than noticing Terri was missing?' Gwen looked pointedly at Terri's lifeless body on the tarpaulin. It was only after the words had left her mouth did she realise the implication of what she'd said. 'Wait, I didn't mean th…'

'You're saying it's *my* fault Terri was violated and murdered?' Jonah roared, his eyes flashing dangerously.

'The girls were adamant Terri had gone home,' Nero added, seeing the rage in Jonah's face at Gwen's words.

Gwen desperately wished she could backtrack. 'I'm sorry. I shouldn't ha…'

'I've just about had enough,' Jonah raged, pacing around the room. 'I've let too many things you've done slide that would have been dealt with had it been anyone else, but this time you've crossed the fucking line.'

Tears spilt down Gwen's cheeks. 'I'm sorry. I didn't mea…'

'First of all you hid your affair with my father; you then felt it your place to tell me to stay clear of Teagan. And let's not forget had you not been so fucking desperate to set me up with Terri Mason and lead the press to believe she was closely involved with me, then maybe she wouldn't be like *that*.' He pointed to the body on the floor.

Nero moved towards Jonah. 'Come on. Let's try and get thi…'

'No! Gwen needs to hear the fucking facts!' Jonah cried. 'She uses the excuse of caring about people to meddle in people's lives. People have *died* because of her, yet she has the cheek to say this is my fault?'

Grabbing Gwen's head, he pushed it towards Terri's corpse. 'You've done this. *You*! Going against my express wishes and putting all of my girls at risk caused this!'

Choking sobs caught in the back of Gwen's throat. Jonah's words cutting like knives. She steadied herself against the wall as her legs threatened to go from under her.

'Jonah…' Nero warned.

'It's time for you to move on, Gwen. I should have let you go when you asked. Remember that, do you? When you tried to slope off under the guise of retiring when really you didn't want me to find out the truth about you and my father?'

Picking up a crowbar from the cellar floor, Jonah laughed seeing Gwen cower. 'You think I'd hit you? You *really* think I'd hit you with this?' he spat. 'I'm not my brother! Or is that something else you've taken upon yourself to assume?'

Jonah launched the crowbar at the wall, the clanging of the metal against the bricks, deafening. 'From now on your meddling and interfering is out of my house and my firm! It's not happening anymore.'

He folded his arms. 'And just for the record, for the first time in my life I want to be with someone and *no one* will stop me! Do you understand?' Jonah glared first at Gwen, then at Nero. Composing himself, he took a deep breath. 'Nero, deal with Terri whilst I work out what the fuck we have to do to find O'Hara for the last and *final* time!'

Slamming the door, Jonah stormed up the cellar stairs. Only on reaching the top did he feel the shaking of his legs and the heaviness in his heart.

THIRTY SIX

WAKING UP ON SUNDAY MORNING with the first rays of sunlight glaring through the window, Heath found himself shivering. The first day of August was hardly cold, so the incessant tremoring in every particle of his body was either from delayed shock or pure unadulterated fear.

Scrabbling in the passenger seat footwell, he reached for the plastic bottle of water and forced his shaking fingers to unscrew the top. Raising it to his mouth, he drank greedily, hoping it would do something to allay the dry burning of his mouth, along with the foul taste.

Heath stretched out his aching limbs, surprised he'd slept long enough to warrant stiffening up and glanced miserably around the layby. *Sleeping in his bloody car? Was this what his life would be like from now on?*

Oh, he could have remained in the house with his father and attempted to comfort the gibbering wreck. He could also have pretended to ignore the knowledge of his mother's dead body crammed inside a compost bin in the shed at the end of the garden. Whilst he was at it, he could have then retired to bed to listen out for the door to slam, signifying his mother's murderer had casually returned to kill the rest of them, but he hadn't done any of those things.

For a start, he couldn't trust himself not to smash his coward of a father's face in for standing by and watching O'Hara murder his wife, let alone think about comforting the man.

And then there was the part that when push came to shove, he was shit scared.

He may think the man a coward, but what did that make him? He'd left his father to the O'Haras and buggered off. But it wasn't just self-preservation that had fuelled his decision to leave.

Heath took another drink of the rather musty tasting water.

Self-preservation and genuine fear were part of it, he'd admit that, but if O'Hara finished him off too, there would be no one left to stop this. And it had to be stopped.

Heath put his head on the steering wheel, refraining from purposely knocking himself out by persistently banging his skull against the steering column.

After listening to his father spouting the things O'Hara had planned, most of which he'd had zilch knowledge of until now, he knew what he had to do. He'd known all along what he *should* do, but now there was absolutely no doubt. There was no other decision but to warn both Teagan *and* Jonah Powell.

He felt like crying out of desperation, guilt and fear.

The main problem - apart from everything, was how to go about it without being killed before he could say what was needed.

Heath's pulse increased. It had to be via Teagan. Out of the available options, she'd offer the best chance of cutting down the chance of immediate death.

Flicking on the ignition, he stared at the dashboard clock. *Christ, it wasn't even 5am.*

How the hell would he speak to Teagan in that apartment she shared with Kim bloody O'Hara without the cross-eyed freak reporting his presence back to O'Hara?

Sweat pooled in Heath's armpits, his shirt stinking to high

heaven.

Phoning Teagan was out too, so there was no other option but to go round. He'd have to pray Kim was either not there or asleep. He'd also have to hope no one was watching the flat. *Like Robert Adams...*

Feeling sicker with every second that passed, Heath reluctantly started the engine and pulled out of the layby.

• • • •

IT TOOK A WHILE for the consistent buzzing to filter into Teagan's brain. Having had very little sleep, courtesy of the delicious memory of Jonah's body on hers, fast morphing into worry about why he'd returned so urgently to the club and the growing suspicion she should have told him about Robert Adams' recent contact, fear mounted.

Her mind span off at various tangents of worrying possibilities.

She was also unnerved about the presence of the security inflicted on her once again. Knowing they were outside watching her every move made her more on edge than the threat of anything else. Again, as before, knowing little or nothing about what the perceived threat actually was didn't help.

On top of that, she'd had to endure Kim's noisy return at 3AM, followed by an hour of extremely loud lovemaking from the adjoining bedroom.

Kim must have brought the dark-haired man back with her. For a split second she'd wondered whether the blonde man had accompanied them too, but being as there wasn't any knocking on her bedroom door during the night, she could only assume they were alone.

The buzzing sounded loudly again, this time for longer and Teagan finally realised it was the intercom. *There was someone at the door...*

The sudden possibility that it might be Jonah - that she was in immediate danger made her scramble from her bed.

Pulling her dressing gown on, Teagan glanced at the clock

on her bedside table. *Just gone 5AM.* Worry pounded as she rushed down the hallway and pressed the button on the intercom. 'Yes?'

'Teagan? Is that you?' a voice crackled through the speaker.

Teagan frowned, her unease increasing. *She half-recognised that voice.* 'W-Who's that?'

'Hea… erm, Darren Harding,' Heath spluttered, belatedly remembering Teagan only knew him from his original alias, which now seemed such a long time ago.

'Darren?' Teagan gasped. 'What are you doing here? How did you know where I liv…'

'No time to explain. Please let me in,' Heath pleaded. 'It's vital I talk to you! It's urgent!'

Teagan heard a scrabbling sound, then the voice of one of the security shouting.

'Teagan! *Please*! I... Get off me!' Heath yelled. 'No, you don't understand! I have to talk to her. I have to talk to Teagan!'

The intercom went dead and before Teagan could question what she was doing, she bolted through the apartment door and rushed down the stairs to the main entrance. Jonah had said to stay inside, but something wasn't right. Although Darren Harding was far from high in her estimation considering he'd disappeared without trace and hadn't bothered getting in contact, something urged her to listen to what he had to say.

At the bottom of the stairs, Teagan slapped the button to release the door and stepped into the early morning light to see Darren Harding pressed against the wall by a burly security guard. 'It's ok. I know him!'

'Teagan?' Heath spluttered, his face crushed against the wall. 'I have to speak to you. It's about...'

'No visitors, mate,' the security barked. 'Strict instructions, so off you fuck.'

'But I need to tell her about what's going on. I need to stop things before they get worse!' Heath blurted. 'Teagan, tell him! Please listen to me!'

Teagan stepped forward. 'Please release him. That's *my*

order!' She had no idea where her assertiveness sprang from, but she'd seen the raw terror in Darren Harding's face and instinct overtook logic.

She looked into the expressionless face of the security guard. 'Listen, I need to speak to this man. By all means call Mr Powell and tell him what I have requested. You're also welcome to stand outside the inner apartment if you wish.' She smiled as best as she could. 'I'll call for you should there be an issue.' She held her breath whilst the man weighed up the options.

'Jonah Powell will want to know what I've got to say,' Heath squawked. 'Please! There's little time! We must hurry.'

Teagan frowned. *Why would Jonah be interested in anything Darren Harding had to say?*

Concern snowballing, Teagan touched the security guard's arm. 'Please. I'll make sure Mr Powell knows how thorough and professional you have been.'

Roughly yanking Heath from the wall, the man scowled. 'If this gets me in the shit...'

'It won't. I'll make sure of it,' Teagan said, hoping she'd made the right decision and watched the man frogmarch Darren Harding into the building.

'I'm contacting Mr Powell and I'll remain *inside* the flat, not outside.'

Teagan nodded and rushed up the stairs towards the apartment, hoping Kim and the dark-haired stranger would not surface anytime soon.

• • • •

JONAH'S HAND GROPED around the bedside table to locate his ringing mobile. *Who the bloody hell was calling at this time?*

He blearily stared at the phone's screen:

```
SEC 04 calling...
```

Shit! One of the security guards stationed outside

Teagan's?

He'd already had one call during the night over the appearance of Kim Sutherland and a man, but he'd had little choice but to instruct security not to step in.

Refusing entry to the person accompanying the girl Teagan shared the flat with would have aroused suspicion and then the woman may have called the police. Besides, from the description of the man, Jonah was 100certain the male was that dark-haired one he'd seen Kim all over at Percy's.

Jonah stabbed the answer call button, his eyes registering the time. His brows furrowed as he listened before jumping out of bed. 'I'm coming now.'

Pulling on his clothes, his mind raced. *What the hell was Pointer doing there? And with Teagan?*

Fumbling with his shirt buttons, his fingers clumsy in his haste, Jonah scrolled through his contacts, setting the phone to loudspeaker.

Come on, answer. Answer.

'Nero? Yeah, I need you at the apartment, NOW. Heath Pointer's there,' Jonah panted. 'Yes, that's what I said - Heath Pointer! Security gave the name as Darren Harding, but we all know that's Heath bloody Pointer!'

Shoving his feet into a pair of slip-on loafers, not wanting to waste time tying laces, Jonah grabbed his car keys. 'He's been let in under Teagan's insistence. Security said he was blathering about important info that *I'd* want to know about... I'm on my way now. I'll see you there.'

Ending the call, Jonah raced out of the door. Unlocking his motor, he fired the engine, his hands shaking. What was Heath Pointer at Teagan's apartment for? Furthermore, how did he know where she even lived? His brow creased as the penny dropped.

O'Hara. Pointer's connection with O'Hara. That's how he knew and that's why he was there.

Gravel flying in all directions, Jonah wheelspinned down the drive.

If Teagan was touched... If anything happened to her, not only would he bring the whole place down, he would hang, draw and quarter the fucking security with his bare hands.

THIRTY SEVEN

IN HIS HASTE, Heath hadn't taken on board the consequences of actually going *in* the apartment. His plan was to get Teagan to accompany him to his car to talk, not to go inside.

If Kim saw him, she'd want to know why he was there and if she told O'Hara about him being there...

Heath's mind whirred. If she saw him then he'd have to pretend that he was here to visit her. Perhaps he could pretend his car had broken down and he didn't know what else to do?

His eyes darted around the hallway, painfully aware the security guard standing two feet away was watching his every move. 'Could we go somewhere else?' Heath whispered. 'Somewhere a bit more private?'

'I don't think that's a good idea,' Teagan frowned. 'We'll stay right where we are.' She folded her arms. 'I'm not even sure why you're here, so I suggest you hurry up and tell me.'

She glanced at Kim's bedroom door - for now still firmly closed, but she didn't want to think about how difficult it would be to explain the presence of a security guard as well as Darren Harding in the apartment. And if Kim got wind Jonah had been here last night too, she'd be grilled until the end of time.

Teagan eyed Darren Harding once again, suspicion

brewing. 'You said it was vital to speak with me, but you're saying nothing.'

Heath was sure he'd pass out. This had gone so badly wrong it was crucifying. 'Is she here?' he whispered.

'Is *who* here?' Teagan sighed. 'Look, if you've got nothing to say, then y…'

'Kim!' Heath hissed. 'Is Kim here? Is she in?'

Teagan turned and glanced at the bedroom door. 'Yes, she's in there, but… Wait! What's Kim got to do with this? Do you know her?'

'Shh!' Heath cried. 'Keep your voice down.' His eyes darted around like a startled animal. 'You don't understand. Kim is Lena's sister.'

'Lena?' Teagan frowned. 'Am I supposed to know who that is?' *Wait. Lena? Not as in Lena Taylor, surely? Lena who was engaged to Jonah? The one who was murdered?*

Heath watched Teagan's face pale and could almost taste her thoughts. 'We need to get out of here. I can't have Kim seeing me and…'

'You haven't said how you know Kim!' Teagan cried, her anxiety building further seeing the security guard with his mobile to his ear. She turned to face the man. *None of this added up.* 'I think Mr Harding should leave.'

'NO!' Heath yelled, immediately regretting raising his voice.

'Mr Powell… Yes… The man says the girl who owns the flat is Lena O'Hara's sister. Yes, he just said it… No, nothing else.' The man looked from Heath to Teagan. 'Ok… One moment…' He passed the phone to Teagan. 'He wants to speak to you.'

Teagan took the phone warily. 'Jonah?' As she listened, Jonah's instructions were clear but precise. She itched to know more, but from the tone of his voice she knew there wasn't time. 'Ok,' she muttered, ending the call.

Handing the mobile back to the security guard, Teagan turned to Heath. 'Jonah's almost here. He wants you to go outside and get into his car.'

Heath blinked, the blood rushing to his ears in a pounding avalanche. Jonah Powell wanted him to get into his car voluntarily to be killed with a single gunshot to the temple? No, no, NO! He would die and then be unable to stop this. 'But I can't! I need to tell you abo…'

'It's ok. I'll be following shortly,' Teagan said, her heart smashing from within her chest, unsure she understood this herself. She was still trying to get her head around the bombshell that Kim Sutherland was Lena's sister. *That's if it were true?* Either way, she had to trust what Jonah said to do.

'He'll kill me,' Heath whimpered, flinching as the security guard took a firm hold of his arm.

'No, he won't,' Teagan said reassuringly. 'He wants to listen to what you've got to say.' She wasn't at all sure of that, but considering Jonah had instructed her to follow down the end of the road in five minutes to meet his car, then she felt it unlikely.

'Remember, if you see the girl, say you're going to the shops. Do *not* mention that you know him.' The security guard jerked his head at Heath.

Teagan nodded mutely. Jonah had already told her that. Hearing sudden movement from within Kim's bedroom, her head jerked around. 'She's awake,' she hissed.

'Fuck me, I feel rough!' Kim wailed, stumbling out of the bedroom, then stopping dead seeing the backs of two men disappearing through the front door. Rubbing her eyes, she stared blearily. 'Who the hell were they?'

Teagan smiled, hiding her panic. 'Oh, erm… I…'

'I could have sworn that was Heath,' Kim muttered. 'It wasn't, was it? Was he looking for me?' She raised her hands in the air. 'Bloody typical isn't it? I really quite fancied him and then he turns up when I've got someone else here?' She leaned closer, the stale smell of spirits on her breath overpowering. 'You know I had a bit of a thing with him not long ago.'

'Heath?' Teagan repeated, a horrible dawn glimmered in the back of her mind. *It couldn't be.* But it would make sense as to how Darren Harding was aware of Lena, the O'Hara's, Jonah and...

Teagan's knees softened and she steadied herself against the wall. Darren Harding wasn't Darren Harding. Darren Harding was Heath Pointer - the bastard who had murdered Dulcie Adams?

Did Jonah know about this? Of course he did. He must do. He must have known of Darren Harding's alias and who he really was all along and hadn't said a word? *Wait... This meant Darren, or rather Heath, was also related to Robert Adams.*

Nausea bubbled. That's why Robert had turned up again. But what did it all mean?

Kim watched Teagan's reaction and felt panic stir through the heavy veil of her hangover. She shouldn't have mentioned Heath. Uncle Ron would go mad. *Shit. Had she screwed up?* 'Do you know him?'

'Who?' Teagan spluttered, buying time to mask her shock. *She must act normal. Fast.* 'Those blokes, you mean? No, I don't know them.' She shrugged. 'Besides, it couldn't be that bloke you're talking about because they were looking for a mate who's been at an all-night party. I told them they'd got the wrong flat.'

'Oh,' Kim said. From the glimpse she'd seen, that bloke looked just like Heath. Jeez, she must be still a lot more pissed from last night than she'd thought.

Teagan watched Kim mentally querying her judgement. *Keep the game going, Teagan, come on.* She nodded to the bedroom. 'You brought your conquest back?'

Kim followed Teagan's eyes to the ajar door, hearing the loud snoring and grinned. 'Keep you awake, did we?'

'You could say that!' Teagan forced out a laugh, thinking five minutes must have elapsed by now.

'You're jealous!' Kim scoffed. 'You should have bagged the blonde bloke whilst you had the chance. Hey! Am I right in remembering through my tequila-soaked brain that Jonah Powell was at Percy's last night?' Her mouth cracked into a knowing smile. 'I'm surprised you didn't drag him back here.' She blew through her teeth. 'You should have. I wouldn't bloody say no! Hot as…!'

Teagan made a sound that sounded more like strangulation than a laugh. *Kim wouldn't say no to anyone....* She surreptitiously found herself eyeing the woman for resemblance to Lena from the photographs she'd seen in Jonah's house. *Could Kim really be Lena's sister?*

She quickly pulled her gaze away. 'It's hardly likely he'd be there for me,' Teagan added. 'He's got a girlfriend.' *Except according to Jonah he hadn't. If she believed him, that was.*

'Oh yeah, that bird from the magazine,' Kim said, her interest piquing as Teagan slipped on her shoes and picked up her bag. 'Where are you going?'

Teagan shrugged dismissively. 'Just to the shop to get some paracetamol.' She gestured to her head. 'Bit of a headache. I blame you and the tequila!'

Kim laughed. 'Fuck yeah, me too! Hurry up then, cos I need a few of them!' Suddenly frowning, she looked at Teagan. 'You're going in your pyjamas?'

Teagan looked down at herself. *Shit. She'd forgotten she wasn't dressed.* 'It's only down the road.'

'It won't be open yet, will it?' Kim frowned. 'It's not even six.'

Teagan felt panic stir. *She had to get out of here and fast.* 'I think it opens at six. I'll be back in a minute. I've got to do something to stop my head banging.'

Before Kim could say anything further, Teagan slipped out of the front door and hurried down the stairs, still able to feel the suspicion burning into her back.

• • • •

JONAH'S EYES REMAINED COLD listening to Heath Pointer talk. Now Teagan was safely in the car he could relax to a point, but it didn't change what this bloke was saying blew his mind.

He rested his eyes on Nero who, on arriving at the designated meeting point, had clambered into the back of the motor, his big frame squeezed up against the smaller man.

It seemed implausible what Pointer was telling them could be true, but why else would he be sitting here? The man was desperate enough to risk death by coming to him and even the most convoluted scheme wouldn't chance that by anyone with functioning brain cells.

Jonah frowned. By rights, he should immediately kill Pointer for what he had done in the past and what, if he was telling the truth, was party to now, but whether he liked it or not, the man was the only link to break the chain, enabling him to get his hands on O'Hara. Pointer was bang in the middle of everything and had access to the lot.

'You're telling me you didn't know this additional information until last night, but knew the rest?' Jonah snapped, his expression unreadable.

Heath nodded, surprised he hadn't emptied the contents of his bowel over the black leather car seats by now. He fruitlessly inched along the seat away from the imposing and worrying presence of Nero, who left no doubt that any attempt to vacate the vehicle would result in the loss of his life. After all this, the chances of that happening was high regardless, but at least he was doing what he knew he must do. Someone had to stop this madness.

'After I found my mother dead last night, my father told me the rest of what O'Hara and Adams have planned. Including the stuff he was keeping from me.' Heath pulled his hand over his face, wiping away the sweat dripping into his eyes.

'Did you say, your mother is *dead*?' Jonah frowned.

Heath nodded, the lump in his throat threatening to render him speechless. He had to keep it together and tell these people everything. 'O'Hara did it. My mother overheard some stuff.' He blinked back the brewing tears. 'She threatened to call the police…'

Jonah glanced at Nero, concern growing. *Was O'Hara*

taking out anybody and everybody?

'I wasn't there, but when I got back my father was in a right state. O'Hara and Kieran had gone. My dad tried to pretend my mother had left him.' Heath's face morphed into a scowl. 'It's what O'Hara told him to say, but I knew he was lying, the fucking coward. He even watched O'Hara kill her. They... they put her in the shed... In the compost bin...'

Teagan gasped audibly. 'Oh my God! The compost bin?'

'Jesus!' Jonah muttered. *There were lots of questions he wanted to ask, but had to let Pointer talk.* 'Go on...'

'I also overheard a conversation a couple of days ago regarding Adams. The deal was O'Hara will let Adams have Teagan once he's done his part in overseeing the tracking of the diamond interception.'

Heath averted his eyes from Teagan's accusing glare. She hated him, *despised* him even and he couldn't say he blamed her.

He made himself look back at Jonah even though it was difficult. 'Since then I've been trying to work out how I could warn Teagan, but couldn't think of a way,' he continued. 'It was only after my father told me Adams is planning on snatching her to keep for his own use and God knows what else that I had to step in whatever the cost.'

He finally met Teagan's accusing eyes. 'I know I used you in the past and I'm sorry, I really am. I wish I'd never got involved in any of this... The only thing I wanted was the diamonds I believed belonged to my Grandfather, but it's spiralled out of control. I never wanted anyone to get hurt.'

Teagan burnt with humiliation. It was hard knowing that Darren, or rather, Heath, pretending to be a schoolmate, then making out he wanted something more had all been fake. She'd just been a means to get to the diamonds. *Those bloody things all along.*

She glanced at Jonah. *Everyone* knew everything apart from her. Anger bubbled and bile rose up her throat. *Robert Adams was planning to abduct her and keep her prisoner... like Saul*

Powell...

Seeing Teagan's mounting distress, Jonah placed his hand on hers. 'Adams won't get to you. I can assure that.'

'You knew all along,' Teagan whispered, her voice trailing off. *Could she trust no one?* 'You knew and didn't warn me?'

Jonah gave a slight shake of his head. 'I didn't know for certain. I suspected there was something going on with him, yes, but what exactly, I didn't know. Now I do.' *And Adams would die for it, but he'd keep that bit to himself for now.*

'And you knew Robert killed Dulcie, rather than *him*,' Teagan cried, her head jerking to Heath in the back seat.

Teagan saw Jonah nod in confirmation. After finally being made aware of the things Dulcie had actually done; all the manipulation and scheming, the worst was discovering how the old lady she'd cared so much for had planned to offload her too.

She scraped her hair off her face, her heart pounding. It was only Robert's obsession which had stopped his mother from killing her because he'd got in first. Teagan shuddered, the whole concept making her blood run cold. Robert was a psycho and as unhinged as Saul Powell, yet she'd failed to notice. *Christ. She'd even felt sorry for him.*

'Don't you see?' Heath interrupted. 'Adams is counting on getting Teagan once the diamonds are lifted but he doesn't realise O'Hara is planning to her take instead.'

Teagan stared wide eyed and felt the trembling in her body increase, but willed herself to remain calm. O'Hara was going to kidnap her instead of it being Robert? The man who was killing everybody around them?

Jonah stiffened, his veins throbbing with the need to strangle the last breath of air out of both O'Hara and Adams.

'They fucked up with Terri Mason - realising after th…'

'Wait! What happened to Terri?' Teagan cried, even the ends of her hair now tingling with dread.

Jonah cut Heath a glare, not having yet told Teagan of what had happened.

'Terri was dumped outside the Feathers last night.' Nero

stepped in, seeing Jonah's stress. 'Raped and murdered.'

Teagan's hand flew to her mouth. 'Oh my God! *That's* why you needed to leave, Jonah? That's why you...' She frowned, the truth dawning. 'Terri was taken from Percy's last night? O'Hara was there?'

Jonah nodded. 'All true. Hence why I wanted you out.' He looked down, guilt raging. 'I'd been informed by the other girls that Terri had gone home. I might have been able to stop it and I don't think I'll ever forgive myself for that.'

'She was intercepted. There's nothing you could have done.' Nero added.

'O'Hara now knows Terri was the wrong target.' Heath nodded at Teagan. 'He wants to pay Jonah back for what happened to Lena, but now knows Jonah's in love with you, that's why I had to come. O'Hara will take you next Teagan.'

'No he fucking won't!' Jonah snarled, glossing over Pointer's remark about him being in love with Teagan. It was a shocking revelation to realise that it was true and even more shocking that it was so bloody obvious. This was unchartered territory and that alone was unnerving. He'd like to have got his own head around it before it was openly discussed.

Jonah felt his cheeks burn and knew Teagan was sneaking a glance at him. Still, he didn't have time to worry about his raw emotions being bandied about when so much else was at stake.

THIRTY EIGHT

'YOU'RE SURE KIM IS LENA'S SISTER?' Nero eyed Heath Pointer curiously. He'd seen the girl himself and although Lena had made it her life's work applying more makeup than a beautician on a department store counter, the woman must have shelled out thousands on cosmetic surgery to delete the family likeness if Kim was anything to go by. Despite having a decent figure and a nicely stacked chest, the woman was an abject monster in the looks department and he'd never have put Lena and Kim as related in a million years.

'She's definitely Lena's sister,' Heath confirmed. 'There's a brother too – Kieran. He's at the house as well as the car lot. I fucking hate him. He's a right thick cunt.'

Nero's eyes shot to Jonah. 'I've seen him too. That's the younger one. The one that just sits there on his phone.'

Heath nodded. 'That's the one.'

'Kieran? No, that's Kim's boyfriend,' Teagan said. 'I've met him a few times. He comes around the flat. Although Kim isn't very faithful to him. She brought another man back last night.'

'Nope. That's her brother,' Heath repeated, his lip curling in contempt. 'Have you not noticed how they've both got the same weird close-set eyes?'

Teagan paled. Come to think of it she had thought once how similar in certain respects they looked. 'He's her *brother*?'

Heath nodded. 'Revolting isn't it? She's probably shagging her uncle as well while she's at it!'

'Fucking hell!' Jonah muttered, shaking his head. 'As disgusting as it is, I don't give a shit what weird crap goes on between them. All I care about is sorting *this*.'

Heath blinked. It was strange. The longer he'd been talking, the more it felt like he could speak easy, like it was normal. *But it wasn't normal.*

He quickly reminded himself who these people in this car actually were and where he stood. It was foolish to become complacent just because he was giving them the information needed.

Jonah turned to Teagan. 'Are you ok?'

Teagan shrugged. 'I don't know what to make of any of it. But it does explain why both Kieran and Kim were constantly questioning me about you.' She looked at Jonah. 'Kim even mentioned the diamonds.' She put her head in her hands. 'I should have known there was something far too suspicious to be coincidence or celebrity obsession.'

'I'm hardly a bloody celebrity,' Jonah muttered.

'So we know O'Hara is planning on intercepting the diamonds when the sale goes down on Thursday,' Nero said, moving the subject forward.

Jonah's eyes narrowed, realisation dawning. 'Benowitz is a fucking snout for O'Hara?' He clenched his fist. 'My father swore by him so I thought I could trust him, yet he's turning me over as well. I'll kill the old bastard!'

'No,' Heath cried. 'Not unless his name is Stan. O'Hara's been getting his info from a bloke called Stan.'

'The other bloke in the shop?' Nero looked at Jonah. 'Benowitz's helper?'

Jonah sat silently for a moment, his mind ticking. 'How is O'Hara planning on doing this?'

Heath shrugged. 'I don't know the full details. I don't even think O'Hara has told my father. All I know is that he's planning to intercept you on the way to the sale and needs Adams for tracking purposes. There's a tracker in your wallet...'

Jonah's eyes narrowed. That fucker had been watching him all along? It proved Adams was working alongside O'Hara on this. Adams must have planted the tracker in his wallet before he took off from the house, the sneaky bastard.

Pulling out his leather wallet, Jonah stared at it. From now on, this tracker would work to *his* advantage, not Adams' and O'Hara's. 'The sale will proceed as planned.'

'Didn't you hear what he just said? O'Hara will kill you to take the diamonds!' Teagan yelped.

Jonah smiled. 'No he won't.' He had an idea. An idea that was fast forming into a plan. One that may be high risk, but if it pulled off then it would be perfect. Again, this he would keep to himself until he'd got the details straight in his head of how he would go about it.

'When they realise I'm not at the house any longer they'll kill me,' Heath said, the full weight of opting to inform on O'Hara weighing heavily. 'And once Kim tells them Teagan's gone too, they'll know for sure they've been rumbled.'

Panic glimmered and not for the first time he felt like running off into the sunset, deducing that he'd made a horrendous mistake by choosing to become involved with the other side.

Teagan frowned. 'What do you mean, when I've gone? I'm going *nowhere!*'

Jonah's head snapped from Heath to Teagan. 'You're not returning to that apartment as from *now*. If you think I'll let y...'

'But Heath's right! If I'm not there, they'll know that *you* know.' Finding a new resolve, Teagan folded her arms. 'If that happens you'll never be rid of this O'Hara person and I'll never be rid of Adams. You also won't be rid of the diamonds...' She stared at him pointedly.

Jonah stared at Teagan incredulously. 'I'll not risk you. I'll...'

'You have to. You need to let me help,' Teagan stated bluntly, her cheeks flushing. 'If we're going to be together, then I need to do this. Let me keep up the pretence.' She looked at Nero pleadingly, hoping he'd seen the sense in her words. 'As far as Kim's aware, I've gone to the shop, but I've already been far too long so I'll go back and act as if nothing has changed. She's getting suspicious, but I'll smooth things over. I'll be your eyes from the inside.' She turned to the back seat. 'Heath must do likewise at his father's house.'

Heath paled. *Wait a minute. He hadn't signed up for that.* 'Hang on... I...'

'I'd take that option if I were you,' Nero grinned. 'Don't forget you're part of the enemy's camp. Doing this for us will be the only thing that might enable you to eventually walk away.' He raised his eyebrows. '*Might* being the operative word...'

'I agree with that.' Jonah's eyes narrowed. 'But if you even think about betraying me, Pointer...'

Heath shook his head. 'I-I won't. I just want this to be over.' The reminder his head was still firmly in the noose only accentuated that.

'But,' Jonah held up his hand. 'I cannot allow Teagan to do likewise. It's too dangerous. Adams or O'Hara could come for her at any time and I won't risk it.'

Teagan sighed. 'From what's been said, O'Hara needs the interception to happen before he comes for me. Plus, I'll be careful.' Gingerly, she reached out, her hand brushing Jonah's, hoping her theory was correct.

Jonah leant back against the headrest, and closed his eyes. Teagan's reference to them being together was music to his ears, but was well aware Nero had also put two and two together. The warm glow of her admission clashed horribly with what she was suggesting she do. *What a conflict.*

He wasn't remotely happy about her returning to the

apartment, but whether he liked it or not and he *didn't,* Teagan was right. It was the only way this could be brought to an end. *But if anything went wrong. If anything happened to her because of this...*

Taking Jonah's silence as agreement, Teagan grabbed her bag from the footwell. 'I'll need a phone.'

'Take this spare burner.' Nero passed a small mobile from one of his inside pockets. 'And before you dash off, there are some important ground rules that you mustn't forget.'

· · · ·

MIKE HAD BEEN EXPECTING THIS, but the raw hatred in O'Hara's strange eyes made him feel more unnerved than ever. The man looked more psychotic than usual.

He knew what was likely to happen and the expression on O'Hara's face made it pretty much of a dead cert, but that was ok. He wasn't frightened anymore. Not about what would befall him, at least. In all truth, it would be a relief. He'd be able to see his Tammy again and make things up to her.

Mike's eyes tracked to the clock on the mantlepiece. That this moment had been avoided until now was a godsend. Had O'Hara noticed Heath's absence when he'd returned last night, the chances of being able to do this one last worthwhile thing in what remained of his own pitiful existence would have been zero, but as it stood now, things might still happen.

The small glimmer of lucidity pushing through the black hole of his mind last night had given him the impetus to tell Heath every single thing he knew. That was the only saving grace. If his son had the brains he believed he possessed, then it would be in motion, or better still, would already have been done.

He didn't want to acknowledge the prospect that it had backfired and the Powells had removed Heath before he'd had chance. Neither did he want to think if Heath hadn't acted in the way he was counting on, then everything would have been for nothing. Mike could only hope that he was right.

At least he didn't have to worry O'Hara had already dispatched Heath because otherwise he wouldn't be standing here raving about his absence.

Ron eyed Mike malevolently. He just about had enough. Feeling his mobile buzzing, he yanked it out of his pocket:

```
Kim calling...
```

Buttoning the call, he wanted to smash the phone up. That was the second time Kim had called. She'd have to bloody wait. The most important thing was finding where this dickhead's son had buggered off to. If this moron had opened his gob and Heath had discovered what had happened to his mother, then there was no guessing what shit could be around the bloody corner.

'I won't ask you again, prick!' Ron roared. 'Where the fuck is your shit-for-brains son? And why do you keep looking at the clock? Expecting someone?'

'Heath's out and I'm only looking at the time,' Mike mumbled, his voice monotonous. He didn't need to fake a bereft act, because he felt every inch genuinely gutted.

'I can see he's not here, but where is he?' Ron snarled. 'What have you said to him? Does he know about the wife?' His eyes flicked to the garden shed just visible from the lounge window. 'Have you told him?'

Even though Mike thought there was nothing left within him to cause a reaction, as O'Hara's voice raised to fever pitch, he flinched regardless. He willed his mind to stay focused and not loop back into the bottomless hole of despair; the one which stopped him from moving. Instead, he dragged his eyes from where he knew his wife's body lay, to the ugly mess of O'Hara's face. 'Heath thinks Tammy has left me. I told him she's gone and wants a divorce.'

Ron eyed Mike suspiciously. 'I don't believe you.'

Mike stared at his hands blankly. 'Think what you want, but that's what I said to him.'

A swift punch to the side of Mike's jaw bounced his head

off the armchair's headrest. 'Don't get smart, you bastard,' Ron snarled. 'You're lying.'

Mike spat out a mouthful of blood, the acute pain a welcome distraction. How he hated this man. *Hated* him. But not as much as he hated himself. 'Heath didn't believe me either at first, but after I told him Tammy had discovered my debts, then he did,' he mumbled, his face a sea of pain.

Kieran moved to stand next to his uncle. 'Didn't Heath find it strange her handbag was left here?'

Ron glanced up, surprised Kieran had managed something so astute. 'Well?'

Mike stared at the handbag. *Yes, Heath had noticed it. That's why he had to tell him the truth.* 'Heath was too busy shouting at me to notice,' he lied. 'He was upset and angry.'

A smirk broke out on Ron's face before it relaxed back into his usual twisted sneer. 'So where's he gone?'

Mike shrugged. 'He stormed off. Said he was going to get pissed.'

Ron paused, weighing up the situation. 'What else did he say?'

Mike sighed. 'That it was my fault... That he hated me... That I was pathetic and a coward...'

'At least your stupid son finally got the measure of you!' Ron sneered.

Mike continued staring at his hands, transfixed by the steady spots of blood dripping from his chin onto them. It was true Heath had said that and with shame, knew his son *did* think him a loser and a coward and he was right. He *was* a coward. And a loser.

He should have stopped this a long time ago and hadn't because he'd been shit scared. Shit scared of *everything*. It had been easier allowing things to carry on, continue burying his head in the sand and lying to everyone. Lying to his wife - the woman he'd always loved - the woman he'd stood by and allowed O'Hara to kill. And what had he done about it?

Fuck all. He'd done nothing. Yep - a loser to the end.

Apart from one thing... Mike may be a coward, but prayed his last ditch attempt would work by trusting Heath to pass on every single morsel of information he'd spouted to the right person - the *only* person who would have the balls and the ability to raze Ron-fucking-O'Hara off the face of the earth.

Ron's face morphed into a scowl as his mobile buzzed yet again. Snatching it from his pocket he stared at the screen:

    Voicemail...

Sighing, he held the phone to his ear, watching Mike rubbing his bleeding mouth. He may as well listen to the message and see if the break gave this muppet time to think about whether there was anything else he wanted to say.

Ron's face contorted into a hideous grimace as he listened to Kim's message. It may have been garbled - the girl sounded half-cut, but garbled or not, it gave him enough to grasp the gist.

Shoving the phone back into his pocket, Ron's fury built. *The two-faced piece of...*

'So Pointer,' he roared, pulling Mike's head back by his hair. 'My Kim reckons something funny is going on...'

Mike winced, his hair tugging mercilessly against his scalp. 'W-What do you mean?'

'I mean...' Ron leant closer to Mike's face, spittle spraying onto his cheek. 'My niece is sure Heath and another bloke were at her apartment this morning... What do you know about that?'

'What? No!' Mike spluttered. 'Why would Heath go there? Unless he went to see Kim?'

'And then they disappeared...' Ron continued. 'Now Teagan's gone somewhere too! You're lying, Pointer, so you'd best tell me what your wanker of a son is *really* up to.'

Mike winced once again as O'Hara tightened the grip on his hair. He had no clue what Heath was doing or planned to do with the information he had. He didn't know where he'd gone either.

All he could do was pray he'd given Heath enough time to

get the ball rolling and to start what needed to be done. And he hoped even more that it would be acted on because this and this alone was the only thing left to bring him a shred of redemption on judgement day.

THIRTY NINE

'YOU'VE BEEN AGES.' Kim poured herself a glass of wine and studied Teagan closely. She knew the signs to look out for if someone wasn't telling the truth - one of the few things Lena had shared with her.

Kim reckoned her sister only spoke of her perceived super-ability in reading people's body language because she thought it made her look important. At the time, Kim was suitably impressed, always a little in awe of how Lena could manipulate everything and everybody around her, but not anymore.

It wasn't like Lena had succeeded in the end, was it?

Kim's lips tightened. But *she* would. *She* would cash in on her sister's groundwork, with the exception of bagging Jonah Powell. Although that might be an option, depending if Uncle Ron decided against certain aspects of his plan.

A small smile formed. The plan her uncle now deemed her important enough to be part of. *How things had changed.*

Kim continued watching Teagan fidget with her bag on the kitchen work top. 'Did you hear me?' she repeated. 'I said, you've been ages!'

Teagan rolled her eyes, trying not to stare at the semi-naked man sprawled on the sofa. 'You were right. The shop at the end of the road was closed. I ended up walking a bloody mile to the next one!' She continued rummaging in her bag. 'My feet are killing and my headache is even worse than ever!' She nodded at the glass of wine. 'You've started early.'

Kim grinned. 'Waste not, want not. It's daylight, so that counts.' *Teagan was trying to deflect. Been to another shop, my arse.* 'Chuck us a couple then.'

Teagan frowned. 'Couple of what?'

Kim sighed. *Gotcha, you lying bitch.* 'The pills? You went to get paracetamol?'

'Oh!' Teagan pulled a box of tablets from her handbag. 'My head's mashed. I had no idea what you were going on about then!' *Nero was spot on to suggest they nip to the shop and pick up pills before dropping her back.*

Christ, she had a lot to learn. Covering her tracks and hiding things wasn't something which came naturally. It never had been anything she'd needed to do, but now it was. Now it was *vital* and she mustn't slip up. If Jonah felt she wasn't hacking it or suspected suspicion was aroused, he'd immediately pull the plug on what she'd insisted herself capable of, despite what repercussions that would mean for everyone else.

Clocking Kim's expression, Teagan's resolve grew further. It had only been for a millisecond before the woman masked it, but she'd seen it all the same. Kim had expected her not to be unable to produce the tablets. That alone showed Teagan there was no room for error. The woman was watching everything she did and she must not screw up. Not even by a cat's whisker. It wasn't just her safety being gambled here, it was *everyone's*. If she ballsed up, everyone's necks were on the line.

A steely determination formed in Teagan's heart. Jonah and his staff had risked their lives countless times for her in the short time she'd known them and were continuing to do so. She knew Jonah didn't want her in this position, but for the first time ever she realised despite being unwittingly dragged into this cesspool of lies and deceit, she would do everything in her power to break the hold of those diamonds.

Teagan wanted to be with Jonah despite the ramifications of what that could mean. She was sick to death of people causing problems. These people would forever make her watch over her shoulder with or *without* Jonah.

It was time to put her big girls pants on.

'You alright?' Kim's voice cut into Teagan's wandering thoughts. 'You've got a weird look on your face.'

Teagan flapped her hand dismissively. 'I'm off with the fairies. Can I have a drop of your wine to take these with?' She popped two paracetamol out of the blister pack and pretended to rub her temples. 'The sooner I get these down my neck, the sooner I rejoin the human race!'

She hadn't got a headache, didn't need any painkillers and certainly didn't want a glass of cheap wine at 8 in the morning, but none of it would kill her. 'Are we going out tonight?'

Kim raised her eyebrows. 'Finally stopped being boring have you? You were the one who went home early last night!'

Teagan grinned bashfully. 'Yeah, sorry about that. I'm much better today, so I'm up for a night out - if you're not already booked...' She nodded at the semi-naked stranger on the sofa, engrossed in cartoons on the TV.

Satisfied she'd jumped to the wrong conclusion about Teagan, Kim grinned. 'To be honest I've been trying to work out how to get rid of him. He's good in the sack, but apart from that, a waste of oxygen.' She nudged Teagan in the ribs. 'I still don't know his name!'

Teagan forced herself to laugh and braced herself to ask the next question. Even thinking about it made her feel sick. 'What about Kieran?' she whispered.

Kim sneered. 'He'll put up with anything that one!'

Teagan turned away to reach for a glass of wine, but really it was because she couldn't bear to look at Kim any longer.

She forced herself to gulp at the bitter tasting liquid. Could it really be true that Kieran was Kim's brother? Was she *really* sleeping with him or was it part of the act? Either way, it was vital she acted like she knew nothing. *Nothing at all.*

Seeing Kim move out into the hallway, Teagan walked to the fridge, pretending to get a top-up, when really it was so she could see through the crack in the door and watched Kim stab out a text before shoving the mobile back into her pocket.

She'd hazard a guess whatever Kim had messaged was heading straight through the ether to either Kieran or O'Hara himself and that it was about *her.*

She swallowed, hoping she'd successfully allayed Kim's suspicions. If she hadn't, then she'd already screwed up.

Teagan's eyes moved to her own handbag where the mobile Nero had given her remained concealed in a zipped compartment. She would text Jonah as soon as she could.

• • • •

'GO AND LOOK... *CAREFULLY,*' Ron hissed, his arms aching. This bastard weighed a bloody ton and if Kieran didn't pull his finger out and put his back into it, he'd lose his temper. He didn't have time to fanny around and certainly couldn't leave *this* lying about.

Seeing his nephew hesitate, jigging from one foot to the other, Ron gritted his teeth. 'I said, go and look, but don't move the curtains.'

Jolted from his stupor, Kieran pulled his eyes away from Mike Pointer. The way his tongue protruded from his mouth through his half-clenched teeth created the oddest expression and he was strangely fascinated by it, but the urgent tone of his uncle's voice dripped into his stunned brain and so he mechanically moved towards the window, quietly wondering how he was supposed to look to see who was hammering at the door without moving the curtains.

Couldn't they just ignore it? What if it was the police?

Kieran glanced back at the body on the floor and the familiar tendrils of panic gripped his insides like they had been doing more and more frequently of late. If it *was* the police, they'd be done for. There were now two bodies on the premises.

'Get a fucking move on!' Ron hissed, blowing like a train as he continued dragging Mike further towards the back of the room by his feet.

Edging towards the window, Kieran pressed himself up against the wall, the reverberations from the pounding on the door so strong it was like being battered by a sledgehammer.

Putting his face almost flat to the wall, Kieran peered through a tiny crack where the curtains met the frame and forced his eyes as far over to once side as possible to glimpse the outside of the semi-detached.

'It's Adams,' he whispered, relief washing over him.

'What the fuck is he doing here?' Ron spat, dropping Mike Pointer's legs to the floor with a thump. 'How did he get this bloody address?'

Wiping his brow with the back of his sleeve, he stormed to the front door ready to give Adams a round of abuse for descending on them like this. The man knew he could not risk leading anyone to this door. *Especially the Powells.*

Ron yanked the door open, his face twisted in fury, which turned to surprise as Robert Adams grabbed him around the throat and pushed him backwards into the hallway. 'What the...?'

'What are you playing at?' Robert roared, kicking the door shut. 'Why have you gone back on your word? I'm telling you now, it stops here. I've come to speak to Mike and if y...'

Robert stopped dead, his grip dropping from O'Hara's neck as he glimpsed inside the lounge. Storming into the room, he stared at his half-brother, then his eyes moved to a worried-looking Kieran. 'Is he dead?'

Seeing the slight nod on the younger man's face, Robert sighed. *This ruined his plan of getting Mike to do his bidding.* His head flicked back to O'Hara. 'What the hell have you done?'

Ron raised his hands. 'Look mate, I know he's your brother and all that, but he was becoming a liability. I had no choice. I had to do this after wh...'

'Stop the shit!' Robert barked. 'He's no real brother of mine. What are you going to do with him?'

'Put him with his missus for now.' Ron wiped the rest of the sweat off his face. 'I'm glad you're here actually. This one's no bloody use.' He jerked his head at Kieran.

'His missus?' Robert frowned, liking the sound of that even less.

'She's in the shed,' Kieran said hollowly. 'She's dead too.'

'Christ...' Robert hissed. *Was O'Hara trying to get them all banged up?* 'And the boy? Heath?'

'I'm just here,' Heath said, walking into the lounge and stared at the body of his father.

Ron braced himself for Heath to melt down and flexed his fists ready to deal with any ensuing issues. 'Sorry son,' O'Hara said. 'It had to be done.'

Heath nodded, knowing O'Hara's slight remorse to be as fake as the rest of them, but that was ok. *He'd go with it.* 'I understand,' he muttered. 'I'm well aware my father was a liability.'

And he *had* believed that. He'd believed it right up until an hour ago. It was what happened from *here* that counted. Although he'd half- expected to find this after he'd left last night. No, he *had* expected this, but he'd also expected to *feel* something too.

But that was the point. Too much had happened and he felt punch-drunk; his brain unable to process anything in the normal way.

What Jonah Powell said after they'd dropped Teagan back at the apartment had done it. By chanting the mantra over and over in his head, he found it actually worked and could stay on top of the base emotions threatening to overspill.

Remember the plan. Remember it was the only thing left to do.

And it *was* the only thing left to do - the thing his father had made possible.

Yes, Jonah Powell was right on that as well.

At first Heath hadn't believed it, but it was. Mike had made out he'd lost it to ensure Heath got the information needed and had counted on him doing the right thing.

And he had. Heath had done exactly what his father had hoped and believed he'd do so this nightmare could end.

Heath repeated the mantra once more, overriding the sting in the back of his eyes.

His father was no coward. It was the opposite. His father had foreseen Heath would start the process to end it. The only way to grant the time to do this was for Mike to sacrifice himself, therefore deflecting O'Hara. *I won't let you down, Dad*, Heath thought.

'Where have you been?' O'Hara pressed.

Heath had already thought about this and hoped he was right second guessing what his father might have given as the reason for his absence.

'I got pissed,' Heath muttered. 'My mum's left and I can't say I blame her.' Against every instinct, he found himself digging his dead father in the ribs with the toe of his boot. 'Anything to get away from this loser.'

He then turned to face Robert who he suddenly noticed was also present. Much as he wanted to smash the bloke in the teeth for framing him for murder, he had to play the game. *Time will out.* 'I didn't kill your mother, Robert. The Powells did,' he lied. 'And I want to see them pay. You may not believe me, but it's all I've got right now. I want them to pay for *everything* and I want both of you to trust me to be part of it.'

Heath watched Robert glance at O'Hara and knew before either of them said anything that he was in. Casually stepping over the corpse of his father, he smiled.

FORTY

PUTTING THE PHONE DOWN, Jonah looked at Nero. 'It will be sometime tomorrow. I said we needed to speak personally.'

It wasn't altogether surprising his words had been met with suspicion. He just had to hope it was taken as being imperative. If it wasn't, then none of this could work.

Jonah dragged his hand across his mouth, the pressure taking its toll.

'And Pointer knows to inform us the second the coast is clear?' Nero asked.

Jonah nodded. It wasn't the best relying on Heath Pointer for anything, but there was no other way.

Nero folded his arms and studied his boss, not liking how this was unfolding. He'd listened very carefully to Jonah's plan and it was good. With timing, cleverness and a hell of a lot of luck, it was just about feasible. But that was the thing... *Just about...*

Even with the most experienced men involved it was a longshot. There too many variables and the people involved were those whose trustworthiness and experience was questionable. Sure, he knew they were between a rock and a hard place, but this was a huge gamble.

Hearing clattering from the office next door, Nero looked up. 'Gwen's still going then?'

Jonah frowned. 'It sounds like it. She went back to her maisonette last night and I haven't seen her today. She's keeping out of my way.'

'Do you think you might have been too hard on her? Too hasty?' Nero asked tentatively.

Jonah's eyes hardened. 'No, I don't. Too many things, Nero. Too many things...'

But it *had* crossed his mind he might have been too hard. He couldn't imagine life without Gwen in it. She'd been the one constant, stable force in his life since his mother had died. She didn't have a bad bone in her body and had been acting in his best interests, but whatever anyone said, she'd lost sight of the line that shouldn't be crossed.

As well as everything else, her judgement had got one girl killed and almost cost him Teagan too, but to banish her? And banish her when everybody was a target?

Jonah hadn't forgotten Nero's involvement either. He sighed. 'Perhaps I should tell her to remain until this business is sorted.'

'I need to ask you something else.' Nero stretched his legs out to the side of Jonah's desk. 'Can we rely on them? Heath Pointer and, well… *Teagan*?'

Jonah stiffened. He had no choice but to trust Heath Pointer, but Teagan was a different matter entirely. Aside from that she was green in this sort of thing, he didn't want her involved full stop. He wanted to *be* with her, not get her killed - get them *all* killed.

The burden of that responsibility gnawed away at him like a rabid rat.

It had only been a few hours since agreeing to her involvement and already it was driving him to distraction. That she'd be out at this very moment putting herself in full view, opening herself up to be a target yet again to plant information for *him* didn't sit well. And should he be wrong on his forecast of how O'Hara or Adams would move next, he'd put her in even graver danger than she was already in.

Aside from wanting Teagan in his arms, which couldn't happen until this was all finished, was frustrating enough, but he couldn't help but worry whether she'd even *want* to be anywhere near him after this.

The parts of the plan he was unable to tell her could be enough to make her walk away for good this time. And that was if everything worked. *God forbid if it didn't...*

The first time in his life Jonah had wanted someone permanently in it and he was risking it all before it had even started?

Nero watched Jonah. He could see the conflicting emotions. 'Mate, I know you're in love with her, but Christ, is Teagan going to be up to this?'

Jonah put his head in his hands and sighed. 'I don't know, but I fucking hope so.'

'So do I,' Nero muttered.

. . . .

TEAGAN HAD LISTENED very carefully to everything Nero and Jonah said. Although the conversation was rushed and thirty years wouldn't be enough to make her feel any more confident, she had to pray her nervousness wasn't visible.

So far so good. Kim seemed none the wiser. Each time it was Teagan's turn to go to the bar, only Kim's drink contained vodka, *her's* was water. She'd also made sure each time she was served a different bartender pulled the drinks. The last thing she wanted when Kim bought a round was a well-meaning barman saying, *"another water for your friend?"*

Teagan had astounded herself by how quickly she'd picked up this covert way of acting. Once she'd put her mind to what was needed it was a lot easier than she'd expected.

She grinned at Kim, agreeing the man she pointed out across the bar was hot and giggled drunkenly, like expected. Soon she wouldn't even have to bother acting hammered because Kim was close to the point where she wouldn't notice how sober Teagan really was.

But she mustn't get overconfident. It was early days and there was lots that could go wrong if she became too lax.

Kim swigged from her drink and grinned. 'I'm glad you've come out of your shell,' she said. 'I was starting to worry I was sharing my flat with a dork!'

Teagan laughed, but Kim's comment stung. *Was she really that dull?* Shaking off her self-consciousness, she shrugged. 'I'm over that now.' *And that much was true.*

Kim leant forward, her elbow slipping off the table. 'You mean men? Come on, be honest. You *did* have a thing with Jonah Powell, didn't you?' Her drunken eyes sparkled with mischief. It wasn't relevant, but she wanted to know. Despite this thing she was doing for Uncle Ron, she liked Teagan.

Teagan smiled. *Now onto the plan.* Pretend to let Kim into her confidence like Jonah said. Tell her things which would go straight back to O'Hara.

That was all very well and good, but she couldn't just blurt out stuff. It had to happen gradually. Kim might be half sloshed, but she wasn't stupid.

She looked at Kim coyly. 'Alright... I did have a bit of a thing about him.' *And she still did.* A bloody big thing, but that was on the back burner for the time being. It had to be.

'And...?'

Teagan frowned. 'And what?'

'Did you...? You know... Is he any good?'

Taking a sip of her water, Teagan played for time. She'd never usually gossip about things like this, but needs must... 'He knows what he's doing, that's for sure.' Even though the conversation was necessary, she still found herself blushing. Probably because what she'd said was true...

Kim struggled to light her cigarette, her hands fumbling over the lighter. 'So it was *him* you were pissed off with the night I met you? Wow!'

Teagan nodded grudgingly. *That was true too.* 'Yeah, but

there's nothing I could do about it when he was more interested in someone else.'

'What? That slapper from the auction?' Kim raised her over plucked eyebrows. 'She hasn't got a patch on you!'

Teagan found the radiating inner glow from the compliment made her feel worse. Terri Mason was dead and she was having to badmouth her? It showed one thing though. Kim wasn't aware of what had happened to Terri, so O'Hara didn't tell her *everything*. 'She's welcome to him. He might be good in bed, but I won't put up with being one of his many bloody women!'

Teagan squirmed on the stool, the memory of Jonah's body on hers still fresh.

Kim leant forward conspiringly. 'I thought he might be making another play for you when he turned up at Percy's?'

Teagan shook her head. 'Nah.' She flapped her hand. 'Anyway, I'm over it. I can't be bothered with all the hassle.'

'Hassle?' Kim's ears pricked up.

Teagan silently noted Kim's attention changing. The woman may well be on the way to being off her head, but she was still digging. *Time to play the game.* Leaning forward, she mirrored Kim's body language. 'I don't know how true it is, but... You know you asked about those diamonds...?'

'You *have* seen them?' Kim cried far too enthusiastically. Reining herself in, she held her breath in anticipation.

'No,' Teagan lied. 'But I *did* hear he's selling them. And...' She glanced over her shoulder. 'They're worth millions!'

Kim blew through her teeth in fake surprise. She knew how much those things would fetch. She'd heard nothing but that for God knows how long. 'Isn't that another reason why you should have bagged him when you got the chance? Not allowed that Terri tart to get her claws in?'

She tried to keep the resentment out of her voice but it was difficult. Lena should be the one benefiting from the diamonds sale. As her sister, Kim knew a percentage would have come straight to the family – and in turn, *her*. But then again, it would be happening anyway now Uncle Ron was ready.

'Well it's too late.' Teagan smiled inwardly, watching Kim as she spoke. Regardless of what she said, the woman wasn't compos mentis enough to mask her feelings. Her face was an open book. *Now think. Jonah said if the opportunity arose she must leave breadcrumbs. She had to get this right.*

'Nothing's ever straightforward is it? And, like I said, I don't want the hassle.' She lowered her voice as much as possible to be just audible over the background music of the wine bar. 'I heard he's moving the sale arrangements.' She shook her head in irritation. 'The man is paranoid and always convinced someone is following him or out to get him. I think I was wrong when I said he doesn't take his own coke!'

'Who told you that?' Kim squawked. 'Where did you hear that about the arrangements?'

'Oh, just a girl from the Feathers. They were in Percy's last night, remember? I knew her from before and well, people love to gossip.'

'Which girl?' Kim pushed, remembering belatedly that she shouldn't act too nosy.

'Just one of the dancers, erm, Patty,' Teagan said, sincerely hoping there was no dancer called Patty.

Worry glimmered. She hadn't expected Kim to present this opportunity and it caught her on the hop. She must bring this down otherwise it could look obvious. 'What does it matter anyway?' Teagan made a big point of knocking her drink back in one. 'Jonah Powell can do what he likes. I'm well out of it.' She nodded to Kim's glass. 'I'll get us some more, shall I?'

The second Teagan had got up from her stool and walked towards the bar, Kim scrabbled for her phone. *This couldn't wait.* Ron would want to know immediately that the arrangements for Thursday could have changed and would owe her *big time* for this, if they had.

FORTY ONE

HOLDING HIS PHONE UNDERNEATH the desk, Heath pressed in the digits of his PIN number, his annoyance rankling to get it wrong for the third time. *Jesus, he'd get locked out at this rate. Come on, how bloody hard could it be?*

Trying not to draw attention to himself, he guessed at the positioning of the numbers once again, whilst feigning unusual interest in this weeks' sales spreadsheet, which was difficult, considering it was completely blank.

Relieved to feel a slight buzz signifying his phone had unlocked, Heath glanced at it. If O'Hara didn't make tracks soon, he'd need to let Jonah know to abandon his visit.

Heath's eyes followed O'Hara stalking across the fishbowl office acting like he owned the place. He'd said he was going an hour ago, yet had made no movement to do so. *What was the bloody holdup?*

'No customers again,' Ron muttered, spinning on his heels to stare at Kieran. 'Are you planning on making the effort any time soon to increase footfall like we talked about?' His mouth cracked into a sneer. 'I mean, it shouldn't be too difficult being as we're now the sole recipients of the profits being as Mike has moved to pastures new?'

Getting no response from his nephew, he paused for effect, his eyes creeping in Heath's direction for a reaction.

Heath refused to divert his attention from the glaringly blank spreadsheet. As much as he wanted to rise to O'Hara's dig of the loss of his father, he wouldn't. He'd wait. O'Hara's comeuppance was only a few days away and was the one thing stopping him from doing what he really wanted - mangling O'Hara underneath one of the many unsold cars on the forecourt.

Unable to help it, Heath's gaze moved to the empty desk belonging to his father, not having properly sunk in he'd never see the man again.

A Monday morning – the start of a brand new week and the first of every week from now on he'd have to get used to not seeing his father sitting there stressing over rows of figures that never tallied, the way he'd done every single Monday for the past however many years since Heath had first joined the business.

Now that business was wrecked and worse, O'Hara believed he had complete ownership of it, like no one else existed.

Heath's lips set in a thin line. Well, *he* existed alright and O'Hara would soon realise that. O'Hara would pay for bulldozing his family, but for now, he would sit here like the stupid individual O'Hara believed him to be and swallow everything being dished out. He'd also continue playing the part of aiding O'Hara in his quest.

'What are you staring at, you gormless prick?' Ron barked.

Heath looked up to find O'Hara staring at him.

'You got a problem with something I said?' O'Hara pushed, his stance threatening.

Heath shook his head. 'I was just wondering why the plan's changed. I thought you said it was definitely happening on Thursday?' *Would that prompt O'Hara to explain why he was still here and not with Stan?*

'It *is* happening on Thursday,' Ron snapped. 'I've already

told you that. It's just a change to the setup, that's all.' And there was no way he'd let what Kim had texted last night become common knowledge. It was bad enough Heath Pointer being involved in this and as for Kieran, well, he'd just flap if he thought things were getting complicated.

'Like what?' Heath pressed. *Come on, O'Hara. Let's see how much you actually know or rather, Stan knows…*

Ron scowled. 'Fucking nosey, aren't you? I don't know yet, that's why I'm meeting Stan. He said it was too complicated to explain over the phone. Don't you listen?' It wouldn't be anything major. It couldn't be – not at this stage. There was no way Powell would pull out of hauling in that amount of money.

Heath prayed the sarcastic smile forming would remain hidden. 'Of course I listen. You said you were meeting Stan, so has he cancelled or something?'

'Why would h…' Stopping, Ron caught sight of the clock. 'Fuck! Why didn't you tell me? I'll be bloody late now.' He grabbed his jacket. 'The bastard better wait until I get there.'

He had to know what the problem was and if it turned out this was all to do with Stan Leyton wanting a bigger earner for his services, then the man could go jump. He'd already promised the greedy bastard an over the odds earner for his assistance in this matter, and if the bloke thought he could twist another few quid out of him at the last minute, then he'd fast discover he'd played the wrong person to mug off.

Rushing towards the door, Ron turned back. 'Text Adams and tell him to let me know immediately if Powell's tracker moves. I'm not walking into a bloody set up.'

Heath nodded. 'Ok, no problem.' *No need to thank me for reminding you*, he thought snarkily.

Pulling his phone out, he stabbed out a text to Adams. Robert Adams could watch Jonah's tracker all he liked but now its presence was known, today the tracker would only show the man remained firmly at the Feathers.

As O'Hara strode through the showroom and got into the Lexus - *Heath's* Lexus, Heath grinned, quickly sending another text to Jonah Powell's second burner phone:

```
OH on the move. Clear to go.
```

Deleting the sent text, Heath turned to Kieran. 'I suppose we'd better try and find some customers then?'

• • • •

RUSHING UP THE ROAD, Ron checked his mobile for the umpteenth time since clambering into the motor. *Still nothing...*

He chucked his half-smoked fag out of the window and gnashed his teeth at the building traffic approaching Hammersmith. Why meet at the bloody Nags Head again? It was too far out of the way and took an age to get to.

He'd texted Stan, he'd even tried to call to let him know he was running late, but had received no response and was getting more stressed by the minute.

If Stan Leyton hadn't waited; if the man was pulling rank, being as he knew his information was imperative at this stage of the game, then it wouldn't go down well.

Ron scowled inwardly. He wasn't in the mood to be jerked about. And he'd had no word from Adams either.

Snatching his phone he balanced it on his knees, using his elbow to steady the steering wheel whilst his pudgy fingers scrolled through his contacts. He prodded the call button against Robert Adams' number.

Feeling like he'd shortly blow a gasket, Ron shoved the phone under his chin, and swerved around the corner onto the main road, keeping his eyes peeled for the hidden entrance to the NCP, his teeth grating every time the phone rang out.

Answer the fucking phone, Adams, Ron snarled, swinging into the tight turning for the car park and cringing as he took the ramp too fast, the grinding noise of the cars' sump scraping against the concrete not helping his already frayed nerves.

'Yeah?'

'Bloody finally!' Ron spat. 'Is it clear?'

'What? Is *what* clear?' Robert growled.

'For me! Is Powell on the move?' Was everyone around him stupid? Had that joker, Heath, not even contacted Adams like he'd instructed? *If this was a bloody set up, then he'd...*

'Of course it's clear! Pointer said to let you know if it wasn't. That's what you said, was it not?' Robert snapped. He'd had enough of O'Hara and his demands, the useless, ugly twat.

'Right, right,' Ron blathered. He needed to calm down. He was becoming as paranoid as the rest of them and he couldn't have that happen because that's when mistakes were made.

'Powell's tracker is still registering static at the Feathers, like I expected,' Robert continued. 'In fact, I'm looking at it right now.'

Reversing into a parking space, the mobile still wedged under his chin, Ron winced feeling something click in his neck as he wrenched his head around to look behind him. 'Have you heard of a dancer from the Feathers called Patty?'

'Why the hell would I have heard of her?' Robert spluttered. 'What's that prick, Heath Pointer said to put the wind up you?'

He'd *known* it was a bad idea to allow that shit-for-brains be involved in this, but O'Hara was insistent the idiot could be useful. Robert would string the toerag up himself if he slowed up the ultimate finale.

'It was something Teagan said to Kim last night,' Ron gabbled, rubbing his neck.

Robert's pulse increased at the mention of Teagan's name. 'What's going on, O'Hara?'

'Nothing... Nothing at all.' Ron took the stone steps from the car park to the road two at a time, refusing to inhale the overwhelming stench of urine assaulting his nostrils. 'Look, I've got to go... I'm meeting someone. And you're *sure* it's clear?'

'I'm sure!' Robert sighed, his anger worsening when O'Hara hung up on him.

. . . .

ABOUT TO WALK into the lounge, Teagan froze against the hallway wall and watched Kim rifle through her handbag. *Kim was going through her stuff?*

Her heart pounded, anger growing for being so stupid to leave her bag on the side whilst she'd gone to the toilet. She'd only been gone a few minutes, but she took her bag to bed with her every night for this very reason.

She hadn't even heard Kim get up. It was almost lunchtime and there had been no sign of her.

Not daring to breathe in case it gave her presence away, Teagan watched Kim pull the phone Nero had given her from the bag and stared open mouthed after it was successfully unlocked following a couple of failed attempts. Her brain rushed through what she'd done after she'd spoken to Jonah last night.

Had she deleted the call log? She thought so, but now she couldn't be sure. *Think, Teagan*, she panicked. She *must* do better than this. This is why no one believed she was capable of pulling off what she promised.

Panic intensified. Closing her eyes momentarily, Teagan fought to remain calm.

After sneaking in the hasty call to Jonah once she was sure Kim was unconscious and well past being woken last night, she'd filled him with what had been said during the evening at the wine bar.

Although she'd been longing to hear his voice; that gravelly edge which made her stomach flip and fill with butterflies, she'd also wanted to know what else to do.

Jonah had seemed happy enough with what she'd told him. At least that was what he'd said, but she'd also detected the worry in his voice and the standoffish tone of his words. The real fear things between them were already evaporating reared its ugly head.

Jonah said he'd text her today, but he hadn't as yet. What if he'd texted while she was in the loo and Kim had seen it? Christ, she'd been stupid. She should have taken the bloody phone with her wherever she went.

Through the crack of the door, Teagan watched Kim still avidly looking at the mobile. *Please don't let Jonah have sent a text, please*, she begged silently.

This proved everything. Kim may act like she suspected nothing, but she was watching *everything*.

Fear rumbled. *How would she play it now?*

Teagan inched back in the direction of the bathroom, deciding the best way to play this was to give the woman warning of her presence before walking back in and would pretend she had no idea she'd seen what Kim was doing.

Pretending to come out of the bathroom, Teagan faked several coughs and a sneeze. 'Bloody hayfever,' she said loudly.

Taking her time to walk down the hallway, Teagan walked into the open-plan living area. 'Oh!' she exclaimed. 'You've surfaced!' Plastering on a relaxed smile, she continued into the room. 'How are you feeling today?'

Ignoring her handbag was replaced exactly where she'd left it, she hid her amazement how Kim had managed this and was sitting on the sofa, painting her nails with a mandarin-coloured varnish, like she'd been doing nothing else for the last ten minutes.

'A bit rough,' Kim grinned.

'Not going into work today?' Teagan asked, hoping Kim would. She was itching to see if a text had arrived. It meant her cover was blown and she, as well as everyone else was in danger.

Do not panic, Teagan repeated in her mind. *Do not panic. Not yet.*

'Work?' Kim's face screwed up. 'Nah. They won't miss me.'

FORTY TWO

IT SEEMED JONAH had been waiting several months for Benowitz to respond, when in reality it was only minutes.

He kept his face perfectly static, the usual air of confidence and assurance firmly in place, even though he felt the opposite. It was a tall order expecting the man to go with what he'd asked. Their only connection was Jonah's father. And he could only hope the man's liking and trust of Jacky Powell, although years ago, would be enough to suffice taking what he'd said at face value.

Jonah eyed the man in front of him, his rheumy eyes as sharp as ever, yet now holding a slight, yet distinct hint of disappointment.

He could only hope the disappointment wasn't to do with him and instead, to do with the man Benowitz trusted within his business.

Businesses such as these - fronts for fencing, were tricky at the best of times and it was everyone's worst nightmare to discover a trusted member of staff was, in fact, an enemy.

And Jonah would know. Oh yes, he'd know all about that and knew exactly how both infuriating and devastating it was on several levels.

Reluctantly coming to the conclusion that Abe Benowitz wasn't prepared to believe him after all, or did believe him, but wouldn't be party to the requests, Jonah realised he'd have to accept defeat.

His stomach sank. He had relied on swinging this. And if he couldn't swing it, then...

'Your father and I go back a long way,' the rusty voice crackled suddenly and Jonah pulled his attention back to the wizened old man behind the tiny desk in front of him. He watched the man fold the piece of paper up and place it in the breast pocket of his jacket.

Benowitz folded his arms across his chest, the suit jacket outlining his stick thin arms. 'You're asking a hell of a lot here, son...' He tapped his pen on the desk rhythmically.

Jonah nodded. 'I realise that, Mr Benowitz. I'm also sorry to be the bearer of bad news. I can assure you it gives me no pleasure to have told you this.'

Benowitz nodded. He opened the top drawer of his old desk and pulled from it a notepad.

Jonah watched the old man scribble a number onto the paper.

'Memorise this and then dispose of it.' Benowitz held out the piece of paper.

Confused, Jonah took the scrap of paper from between Benowitz's old fingers.

'I'll act on what you've told me, boy. For your father, you understand?' Benowitz held Jonah's gaze with his watery eyes. 'Take it things will proceed as agreed. Any changes and you'll be contacted by the number on that paper.' He slowly rose from his chair. 'If you do not receive a call from that number, then everything will proceed as outlined on Thursday.'

Jonah's relief was palpable, but he remained outwardly collected. He nodded courteously. 'Thank you. All being well, I shall see you on Thursday then.'

Leaving Benowitz's Fine Jewels, Jonah strode down Grenville Street and fired a text off to Nero to collect him.

He pulled his cigarettes from his pocket and lit one, noticing the slight tremor of his fingers. He hadn't thought things were going to work out there, but he was very glad they had.

And best of all, there was no sign of Stan Leyton.

· · · ·

'YOU DON'T NEED TO WORRY, RON,' Stan Leyton assured, waiting for the head of his pint of Guinness to settle. 'It's all in hand.'

Ron scowled. But he *was* worrying. And worrying a *lot*. By the looks of it, this bloody journey was a wasted one. For all of Stan's blustering and promises of important updates, the man was still as much in the dark about what was going on, or what *could* be going on, as he was himself. And that was no use.

'You said there were changes?' Ron snarled. 'So what the fuck are those changes?'

Stan shrugged his big shoulders. 'I don't know yet. And I should add, neither does Benowitz.' He took a long slurp from his pint. 'He had a phone call and told me stuff needed to be followed up and we'd soon know more.'

Ron wanted to scrape the white froth from Stan Leyton's face with his nails, leaving big bleeding gouges down his mug. 'So basically, I've come all the way here for nothing?' he spat. 'Is Powell coming back down to the Gardens to see Benowitz? Is that what you're saying?'

Stan laughed, his jowls trembling. 'Powell's hardly going to risk doing that at this stage, is he? No, Benowitz said Powell would be calling or texting with the changes to the arrangements.'

He leant forward, not noticing he'd put his arm in a pool of spilt beer. 'Powell's a paranoid prick. He's got the fear the Old Bill's sniffing around and so wants to alter a few things. I thought he'd have called by now to be honest, that's why I arranged to meet you.'

Ron sat up, sweat forming. 'What if he calls or texts whilst you're here with me?'

Stan laughed once more. 'Oh, ye of little faith!' He opened one half of his tweed sports jacket, revealing the top of a mobile phone in his inside pocket. 'All calls will come through to this because I've diverted them. As I said before, Benowitz struggles to even use a fucking landline, let alone anything else. He won't have a clue I've diverted the line. Besides, like I've already said, he leaves arrangements like texting to me, so either way I'll get wind.'

Ron nodded, feeling less on edge. Jeez, he really was getting uptight, but he couldn't help it. Too many things were riding on this and he'd waited too long for this particular boat to come in for any fuck-ups to appear at last knockings.

'You need to chill out, me old mate,' Stan said, slapping Ron on the back. 'You'll give yourself a heart attack and then what good will all of that money that's about to land in your lap be?'

'You're right,' Ron nodded. *He did need to chill out.* All these extra hurdles popping up the last few days had grated on his nerves and thinking the deal might be off had been the final straw.

'A-ha! See? Bet this is something now!' Hearing the notification ding of a text, Stan pulled his mobile from his pocket. Staring at the phone, his mouth cracked with a smile. 'Yep. Just like I said.'

As Stan turned the phone around, Ron stared at it:

```
Meet at 8.30 instead of 8? Place as stands.
Moving the unicorns will be staggered in case
of tail.
Details later.
```

Ron frowned. 'What the fuck does that mean?'

Stan slugged down the remains of his pint. 'Oh come on, O'Hara. Concentrate man! The meet is at the same place, but a bit later. Unicorn means diamonds and I told you Powell was bleating about being paranoid? Well, he's not going straight from the Feathers to Hatton Garden.'

'Do you think he knows I'm on to him?' Ron asked, worry rising once again.

'And how would he know that? You're the one with tails and trackers, not him.' Stan waved his hand dismissively. 'He's being cautious. Anyone would do the same. And...' He tapped the screen of the mobile. 'More details will follow. When they do, I'll let you know.'

• • • •

'HAS SHE SAID ANYTHING ELSE?' Kieran hissed, watching Kim pour herself yet another glass of wine.

'Shut up!' Kim spat. 'She'll hear you. She's only in there.' Her head jerked towards the bedroom. 'Now why don't we relax and have a few drinks whilst we've got a bit of spare time?'

'I'd have thought you would be more than busy with one of your other men?' Kieran snapped. Kim was the only one getting any fun around here and he'd just about had enough.

'Don't get snarky,' Kim pouted, walking away.

'You haven't been in work for ages either,' Kieran moaned. 'Do you not think you should make the effort?'

Kim swung around, her hands on her hips. 'Do you not think *this* constitutes making the effort? Am I not doing a job in itself here?'

Teagan stood with her back to the bedroom door, her ears straining to hear the conversation. They were talking about her again and Kieran was here too.

Her stomach rolled. *Kim's brother.*

She didn't know how she would cope with having to play dumb. Not with what she now knew.

Shuddering, Teagan stared at her mobile. She'd clutched it in her hand for hours, willing for a call or text to come through from Jonah, but there was still nothing.

She checked once again that she hadn't missed any calls. Having set the phone to silent she was constantly on edge she had missed something, but the call log remained empty.

Taking a deep breath, Teagan prepared to venture from the bedroom when the phone started vibrating. Her heart lurched and she fumbled with the call answer button:

```
JP calling...
```

'Jonah,' she whispered. 'Thank God! What's go…'

'I haven't got long. I'll send you some texts. Let the girl see you being cagey. Reply to the texts - put anything you like. Then delete them and the replies. Let her see you doing that.'

Teagan frowned. 'But what f…'

'It will all be drivel, but then I'll send you a final text. I'll send it at 10. That's the one I want you to leave on the phone.'

'But she's been looking at my phone!' Teagan explained. 'She'll know that y…'

'I *want* her to see this last one. Trust me.' Jonah's voice was clipped, expressionless.

Teagan faltered. She didn't want to talk about this. She wanted to ask about him. *Them.* If there was a "them"? But it was pointless. This had to be done first. Only when this was sorted would there be a chance to see if...

'Listen, I've got to go,' Jonah said hastily. 'You're doing well.'

'Jonah, I...' Teagan stopped, her heart sinking realising the line had gone dead.

Moving into the call log she deleted the one received call and putting the phone back in her pocket, glanced in the mirror, practised a smile, then walked from her bedroom into the lounge.

FORTY THREE

AWKWARD DIDN'T ADEQUATELY describe the atmosphere in the office.

Gwen perched uncomfortably on the chair and covertly read Jonah's face as he stared at the mounting pile of paperwork. If only she could backtrack the decisions she'd made over the last few weeks, then she would. To have alienated Jonah - the man she regarded as the son she'd never had, was the worst thing she could have envisaged.

The image of his father filled her mind once again, like it did every day. Biting the inside of her cheek to the point of pain to maintain an outward composure, Gwen's angst and worry deepened.

She'd been surprised to be told she could stay on until all this business was sorted. It had been Nero who had told her, not Jonah himself, and she knew it was only a temporary reprieve.

Once everything was done and there was no longer a threat, Gwen knew she would have to walk away from the Feathers and from Jonah for the last time. She'd well and truly burnt her bridges. She knew it - *accepted* it even, but the fact still stabbed deep in her heart that she'd interfered with Jonah's life so much he wanted her out of it.

Much to her shame he'd been right with everything he'd said. She'd overstepped the line, she really had, but she'd never, *ever* meant to hurt him. Or hurt *anyone*.

Gwen glanced out of the office door's glass panel, watching the girls dejectedly make their way along the corridor from the stage towards their dressing rooms.

The show had gone ahead, but it was obvious that the spark, vitality and the *energy* were depleted.

There was no chatter or banter. Every single girl was crushed and horrified.

Having to tell them at the meeting Jonah had called this morning about Terri Mason's fate was one of the most difficult things she'd done in a long time. And witnessing their fear when Jonah explained that until further notice, every single one of them was also at risk was equally dreadful.

Even sadder, Josie, whose hen night it had been was so distraught from a combination of fear for her unborn child and misplaced guilt that Terri would still be alive had it not been for the celebrations, had resigned and walked out.

Gwen had tried to convince Josie otherwise, but the girl was adamant. So adamant, she was even talking about cancelling her wedding...

Gwen could have cried. And not for the first time either. There was no guilt on Josie's - or *any* of those girls' parts. They hadn't known of the threats.

She swallowed painfully. But *she* had. *She* had known and she had dismissed them.

Terri's death, although not by her hand, was *her* fault. Another example of how her actions, judgement and need to override Jonah had caused irreparable damage.

And how could she have risked pushing Teagan away? What right was it of hers to decide the girl and Jonah couldn't be together?

None.

Gwen had attempted to talk to Nero about how dreadful she felt, but he'd cut her short, plain to see he was questioning his own part in all this. Instead, all he said was they should just concentrate on ending this business, rather than dwell on things they could no longer change.

Gwen's face crumpled. But she couldn't help but dwell on it. Because of *her*, Teagan was now a sitting target for O'Hara and Adams. And Jonah must only despise her more than she wanted to think for forcing a situation that was now their only option to stop these bastards.

She looked once again at Jonah, the worry deeply ingrained on his face. *The worries she'd caused.*

How could she ever make this up to him? To *any* of them?

The answer was, she couldn't and that was difficult to swallow.

All she could do now with the remaining time with Jonah and the Feathers before he pushed her away forever, was to make sure she did nothing else to impede anything.

· · · ·

TAPPING OUT THE FIRST TEXT, Jonah deleted it then re-entered the words. He frowned. What should he say?

His fingers faltered over the keys. Perhaps she'd read through the lines and see that he meant it. *Every single word.*

        I wish I was with you.

Pressing send before he could change his mind, Jonah exhaled sharply, suddenly feeling fourteen years old. Never in his life had he said anything like this to anyone, let alone *meant* it.

At least Teagan couldn't see his face and realise exactly how nervous he was.

Because it was true. And that knowledge crucified him. It left him wide open because he *did* wish he was with Teagan. He could be with a whole host of women, yet the one he *really* wanted, the one who said she also wanted to be with him, he couldn't. And all because of Ron O'Hara and Robert Adams.

It might only be three days until this was over one way or the other, but that was three whole days of worrying. Worrying that in the end, Teagan wouldn't want him. Worse, knowing he'd sanctioned putting her in the position of being a decoy rubbed against every nerve in his body.

And he hated every single bloody thing about that.

Jonah glanced up, conscious both Nero and Gwen were watching him, which didn't help.

His resentment over Gwen's part clawed the inside of his brain. Nero was correct that Gwen should remain within the firm's protection until this business was over - if it ever was over? But the festering anger he felt towards her built steadily. His feelings may be out of proportion, but he had to blame someone – *anyone* for this mess.

Jonah frowned. His plan may be in place, but there was so much riding on everything coming together at the right time, it made things extremely difficult. Neither did it help people that he had no trust in, such as Heath Pointer, were involved.

Even Benowitz's involvement was dubious. Would he stick to what was agreed?

He could only trust the old man put the changes into place and even more importantly, at the *right time*. It Benowitz hadn't, or hadn't used the exact times needed, then this whole thing would crash and burn.

Jonah glanced at his mobile. As for Teagan, it wasn't that he didn't trust her, it was that he couldn't tell her what was planned. He wanted to tell her – *should* tell her, but if she knew it would dilute the effectiveness, yet at the same time carried the very real risk that she'd never forgive him.

Many people had parts in this and he was relying on them to deliver like never before – perhaps *too* much. Only one, aside from himself, knew the full plan of what was hoped would result.

Meeting eyes with Nero, sweat gathered underneath Jonah's collar. *Christ, there was so much that could go wrong. And if it went wrong...*

He shook away the negative thoughts. What would happen, or what he *hoped* would happen, was the only way to finish this properly, but what might be left in the aftermath was a different story.

Jonah was grateful the buzzing of his mobile snapped his concentration back to the here and now:

```
So do I
X
```

Teagan. Hiding the ghost of a smile, Jonah stabbed out his reply:

```
Move in with me.
```

He drummed his fingers on the desk, then pressed send. Did he really want Teagan to move in with him after all of the grief with Lena?

Yes he did.

He waited impatiently.

'Is that about the deal?'

Nero's voice broke the silence and Jonah glanced up. 'What?'

Nero nodded to the burner phone in Jonah's hand. 'The texts?'

Jonah shook his head. 'No, these are for the benefit of Kim O'Hara.'

Gwen looked up, not daring to ask what that was about. Her eyes moved to Nero questioningly. She'd been omitted from the latest developments and understood why, but it was still horrible.

All of these years of being involved behind the scenes with both Jonah and his father appreciating her take, now she was blind to it.

Worry prickled, hoping Jonah was being sensible in whatever he was doing. The only part she'd gleaned was Kim

O'Hara was the woman Teagan had moved in with and also knew the diamonds deal was happening this week, but that was about it.

'Is there anything I can help with?' Gwen asked quietly, her voice small and nervous.

Jonah glanced up, almost surprised Gwen had spoken. 'You could check the girls and see how they are?' he muttered coldly.

Nodding and swallowing the stinging rebuff, Gwen made her way out of the office.

Nero pursed his lips. 'You should involve her. We need all hands on deck.'

Jonah shook his head resolutely. 'The less people involved, the better.'

Receiving another text, he scrambled to open the message:

```
Ha ha. Good job I know you're not serious.
```

Jonah frowned. Well, he had said these initial texts would be drivel. They weren't though. *Change the subject.*

```
Is she there?
```

'How many more of those are you sending?' Nero eyed Jonah suspiciously.

'Like I said, I want to make sure the O'Hara bitch sees Teagan receiving these before sending the final one.'

Nero nodded, his unconvinced expression remaining as another notification sounded on Jonah's phone.

```
Yes. Watching me all night.
```

Jonah grinned. 'I'll send the final one in just a moment.'

```
Delete everything now. You know what to do.
Final one coming next.
```

Tapping out the final text, Jonah's cheeks burnt. He had to make this convincing so Kim believed it. The only problem was that it was true. And that made him feel uncharacteristically vulnerable.

```
My involvement with Terri was a mistake. I know
I've hurt you, but it's you I want.
Meet me Thurs?
```

Pressing send, Jonah sighed. 'It's done and the O'Hara tart is clocking everything. Tomorrow I'll send another telling Teagan where to meet.'

Nero frowned. 'Where *are* you meeting her?'

Jonah stared at the empty glass on his desk, wishing he could justify another whisky. 'I don't know yet, but somewhere out of the way!'

Nero blew through his teeth loudly. 'This will take some fucking doing, won't it?

'You could say that, but it's the only way.'

FORTY FOUR

KIERAN SAUNTERED into the office at City Car Sales, excited that for once he had the chance to impress Uncle Ron.

Had Kim not got so wasted last night she wouldn't still be fast asleep and would have already brought their uncle up to speed instead of giving *him* a long-overdue opportunity to receive some recognition.

'It's all bloody true!' he cried, frowning at the lack of attention from Ron or Heath.

That said everything, did it not? They thought he was a nobody - a nothing.

The thought suddenly occurred that out of principle he could hang on to what he knew instead and say nothing about what Kim had failed to share, but then that would only delay or even *ruin* his chance of getting on a ferry out of this dump back to where he belonged, along with the prize of the century.

Kieran's eyes narrowed. Perhaps if Ron listened then he'd realise Kim wasn't the replacement Golden Child he thought she was.

Walking over to the main desk Ron now resided over, Kieran perched on the edge and looked at his uncle. 'I take it you don't want to know how I have proof of Powell's thing with that Teagan girl and Kim was wrong saying the woman isn't up to anything?' He paused dramatically. 'Because she is…'

Heath's head flicked up a bit too quickly at Kieran's words, worry spawning. Had Teagan been rumbled? Had it been discovered she'd met with Jonah or the rest of them? Including *him*? Fear pooled at the base of his spine.

Ron's disdain for his nephew was obvious. 'What are you talking about? If there were new developments, then I'd have already heard from Kim.' He glanced at his mobile. 'And I haven't…'

A cocky smile spread over Kieran's face. *This was enjoyable.* It served Kim right. 'I'm surprised she didn't tell you last night, but then she was so pissed by the time she crashed out and was still fast asleep when I left to come here.. I think you'll find this interesting…'

Ron sat forward, alert. 'Go on…'

'Well…' Kieran folded his arms, pleased to have a captive audience. 'Teagan was on her mobile texting. She didn't think we were taking notice, but we were. Well, I say *we*, but Kim was pretty smashed and I…'

'Instead of scoring points against your sister, just tell me the fucking upshot!' Ron barked.

Kieran blinked. Even now he was taking Kim's corner, but he continued regardless. 'She was texting Jonah and he was texting her.'

'She's got a phone?' Ron muttered, the hairs on the back of his neck standing up.

Kieran nodded. 'Kim found it the other day. Teagan said she'd bought it when she went shopping, but…'

'Right. And?' Ron snapped impatiently. Kim hadn't filled him with *that* either. 'What did the texts say?'

Kieran grinned. *Now he was getting somewhere.* 'When she went to the bog, I looked, but she'd deleted them.'

Ron sighed loudly. 'You thick fuck! If she deleted them, then we don't know who they were from and what they said! They could have been from anyone! Kim says lots of blokes chat them up when they're out, so it could have been anyone!'

Kieran's cheeks burned. 'The next time Teagan went for a piss another text came through. Kim had passed out by this point, but *I* looked. It had to be from Powell because it said Terri Mason meant nothing and he wants Teagan. He's asked her to meet on Thursday.'

Ron sat forward. *Thursday? The day of the deal?* 'Where? Where is he meeting her?'

Kieran shrugged. 'I don't know because she didn't reply.'

Ron stood up. 'Fuck! You need to get back there and see if she gets any more texts!'

The sly bastard, Powell, was planning on meeting the bird before the deal, wasn't he? That was why he'd bought the deal forward. He'd want to impress her with the promise of big money. What woman didn't fall for that?

Ron paced around, the grin on his face spreading, almost slathering over his good fortune. This was perfect. By the point Powell had arranged to meet Teagan, he'd have the diamonds, the money and Powell would be nicely dispatched. There would be no further use for that silly tart anymore so Adams was welcome to her. He'd finally get that psycho Adams off his back too.

All he needed now was the location.

Ron's eyes swivelled back to Kieran. 'What are you waiting for? Get your arse back to the apartment and find out where the fuck they're meeting and what time.' His attention slithered over to Heath. 'And you! You bring Adams up to speed. Tell him to be on standby for further information.'

Heath reluctantly nodded, watching Kieran fluster.

'What happens if the bird decides she doesn't want to meet Powell?' Kieran panicked.

'Then you or Kim talk her into it. Get Kim to make the tart admit Powell has a thing for her. They get on well, so she'll blab. Women always do.'

• • • •

HEATH'S BLOOD PRESSURE ramped up more than the electricity bill after making the mistake of using an electric heater one year. Not that he needed one anymore because he didn't have his own place and the chances of ever having one again were unlikely.

It was more likely he'd spend the rest of his life behind bars and probably even longer than that by the time this was done.

Walking down the steps from the police station, he gulped in large lungfulls of fresh air.

Even reporting to his probation officer for his weekly check was a pleasant respite from sitting in the car sales showroom with Kieran and Ron O'Hara.

At the cop shop he'd been almost tempted to blurt out the fate of his parents and where their murderer was right at this very moment. *Almost.*

Of course he hadn't, because no matter which way he turned, he was shafted.

He'd either be shafted by Jonah Powell, who he was now roped in with up to his bloody neck or by O'Hara, who he was attempting to take down or he would be literally shafted by a random person when he invariably got sentenced for the murder of Dulcie Adams.

That's if he survived long enough to even make it that far. He was still no wiser even when the court date might be.

Christ, this was bad.

Hurrying along the road, Heath glanced at his watch. Just gone 11, which meant he was late... Still, the less time spent at the car sales place or the house where his parents continued rotting in the shed, the better.

He swiped the back of his hand across his brow and increased his pace. He couldn't stand much more of this, but by Thursday it would be over.

Then he'd join his parents in the shed or be riddled with bullets somewhere.

O'Hara was all but hallucinogenic with excitement about Thursday's unfolding plan and it was becoming increasingly difficult to stomach.

Turning the corner and hurrying down the next street, Heath kept his eyes peeled for Nero's motor. The phone call said to meet somewhere around here...

He was also on the look-out for O'Hara and the Lexus. Paranoia was a given at the moment. Just about everybody was being followed, so why not him?

Hopefully, O'Hara would feel it sensible to stay as far away from police stations as possible, but then the guy was hardly Einstein - unless he was compared with Kieran.

• • • •

THE CAR PULLED UP alongside Heath, the passenger door flung open before he'd even noticed it, drawing vivid attention in his rattled mind that had this been one of the scores of people queuing up to remove him, he wouldn't have stood a chance.

'Get in,' Nero hissed.

Heath scuttled into the car obediently and had barely got his seat belt on before the car screeched off. 'Where are we going?' he asked, his throat constricted with a pile of imaginary fish bones making the act of uttering a sound not unnaturally high-pitched and strangulated nigh on impossible.

'Instructions,' Nero muttered, his attention on the road ahead as he manoeuvred through the traffic.

Heath thought it wise to remain silent and wait for these instructions, rather than making polite conversation and instead continued fiddling with his seat belt.

'Where does O'Hara think you are?' Nero asked, knocking Heath off guard.

Heath frowned. 'He thinks I'm at the police station or on my way back from there.'

Nero stiffened. 'Why does he think you're at the police station?' *Was this prick setting them up after all? If he was in cahoots with O'Hara, then he'd...*

'Probation. It's a weekly thing,' Heath said dully. Saying it out loud underlined exactly how shit his life was. 'He won't be following me because he's gone to Adams' place to inform him of the latest - that Jonah's meeting Teagan on Thursday and that everything's still good to go.'

Nero grinned, placated. *The message had worked then?* The sudden glimpse of possibility glowed.

'Teagan isn't *really* meeting Jonah on Thursday night is she? Adams is planning to lift her, I know he is,' Heath spluttered. *This was out of control. Way out of control.*

'I can't comment on that and you don't need to know anyway.' Nero's tone left no room for debate. *And now onto the next bit.* He'd been loath to risk this part of Jonah's idea, but now... Now it just *might* work if luck remained on their side. *And there was no time like the present.*

Pulling his eyes from the road, Nero shot Heath a glare. 'If O'Hara's gone to see Adams, we'll have time.'

'Time for what?' Heath suddenly noticed they were heading in a different direction from anywhere he had been or *should* be heading. 'Why are w...'

Nero turned the car towards Victoria. 'I'll tell you when we get there.'

Heath sat back in the seat, his blood slowly congealing. Was he about to be mowed down in a hail of bullets 48 hours earlier than expected?

FORTY FIVE

TEAGAN WAS TRYING her utmost to act normal, but it was difficult, her mind still spinning from the text she'd received last night.

How she wished she hadn't had to delete those texts so she could stare at the words Jonah had written again. Her lips flattened, knowing that no matter how many times she stared at them, it would make no difference to their truth or not.

She could analyse the messages until the cows came home and she still wouldn't know whether Jonah meant what he'd written or whether it was for show.

But the unrelenting hum of hope that Jonah's words weren't part of an act thrummed consistently in Teagan's mind.

Wish I was with you...
Move in with me...

Teagan could have kicked herself. She'd been so excited by that first text, she'd momentarily forgotten it was part of a scheme. How she wished she hadn't replied saying she felt the same...

She'd even put a kiss after it.

She scraped her hair away from her face in mounting embarrassment.

It hadn't taken Jonah long to get to the point and ask whether Kim was watching her receive the texts though...

It was all very well wanting whatever was unfolding to end in a fairy-tale, but *wanting* something and it actually happening were two completely separate things. She'd do well to remember that.

The creeping doubt that this whole thing - what Jonah had said to her before; the way he acted; was a convoluted way of manipulating her to achieve his goals slid back into her mind.

Whether it was or not, Teagan didn't know anymore, but she had to remember to take it for what it was.

Against her very best instincts, she was in love with the man, but not everything ended in ways that were good. *She more than most knew that.*

Teagan glanced at Kim sprawled on the sofa. The woman had only just surfaced and she wished more than anything she had a job to go to herself in order to excuse herself from this place for a while.

She was doing this job alright though and was impressed by her acting ability.

Last night, both Kieran and Kim were slyly watching as she received the texts. Oh, she'd done a fine job of making out she was replying on the quiet, but not enough so they didn't notice. Those two pairs of close-set eyes scrutinised her every move.

Teagan shuddered.

And when Kim zonked out before Jonah sent the final text, she'd panicked everything had gone to pot until Kieran stepped in to do the job.

She'd watched him go through her phone through the crack in the door. It had almost been worth putting up with the pair of them all evening now she'd pulled off what had been asked.

But what now?

That final text had now gone too. Once she knew it had been seen, she'd deleted it as agreed, but when would Jonah text again? She needed the time she was supposed to be meeting him to ensure it was passed to O'Hara.

Cold slithered up Teagan's veins. It really was horrible knowing that this woman – the one she'd initially liked, was betraying her. It also begged the question would she have ever noticed, had this not come to light?

Nausea bubbled. The one thing she *had* learned was that no one could be trusted. *And that alone was horrible.*

Teagan found her mind wandering to Gwen. How she missed that woman. She'd love nothing more than to ask for her advice, but it was impossible. She'd really thought Gwen genuine, but she hadn't even attempted to get in contact since Teagan had left.

The apartment doorbell made Teagan jump and she watched nervously when Kim groaned and reluctantly got to her feet.

'I expect that will be Kieran. He said he was coming back,' Kim muttered, moving towards the hallway.

Teagan's heart sank. She could only hope Jonah hurried up and texted her. The sooner these two got the information they wanted, the sooner she wouldn't have to pretend to be the best of friends.

· · · ·

WAITING IN A DROP-OFF POINT at Victoria station, Nero couldn't say he was comfortable with the situation. He stared at his mobile in the dashboard holder. That twat had been gone five minutes already. How much longer would it take?

What if he'd done a runner?

Tapping his screen to bring it to life, Nero pressed the contact for Jonah's direct line at the Feathers, not wanting to risk using his mobile.

No one knew for sure whether Adams had infiltrated the burners again like they'd witnessed him do so efficiently with Pointer's mobile when they'd believed him to be helping them.

How he despised that piece of shit, Adams.

Nero impatiently listened to the phone ringing out. *Come on Jonah, pick up. If he wasn't in his office, where the hell was he?*

Jonah's voice down the other end of the line made Nero sigh with relief. 'He's been in there five minutes. How long do I give it before going in?'

The couple of seconds before Jonah answered felt like an hour and Nero frowned at the response. 'Ok... If you're sure? O'Hara's gone round Adams' place. He's acting on the messages... Yes, ok... I will do.'

He paused, not really wanting to voice what was on his mind, but it *was* on his mind and glaringly so. 'What do you want me to do if Pointer doesn't show?'

Nero kept a constant watch in his rear view mirror, alert for a sign anyone was watching and nodded, mentally acknowledging Jonah's response, although he couldn't say he was as confident.

Pointer had already proved a snake before, so why not now? But then, orders were orders and he just had to hope Jonah was correct in his assumptions.

'And the next part is still as planned? Yep... Alright, I'll be back later.'

Ending the call, Nero spotted a traffic warden making his way slowly up the road checking all cars parked in the designated waiting bays. He mentally calculated he'd got less than three minutes before the warden reached this motor and he couldn't have the car being clocked here.

'Come on Pointer,' he muttered, refraining from sparking up yet another cigarette, his foot hovering over the accelerator pedal.

With one eye on the approaching traffic warden, Nero started the engine. He couldn't leave Pointer here - it was too risky, but then he couldn't hang around either...

Shit, shit, shit!

Perhaps he could swing out of the car park then come back in?

Ah, thank Christ!

Heath fumbled with the door handle and bundled into the car and Nero wasted no time in exiting the drop-off point, making his way rapidly towards the station exit.

Heath rested his head back against the headrest and struggled getting his lungs to function, sure he was about to have a heart attack.

'Well?' Nero spat. *The prick had been ages, got back to the bloody car, yet not said a word?* 'Did you do it?'

'Yes,' Heath croaked, his throat dry. 'Have you got a drink? I'm gasping.'

'What do you think this is? A fucking bar on wheels?' Nero snarled.

'I-I meant water. My throat's dry... I...'

'Was anyone there? What took you so bloody long?' If looks could kill, Pointer would be dead twice over.

Heath dared to glance at Nero. *Jesus, what did the bloke expect?* 'Those things were right the other end of the bloody station! I didn't even know where to look!'

Nero scowled. 'You didn't ask anyone did you?'

Heath shook his head. 'No. You said not to speak to anyone and I didn't. I'm doing exactly what you're asking here.' *And he liked none of it.*

He'd be surprised if his heart ever slowed to a normal level. Being convinced he was about to be blown to smithereens in broad daylight in the middle of a packed London station may sound far-fetched and unlikely to a normal person, but these people *weren't* normal. *None of this was...*

Although Heath had no idea what he'd just done, he did have the distinct and horribly worrying feeling he'd just been part of something that wasn't good. The very real possibility he was being used as collateral damage filtered back into his mind, like it had done countless times over the past few days and none more than since being dropped off outside Victoria not ten minutes ago.

'What was it in it anyway?' He found himself asking,

belatedly realising he may be better off not knowing.

'That's not your concern,' Nero said bluntly. 'All you need to know is to be certain that it was put exactly where I specified.'

Heath felt strangely relieved not to be party to the contents of the envelope and even more relieved that whatever it contained was no longer on his person. 'Yes, it went exactly where you said. And no one was there. Well, there were plenty of people about, but no one was watching me.'

'Good,' Nero muttered, putting his foot down as they moved further away from Victoria. 'I'll drop you back near the car sales place.'

Heath stiffened. 'You're taking me back *there*? What if...'

'I ain't walking you in, if that's what you mean! But they'll be suspicious if you're not back soon. It will take you ages otherwise.'

Heath had to reluctantly agree with that and although the prospect of being back in the same space as Kieran was not a warming prospect, with any luck O'Hara would still be at Adams' place.

Nero pulled up opposite the nearest bus stop in White City. 'At least you know where to go in Victoria now.'

Heath was reaching for the door handle when he froze. 'Going back?' His eyes swivelled to Nero. 'Why do I have to go back? I put it where you s...'

'First though you need to find a reason to get out undetected on Thursday and make your way to the Feathers,' Nero continued.

Heath blinked. 'The Feathers? On Thursday? Wh...'

'The road behind is a service road for deliveries. Be there at 7 and I'll give you the rest of the instructions.'

Heath's hand was unwilling to close around the handle even though it offered escape. 'But...'

'Thursday at 7. Unless you hear otherwise,' Nero repeated. 'Anything else you hear from O'Hara or *anyone*, let me know on the burner.' He jerked his head at the door. 'Thursday. 7.

Service road. Got that?'

'I've got it,' Heath mumbled and got out of the car, feeling even more apprehensive than before. *Could things get any worse?*

FORTY SIX

ROBERT STARED AT THE unpleasant sight as he opened the door to his room. 'What the hell are you doing here?'

O'Hara had said on so many occasions they were not to be seen together, yet he turns up at the B&B? *What was he playing at?*

'Are you letting me in or what?' Ron pushed his foot against the flimsy hardboard door. 'I'm not discussing this through the crack.'

Robert scowled. 'Go back to your car and I'll meet you down there in five minutes.' He went to shut the door, taken off guard when it rebounded back. He stumbled back into his room, his face a picture of shock. 'What the...?'

Ron pushed his way into the room and slammed the door behind him. 'I haven't got time to fuck about, Adams. There's too much I need to tell y...' He stopped, his eyes glued to the walls covered with cuttings of Teagan. 'What the fuck is all that?'

Robert glowered with rage. How dare O'Hara barge in and look at his things. This was *his* space. *HIS.*

Panic replaced his anger, watching O'Hara digest his masterpiece. Now he'd seen the montage, the bastard had ruined everything. No one was allowed to see his work. *No one.* But now O'Hara had seen it before Teagan. *No!*

Regaining control, Robert scrambled towards O'Hara. 'Don't fucking look at it! It's mine!' he roared, his eyes wild.

O'Hara stepped back in surprise. *This guy was screwed up with a capital S.*

'You've spoilt it now!' Robert raged. 'Fucking spoilt it and it will dilute my plan. No one can see this apart from me and her.' His big hands lurched towards O'Hara's throat. *There could be no witnesses diluting the power.*

Raising his hands to protect his face, Ron had to think quickly. Adams was tapped. His initial reaction was to just kill the fucker, but he still needed him for two more days. 'Seen what?' He raised an eyebrow. 'What's the matter?'

Robert blinked. *Was O'Hara being legit? Had he not noticed the wall? The protection had worked?*

Two nights now he'd envisaged a force-field surrounding the masterpiece. The old cow who owned this dump had bleated about needing to change his sheets so it was only a matter of time before she let herself in.

Robert's eyes darted back to the wall. That was also why he'd not stepped outside for the last couple of days. Staying indoors also stopped his now uncontrollable urge to watch Teagan.

He fixated on the large image forming the centrepiece of his second montage - the one where Teagan's eyes were wide and clear, taken the night in the wine bar.

It had worked. No one apart from *him* could see it. And no one would - apart from Teagan when it was time.

Ron watched Robert closely, seeing the cogs in his brain turning. The man had completely lost it. It was time to deflect him from the madness whilst he still had the chance. 'I came to tell you you'll get what you want on Thursday for definite.'

Robert froze, his eyes moving slowly to O'Hara. 'You'd better not be winding me up,' he spat. If O'Hara slowed up his pay-out again he'd kill him this time. *That* was definite.

Moving further into the room, Ron sat uninvited on the bed, making doubly sure his eyes didn't stray to the walls, but that was difficult because it was all he could see. Photo after photo of that woman. *The man was barking mad.*

'I'm not the sort to go back on my promises.' Ron's voice sounded uncharacteristically jovial.

Robert flinched, knitting his fingers together behind his back to quell the urge to rip O'Hara off his bed. *He'd creased the duvet. He actually creased the bloody duvet!*

'Powell's arranged to meet Teagan on Thursday,' Ron continued. 'He's been pissing about with the plans by moving the time by half an hour, but at a guess he's meeting her at some point before and after the deal.'

'When and where?' Robert's voice was hoarse, the need fierce. *This was it.*

'I'm awaiting confirmation, but don't worry, I'll get it.' Ron watched Robert mull over his words, unable to decide whether the man was about to launch himself back around his throat or whether he'd accepted the situation.

Feeling his phone vibrate, he snatched it from his pocket. *This might be Kieran now. The dozy bastard had had ample time back at the apartment.*

Unicorns to be collected from Victoria

Ron frowned. *The unicorns would be picked up from who?*

'What's that?' Robert barked. 'Have you received the time Powell's meeting Teagan?'

Ron shook his head. 'This is from my contact at the jewellers.' He showed Adams the phone. 'What do you make of it? I knew Powell was changing how the diamonds would get from the Feathers to Hatton Garden. Got himself convinced the Old Bill's watching him, but I don't get this.'

Sidetracked with the question, Robert stared at the message.

'Who's Victoria?' Ron asked, almost to himself rather than Robert. 'Is that another code word like this unicorn bullshit?'

Robert rubbed his fingers across his chin, disturbed to feel stubble. He'd only shaved last night. He needed to look his best. *Only perfect would do.*

His eyebrows knitted as his brain scrolled through scenarios. 'He's breaking the journey up you say?' Seeing O'Hara nod, Robert hummed to himself. 'Yeah, I think I know what they're doing.'

Ron hid the forming scowl. *Was Adams going to tell him then or what?*

'Victoria isn't a person, it's the station.' Robert said calmly, as if the last ten minutes of rage hadn't occurred. 'London Victoria. *That's* the halfway point - the destination to break up the journey.'

Picking up a pen from the collection of neatly lined up ones on his desk, Robert tapped it on the side of the phone. 'Yes, I get it. The diamonds - the *unicorns* will be dropped there for someone else to collect.'

Ron raised his eyebrows. 'Are you mad? How do you work that out? Who in their right mind would leave millions of pounds worth of jewels at a fucking station?' And why was he even bothering asking if Adams was mad - that much was obvious. He should never have thought him able to look at this logically.

A flash of indignation passed through Robert's eyes before the shutters came down once more. 'Security boxes - lockers for valuables. I should know. I wrote the code for the programme which generates the unique references.'

'References?'

'People get automatically generated codes to access their boxes.' Robert's brow creased in thought, his mouth forming a rare smile. 'Powell will get the diamonds put there or has already done it and then he or someone else will collect them to take to the deal.'

Ron frowned. *Was that even feasible?* 'But wh…'

'By meeting Teagan, Powell will have an alibi. Don't you see? They're planning for someone else to do the deal in

Powell's place whilst he goes for Teagan should it go tits up. He gets the girl *and* the alibi.'

Ron's brain whirred. *Fuck! Adams could well be right.* 'How can I do this then? How can I get in first? I need to get to those diamonds.'

'You get the code,' Robert said abruptly. 'Get the code, lift the diamonds, then go to the meet yourself and do the deal.'

'He's not likely to give Benowitz the code is he?' Ron snarled, losing patience. *Oh, he'd thought he'd had it then too. He'd thought this was all coming together perfectly.*

Robert raised his hand. 'But you're forgetting… Get me the new number Powell's been texting Teagan on and then I'll hack it. I guarantee he'll either phone someone to give them the code or text it. I'll monitor his phone as well as the tracker.'

A smug grin wormed its way onto Ron's face. Adams might be more fucked in the head then a prize fighter, but he was damn cracking at certain stuff. And if he could do this, then how it could unfold would be even more gratifying.

• • • •

'I'M TELLING YOU, she doesn't suspect anything,' Kim hissed, checking Teagan was out of earshot. 'She'll keep me informed without even realising it.'

Kieran couldn't help but sneer. 'From what Ron's just told me she probably won't need to bother!'

Kim folded her arms. 'Has he called? What's he said? Why would he tell *you* something over me?'

Kieran nodded, enjoying the irritation on his sister's face. 'He probably assumed you're pissed again and I'm the best bet. Good job I had the foresight to tell him about that text otherwise we wouldn't be in such a good position.'

Kim swallowed down her rising anger. *The fucking snake.* Kieran had gone behind her back, making her out to be incapable? Trying to get ahead again was he? 'You think you're so fucking clever Kieran, well you're not. Y...'

'Keep your voice down!' Kieran hissed, enjoying this more

than expected. 'She'll hear you if you carry on. Luckily I made a note of the mobile number that must be Powells last night and Ron's got that now, so...'

Refusing to listen to any more of Kieran's "achievements", Kim flounced out of the bathroom and made her way to the lounge. 'We off out tonight, babe? Fancy some drinks?

Teagan smiled, although she was anything but happy. She knew Kieran and Kim had just discussed her. 'I think I'll just chill out tonight.'

Kim perched on the edge of the sofa, her mini-skirt riding up even higher. 'Oh come on. You're mooning over whoever you were texting last night, aren't you?'

Teagan forced herself to look suitably surprised. 'What? I...'

Kim grinned knowingly and gave Kieran an "I-told-you-so" look. 'Come on... Who was it? You can tell me...'

Teagan laughed, amazed it sounded so natural and tapped the end of her nose. 'I'll tell you if anything comes of it. I don't want to tempt fate.'

Come on Teagan, think, think. Worry prickled. She couldn't balls this up now. She was on the spot here and she knew it. She couldn't make this too easy – too obvious. Everyone thought these two were thick as mud, but Kim especially was more switched on than people assumed.

The call she received from the unknown number earlier she'd thought to be Nero, was Heath. He'd spluttered a condensed version of what O'Hara had recounted about visiting Robert, telling her the phones would shortly all be tracked. All calls or texts from now on would be visible to O'Hara and Robert if they weren't already, which meant she was now on her own...

Teagan felt sick just from the thought of it. She had no means of getting further instructions. No means of talking to anyone or warning Jonah should something happen.

She was only on the call for less than a minute, but it was long enough to hear the fear in his voice. There was something he wasn't saying and she strongly suspected it was about her.

Didn't she deserve to know? But she couldn't ask. Kieran and Kim were everywhere she went. It was only fortunate she'd received the call whilst in the bathroom.

The last thing Heath said before ringing off was to expect a call from Jonah. *Tonight.* She should follow what was said to the letter. The call would be overheard, but to play along.

Teagan was now even more nervous than before and quickly picked up a magazine to hide her building anxiety.

'Oi!' Kim cried. 'Don't sit there and read mags. I want some goss!' Ignoring the warning looks Kieran threw at her, she pushed on. 'If you don't fancy going out, let's have a few drinks here?'

'Oh, go on then,' Teagan agreed, wishing she was anywhere but here.

'You having a beer, Kieran or shooting off,' Kim cried, her tone playful, but her eyes conveyed bitterness. She nudged Teagan. 'He shoots off quite quickly. I don't know why I bother!'

Teagan laughed again, but found that comment with its thinly-veiled reference even harder to fake. 'Grab the drinks then,' she chirped, moving to sit cross-legged on the sofa, making sure her phone was within reach and the volume up. There was no way she could miss this call whenever it happened.

$\bullet \; \bullet \; \bullet \; \bullet$

'I'VE SENT IT,' Jonah said. '90524'.

Hearing the expected ding on his mobile, Nero opened the text. 'Received. I hope that bastard is enjoying seeing this, thinking he's doing well.'

Jonah gritted his teeth. 'He'll see it.' He stabbed out a further text:

No 128 red

Nero tapped out a reply:

```
Will collect at 7:30 tomro
```

'It seems insane texting each other when we're in the same room,' Nero grinned.

'Just giving them what they're looking for.' Jonah moved to the metal cupboard at the back of his office. 'Right everything is loaded and ready. And I've got my bag.'

Nero sighed. 'Are you sure about this?'

'What fucking choice do I have?'

Nero nodded sadly. *There wasn't an answer to that. Not one they both didn't already know.*

'And Pointer is coming when?'

'7. I've arranged to meet him in the service road.' Nero watched Jonah doing yet another double-check on the contents of the small leather holdall. 'You taking that or putting it in place first?'

'It will go in place. I'm not messing about with that the other end. I presume Pointer knows what he's doing?' Jonah's concerns over that man were still clanging.

Nero nodded and glanced at the clock. 'Time?'

Sighing, Jonah walked back to his desk and pulled out his mobile. Just the thought of Adams having control of his bloody phone boiled his piss. It boiled his piss even more than he could no longer get word to Teagan without an audience.

He waited as the phone rang out. *Pick up Teagan.*

Jonah's heart lurched hearing Teagan's voice, breathless, tempting... 'It's about Thursday...' he murmured, aware the time he spoke to her was limited. Everything he said must be relevant. It must not hold any hint to give O'Hara and Adams wind of anything being other than genuine, but how he wished he could tell Teagan not to worry, however futile that was. 'I texted you last night, but you haven't responded?'

Teagan glanced at Kieran and Kim. Kim was excitedly mouthing something, so she turned away, knowing she must make this look real, but her mind was scrambling for the strength to work out how she was supposed to act.

Aware Teagan still hadn't responded, Jonah developed the real worry that he'd put her in an untenable position. What if her silence was conveying she was in trouble? What if he'd misjudged what O'Hara or Adams would do and one or both of them were with her right now?

Had they rumbled him? Or was Teagan unable to adlib? Was she not able to pull this off in the way he'd counted on? It was a big ask - a big presumption and she had no experience.

He swallowed drily, his mind churning. How he longed to give her words of reassurance, but he dared not. Doing that would not only blow the whole operation, but would place her at risk too. One thing was for sure and if she didn't pick up the flow, then he'd pull everything. He'd go and get her himself – O'Hara, Adams, deal or not. He would not allow Teagan to become collateral damage.

'Teagan? Can you hear me?' Jonah expelled a loud breath. 'Christ! I've said I'm bloody sorry and I meant it. What else do you want me to say?'

'I can hear you...' Teagan muttered, willing her heart to still. *Concentrate, concentrate.* She blanked out the eyes boring into her back.

'Are you meeting me on Thursday?' Jonah continued. Scraping his hand through his hair, he glanced at Nero busy listening. 'I want to see you...'

'Why?' Teagan whispered. 'Why should I want to see *you*?' She prayed this was the correct way to play it.

'Fuck's sake! You're not making this easy!' Jonah snapped, getting into character. 'I'm not going to beg, but I want you to meet me. I think you'll like what I have to offer you...' *Come on Teagan, pick up the trail.*

Sweat gathering in Teagan's armpits. *Should she mention the jewels? Oh Christ, she didn't know...* 'T-To offer me?' she stuttered. 'Is this something to do with the dia…'

'Don't say another word!' Jonah snapped. *Well done*

Teagan, exactly what I wanted you to do. 'I can't be sure my phone isn't tapped. The cops might be watching me.'

'The police? I...'

'Look, come and meet me at 8. I'll tell you about it face to face. I know you want me and I want you, so meet me, then wait while I do the deal and then we can be together.'

And he meant it. He could only pray she would still want him if this played out the way he planned.

Teagan's brain frantically digested what Jonah was saying. Was any of it true or was it for the benefit of the audience?

She took a deep breath. What did it matter? Play along, Heath had said, but was she supposed to agree to meet Jonah or not? *God, this was difficult.* 'You seem very sure I want you Jonah,' she said.

Jonah gritted his teeth. *Don't play too hard to get, they'll know I wouldn't beg.* 'You want me and I know because you're a shit actress. If you're trying to make me pay further for my dalliance with the dancer, then it won't work.'

Teagan knew she mustn't forget herself. She'd heard the reminder loud and clear within his dig about her acting skills. She sighed resignedly. 'Ok, I'll meet you. Where?'

'I'll meet you on route to the deal. Teller Street, St Giles. 8PM.'

'Where do I go while you're doing the deal and what happens after that?' Teagan blustered. *Give me a hint, Jonah, please...*

'I'll arrange something, ok?' Jonah could hear the waiver in Teagan's voice. She'd done well, but how he wished above all else that he could offer her reassurance. Even if he were able to speak freely, that was the *one* thing he couldn't give her.

His frown deepened. But he could give her *something* - something in case this went wrong and could only hope she read between the lines. 'Whatever happens...' *Word this properly Jonah, they're listening.* 'And whatever your decision is after I tell you what I can offer... If what happens doesn't turn out the way I'm *hoping* - your decision, I mean,' he added quickly.

'Then I want you to know that… that I love you…'

Teagan felt faint with shock. *Loved her? Did he mean that? Whatever happens…? That wasn't about her decision.* Panic swirled. 'Jonah… I…'

'8 o'clock.' Jonah ended the call before Teagan could say anything else. He looked at Nero. 'She did well.'

Nero nodded, inwardly smiling at the colour infusing Jonah's cheeks.

FORTY SEVEN

'IF IT'S GOOD ENOUGH for you to come to my place of accommodation, then it's good enough for me to pretend I'd like a new car, is it not?' Robert said pompously, ignoring O'Hara's irritated expression as he feigned interest in a Mazda on the forecourt of City Car Sales.

Ron scowled. Adams really was a prize irritating bastard and it was wearing his patience thin. The prick had him over a barrel, but not for much longer. As it was, he'd been up all night waiting for the man to get in contact, but he'd dragged it out until this morning?

'You're taking the piss! I know Powell called last night. 10PM if what Kim said is correct, yet what have I heard from you? Fuck all, that's what!' he snapped.

Robert shrugged. 'I've been busy.' And he *had* been busy. Busy planning exactly how he would use the information and busy working out how he would get what he wanted.

His eyes narrowed. It had been a toss-up deciding whether to give O'Hara the information he'd gleaned last night and was leaning towards not.

He had everything he needed now to act, so there was no pressing need to tell O'Hara *anything*. After all, the Irish bastard had been the one who'd put the brakes on him getting his part of the deal for long enough. And he'd have stuck with that decision too had he not been aware the ugly niece, Kim, would flap her plastic mouth to her thick fuck of an uncle, so O'Hara would already know the call they had been waiting for had happened.

Furthermore, Robert didn't trust O'Hara not to put a bullet in his head. And that would not happen. Not now he had so much to live for.

Robert inwardly smiled. Tomorrow night and Teagan would be his. O'Hara could take the diamonds and fuck off. He had his plans set in stone now and that was all that mattered.

He leant against the Mazda. 'Powell's meeting Teagan at 8.30.'

O'Hara nodded. 'I know, Kim told me. She was in the room when the girl took the call and got some more details from her afterwards. She also confirmed it was Powell.'

'I *know* it was Powell! I had to listen to his fucking voice!' Robert seethed.

And he'd heard Powell tell Teagan that he loved her. *Loved her?* People like that didn't *love*. Love was irrelevant. It was ownership and control. The one and only thing he shared with pond life such as Jonah Powell.

But Teagan was not Powell's to own. Teagan was his. *But what if Powell actually had awakened to real emotions? Did that make him better? No, it fucking didn't.*

'Where are they meeting?' O'Hara hissed.

'Where they're meeting is irrelevant. It is happening at 8 and then Powell will go to do the deal. He's planning on meeting her again afterwards.'

'Yes, but I want to know *where* he's meeting her. I haven't got the diamonds, so I need to jump him and get them from him.' O'Hara clenched his fist. 'Adams, don't fuck around. You need to te…'

'You don't need to get the jewels from Powell,' Robert said slowly. Furthermore, O'Hara would *not* be jumping Powell. He would be having *nothing* to do with him. The man wouldn't be laying a finger on Jonah Powell or touching a hair on his head because that was *his* for the taking.

His face morphed into a gratified sneer. He owed Powell one and *he'd* be serving justice, not O'Hara. The Powells had spoilt things and now it was *his* turn to put that straight. Not that he'd tell O'Hara that.

Ron felt his last shreds of patience slipping away. 'Adams, I need the fucking jewels. You need to tell me where Pow...'

'You'll get your diamonds, O'Hara,' Robert said. 'I have the code for the security box.' He fished out a scrap of paper from his pocket and handed it over. 'Now you can go and get them. You'll need to wait until tomorrow though in case anyone is sent to double check they're still in place. But when you go, I'll watch the tracker to make sure Powell isn't there. Once you've got them, go straight to the meet at the jewellers.'

He watched O'Hara staring at the security box code. 'I'll warn you you'll be cutting it fine. Once Powell realises the jewels have gone, he'll have to explain to the buyer.'

Ron's face split into a grin. 'My contact tells me the buyers are the Russians. They're due to be there by 8:30.'

'Then make sure you're there first,' Robert said casually. 'You'll have a bit of time though as Powell will still go and meet Teagan.'

Ron stared at Robert incredulously. 'The man's hardly likely to go and see some bird when the family's heist has just been lifted.'

'He will, trust me,' Robert snarled, the smile on his face turning menacing. 'That fucker is in love with Teagan, so he'll go and see her regardless.' How it pained him to say that. How it pained him to have to say that a Powell may have managed something he couldn't. *Emotions.*

'If Powell makes a move to head to the deal instead I'll find a way to deflect him,' Robert added.

Ron eyed Robert with malice. 'You're not to fuck Powell up. That's my bag. He's going to pay for my Lena.'

Robert shrugged. 'For Christ's sake, O'Hara. I don't want Powell, your prize is safe. All I want is the girl, like agreed.'

A wide smile broke out on Ron's face. This really was doable. He would finally get the diamonds *and* avenge his brother and niece. 'Let's hope the Russians are running early, shall we?'

Robert nodded. Personally he didn't care what the Russians were doing. In just over 24 hours from now his life would be on track and he could move forward with everything he'd dreamt of for so long.

· · · ·

HEATH STARED IN FASCINATION at the contents of the envelope O'Hara emptied onto the desk.

Ron's tongue traced over his fat lips. 'Aren't they beauties?'

'A-Are those what I think they are?' Heath spluttered. 'The pink diamonds? H-How…?'

Ron thumped his chest, glowing with self-importance. 'They're exactly what you think they are. Have you any idea how much these are worth?'

Heath nodded, knowing *exactly* how much they were worth. He knew because he'd calculated it himself when his initial plan had grown to its doomed fruition. His eyes then tracked back to the envelope the diamonds were emptied from. *That looked like…*

Didn't most brown envelopes look the same? No, it *was* the same one. The one he placed in the security box had a coffee stain on the very left hand corner - *exactly* the same as this one…

Sickness rose. So that was what he'd placed in the locker at the station? *Fucking hell! He could have been stopped, shot, anything!*

Colours flashed in the back of Heath's mind as panic threatened to engulf him and he fought to remove any recognition from his face. If O'Hara caught on he'd been the one to place them and that he knew where they had been kept…

'H-How did you manage to get th…'

'Don't concern yourself with that.' Ron shot Heath a look that cut him stone dead. 'You don't need to know. You don't need to know *anything*.' This idiot would be dispatched like the rest of them by tomorrow night. He was only still breathing in case he was required for last minute alterations.

Heath peered at the diamonds again. 'Is that all of them? I thought there would be more.'

'What do you mean?' Ron snapped. 'Being as you did your homework on this in the first place, you'll know several went as payment back in the day. Benowitz will have taken one or two for valuation purposes as well. Were you there at the time the heist took place? Did you know how many were there to start with?'

He stared at Heath knowingly. 'No? Well, *I* was told at the time and with everything that's happened, I'd say this was about right. Plus, that old cow you killed would have flogged a few over the years as well to fund her fucking lifestyle, I don't doubt.'

Heath slunk back to his side of the office. How could he get word to Jonah that his jewels had gone? That the rigmarole Nero had put him through the other day was for nothing?

He felt like crying. O'Hara had the got the jewels after all and his father's last wish was a pile of dust.

FORTY EIGHT

'OH, HELLO KIERAN!' Teagan pulled her dressing gown around her as she walked out of the bathroom. 'I didn't realise you were here. No work today?'

Kieran's eyes lingered on Teagan as if staring would force her robe to fall open on command. 'Nah, we've been given the day off.'

Teagan squeezed past Kieran, cringing when she was forced to brush against him.

Her nerves fluttered. It was Thursday - the day she was meeting Jonah and the day the diamonds deal was going ahead. She still had no idea what part she was playing - that's if she *was*? Maybe she was meeting Jonah because he would tell her it had all gone wrong? What if something she'd done or *hadn't* done had ruined the plan?

Frustration ballooned. If she knew the details, she'd be in a better position. Why wouldn't he tell her?

Aware Kieran was trailing her down the hall, Teagan hurried into the living area. Was he here to keep tabs on her? How would she get out of here later without them knowing?

'Ah-ha! You've surfaced!' Kim looked up from her magazine and stubbed her cigarette out in the ashtray. 'It's not like you to sleep until lunchtime? I thought I was the only one who did that!'

Teagan's stomach lurched. 'Lunchtime? Is it really?' She knew she'd had little sleep, but this was ridiculous.

'Ooh, look at your face,' Kim giggled. 'Don't panic. You've got plenty of time to make yourself look ravishing before tonight.'

'T-Tonight?'

'Oh come on! How long can you keep it under wraps for?' Kim folded her arms. 'We know you're meeting Jonah Powell. We heard you on the phone to this "mystery" man last night, which is *obviously* him!'

Teagan pretended to search for a glass, hoping to God she'd played this the right way and would *continue* to play it the right way. She turned the tap on full blast, waiting for the water from the mixer tap to run cold.

'When will you admit you're seeing Jonah Powell?' Kim pressed. 'You said you'd tell me once there was something to report.'

Teagan turned around. Leaning on the work surface, she sipped her water and gave Kim what she hoped was a mischievous look rather than one belonging to someone about to go to the guillotine. 'I haven't said anything because there's nothing to report... *Yet...*'

'What's Jonah Powell up to?' Kim shuffled forward to perch on the edge of the sofa. 'What's he planning? Is he going to propose or something?'

Teagan laughed despite herself. 'I doubt it! He's only just got rid of his last one - that tart dancer and before that the Lena woman. He won't be in any rush to get engaged again.'

As soon as she'd said it and saw the accompanying flash of pure hate behind Kim's eyes, Teagan knew she'd made a mistake. 'I wonder where she's gone?' she continued, wracking her brains for something that would turn this around. 'If that Lena woman has any sense, she'll file a lawsuit for some of his money!'

Kim's eyes flashed with malice. 'Yeah, you'd think so wouldn't you, except th…'

'Except by now she's probably involved with someone with even more brass than Jonah Powell,' Kieran cut in, glaring at his sister, sure she'd been about to say something stupid like Lena was dead.

Teagan watched Kieran's reaction with interest. Kim had almost forgotten herself then. Regaining her confidence, she knew she could work this to her advantage. An advantage Kim would understand. 'Well, all I know is it's good for me. I'm more than happy to take his money.'

Kim bit back her anger. For Kieran to have stepped in to stop her from putting her foot in it was unheard of. *Was she losing it?* 'That's the way to look at it. Go after his money and do whatever you need to do to get it!' She laughed shrilly.

Teagan relaxed. *She'd got away with her faux pas.* 'I'd best go and get showered.'

Kieran waited until Teagan had moved out of the living area and heard the bathroom door close before turning to Kim. 'That was fucking stupid! You almost sa…'

'I almost said nothing!' Kim snapped. 'Shut the fuck up, Kieran, you're getting on my tits. What do you know anyway?'

Ok, so she *had* almost ballsed up, but it made little difference. Teagan hadn't noticed. Why would she? Teagan wouldn't be getting her greedy little mitts on Powell's money. That was *hers*. It should have been hers anyway - at least some of it if the bastard hadn't killed her sister, but now, come hell or high water, it was still coming to her courtesy of Uncle Ron. *And she couldn't wait!*

• • • •

JONAH SCANNED the sea of faces in front of him, ensuring he made eye contact with every single person, wishing to silently convey that each member of his staff mattered, just like his father would have done.

This might be the last time he ever saw these people and

without uttering that in so many words, it was important they knew that they, as well as their hard work was appreciated.

'Thank you everyone. I know it isn't usual having a meeting for all staff like this, but I felt I should call it.' Jonah folded his arms across his chest and smiled confidently, without coming over as happy.

Happy would not be the right look and, in all fairness, would be impossible to pull off. Ask him again in a few hours' time and the answer may be different, but even then it wouldn't change the gravity of the situation. These people - every single one of them needed and *deserved* his sincerity. And that is what they would receive.

'I'm well aware things have been difficult after what happened to Terri.' Jonah's eyes moved to Sally - the dancer who out of everyone, seemed to hold him personally responsible for Terri's death. 'What happened was clearly not something that should have occurred.'

He moved his eyes back to the general audience. 'I also know the instructions to go nowhere unaccompanied without being given an explanation is difficult and I appreciate many of you have worries about this. Again, the details are unfortunately not something I can divulge, but what I *can* say is that very soon I hope to be able to tell you that is no longer the case.'

He clasped his hands together. 'There will be a full remembrance service here next week in Terri's memory and I would like everybody to attend.' Jonah smiled thinly. 'Finally, I want you to know your hard work and support to this business is valued... Each of you... That's it from me for now, so well done everybody. Oh, and just to let you know, the yearly audit is underway so I'll be up to my neck with accountants for the rest of the day.' He nodded in Nero's direction. 'Nero will also be unavailable for the same reason, so if there's any pressing matters from either side of the business then please let me know now.'

A lie, but he couldn't have the enforcement teams, nor any of the cabaret suddenly feeling the need to speak to him. It was vital everyone believed he was on site and not anywhere near where he would *really* be.

Jonah paused, grateful there were no takers, then left the room.

Making his way back to his office, he glanced at his watch, finding his mind moving back to Teagan.

Would this go as planned?

His lips pursed. It *had* to. If it didn't, then he trusted Nero to ensure Teagan and everyone else was well looked after and catered for. What else could he do short of that?

Shutting the office door, Jonah poured a tot of brandy and wasted no time tipping it down his throat. Replacing the thick tumbler on the tray, he turned the lead crystal decanter around.

I hope this works, Dad, Jonah thought. *I hope I can finally put an end to this.*

FORTY NINE

AS TIME MOVED ON, Heath became more and more uneasy. He watched O'Hara fixated on his phone and wondered what he was expecting.

He purposefully sat with his back to the lounge window so that his eyes wouldn't wander in the direction of the shed. His parents were still in there. At least he thought they must be because he hadn't seen anyone move them.

But it might have happened without his knowledge? His parents could have been disposed of like rubbish and he'd never know.

There was only two hours before meeting Nero and the prospect rested in the base of Heath's stomach like a lead weight.

Countless times he'd picked up his own phone, toying with whether to call the man and tell him O'Hara had the diamonds and that their plan was screwed, but he hadn't. This was because he didn't know whether that raving weirdo, Adams, was tracking *his* phone in addition to everyone else's.

He'd tried to convince himself Adams wasn't and that he was being stupid and paranoid because as far as that lot believed, weren't they all on the same side?

Heath swallowed uncomfortably. He had no real idea what

went through that bizarre brain of Adams. Certainly nothing that would go through anyone else's.

Heath's eyes tracked to O'Hara. Aside from *his* brain, perhaps?

Christ, this was a nightmare. Had O'Hara discovered his part in it? Was the man biding his time?

'What the fuck is the matter with you?' Ron barked, making Heath physically jump.

'Nothing,' Heath spluttered. 'I'm just tired.'

'Tired? It's hardly like you've been run off your feet!' Ron snatched his phone up as a notification sounded.

Heath watched O'Hara staring at the mobile, a sickening grin spreading onto that face of his. He waited to see if anything was mentioned, but it wasn't.

Sweat beaded on Heath's brow and he willed it to evaporate before O'Hara noticed. Should he ask? *Yes, he'd ask.* 'Everything still on?'

Ron pulled his eyes away from the phone. 'Why wouldn't it be?'

Heath shrugged. 'No reason. I guess I'm just nervous.'

Ron's eyes narrowed. 'Why would you be nervous?'

Heath smiled, yet had no idea why. *What was he smiling for? Christ!* 'It's kind of a big deal!'

'Everything's fine,' Ron growled. 'That's all you need to know.' He closed the email app on his phone. The email confirmation of three tickets waiting at the port for the first departure of the day tomorrow was music to his ears.

His lips curled into a sneer. In a few hours from now he'd have everything. Powell would be dead, Adams would be out of his life to do what the hell he wanted with that bimbo and by the morning, he'd be on the ferry with enough brass to enable him and his entire family to retire three times over.

It was unfortunate he couldn't leave Kim and Kieran in this English shithole, but he'd never hear the fucking last of it from the wife if he did that.

His owl-like eyes gravitated towards Heath. And *he*

wouldn't have anything left to worry about either. *Bye bye, Heath*, he thought happily.

He'd off this prat just before they made their way to Dover later.

• • • •

NERO WAS STILL ON THE PHONE and Jonah had double-checked his holdall for the last time when Gwen tapped on the office door. 'Come in.'

'I take it I'm exempt from the "no one to disturb you this evening" rule,' Gwen smiled, pleased things had become more civil between her and Jonah over the last day or so.

'No one's asked to see me?' Jonah asked, inspecting himself in the mirror against the back wall.

Gwen shook her head. 'No.' She smiled again, nervous to broach the subject considering the angst it had previously caused. 'Calling that meeting today and what you said about Terri... It put people - especially the girls, in a much better frame of mind and that can only be good.'

'Good, good. That's good...' Jonah acknowledged, adjusting his tie. He checked his watch. Soon everything would be underway. The time of reckoning was approaching and all he could do was hope and pray timing and a huge helping of luck was on his side.

He glanced in the direction of the safe. Phase one had gone well, which was one less thing to worry about, but now that was done it left the huge chunk of what he dreaded most to deal with.

'I have to say you look very smart,' Gwen said as Jonah lined his cuffs up with meticulous precision.

'What? Oh, thanks,' Jonah said dismissively, half an ear on the conversation Nero was having. He needed to wrap that call up and get going. He motioned towards his right hand man.

'Thanks Lenny. I appreciate it. I'll call you on this number, yes?' Cutting the call, Nero nodded at Jonah. 'Sorted!'

Gwen frowned. 'Lenny? As in Lenny Dust?'

'Yeah, he's picking up the old chairs that have been

knocking around in one of the stockrooms for ages,' Nero lied, retrieving his jacket from the back of his chair.

He'd like to shake Jonah's hand, but even if Gwen wasn't here, he wouldn't. It was akin to tempting fate and there was no real reason why either he or Jonah wouldn't be back later. Actually, there were several, but he wouldn't dwell on those. Neither was there any need to go through the plan again. They'd discussed it enough.

Nero trusted Jonah to stick to the timings with military precision and knew his boss and friend of old could say the same about him. Slipping his jacket on, he brushed his hand against the gun placed in his inside pocket. *All set.*

He cut Jonah a look, the ghost of a smile across his lips. 'I'll be off then.'

Jonah nodded. 'Ok, mate. Thanks.'

Gwen watched Nero stride out of the office, shutting the door behind him, desperate to ask what was going on, but she didn't. If Jonah wanted her involved, then he'd have done so already.

She looked at Jonah staring wistfully at the framed photograph of his father. The photo she had to actively avert her eyes from every time she entered the office save it push her over the edge with how much she missed Jacky Powell.

Her gaze moved back to the faintest hint visible on Jonah's face showing the young boy she'd first taken under her wing as he stared at the faded image of his father.

Sensing Gwen's attention, Jonah pulled his eyes from the photograph, the mask of cold neutrality falling down over his rugged features and felt the overwhelming urge to hug the woman.

Regardless of what had occurred to push him away from her and whatever she'd done to incense him, Gwen was still the one fixture in his life that tied him to his father. This was the woman who, without asking for anything in return, had treated both him and his brother like sons and who had, faults aside, done everything she could possibly do for him.

She may have screwed up and overstepped the line, but her intentions had been good. The approaching prospect of what was about to happen reminded him that now was the very real possibility of being the last time he'd ever see her and he didn't want that to be tinged with bad feeling.

Moving towards Gwen, Jonah smiled then bent to kiss her cheek. He didn't say anything. He didn't need to.

Gwen blinked away the forming tears. Now she knew exactly what was going on. It was crystal clear. The deal was happening and it was happening tonight.

She grabbed Jonah's suit jacket sleeve. 'Good luck, love' she whispered. 'You be careful, do you hear me? All of you. I want you back in one piece.'

HEATH HADN'T EXPECTED the blue saloon to reverse down the service road. He hadn't expected *any* car to appear either forward or backwards. All deliveries for the day were over and no other motors used this wide alley, not even waiting taxis.

His first and immediate thought was an ambush. *O'Hara had followed him and was about to blow his brains out.*

Heath slunk against the wall, pointlessly attempting to merge into the brickwork.

He'd thought it was too easy to leave the house. O'Hara had already left and there was no sign of Kieran. Now it was obvious why. They'd been waiting and watching. Waiting and watching to see if he also left and then where he went.

And where had he gone? Around the back of the Feathers...

Aware his whole body was shaking, Heath held his breath for the expected gunshot. By the time he heard it he'd be dead. *It wouldn't be long...*

'What the fuck are you doing, you prick?'

Heath opened his tightly closed eyes to see Nero behind the wheel of the unknown blue car. He robotically scrambled into the passenger seat. 'I-I thought... I...'

'I'm not even going to ask,' Nero muttered, backing out of the service road with speed, then swinging the car onto the main road out. 'Here - take this.'

Heath stared at what was thrust into his hands. *The wallet... Jonah Powell's wallet containing the tracker...*

His eyes darted to Nero - the relief at not being gunned down replaced by fear. 'Wait! You...'

'Put it in your pocket, Pointer,' Nero growled, concentrating on weaving through the traffic.

'But you don't understand!' Heath garbled, suddenly spying the sign for London Victoria. 'We're going back to the station? There's no point beca...'

'I said, shut up!' Nero hissed, his nerves already shot to buggery without this eejit bleating down his ear. 'All you've got to do is walk into the station, stand there for a couple of minutes and th...'

'But you don't get it!' Heath screamed, pulling at one of Nero's arms in panic.

Nero jerked his arm out of Heath's grip, his movement causing the car to swerve. 'Don't be a fucking idiot! I don't need *you* getting us killed!'

'O'Hara has the diamonds! He's fucking got them.' Heath yelled. 'That's what I'm trying to tell you. The plan has gone to shit and th...'

'Yeah, I know he's got them,' Nero sighed, flicking on the indicator.

'W-What?' Heath blathered. 'What do you mean, you *know*? How do y...'

'Don't worry.' Nero pulled into one of the designated drop-off points outside the front of the large station. 'Just do what I've told you.'

Heath remained stuck to the passenger seat. This made no sense. If they knew O'Hara had the diamonds, why was he sitting here with Jonah Powell's wallet?

Suddenly a horrible thought slithered into his brain. O'Hara wanted to kill Jonah Powell. Heath had heard him rant about it enough times and Adams tracked Jonah using the wallet... *He was being placed as the target. He was taking Jonah Powell's place - a sitting duck.*

Heath stared at the monogrammed leather wallet in his hand, the urge to sling it out of the window, strong. *He was walking headfirst into a trap.*

His mouth flapped up and down, but nothing came out, the screams stuck in the back of his throat.

'What the fuck are you waiting for?' Nero shouted, leaning over Heath and shoving the passenger door open. 'Go on. Go in and walk to the lockers. Wait for two minutes and then come back and get in the car. It's not difficult.'

Heath finally forced his voice box to engage. 'B-But they'll shoot me. They'll think I'm him. They...'

'No they won't. They're busy,' Nero snapped. That's what was assumed, but it could be wrong. Heath might be correct in his assumptions, but either way this had to go ahead.

Heath was about to argue, but catching a glimpse of Nero's expression made him change his mind. His legs moved against his will and before he knew it, found himself heading towards the entrance to London Victoria.

• • • •

PARKED UP one block down from Teller Street, Robert stayed focused on the tracker app. His engine remained running, his mobile plugged into the charger wedged into the cigarette lighter socket. He couldn't risk his phone battery getting low.

Reluctant to blink in case he missed something, he continued watching the coordinates move. Powell had set off from the Feathers and was heading quickly in the expected direction, but always suspicious of a double-backed route, Robert waited for the confirmation.

And now he'd got it. Powell was definitely at Victoria.

Minimising the tracker, he tapped out a text:

He's there. Clear to move. GO.

Pressing send, Robert brought the tracker back to fill the small screen of his mobile and his eyes moved to the dashboard clock. *7.45*.

O'Hara had better be ready to enter Benowitz's. This would go off quickly. Robert hoped his instinct about Powell was right and that he'd go ahead meeting Teagan, despite realising his family's nest egg had disappeared from right under his nose.

Despite his apprehension, Robert couldn't stop his mouth from curling into a smile. How he'd love to see Jonah Powell's face when he opened that locker to find it empty.

His eyes moved back to the tracker. *Still in the station*. No doubt ranting at an official that his security box had been interfered with.

Ah, but he couldn't because then the police would become involved.

Oh, it was brilliant. Just brilliant.

Regardless of the instructions Robert laid out to himself over and over during the past day of intense concentration to keep fully in control and to remain calm and constant, he could feel his pulse accelerating with the building anticipation.

His eyes flicked back to the clock. *She would be here soon.*

Teagan would be here and then it was *his* time to shine. He could prove to himself, the world and his dead bitch of a mother, that he was just like everybody else. That he had a normal relationship and functioned in a completely standard way along with the rest of society that was always held in such high regard.

Robert dared to shift his concentration away from the tracker and the clock. He pulled down his sun visor and looked at his reflection in the vanity mirror, nodding in appreciation.

He looked perfect; groomed, presentable and *normal*. He looked just like everybody else and now he would *be* like everybody else.

The buzzing of his phone alerted Robert back to the task in hand and with irritation, slapped the sun visor back into position and snatched up his phone:

> I'm in but they not here yet

Robert frowned. *O'Hara.*

It wasn't altogether surprising the buyers were yet to arrive. They had stated 8:30 which was still just under three-quarters of an hour away, but that was ok.

Robert's lips twisted into a sneer. He would find it most satisfactory deflecting Powell and preventing him from making the rest of his journey to Hatton Garden.

He placed his phone back on the passenger seat and trained his eyes back along the road, waiting for Teagan to come into view. Then and only then could he move into position.

FIFTY ONE

TEAGAN HURRIED ALONG the road to where she had agreed to meet Jonah, her heart thumping. She refrained from looking over her shoulder, having already done that several times since getting out of the taxi. She didn't want to draw attention to how nervous she was.

But that was an understatement. She wasn't just nervous, she was utterly *terrified*, convinced any second now she'd be bundled into a car and spirited away somewhere no one would ever find her.

It had been stupid not to double-check the location. She thought she'd got it right, but not wanting to spend too long on the internet, unsure whether she could be certain of deleting all the history, she'd failed to notice the road where the taxi had dropped her was an extremely long one - a lot longer than she'd envisaged, which meant she'd got a ten minute walk.

Teagan continued, keeping her eyes fixed ahead rather than allowing them to skitter in every direction like they wanted to and urged herself to keep calm. *You'll be there soon*, she repeated in her mind. *You'll be there and then it will be ok.*

But however much she kept telling herself that; however much she'd repeated that same sentence over and over all evening, afternoon and most of the previous night as she'd lain awake, Teagan had been unable to shake off the very real and consistently clamouring voice that kept telling her it *wasn't* ok.

None of this was ok and it was pushing her to the very limits of sanity.

She glanced at the numbers on the shops as best as she could without losing track of where she was walking. *Still quite a way to go.*

As far as she could see there was no turning anywhere up ahead signalling the road she needed to turn down to find the meeting place. *Wasn't meeting around the back of somewhere, rather than in the open, risky?*

Fear travelled further up Teagan's legs, making the brisk walk even more arduous. Her calf muscles were already burning and the shoes she wore were a bad decision with the distance she found herself travelling. *She really had messed this up.*

'Not long,' she muttered - anything to distract from the fast-forming blisters on her heels.

Teagan's mind moved to Kim. Kim *knew* she was meeting Jonah - that much was obvious and exactly what she'd been told to expect, but the question was, was she being followed?

Would she even know?

Oh God, she wasn't any good at this sort of stuff.

Walking into someone, Teagan almost died of fright, her panicked eyes darting up to the stranger she'd just collided with.

See, her concentration had been elsewhere. Stupid, stupid. Would she ever learn? Was this man something to do with O'Hara? Would he drag her off?

'I'm sorry,' Teagan garbled. 'I...'

'Are you alright?' The man asked, concern in his eyes. He reached out to steady the young woman as she wobbled.

'I'm fine,' Teagan cried, jerking out of the man's reach. Ignoring his confused expression, she hurried off as fast as possible, the pain of her rubbing shoes now entirely irrelevant.

. . . .

'LET'S GO,' Nero muttered the second Heath opened the car door, refusing to show relief that the man had actually done as instructed. For a very long couple of minutes he'd been convinced Pointer would do a runner and screw up the entire operation.

But now, both Pointer and Jonah Powell's wallet were safely back in the car, which was one thing less to worry about. *But only one…*

'Thank God for that!' Heath exclaimed, his breath coming in ragged bursts as he fumbled with his seat belt, aware the car was already rapidly heading out of the station. 'There was no one there.'

He still couldn't quite believe nothing had happened to him whilst he'd lurked around the security boxes. He'd genuinely expected a hail of bullets to fly in his direction, but there was nothing. *Nothing at all.*

'I didn't expect there to be,' Nero said. *And that confirmed that so far, it was all good.*

He glanced at the clock, knowing he needed to get a shift on. Time was tight. A few minutes to reach the pickup point, but providing the traffic didn't snarl up, he'd be bang on time.

'Are you dropping me back now?' Heath asked, glad his heart rate was returning to a rhythm compatible with life.

'Back?' Nero frowned. 'No. It's on to the next bit now.'

'What?' Heath screeched. 'You didn't say anything about a next bit!'

'That's because should you have been accosted, you wouldn't have given anything up under torture.'

Heath remained silent as they continued up the road, numbly acknowledging that torture could have been a possibility.

A part of him wanted to ask what the next bit was, but knew it was pointless.

Swinging down another road, Nero clocked what he was

looking for and pulled over.

Heath's eyes darted around. 'What are we stopping for?'

'Give me the wallet!' Nero barked, his eyes trained in the rear view mirror on the car he'd pulled in front of, watching as the occupant got out.

'The wallet?' Heath fumbled in his pocket, his heart lurching into his throat as the back door flew open. *Christ! Was it O'Hara?*

'Right, go!' Jonah yelled, swinging his legs into the car and slamming the door.

Leaning forward, he slapped Heath on the shoulder. 'I take it that went off without a hitch? Nice work. Now, give me the wallet.'

Heath robotically passed the wallet into the back seat, his fear intensifying.

Nero sped back off up the road, jerking his head in the direction of the car they had left behind. 'That motor will be removed. We'll go to the next one now. It's in place.'

Heath wanted to ask what was happening, but even if he thought he'd get an answer, his tongue was glued to the roof of his mouth. All he could do was wait. He'd be told nothing and could do jack shit about that, apart from accept whatever his next instructions might be. He instead closed his eyes in desperation as Nero jolted over a series of speed humps.

Jonah's eyes remained glued to his wristwatch. He had five minutes to pick up the next untraceable motor and reach the meeting point.

It was cutting it fine. *Really* fine, but he'd drive through every single red light if he had to. He could only hope Teagan hadn't arrived early. Adams would be waiting, that was guaranteed and if he was late, Adams may decide to bypass him and take off with Teagan instead.

He could only hope his instinct about what else Adams wanted was equal to what was driving his obsession with Teagan.

'At this next drop Pointer, you can get out too. It's only a couple of minutes walk to the flat from there,' Jonah said.

'Flat?' Heath repeated, unsure he actually wanted to know when it came down to it.

'You're paying the fucked-up twins a visit,' Nero growled. 'Make sure they don't leave the place.'

Heath's eyes widened. 'You want me to go to Kim's flat?'

'We don't *want* you to go, Pointer,' Jonah spat. 'You *are* going. They know the deal is going down and that Teagan's meeting me, so I don't want them getting twitchy and deciding to take in upon themselves to stick their oar in.'

Heath blinked. 'B-But what should I say? What do I do if...'

'Do and say whatever you want!' Jonah yelled, his hand ready on the door handle as Nero screeched up behind a red motor. 'But keep them there by whatever means.'

'The keys are behind the front wheel arch.' Nero met eyes with Jonah in the rear view mirror. 'Good luck. I'll be in position.'

Nodding, Jonah jabbed Heath in the shoulder with his finger. 'And you. Out! The flat's on the next road.' With that, Jonah leapt from the car and dashed to the other motor.

FIFTY TWO

SITTING THE OPPOSITE SIDE of the desk in Benowitz's cramped backroom, Ron O'Hara quelled his rising agitation, but found it increasingly difficult. It was almost 8 and *still* no sign of the Russians.

Acutely aware this fossilised specimen of a man was scrutinising him with beady eyes, Ron refused to give Benowitz further ammunition to suspect him by looking at his watch again and instead cranked his face into a strange-looking smile. 'Nice place you've got here.'

No it wasn't. It was a crummy shithole and even if Benowitz's Fine Jewels wasn't shamed enough by being sandwiched between two of the swishest-looking jewellers in the Garden just to accentuate its shabbiness, it was still a dump better suited to a ghetto. But even ghetto shops would have had a paint job over the last sixty years.

When he'd first approached, he'd taken one look at the crumbling façade and thought for a fleeting moment the whole thing must be a wind-up. That was until he'd gone inside and seen Stan Leyton.

But, Ron acknowledged with an internal smirk, crappy façade or not, the place was packed to the rafters with millions worth of clobber. And had he not known that any minute now he stood to walk away a multimillionaire, he'd bash this frail old codger to the floor and shove as much of the contents of this doss hole as possible into his bag.

Something to consider for the future, perhaps?

Ron almost laughed. *What was he thinking?* He wouldn't need to pull off any more jobs ever again after tonight.

'I have to say, Mr...'

Ron's head snapped away from the tray of top quality sapphires on the desk when the man spoke. 'Taylor. Ronald Taylor.' *He might as well adopt the name Lena had used and honour her once again.*

'Yes, Mr Taylor. I have to say I'm a little surprised you have come in place of the original seller.' Benowitz eyed O'Hara suspiciously.

'Mr Powell, you mean? He assured me he'd already told you of the situation. A problem arose at the club,' Ron explained. 'An unfortunate accident with one of the dancers. He asked me to conduct the deal being as I'm aware of all the details.'

Benowitz frowned. 'It's very unusual...'

Ron hid his panic. He hadn't factored the old boy might prove a spanner in the works. *Christ.* He didn't want to have to kill the old fart. The Russians wouldn't want to deal with anyone who wasn't sanctioned - not with shit like this. His eyes darted to Stan Leyton.

'I don't wish to interrupt, Mr Benowitz,' Stan said, 'but Mr Powell *did* call earlier. I mentioned it, but I think you were occupied with costing. Perhaps you didn't take in what I said?'

Benowitz glanced at the extra-large sapphire in the centre of the tray on his desk. 'Did I...?'

Ron bit back a smile, not knowing why he'd even worried. The old fucker was clearly demented. *Nice one, Stan.* 'Rest assured, Mr Benowitz, this is all perfectly above board and fully sanctioned by Mr Powell. If you'd rather, you can call to check, although I don't know if you'll get hold of him.' *And no one will ever again by the time I'm finished.*

Benowitz flapped his arthritic hand in O'Hara's direction. 'If he's already called, then that's fine. These days I get so engrossed in things I sometimes pay little attention to anything else.'

Ron nodded sympathetically. 'I get like that,' he lied. *The mad old coot.* 'I meant to say, I'm sorry I'm a bit early. The taxi made really good time. I wonder if the buyers will arrive any time soon? I'm eager to get this sorted. It will be a huge weight off Mr Powell's mind.'

Benowitz leant forward. They'll be here, don't you fret.' His long fingers knitted together. 'Would you like to get the "unicorns" out ready?'

Ron faltered. Should he get the prize out before seeing the colour of the Russians' money? He glanced at Stan, seeing an imperceptible nod.

Assured, O'Hara pulled the envelope from his pocket and savouring the moment, spent a long time undoing it. He slowly tipped the collection of pink diamonds onto the newly laid piece of black velvet spread in a vacant part of the cluttered desk. 'Here we go… The rest of the unicorns.'

Benowitz sucked air between his teeth in appreciation and picked up his loupe. 'Magnificent. Absolutely magnificent,' he muttered.

O'Hara smiled ingratiatingly and watched Benowitz start examining the glittering jewels. Revelling in the kudos that accompanied his ability to deliver such fine pieces, he decided to use this time Benowitz was otherwise distracted and while waiting for the Russians, to drop Adams a quick text.

By now, Powell would know the diamonds had gone and he wanted to make sure the bastard wasn't on route here.

• • • •

ROBERT TUTTED with irritation as his phone buzzed again:

Still waiting. Make sure JP nowhere near.

Cancelling the message, Robert hastily refreshed the tracker, his impatience unbearable. It was 8 o'clock. Teagan was still not here and neither was Powell...

As Jonah Powell's coordinates scrolled up the screen, anticipation replaced Robert's building anxiety.

Powell was approaching the meeting point. O'Hara need not worry, he was not heading to Hatton Garden. The stupid bastard was so obsessed with Teagan he was heading *here* just as foreseen. He'd miss his diamonds being sold from under his nose.

But Robert wouldn't bother wasting time putting O'Hara's mind at rest. There were too many pressing things to do.

Opening the glove box, Robert pulled out the towel-wrapped gun. Chucking the towel to one side, he checked the gun was properly loaded and the safety catch off. 'Thank you, mummy dearest,' he smiled.

Shoving the gun in his inside pocket, Robert saw her before the figure was barely recognisable.

Teagan.

He'd recognise her from the shape of her legs; from the way her shoulders were positioned with a handbag on one side. He didn't need to see her face. *It was her.*

Robert's mind clamoured with an unusual cacophony of conflicting sounds and thoughts. Deviations to an agreed plan *never* happened, but it was happening.

He gripped the steering wheel to steady the rising tremoring of his fingers. He could not deviate. *Would* not deviate. He'd prepared for this. It was almost time and he couldn't change it now...

But it was strong. *Very strong...*

Robert bit into his bottom lip, fighting against the rolling thoughts.

But he *could* do it... He could take Teagan now. He could drive up the street and she would get in his car. It was unlikely he'd have to force her because she would be obedient, like the puppet she was.

He could take her and be gone before Powell even arrived.

Robert's eyes flicked to the tracker once again, his fingers twitching, then physically shook his head, anger with himself mounting.

She'd done it again. The vile temptress had infiltrated his brain, causing it to malfunction and urge him to follow a path not on the planned route.

Robert's jaw clenched. Well, he wouldn't allow it. This was prearranged and decided.

He needed to pay the Powells back, remember?

'Do you remember?' Robert said loudly, his voice echoing around the interior of the car. He'd promised himself he would make them pay for everything they had done. *Everything*. How would they pay if Jonah Powell was allowed to walk free and escape his designated punishment? To escape the arranged end?

'Nearly, Teagan, you little whore. *Nearly*, but not quite,' Robert muttered. 'You almost tricked me, but you failed. I, however, will not!'

Resolute, he started the engine and pulled out of the road into the next one, parking up not 300 yards from where he'd previously been.

Arranging the position of his rear view mirror, Robert trained his eyes on the road behind.

The second Teagan crossed that road to walk around to the back where he'd heard with his very own ears Powell telling her they'd meet, then he'd move again.

Robert couldn't wait to see Teagan's face. How he'd dreamt of this moment and it was *finally* here. And in the very exact way he'd planned.

FIFTY THREE

PRESSING THE INTERCOM, Heath waited, deciding he'd rather lie face down in the sewer being gnawed by rats than come here, but what was the alternative?

He sighed resignedly. He was finished whichever way he looked at it, so he may as well just take it on the chin. There was nowhere to run. Nowhere to hide. And time had run out.

Either way, tonight he would be removed from existence and despite his initial theory about Jonah Powell, he knew that out of all of them, the man wasn't what he'd always thought.

If Heath could pick which one of them he'd prefer to knock him off this mortal coil, it would be Jonah Powell. At least the man would undertake the job without gloating, so if having to spend his last few hours in the company of Kieran and Kim O'Hara would help to ensure Ron O'Hara wasn't the executioner left standing at the end of this, then he'd do his very best to achieve that.

'Yeah?' A voice crackled.

Hearing Kim's voice through the intercom immediately made Heath's skin feel infested with ants, but dismissed his internal shudder. 'Kim, it's Heath. Can I come in?'

The buzzer released the door and Heath reluctantly made

his way up the stairs to the apartment, a plan formulating in his mind.

It may work, it may not. If it didn't, then he'd think of something else, but he suspected this might just be enough to keep them here and hanging on his every word.

How long he was expected to babysit these two, he didn't know, but guessed it all depended on the outcome. And it was probably best not to dwell on what that outcome could be.

'What do you want?' Kim scowled at Heath standing at her door. 'Didn't think you bothered paying me social calls? If you've come round because you've decided you fancy me after all, then you're too fucking late!'

His rebuff of her advances at the start still stung and she wasn't in the mood to be pleasant because she was worried and on edge. It *had* to go well tonight otherwise this charade would have been for nothing.

Heath stared at the obligatory glass of wine in Kim's hand. 'I can assure you that's not why I'm here.' The thought made him feel just as horrific as it had done the first time around.

Kim's mouth twisted into an ugly grimace. 'Then you might as well piss off!' She went to slam the door in Heath's face, finding his foot stuck in it.

'Kim, let him in.' Kieran rushed into the hallway. 'He might have some news.'

'Finally something sensible comes out of your mouth Kieran,' Heath sniped. He might as well get a few digs in while there was still time.

Scowling, Kim released the door and Heath stepped inside and moved into the living area.

'Well?' Kieran cried impatiently. 'What have you heard?'

Heath had to admit that despite the circumstances he was looking forward to upsetting this pair, even if it ended up being short-lived.

He spent an unnaturally long amount of time making himself comfortable on the sofa before moulding his face into something that passed for sincerity. 'I don't want to worry you unnecessarily, but I think something might have happened to Ron.'

'What?' Kim screeched, spilling her wine down her orange mini-dress. 'What's happened?'

Heath shook his head. 'I don't know anything for sure.' He leant forward conspiringly. 'But I think we could have been set-up, so we need to be extra careful. That's why I'm here.'

Kieran frowned. 'What do you mean, set up?' He pulled his phone from his pocket. 'Uncle Ron should have done the deal by now. I'm calling him.'

'Don't be crazy!' Heath cried, snatching the mobile from Kieran's hand. 'That's what I've come to tell you.' He pulled the back off the phone and yanked out the SIM card.

'What are you doing?' Kieran screeched, his hand reaching towards his phone.

'Seriously, leave it. And you, Kim. Take your SIM card out now. Quickly!' Heath hissed. *This was fun. And now Kieran had lost his progress on snakes. Ha ha ha.*

Kim fumbled to remove the back of her phone, her fake nails hinging off in the process. 'I can't do it.'

'Here, let me.' Heath took the phone and hastily removed the SIM. *Now they couldn't call anyone. Not that, with any luck, they'd have anyone to call.*

'Where's Ron?' Kim cried. 'What's going on, Heath?'

'I think the police might have him.' Heath nodded to the SIM cards he'd placed on the table. 'That's why I'm making sure none of us can be located via our mobile phones.'

'You mean like Robert Adams was doing to Powell?' Kieran said, his voice holding a hint of suspicion.

Heath's eyes narrowed. *One for you Adams.* 'I think Adams could be the one behind this.' He lowered his voice to a whisper, almost laughing at the suspense he could see on these idiots' faces. 'I think Robert Adams might be an undercover cop.'

'What?' Kieran roared. 'The fucking snake!'

'Yeah,' Heath nodded. 'That's exactly what I thought. It now makes sense why Adams offered Ron the money to buy my debts, remember? It was obviously part of an undercover operation.'

'Fucking hell!' Kieran exclaimed. 'Does Ron know?'

'If it's true, he probably does by now,' Heath said. And if the worst happened and O'Hara walked away from this, then at least he could take pinch of solace that Robert Adams would be next in line for the chop if it was believed he was a copper.

'Wait a minute,' Kim frowned. 'If Ron doesn't know and hasn't told you this, then I don't think Robert Adams would have suddenly come out and told you he's a cop, so how do *you* know this?'

Heath blinked. *Bollocks. He hadn't thought of that. Shit. Quick, think...*

'I don't know anything for certain. All I know is that the deal is going down tonight. It should have already been done. We know that, right? Well, Adams was supposed to be in contact with Ron, and us, but I've heard nothing. I've tried to call him three times, but it goes to voicemail.'

Kim frowned. 'That doesn't make him a copper though, does it? Maybe *he's* been nicked?'

Heath shook his head. 'No it doesn't make him a copper, but think about it... Why would he have all that knowledge, as well as the kit to track people? Our phones are probably bugged too.'

Kim glanced at Kieran. *It made sense. Shit.* 'But where's Ron? Has he been arrested?'

Heath shrugged. 'I don't know. All I know is that I can't get in contact with Adams and he's the one who was supposed to be laying the road clear for Ron...'

Kieran folded his arms and stared from his sister to Heath. 'Or what if the deal *has* been done and Ron has done one and cut us out?'

'Uncle Ron wouldn't do that to us. To *me*,' Kim cried indignantly.

'Wouldn't he?' Kieran raised an eyebrow. The way Ron treated him half the time that would be something he expected might just happen.

'Look, I don't profess to know the answers, but I think it's sensible if we lie low. Certainly until we get word from *someone*.' Heath sat back and watched him and Kieran bat around their analysis. One way of passing the time and he'd done well there. He just hoped it wouldn't be too long.

• • • •

SWERVING INTO THE ROAD behind the line of shops, Jonah's heart raced. *There she was, thank Christ!*

Pleased to see the area deserted, Jonah pulled alongside Teagan. Despite his growing fear for what might unfold, seeing her eyes light up, his heart swelled.

Oh, for this to be normal.

Wincing at the tightness of his suit, Jonah leant across and pulled the door handle. 'Get in.'

Teagan scrambled into the car. 'Jonah,' she gasped. 'What's going on? You've got to tell me. This is j…'

Jonah silenced Teagan with his mouth. He had to kiss her. *Needed* to kiss her. He had to at least do that before anything else.

Feeling the overwhelming urge to shove everything else aside, Jonah reluctantly pulled away before the temptation overtook him. His eyes searched hers. 'I'm so glad you're here,' he said, a trace of a smile on his lips.

Breathless, Teagan laid a trembling hand on Jonah's cheek. 'Please tell me what's going on. What's happening? I need to...'

'There's no time,' Jonah said, knowing Adams must be here by now. 'You need to trust me on this and do exactly as I say.'

Teagan frowned. 'But, I...'

'*Please* Teagan,' Jonah cried. 'There's no time. I want you to get out of the car.'

'What?' Teagan searched Jonah's eyes. *After all of this he wanted her to get out of the car?*

'Pretend we're having an argument. Say whatever you like. Just make it look real.'

'What?' Teagan shrieked again. 'Jonah, I don't understand. I...'

'Just do it,' Jonah yelled, then lowered his voice. 'Please just do it. Go. Go now!'

Teagan reached for the door handle in a state of confusion, when Jonah grabbed her arm. 'And I meant what I said the other night.'

Teagan swung around to face Jonah. *He loved her, yet wanted a row?* She didn't understand this, but the urge to melt into his arms and tell him to stop whatever he was doing burnt.

'Go!' Jonah hissed.

Hurrying out of the door, Teagan slammed it and moved to walk away.

Jonah scrambled out of the car behind Teagan. 'Don't walk away from me!' he screamed at her retreating back.

Teagan turned around, confusion hammering inside her skull. Seeing the hint of pleading in Jonah's eyes she knew he was deadly serious. She had no idea what was going on or why, but much as it didn't make sense, knew she must do what he asked. 'I'm not falling for it!' she cried, resisting the urge to laugh at this bizarre drama.

'At least take the flowers.' Jonah thrust a large bouquet into Teagan's arms. 'I've said I'm sorry and that should be good enough.'

Teagan laughed bitterly. 'You think a bunch of flowers will sort this? Forget it!' Throwing the flowers onto the floor, she stared at Jonah.

'I won't apologise again,' Jonah spat. 'You're lucky to even get that! Most people don't!'

'And we all know what most people get!' Teagan called over her shoulder.

'Walk away from me and it will be the last time, you ungrateful bitch! First you play games with my brother and now me?' Jonah hissed, hating himself for saying such things. He had to make Teagan's hate look real and only hoped she would understand. *Come on, Adams - where the fuck are you? I know you're here somewhere...*

Teagan froze for a split second. How could Jonah say that? How could he mention that bastard? His voice; the way he'd sounded... He'd sounded just like... like his brother...

'I think you've said enough,' she said quietly. 'And I won't be coming back.'

Continuing walking, Teagan suddenly came to the conclusion this was nothing to do with anything. This was an extravagant game set up to control her and manipulate her and she'd fallen for it...

A lone tear rolled down Teagan's face. *Jonah wasn't following. This was real. How could he? How could he do this to her?*

Teagan didn't even notice the figure loom out from behind the jutting wall until he was over her with his hands on her shoulders. She yelped in fright, then seeing who it was, froze, too terrified to even scream.

Robert pulled Teagan towards him. 'Finally!'

'R-Robert!' Teagan cried. 'What are you doing here? Get away from me!'

'Adams!' Jonah roared, his footsteps loud in the empty space.

With his face locked in a grimace of pure hatred, Robert dragged Teagan to the side, watching Jonah Powell's hand fumbling inside his jacket.

Powell hadn't expected this, the loser. The man would never risk shooting with Teagan so close. Besides, he was taking too long fumbling for his gun, the fool. Powell was disorganised. Distracted. Too late.

But he wasn't...

Robert pulled his gun. 'You're finished, Powell!'

Sweat poured down Teagan's face, panic intensifying. He was going to shoot Jonah. *Oh no, no, NO!*

She flailed around as much as possible to free her arms from Robert's grip and deflect him or knock him off centre. 'Robert! STOP!'

'Teagan, leave it!' Jonah called.

'You're finished, Powell,' Robert repeated, his voice crystal clear and monotonous. His joy was so compounded he could barely get his words out. 'You dare to take something of mine. Now you will pay.'

'ROBERT!' Teagan screamed, the noise of the gunshot drowning out her plea.

She watched in terror as Jonah was knocked backwards when the bullet hit him squarely in the chest, his own gun clattering to the floor.

'No! NOOOO!' Teagan shrieked, her fists blindly pummelling Robert's side. He'd shot Jonah. Robert Adams had shot Jonah. He'd shot the man she loved. 'JONAH!' she screamed, desperate to go to him.

'Keep away from him,' Robert snarled, dragging Teagan with him as he edged forward.

Powell was dead. Admittedly, he was a tad disappointed he'd failed to list the reasons why he'd had to die, like he'd planned, but it didn't matter. Teagan was what mattered and now she was *his*.

Teagan's lungs fought to drag in oxygen, her breaths coming in heaving gasps. Her legs buckled and the guttural roaring within her own mind she slowly realised was coming from her mouth.

Was he dead? Was Jonah dead?

Robert dragged Teagan further forward. He just needed to check. He could always put a few more bullets in the fucker, but he couldn't risk bringing attention by more gunfire unless he had to. The one shot he'd taken would probably go unnoticed.

Nearing the body, Robert could already see Powell's awful blue eyes staring, unblinking at the darkening sky. 'Now you're mine,' he whispered, his lips against Teagan's ear.

Teagan gagged as Robert pulled her tighter and forced herself to stare at the man on the floor.

'We need to go,' Robert muttered.

Teagan clawed at Robert's sleeve as he began pulling her slowly back in the opposite direction. 'I can't leave him. I...'

'That man is of no concern of yours.'

Robert saw the flash of the metal too late. The bullet had already left Jonah Powell's gun in an exact trajectory into his right temple and could not be avoided.

Teagan stood motionless, blood and tissue splattering the side of her face from Robert's exploding skull and watched transfixed as the man crashed in slow-motion to the floor.

FIFTY FOUR

TEAGAN SANK TO HER KNEES, unable and unwilling to process the situation.

Scrambling from the ground, Jonah rushed to Teagan's side, desperate to ensure she was unharmed. He prided himself on being a good aim, but there was always a chance the shot that hit Adams could have grazed her.

Squatting on his haunches, he pulled her into his arms. 'Are you ok? Tell me you're ok,' he cried. 'You're not hurt?'

Teagan stared at Jonah blankly, her eyes unseeing.

'The vest worked then?' Nero moved from his position at the end of the service road. 'Come on. You two need to disappear.'

Teagan's glazed eyes shot from Jonah to Nero, then back to Jonah, before she looked back to Robert Adams' body, her mind rolling in waves of horror and disbelief.

Jonah wasn't dead? He wasn't dead? But...

Her shaking hand moved slowly to her face, her fingertips touching lumps of gelatinous mess. Jerking her hand away, she stared at the bloodied tissue on her fingers and it was then that the uncontrollable screaming started.

Jonah pulled Teagan closer, both to comfort and silence her.

'Shh, shh, It's ok.'

'Get away from me!' Teagan screamed, her bloodied hands lashing out wildly, pounding at Jonah's chest.

Jonah turned to Nero in desperation. 'She's hysterical! I need to get her out of here before she alerts attention.' Getting to his feet he dragged Teagan with him, but she was like a woman possessed. He winced against the screams splintering his ear drums, then reluctantly slapped his hand over her mouth, muffling the noise. 'Teagan! *Listen* to me! You need to be quiet,'

'NNNNN!' Teagan squawked, thrashing about harder, almost pulling Jonah off balance.

'Sorry mate.' Nero stepped forward and raised his hand. 'I'm going to have to slap her. She's going to fuck this up.'

'No you won't!' Gwen cried, pulling Teagan out of Jonah's arms and into hers. She enveloped the wildly convulsing body and began speaking softly and slowly into Teagan's ear. She then turned to Jonah. 'Get in your car.'

Nero stared in astonishment. 'What's Gwen doing here?'

Jonah almost sagged with relief. He hadn't thought she would make it in time. 'I listened to what you said and brought her back in. I'll explain later.' He jerked his head at Robert Adams' body. 'Do what you need to do and I'll meet you at Benowitz's.'

Quickly following as Gwen led Teagan towards the car, Jonah threw himself in the driver's seat and started the engine.

Nero shook his head in silent confusion and watched Jonah's car disappear from the service road, then took a deep breath to realign his thoughts.

He pressed his hand against his jacket, double-checking the envelope was still in situ. Bulletproof vests always made things difficult to feel. They bloody worked though, thankfully.

A grin cracked his face. Jonah had done well.

Even from behind the trade bins, Nero had seen how tight the shot was for Jonah to take. One slight movement at the wrong time and Teagan would have been a goner. And to do that from his position on the floor made it doubly difficult, but fuck, he'd pulled it off.

Standing over Adams, Nero stared expressionlessly at the remains of the man's skull. 'You fucking mad bastard!' he spat.

Hearing the unmistakable and increasing sound of police sirens in the distance, Nero unzipped his bomber jacket and pulled out the envelope. Shoving it in the inside pocket of Adams' suit jacket, he hastily made his way from the road and back to his car two streets away.

It would only be a few minutes before the police arrived. They could draw their own conclusions, but for now there was no time to waste getting to Benowitz's, meeting Jonah and completing the last part of this plan.

• • • •

RON WAS BECOMING more twitchy with every second that passed. 8.20 and still no sign of the bloody Russians. It looked like the bastards would turn up bang on fucking time, rather than early? *Bloody typical.*

He'd have thought they would be eager to get their hands on this collection that would rake them in a mint.

His eyes moved back to his mobile. Still no texts from Adams. Four he'd sent now without Benowitz noticing and still not a peep from that weird fuck. What was betting he'd got his hands on Teagan and was busy wanking over her back at his poxy B&B with that creepy backdrop of pictures.

They'd had a deal and Adams had welched on it.

Ron scowled. Adams had promised he'd text to say when Powell was on the move and by Christ, no matter how much the man was in love with a stupid woman, he wouldn't miss out on the chance of trying to catch whoever had filched the diamonds from under his nose, would he?

The Russians had to hurry up and get here before Powell turned up. That's if Powell was insane enough to risk the ire of turning up to a deal empty handed?

Unlikely.

Regardless, Ron had to get the money and get out of here before anyone came looking.

He glanced at his phone again, then cut Stan a look, receiving a raise of an eyebrow in return.

The buzzer of the shop startled Ron enough for his phone to slip from his hands and clatter to the floor.

'That must be our customers.' Stan shot Ron a hidden wink. 'I'll let them in, shall I, Mr Benowitz?'

Benowitz looked up. 'No. I must go. The Russians will not deal with anyone they are not familiar with. It has to be me.'

Ron was convinced he heard a loud creak as Benowitz painstakingly pushed himself to his feet. His movements were so slow they all but defied gravity.

Come on, come on, Ron willed, the palms his hands leaving sweaty patches on his trousers.

His teeth cut into his cheek with the effort of refraining from shouting at the crippled old goat to hurry the fuck up. Waiting on the doorstep with millions in their briefcases whilst an old codger shuffled through a shop to open the bastard door, wasn't the best way to pull off a swift and easy deal.

FIFTY FIVE

JONAH RACED towards Hatton Garden. It had been less than a two-minute diversion dropping Gwen and Teagan where he'd told Gwen to leave her car, but every second was another second longer before he could return to his life and finally say all of this was over.

And it wouldn't be a second too soon.

Taking the corner a bit too fast, Jonah stabbed the button for the electric window, sweat running freely down his brow.

The added layers and bulk of the bulletproof vest was taking its toll and it felt like he was in a sauna, but by God, it had served him well.

And he may have cause to rely on it again.

He'd hated leaving Teagan in the state she was in, but he had little choice.

Worry churned. He'd seen the disgust on her face; the hatred shining like a laser beam through the splatters of gore on her beautiful face.

How he wished he could have warned her what would happen - or what he *hoped* would happen. It wouldn't have been so much of a shock.

Jonah's fingers fumbled for a much needed cigarette. How

could he have told her? She would have made it nigh on impossible for him to do what was needed.

If she'd realised the whole thing was such a gamble and he could have been the one lying dead on the floor like she'd initially believed, then she'd have begged him not to go through with it.

Jonah dragged deeply from his cigarette and stamped his foot down harder on the accelerator.

Yes, she'd have pleaded and begged and if she had, he might have relented and abandoned the idea.

Why?

Because he'd do anything for her.

Would she ever forgive him for allowing her to think him dead? Would she feel he'd placed her at risk?

It may have looked like she'd been at risk, but Nero would have offed Adams before that happened. Nero was waiting gun poised, to step in if needed the whole time. Jonah knew that without a shadow of a doubt, he would have done exactly that.

He dragged his hand through his hair, wincing as he twisted, the bruising on his ribs coming out already. Bulletproof vest or not, where that bullet had struck him bloody hurt.

He glared at the hole in his shirt. *Christ.*

Would Teagan ever forgive him? He'd heard her screaming. Her anguish when she'd thought him dead. But it was the only way. And the way he would do *this* too.

Pulling up behind Nero's car, Jonah checked his gun, then stashed it back in his pocket. Taking a final glance in the mirror at the road behind, he got out of the car.

• • • •

RON LOOKED AT STAN, desperation in his eyes. 'Christ,' he muttered, glancing back at the time on his phone, grateful the screen hadn't smashed when he'd dropped it.

He had to do this quick and get the hell out of here. Time was now very much of the essence.

Hearing voices, he found himself self-consciously

adjusting his tie and raising himself from the chair. The ironed-on smile on his face held firm only until he saw who followed Benowitz into the backroom.

'Good evening, O'Hara,' Jonah said, his voice disturbingly calm as he looked the ugly balding man up and down.

Staring directly into O'Hara's owl-like eyes, Jonah remained alert for any movement the man made towards the loaded gun he knew was undoubtedly on his person, but all he could see on the revolting face in front of him was surprise, mixed with shock, along with a good helping of terror.

Jonah smiled. It would be so easy to truss this bastard up and torture the life from him over the next few days. Although this was something he would usually relish in an opportunity such as this, he felt only the need to finish it for good so he could go home.

But he couldn't do that without at least letting this pathetic creature know exactly how much he had failed.

Remembering himself, Ron wiped the shock from his face. Powell had the fucking cheek to barge in on his deal? He may have caught him off guard, but the jumped-up prick had failed when it came to making sure he looked after his own goods. Powell may not have a gun in his hand, he didn't doubt that it wasn't on his person. But that was ok because he had thought of that.

An invisible smirk played at the corner of Ron's mouth. He'd foreseen the possibility of a double cross. Ok, so he'd thought it would most likely be in the guise of the Russians, but it made no difference. He had the backup and he knew it.

He drummed his fingers on the desk - the sign for Stan Leyton to get into position and ready.

Jonah moved further into the small room, waiting as Benowitz shuffled to lean unsteadily against a metal filing cabinet. He peered at the selection of pink diamonds on the black velvet. 'Expecting someone else?'

A full smile slid onto Ron's lips. 'What are you going to do now then Powell? Shoot me?'

Jonah raised his eyebrows and smiled coldly. 'Why would I want to shoot you, O'Hara? For killing one of my best men? For raping and murdering one of my staff? For having a plan with Robert Adams to kidnap the woman I love, or perhaps just for stealing my father's goods? Which one? All of them? What would you suggest?'

'These diamonds are mine now, Powell,' Ron spat. 'They were mine anyway. It was *your* family who ripped off mine and it was *you* who killed my niece.'

'But the one thing I wouldn't bother wasting a bullet for would be *those*.' Jonah nodded at the diamonds.

O'Hara laughed, his yellow teeth looking worse in the dingy orange light of the room. *Yeah, yeah play it down Powell. You know as well as I do this is a stand off and I've got one up on you....*

'I'd be careful, Powell. You may think you're all that for working out Adams' plan for the woman you fancy a bit with - silly tart that she is, but the fact that you're here shows that you were too fucking late!' Ron snarled.

Seeing a vein pulsating in Powell's clenched jaw, Ron jutted out his chin, all mirth gone from his ugly face. 'You haven't seen what Adams has done to that room of his ready for that bird of yours, but I have...' He whistled through his teeth. 'Fucking madder than a bat Adams is. But your tart will lap up the attention, I'm sure. Slags always do, don't they?'

Jonah tensed, ready to strike O'Hara, but reined himself in.

Pleased to get the desired reaction, Ron continued. 'Plastered his walls full of photos of her he has, but now he's got the real deal.' He shrugged his big shoulders. 'Personally, he'd have been better setting his sights on that other slut of yours. I know from personal experience her tits are a lot bigger, even if they were fucking fake!'

A vein pulsing in his temple, Jonah wanted to torture this bastard after all, but getting the job completed was more important. 'Hmm, so you say, but unfortunately I shot Adams dead only minutes ago, so that's pissed on your theory.' *And now to really get him...*

'I should also add the Russians were pleased with the sale.' Jonah casually picked up a sapphire and turned it around in the light. 'It was a shame you missed it really.' He nodded back at the diamonds. 'Then again, Russians aren't usually interested in fakes.'

Ron blinked. *Fakes?* Trickles of icy-cold filtering through his veins *These were fakes?*

Watching O'Hara's dawning reality, Jonah smiled. 'Yeah, shame you didn't notice. You'd have saved yourself the grief. Mr Benowitz here was good enough to loan me those glass diamonds which I left for you. You know, the ones you lifted from the security box.'

Leaning nonchalantly against the wall, he put his hands in his trousers pockets and sighed. 'I've done you a favour really, because the Russians would have blown your head off for attempting to turn them over. Still, when I concluded the deal with them earlier this evening whilst your expert tracker was following my wallet to the station, they left happy customers. It's a shame Adams is no longer around, but hey, shit happens...'

Nausea bubbled in Ron's throat, quickly replaced with rage. His head swung to the pink diamonds. *His pink diamonds were fakes?*

Sweat poured down his back. He'd been tucked up by this old bastard, Benowitz? And he'd done it for Powell? 'You piece of shit,' he growled at the old man.

Whether he liked it or not, Ron knew he'd lost out on the money, but he wasn't losing out on *everything*. A percentage of this was salvageable. Taking Powell out, along with his fucking monkey sidekick and the old bastard would do and then he'd lift the contents of this mouldy shop.

He tapped his finger on the table three times, pretending to think, knowing it was the final signal Stan Leyton was waiting for. *The one that would take this sly cunt by surprise.*

Ron's eyes flashed with malice. 'Think you're fucking

clever, Powell? Well, think again!'

The sudden movement as O'Hara rapidly made for his gun was enough to divert both Nero and Jonah's attention, not seeing Leyton also pull a gun from the other direction.

Ron's mouth cranked into a smile when the gunshot rang out. Now, in the confusion he'd finish the ones left.

His smirk dropped watching Stan Leyton suddenly crumple to the ground, a bullet hole in the centre of his forehead and his eyes darted to the gun in Benowitz's hand. *The old fucker had shot Leyton? Shit. SHIT.*

Finally pulling his own weapon, Ron's mind scrambled who to aim for and got as far as raising the gun to his hip before his world went black.

FIFTY SIX

NERO STEPPED TOWARDS O'Hara's body and planted another bullet in the man's temple for good measure, chuffed Jonah had given him the ok to be the one to take this piece of shit out.

He knew Jonah had his own reasons to want to finish O'Hara and was grateful to be granted the job. 'That's for you, Paul,' Nero muttered, spitting on the crumpled corpse.

Jonah nodded. The killing of Paul Bannister had bothered Nero deeply and although he wanted to take O'Hara out himself, he owed Nero enough to grant him the pleasure.

And as for Mr Benowitz...

Outstretching his hand, Jonah shook the old man's firmly, having nothing but full admiration. He hadn't expected Benowitz to save the day in that way. Not for a minute.

Mr Benowitz grinned. 'You've no idea how difficult it's been putting up with that two-faced rat, Leyton, since I learned he thought it acceptable to betray my trust.'

'I sincerely appreciate your help in this. *All* of it.' Jonah said.

Benowitz opened one of his many safes. Bending down, he grunted with exertion as he pulled two briefcases from the space. 'These I think, are yours…'

Jonah grinned. 'Thanks for holding onto these.' Taking the briefcases, he then handed one of the cases back. 'I'd like you to keep one.'

Shaking his head, Benowitz pushed the case back to Jonah. 'You've already paid my cut, son.'

'You've gone above and beyond for me Mr Benowitz. You took everything I said at face value. You didn't have to do that,' Jonah said, his face grave.

Benowitz laid his withered hand on Jonah's shoulders and smiled, his watery eyes twinkling. 'Listen son, I've no family to leave that sort of money to and there's no pockets in a shroud. Take it as a gift from me on your father's behalf. I know he'd be more than proud of you.'

Feeling a lump constrict his throat, Jonah nodded and turned away.

Hearing the rumble of an engine, Nero slapped Jonah on the back in a bid to save his friend the embarrassment about to avalanche. 'That will be Lenny Dust.'

Jonah nodded, grateful for the distraction. 'We'll get this place cleaned up now.'

Benowitz glanced uncertainly at the two bodies sprawled on his floor and the liberal amount of blood.

Nero jerked his head at O'Hara's corpse. 'This one's booked to be picked up, so one more in the back of a dustcart will make no difference.'

Jonah couldn't help but grin. The relief things had gone to plan was palpable. Slipping his jacket off, he rolled up his sleeves ready for the clean-up. For this one, aside from the help with disposal from his contact in the refuse trade, the rest was down to himself and Nero.

And the sooner they got stuck in, the sooner he could return back to the house, where hopefully he would find Teagan still waiting for him.

. . . .

THE SHOWER THAT WASHED the nightmarish remains of the contents of Robert Adams' skull from Teagan's hair and face had helped somewhat, but watching the chunks of tissue gather in the plug hole before disappearing forever was still fresh in her mind, along with the rivulets of red water cascading over her body which took an age to run clear.

Despite the frantic scrubbing, that image was a constant burning reminder and she wondered whether it would ever go away.

Would the image remain permanently ingrained in her mind's eye, along with the glaring memory of Robert's body?

Feeling her all-over tremoring start again, Teagan knew the vision of Jonah being flung backwards when the bullet hit his chest and that all-encompassing desolation she'd experienced as his body crashed to the floor would take a long time to leave her - if *ever*.

'Come and sit down,' Gwen said, watching Teagan's shock resurface again. She led her over to the sofa and placed a replenished glass of brandy in her shaking hands. 'Drink.'

Gwen knew something big was going down when Jonah had asked her to come to Teller Street at an exact time, but she still hadn't expected to see what she'd seen.

She'd been told Teagan would need someone with her regardless of how things played out. What had she expected, she didn't know, just not *that*.

Frowning, Gwen watched Teagan raise the glass to her lips, her shaking hands causing the brandy to slosh down the clean clothes she'd given her. *The poor girl.*

Christ. She knew Jonah wanted this business finished, but to risk himself the way he had made her feel sick to the bone.

Nausea moved from Gwen's stomach into her throat. It could have ended up very differently. And, she thought with trepidation, it still *could* because he wasn't back yet...

Again, she hadn't been made privy to where Jonah had now dashed off to with Nero after instructing her to get Teagan back to the house, but she had a good inkling. And she could only hope and pray he was safe.

'H-He let me believe he was dead...' Teagan's voice was barely more than a whisper. 'I thought he was dead... I...'

'I know you did love,' Gwen soothed, unsure if there was a way to justify what had panned out. Would this girl ever reconcile what she'd witnessed? It was a tall order.

'How could he do that?' Teagan whimpered.

Gwen remained silent. Saying Jonah probably took that measure because he didn't want to worry her would sound lame. It was most likely the case, but she knew what *she* would have said had she known. And that would have been, *don't be so bloody reckless*.

'I'm only sorry you've been brought into this from the start. I'm even sorrier my interference put you in a worse position' Gwen's eyes brimmed. 'I thought I was doing the right thing.'

Teagan nodded blankly. It made little difference knowing Gwen had pushed her away from Jonah. Neither did it matter that she'd fixed it for him to be with Terri Mason. Normally she would be hurt – angry, but now such things seemed somehow irrelevant.

It didn't matter what had been done or how, it changed nothing. She despised Jonah for doing this and nothing changed that either.

'I don't care if I never see him again,' Teagan snapped, knowing she was lying. She *did* care, but couldn't take it. Not knowing whether he was alive or dead for the second time in one evening was too much.

She couldn't live like this - being back in this house... It would never work. And what Jonah had said about Saul? Her mind retreated to a place where thinking was impossible.

'Teagan,' Gwen said. 'When you're in love that person has the power to destroy you.' *She knew that well enough herself.* 'It works two ways though – you have that power over that person too. Jonah's been worried sick about you. You're all he thinks of.'

Snorting in derision, Teagan reached for her brandy.

FIFTY SEVEN

JONAH PICKED AT HIS NAILS, mentally urging Nero to drive faster. He needed to get back to the house and shut the door on this night.

As much as the relief the diamonds were finally gone and the people who threatened everything that mattered were no longer, none of this was fully closed until he knew he hadn't lost the one thing his power and money could not buy.

Pulling his gun from his inside pocket, he emptied the barrel, shoving the remaining bullets in his breast pocket.

'Worried she's going to shoot you?' Nero asked, watching Jonah out of the corner of his eye.

Jonah grimaced. He'd rather Teagan *did* shoot him compared to the prospect of being without her. He'd promised her he'd finish this and he had. Surely she would understand he'd had to do it this way. It was the only way it would work.

Getting no response, Nero didn't push it, suspecting his attempt at humour wasn't appreciated. Despite the acute stress of the evening, personally he was elated with the result. The chances of it going off the way it had hinged on so many things, yet they'd achieved it. *They'd fucking done it.*

Nero watched Jonah place the now empty gun back into his

inside pocket. 'You don't want to go via the Feathers and show our faces? Offload the weapons?'

Jonah nodded, his jaw set. 'I'm sure.' He was going home and closing the door. He would close the door on this chapter and open another. Hopefully it was still attainable.

'What about Pointer? He's still at the flat with the fucked-up twins.'

'They can wait,' Jonah snapped. As much as Pointer had done his bit in aiding the plan, he wasn't spending a minute longer dealing with him or anything else to do with O'Hara tonight. The O'Hara siblings were nonsensical in the big picture and only followed instructions. With the organ grinder gone, they would do nothing, apart from sit and wait until told otherwise.

As Nero turned into the driveway of the house, Jonah itched to get out of the car and the minute the gravel stopped crunching, he was out and rushing up the steps.

Barging through the front door to find the hall in darkness, panic surged. He raced into the living room. 'Teagan? Gwen?'

Jonah's raging anxiety turned to relief seeing Teagan sitting in the chair. 'You're here!'

Teagan stared at Jonah's frame filling the doorway. Her relief at his return conflicted with burning resentment and the two emotions clashed noisily within her head.

'Thank God you're back!' Gwen gasped, jumping up before stopping. Rushing to confirm Jonah's safety was no longer her place. *It was Teagan's.* 'Where's Nero? Is he alright?'

'He's fine. He's just coming.' Jonah answered Gwen's question, but his eyes remained locked on Teagan. She hadn't said a word. Nothing – just stared at him, *through* him. 'Teagan?'

Rising from the chair, Teagan slowly walked across the room, her face poised. Even she didn't know what she would do until she reached two feet away and then it was obvious.

Launching herself at Jonah, she pummelled his chest, her fists lashing out wildly. 'You bastard!' she screamed.

Jonah didn't attempt to deflect the punches raining into him, he could only concentrate on the pain on Teagan's face. *The pain and worry he'd caused.*

Teagan continued punching, screaming and shouting obscenities. She could hear Jonah saying something, but didn't know what. She wanted to rip his soul out, make him feel like she'd felt. Make him hurt like when she'd believed his life to be extinguished.

She continued until her energy depleted and she sagged forward, spent.

'Teagan...' Jonah said softly, grasping her face between his hands.

Teagan realised she was on the floor. How had she ended up on the floor? Jonah tilting her face up to his, but she didn't want to look. Didn't want to look into his eyes.

'Look at me.' Jonah murmured. 'It's over. It's done...' He traced his finger down Teagan's cheek. 'Teagan, look at me!'

Raising her eyes, Teagan knew she was done. She couldn't be without this man and tonight had proved that beyond anything. 'I thought you were dead,' she whispered.

'I know and I'm sorry,' Jonah said, resting his forehead against hers. 'It won't happen again. I swear I will never do that to you again.'

Tasting the salt of Teagan's tears as Jonah's mouth found hers, neither of them noticed Gwen and Nero subtly leave the room.

• • • •

WAKING UP WITH Jonah's big arms still wrapped tightly around her, it took a few moments more before Teagan fully took in what had happened, where she was and exactly what had occurred to bring her here and her mind jolted out of its satiated bliss.

Her eyes moved to the pile of discarded clothes, her gaze locked on the bulletproof vest explaining Jonah's miraculous escape from death.

She hadn't forgiven him for what he'd put her through in his quest tonight, but understood to an extent. It would take some time if not forever to forgive him for splintering her heart, but she loved him too much to let that stop her from being in his life, however difficult that might be. She knew that now.

She couldn't help how she felt and neither it seemed could he.

For the first time, Teagan believed this man needed her as much she needed him. It made no sense, but it was out of her control. And she'd go with it because if she didn't, she would fade away.

Sensing Jonah stirring, Teagan turned to face him. 'We need to talk...'

'Not right now we don't,' Jonah smiled lazily, his hands moving over Teagan's body. 'We'll talk properly in the morning.'

Pulling her on top of him, Teagan knew she was lost.

FIFTY EIGHT

JONAH HANDED THE PAPER across the breakfast table and watched Teagan read the front page.

Although in one respect this was good news and meant things had unfolded the way he'd hoped, it also meant it was only a matter of time before the police came knocking. And that would mean questions, which ran the very real risk of many things being exposed that would prove difficult, if not *catastrophic*.

Despite his worry, Jonah smiled, not wanting to alert Teagan to the concern swirling in his mind. As much as he wanted to remain with her in the cocoon of the bedroom, he had to get back to things and prepare.

The main part was over, but the aftermath was not.

Teagan stared at the paper in front of her. This morning, after the first proper night she'd ever spent with Jonah, they'd talked.

Surrounded with the warming glow of early morning love making, Jonah had explained a lot of things, but there were still many unanswered questions she needed to ask.

Teagan frowned as she read the article for the second time.

Violent Death Uncovers Clues to 30 Year-Old Mystery

A man found dead last night with gunshot wounds in the St Giles area of London is believed to be connected to several incidents, as well shedding light on a 30-year-old unsolved case.

Robert Adams, 40, was in possession of some of the world's rarest diamonds stolen in a robbery in Chelsea during 1968.

A subsequent search of Mr Adams' vehicle and lodgings uncovered other items leading the police to believe he was involved with other recent cases. The most pressing concern at this time, however, is Mr Adams' obsession with a woman, who the police have as yet been unable to trace. Although we cannot publish her name for legal reasons, the police are appealing for her to come forward, believing she is already aware of Mr Adams' obsession.

Any witnesses in the Teller Street area around 8PM on 5th of August please contact the police.

Teagan put down the paper and shuddered. Even looking at Robert Adams' name made her feel nauseous - the image of his shattered skull still far too fresh. Then there was what Jonah had reluctantly repeated of O'Hara's words of Robert's room at the B&B. She dreaded to think what would have happened if Robert and O'Hara had succeeded rather than Jonah.

Getting her head around the success of Jonah's complicated plan was difficult, but thought she'd started to understand.

Jonah said he'd sold the diamonds. She didn't care about the money. Those things were gone, along with the people who had tried so hard to exterminate them all and that was the main thing.

But reading this article, what he'd said didn't make sense.

Teagan frowned. 'I thought you'd sold the diamonds? How can they have been found on Robert Adams?'

Jonah nodded. 'Some of them were. The others were planted on Adams. Fakes were left in the security box at Victoria which O'Hara took as I knew he would. I then did the deal with the Russians for the remaining *real* diamonds whilst O'Hara was busy thinking I'd gone back to the box.'

Teagan listened avidly to Jonah's words.

Jonah shrugged. 'Benowitz briefed the Russians there were less than planned and they accepted it because of this…' He prodded the newspaper.

Teagan frowned. 'I don't understand.'

'I knew the police would connect Adams to the original robbery. Those diamonds are rarer than rocking horse shit!'

The implication of what Jonah had done slowly dropped into place in Teagan's mind and she gasped. It seemed alien to discuss something such as this in a matter of fact way, but realised with a jolt that she'd accepted it. This was Jonah Powell's life and now it was hers.

'So, this means that any involvement from your firm to this or to the original robbery that your father organised will not be connected?' she asked.

'That's the general idea, yes,' Jonah smiled. 'Like I promised, I want to close the legacy my father left and start a new one for my business, the club and most especially *you*.'

He reached for Teagan's hand, his big fingers running over her soft skin, then reluctantly glanced at his watch. 'I'm going to have to go as there's still a lot to sort out. Will you be alright here?'

Teagan's skin trembled from Jonah's touch. How she'd love to lock the door and shut the world out, leaving just him and her together to continue the long-overdue exploration of each other, but she knew there must be loose ends to tie up before they could really relax. And one in particular was bothering her.

'What's going to happen to Kim?' Teagan asked nervously. 'You said she was still at the flat with Heath Pointer and Kieran?' *The apartment that up until a few hours ago had been her home...*

Jonah pulled on his jacket. He'd hoped that question wouldn't be asked. That's where he was going now - to deal with the remaining O'Haras and Heath Pointer with Nero.

'I want you to let Kim go,' Teagan said.

'What?' Jonah cried. *That wasn't feasible.* All that he had to work out was *how* they would be got rid of.

'I do. I want you to let them all go,' Teagan repeated. 'Please Jonah.'

'They were instrumental in setting you up! The O'Haras are dangerous. Even those two remaining ones,' Jonah cried. 'Look, I haven't got time for this.'

'Jonah, please listen. They are victims of circumstances. You've got to see that. It is all because of O'Hara and those *things*. Now the diamonds are out of your life, don't let them claim further casualties.'

Jonah shook his head with exasperation. 'I can't promise anything. I have to do what is necessary.' And he knew *exactly* what he would be doing. Teagan wouldn't like it, but he would however, spare her the details.

Teagan nodded, knowing that was the best response she could hope for. 'In the meantime, I'll go and see them.'

Jonah frowned. 'Don't be ridiculous! You're not going back to that apartment. I'll replace all of your things or they can be collected after th...'

'I didn't mean the flat.' Teagan hadn't missed Jonah's reference to "after". *After he'd killed them?* She knew deep down he had to but wished there was another way.

'Then what the bloody hell are you going on about?'

Teagan smiled warily. 'The police. I'm going to see the police.'

Jonah held Teagan's eyes. *Was she serious?*

'They'll track me down eventually, that's after they've picked you and the Feathers to pieces, so I'm going to do what I have to do so that doesn't happen,' Teagan continued.

Jonah inwardly sighed. Teagan's attitude might be commendable, but she could inadvertently make everything worse. She could even be implicated. 'I don't think that you should.'

'I know what to say,' Teagan added.

Jonah raised an eyebrow. 'You're going to lie?'

Teagan shook her head. 'No. Well not exactly. Only on the extra things Robert bloody Adams can take the wrap for. It won't make any difference to him.' Her eyes narrowed. 'It's not like he doesn't deserve it.'

She watched Jonah studying her, realising that something had hardened within her. She wasn't sure whether she liked it, but it had happened all the same.

She couldn't and *wouldn't* spend the next however long looking over her shoulder waiting for the police to come for her or the people she loved.

Teagan knew if she wanted her life to be with this man, then she needed to act like it and do whatever it took to ensure this episode was wrapped up and finished.

6 Months Later

'IS THIS HIS FAVOURITE ONE?' Teagan looked at Gwen hopefully as she unwrapped the large framed print which had arrived just in time. 'I wanted to get him something new for his study here.'

Gwen gasped, her eyes drinking in the details of the enlarged photograph of Jacky Powell - the man she'd loved with all of her heart. 'H-How did you get this done?'

'They can digitally enhance old prints these days,' Teagan said, pleased by Gwen's reaction. 'Do you think Jonah will like it?'

'Like it? He'll *love* it!' Gwen exclaimed. 'I know he will. It will be like having his father there in person.'

'Not quite, but the next best thing. I won't bother wrapping it. He'll be back soon with Nero.'

Gwen smiled. 'Thanks for inviting me over. I haven't missed one of Jonah's birthday since he was a youngster, but I thought it might be different this year... what with...'

'That's all done and dusted.' Teagan squeezed Gwen's hand. 'Besides we're together now and that's all that matters.'

And so far it had been the best six months of her life.

Teagan moved to the window of the lounge of her new home and looked out over the garden, the plants she'd bought already established in the pretty garden.

It was a thousand times different to the manicured lawns and landscaped beds of the garden at the big house, with not one reminder of Lena or anything else which had happened within those four walls to haunt her.

Sensing Teagan's thoughts, Gwen smiled. 'It's looking really lovely here, sweetheart. It's only been a few months, yet you've done wonders doing the house up.'

A small frown appeared on Teagan's otherwise relaxed face. 'I sometimes wonder if it was the right thing to do...'

'What? Buying a different house?' Gwen cried. 'Oh my life, of *course* it was!' She raised an eyebrow. 'You know what Jonah's like. If he didn't like your idea of moving to a different place, then he wouldn't have bought it.' She folded her arms. 'Besides, I've never seen him happier.'

It was true. How wrong she'd been standing in Teagan and Jonah's way. Teagan had come into her own since the diamonds had gone and she and Jonah had officially become a couple. Plus, Teagan was the one to put the icing on the cake.

If Teagan hadn't gone against everyone's opinions and taken it upon herself to go to the police following the article in the paper and waited for them to come looking for her instead, then they may not have been so inclined to believe what she'd said.

And what she'd said had been perfect.

Teagan's words had corroborated the police's suspicions in the best way possible.

She'd done astoundingly well. Teagan had confirmed to the police that she was indeed the object of Adams obsession and had been ever since she'd started working for his mother, Dulcie.

Gwen smiled, recounting how proud she'd been hearing how Teagan had gone on to say that only days before Robert was found dead, he'd followed her, admitting he killed Dulcie because he wanted the diamonds his father had originally stolen. His mother had been hiding them all of this time at Footlights.

Teagan had been *so* convincing when she'd said she'd wanted to go to the police straightaway, but was too scared - too terrified Robert would do to her what he'd done to his mother.

She told them Robert had said her it was *Dulcie* who had previously killed her own daughter and this statement prompted the police to test the towel found in the glove box of Robert's car, as well as the gun, which proved both had come from Footlights.

But the cleverest bit was when Teagan said Robert planned on selling the diamonds and had to kill his mother in order to do so.

She told them Robert admitted to framing Heath Pointer because he knew the man had been at Footlights that night trying to warn Dulcie. Robert had since also threatened Mike and Tammy Pointer, mistakenly believing they had a claim on the diamonds. And when the bodies of Heath's parents were subsequently uncovered in the shed at the back of the garden at the Pointer's house, Teagan's statement backed up everything.

Although the police were still investigating, it was common knowledge Robert was thought to be the one behind everything.

Hearing the front door shut, Teagan beamed as Jonah made his way into the lounge, followed by Nero.

Taking Teagan into his arms, Jonah kissed her then turned to Gwen. 'Don't mind us,' he grinned.

Gwen laughed good-naturedly, happy to see Jonah so content. 'You're back early.' She glanced at the clock on the inglenook fireplace. 'Is everything alright?'

'Of course it is,' Jonah grinned. 'You know I have a couple of nights a week that I don't stay late at the Feathers anymore.' He kept his arm tightly around Teagan's waist, pulling her closer to him. He'd changed a lot of things and one was to spend more time with the woman he truly loved.

'I'm only pulling your leg,' Gwen smiled, reaching for her handbag and fishing out a card. 'Happy birthday.'

'Thank you,' Jonah smiled, taking the whisky Nero poured. 'We'll have a toast for Nero as well while we're at it.'

'Yes. Congratulations, love,' Gwen said, laughing when Teagan went on tiptoes to kiss Nero on the cheek, making him blush.

'Yep. Cheers, mate. I can't think of anyone more deserving and suited to being my partner in the business.' Jonah raised his glass.

And that was for definite. Nero had been with him from the start and there was no one else he would rather have by his side. Not only had he done more for the firm than anyone, the man was like a real brother. Much more than Saul had ever been or ever *could* have been.

Jonah looked at Teagan. *Apart from her.* He wrapped his arms around her. 'You all might like to know that I had word from Heath Pointer today. All charges against him for Dulcie Adams' murder have been officially dropped.'

Teagan beamed. 'That's wonderful news.' She had been both surprised and pleased with Jonah's decision to take no action against Heath for his previous involvement. Surprised because she hadn't thought he'd do that, but also that he'd listened to her.

Without Heath's actions and help they may not have stopped O'Hara and Adams in time.

Jonah didn't have to put money in City Car Sales either, but since he had, Heath had succeeded in turning it around from the nosedive it had been in.

Jonah fished an envelope out of his pocket and handed it to Teagan. 'This arrived at the Feathers for you today. I think I you'll be happy about it.'

Eyeing Jonah quizzically, Teagan took the envelope, her heart increasing as she viewed the postmark. *Could it be? It wasn't, was it? Jonah had always refused to go into details and so she therefore presumed...*

Her hands taught the envelope. *It was!*

```
Hi babe,


I wanted to write but didn't know whether to.
Just wanted to say thanks. Your man told me it
was down to you. I'm sorry for all the shit.


Friends in another time and place?


All the luck to you and be happy


K

x
```

BTW Kieran wasn't really my BF. Give me some credit!

Teagan's mouth flapped up and down in relief. 'I-It's from Kim. You did what I asked? Why didn't you tell me?'

Jonah smiled. Although it had gone against his instinct to let the O'Hara siblings go, he'd secretly agreed the diamonds should not claim any further victims. 'I heard they had a mark on them back in the Emerald Isle, but I had a feeling if she survived she'd get in touch.' He glanced at the letter and his face screwed up. 'And she wasn't shagging her brother after all, which is least makes letting her go a bit more palatable.'

'Thank you,' Teagan grabbed Jonah's arm. 'I'm glad.'

Jonah squeezed Teagan tightly. 'You'll also want to see this!' He placed the evening edition of the paper on the sofa and watched as Gwen and Teagan both bent to look at it:

Robbery Finally Solved

The case regarding the theft of diamonds from a Chelsea town house in 1968 has finally been closed after some of the diamonds stolen were found on the body of Robert Adams, discovered shot dead in August this year.

Mr Adams, 40, had planned to sell the diamonds stolen by his father, Michael Pointer in 1968, when he was shot dead – presumed by foreign buyers as the deal went wrong.
It has since been revealed that Adams was also responsible for murdering his mother, Dulcie Adams and Mike and Tammy Pointer, in relation to these jewels.

All charges against Heath Pointer, previously wrongly accused of Dulcie Adams' murder and due to stand trail, have been dropped and Mr Pointer has been exonerated from all connection to this crime. The police are no longer looking for anyone else in relation these matters.

Teagan gasped. 'So that's it? They won't be looking into you, your father or the Feathers?'

'Got it in one!' Jonah grinned as Teagan threw herself into his arms.

'That's fantastic!' Gwen beamed. 'I'm so pleased it's finally over after all this time.'

Jonah's expression became stern. 'Not quite…'

'What do you mean?' Gwen blurted. 'Please don't tell me they're investigating you anyway? Have they said that? Have th…'

'They've said absolutely nothing to me. They've never officially investigated me, remember, so they don't keep me abreast of anything. All I know is what's in this paper and what my contacts in the force tell me on the sly,' Jonah explained.

Gwen's eyes flicked to Teagan. 'Then is it you? Have they discovered what you said about Adams killing Heath's parents wasn't true?'

'Relax Gwen. That bit may have not been entirely on the level, but the rest Teagan said was.' Jonah ran his finger down Teagan's cheek. 'Isn't that right, babe?'

'It is,' Teagan agreed. 'Besides, I didn't say Robert killed Heath's parents. I said he *hinted* that. As I said before, he'd done enough so why not let him take the blame for that? If O'Hara had somehow come into the conversation, Jonah would have inevitably been brought into it and...' She wrapped her arms around Jonah's waist. '...I want him with me.'

Jonah's lips moved to Teagan's neck and Gwen sighed impatiently. 'Then what is it?'

Jonah grinned. 'Well, being as you looked after Teagan for me when I asked you and ignoring the small matter of everything else you've done to make me angry in the past...'

'Oh Jonah...' Gwen muttered despondently. *How many times could she apologise for that?*

'It doesn't change that I love you to bits,' Jonah continued, his eyes twinkling. 'And I'm glad you've decided to stick around.'

Gwen breathed a sigh of relief and rolled her eyes. 'Oh, you rotten...

Teagan stuffed the letter from Kim into her pocket. 'And on that note, I've got something for you, Jonah.' With a flourish, she pulled the covering off the photograph of Jacky Powell. 'Happy birthday.'

Jonah silently stared at the photograph, a lump forming in his throat. 'Thank you,' he murmured. *This woman was the best and she was HIS.*

He looked at the photograph of his father, knowing he would be more than happy with what he was about to do. Pulling the box from his pocket, Jonah dropped to his knee. 'Teagan Fraser, I love you with all my heart. Will you marry me?'

Teagan squealed with surprise. 'Oh my God!' She stared with amazement at the velvet ring box in Jonah's hand, then fear suddenly overtook her joy. *It wasn't one of those... those diamonds was it?*

Jonah opened the box revealing a beautiful blue sapphire ring made by Benowitz himself from the jewel he'd admired in the shop that very night the diamonds had gone from his life forever. 'Well?'

'Yes!' Teagan shrieked. 'Yes, I'll marry you!'

Gwen's hand flew to her mouth and she looked from Jonah to Teagan. 'Congratulations!'

Getting off his knee, Jonah slipped the ring onto Teagan's finger and planted a kiss on her lips, then raised his eyebrows at Nero. 'Best man?'

'Of course,' Nero replied, his smile almost as wide as Jonah's.

'I'm in such a good mood, I'll even invite Heath Pointer!' Jonah laughed, picking Teagan up and swinging her around.

'You'll be my maid of honour, won't you, Gwen?' Teagan cried, her excitement brimming over.

'I'd be honoured.' Choked with emotion, Gwen pulled Teagan into a hug. 'I'm so happy for you both.'

Teagan smiled widely. Her life may not have panned out as she'd expected and she could have happily bypassed many of the things that had occurred, but they had all factored into reaching a point where she couldn't be more content and knew whatever being involved with Jonah Powell brought with it in the future, she would be alright with that too.

Thank you!

Thank you for reading *The Final Take*. I hope you enjoyed reading it as much as I did writing it!

If so, would you please consider leaving a review on Amazon and/or Goodreads.

Reviews from readers are SOOOO helpful and especially important to us authors and without you we would have nobody to write for!

Thank you once again and hope you enjoy the rest of my books.

Edie xx

MORE FROM THIS SERIES

RETRIBUTION SERIES:

#1: AN OLD SCORE

Three families... One prize...

Teagan Fraser had no idea what she was getting herself into when she took on an assignment as a live-in carer for Dulcie Adams – a retired dancer from a Soho club. Dulcie has waited forty years for her lover, Michael Pointer, to return, but she's been living in hope for a time that never came and left looking after something important, which Jonah Powell and his firm want back.

In addition to the notorious Powell firm, there are others wanting to claim what they believe is rightfully theirs and they'll do anything to get it back. If only Dulcie wasn't around it would be a lot easier, but she's difficult to shift...

A lot can happen in the space of two weeks and Teagan might wish she'd never become involved.

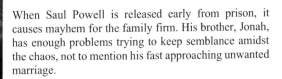

#2: FINDERS KEEPERS

The race is on...

When Saul Powell is released early from prison, it causes mayhem for the family firm. His brother, Jonah, has enough problems trying to keep semblance amidst the chaos, not to mention his fast approaching unwanted marriage.

But even Jonah's problems pale into insignificance compared to what Robert Adams is discovering about his mother, Dulcie – the woman he's always put on a pedestal.

In the meantime, Teagan Fraser is also facing a dilemma – one which could ruin her life completely.

Can anyone come out of this nightmare unscathed?

MORE FROM THIS AUTHOR

ALLEGIANCE SERIES:

#1: TAKEOVER

Samantha Reynold hadn't bargained on unexpectedly needing to step into her father's shoes and take over the family casino business and known nothing about the rules of this glamorous but deadly new world. But she won't let her family down, especially when it looks like they could lose everything to their biggest rivals – the Stoker family.

Eldest son Sebastian hasn't got time to pander to pretty girl Samantha as she plays at being boss. Rumours are swirling around the streets of Birmingham that have the power to rip the Stoker family apart and destroy everything they've built.

#2: FALLOUT

With the odds stacked against her, Samantha Reynold is determined to prove she's tough enough to be the boss. But when a secret from the past threatens to ruin Sam's reputation, she suddenly feels very alone in this dark new world. There's only one man she can turn to – rival club owner, Sebastian Stoker.

Seb knows first-hand how secrets and lies can tear a family apart. He wants to protect Sam at all costs, but siding with her could threaten his own position as head of the Stoker family and risk accusations of betrayal.

With loyalties divided and two families at war – the fallout could be deadly.

#3: VENDETTA

Once bitter enemies, Samantha Reynold and Seb Stoker's powerful alliance enables their firms and casinos to go from strength to strength. With the families no longer in opposition, it seems that Sam and Seb are untouchable...

But not everyone is happy with the new power couple of the club world.

Unbeknownst to everyone, someone new wants to see Sam's perfect life ruined. And they will stop at nothing to seek their revenge – even if it means destroying everything - and everyone - in their path.

MORE FROM THIS AUTHOR

HUNTED SERIES:

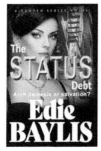

#1: THE STATUS DEBT

Lillian Morgan would do anything to regain the status she lost by marrying beneath her and to cover the sordid details of her husband's death. This includes blackmail and the hand of marriage of her own daughter.

Tori thought her life couldn't get much worse, but someone is not being honest and secrets have the power to rip everyone to shreds.

Especially when life is built on lies.

#2: THE FAMILY LEGACY

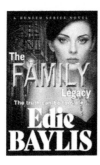

Unsure of whether Matt or Hunter has fathered the child growing inside her, Tori's unwanted wedding to Matt grows closer, but is there light at the end of the tunnel? Unfortunately, Tori hasn't counted on another man present in her life. One who is more instrumental in her misery than she realises.

Sometimes the truth is too late in coming and makes bad things happen and sometimes a hidden legacy can cause the most horrific thing of all…

#3: THE TARGET OF LIES

Neil Sparks has a score to settle. In fact, he has several… His first port of call when returning from France after a five year exile is to catch up with his estranged wife. Secondly, Neil wants to even a score with the people instrumental in his departure and thirdly, he wants an explanation from the man who promised his marriage would be free from hassle. The trouble is, he's not the only one with an agenda…

There are too many people about to become caught in the crossfire and everyone could become a target.

** This series contains written depictions of graphic violence, sex and strong language. It also contains some themes that may be uncomfortable for certain readers. **

More From this Author

DOWNFALL SERIES:

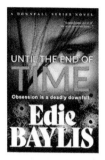

#1 - UNTIL THE END OF TIME

Dive into Seth and Jane's train wreck of a life, where drugs, alcohol and obsessional love means this downright dangerous pair will do *anything* to ensure nothing gets in their way.

They do bad things. *Very* bad things and their promise to love each until the end of time turns into a war against each other.

A war neither of them can win.

#2 - ESCAPING THE PAST

Things have changed and Jane has got on with her life.

Well, not *entirely*…

Embroiled in a bitter feud between two rival firms, it is clear that not everyone is who they proclaim to be.

The net is closing in and some things just can't be changed.

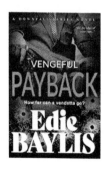

#3 - VENGEFUL PAYBACK

There is something missing. Something *very* important and no one is above suspicion.

Past vendettas are gaining pace and it is vital that whoever is behind this never-ending stream of cleverly engineered payback is discovered before it is too late and everything held dear is ripped apart.

** This series contains written depictions of graphic violence, sex and strong language. It also contains some themes that may be uncomfortable for certain readers. **

ABOUT THE AUTHOR

Over the years Edie has worked all over the UK as well as in several other countries and has met a lot of interesting people - several of whom have supplied ideas for some of the characters in her books! She has now settled back in central England with her partner and children, where she is pursuing writing her gritty gangland and urban fiction novels.

Edie is currently signed to Boldwood Books for a 5-book gangland fiction series set in Birmingham. The first three in the *Allegiance* series, *Takeover*, *Fallout* and *Vendetta* have been released and the fourth in the series, *Payback*, is due to be released in January 2023. She is also concurrently writing the *Scarred* series - the first titled, *Mirrors Never Lie*.

Edie's other series are the *Retribution* series, the *Hunted* series and the *Downfall* series - all trilogies.

When she isn't writing, Edie enjoys reading and is a self-confessed book hoarder. She also enjoys crochet and music as well as loving anything quirky or unusual.

Visit www.ediebaylis.co.uk for the latest news, information about new releases, giveaways and to subscribe to her mailing list.

CWA MEMBER

CONNECT WITH EDIE

https://fb.me/downfallseries

https://www.goodreads.com/author/show/17153586.Edie_Baylis

https://twitter.com/ediebaylis

https://www.amazon.co.uk/Edie-Baylis/e/B075FQHWCZ/

https://www.bookbub.com/authors/edie-baylis

https://ediebaylis.co.uk/

info@ediebaylis.co.uk

https://www.fantasticfiction.com/b/edie-baylis/

https://www.instagram.com/ediebaylis/

https://www.tiktok.com/@edie747

https://www.pinterest.co.uk/ediebaylis/

JOIN EDIE'S MAILING LIST

Subscribe to Edie's mailing list for the latest news on her books, special offers, new releases and competitions.

https://ediebaylis.co.uk/signup.html

Edie Baylis

gangland | crime | urban

THRILLER AUTHOR

ACKNOWLEDGEMENTS

Thanks to the people that kindly read my drafts of *The Final Take* – you know who you are and I appreciate your time and feedback.

I would also like to thank Sue John, Jess Richardson and Caz Finlay – all lovely ladies who never cease offering me their much appreciated support.

Printed in Great Britain
by Amazon

23215634R00239